my Heart

Always in my Heart is Ellie Dean's fifth novel. She lives in Eastbourne, which has been her home for many years and where she raised her three children.

There'll be Blue Skies
Far From Home
Keep Smiling Through
Where the Heart Lies

Ellie Dean

Always in
my Heart

arrow books

Published by Arrow Books 2013

2 4 6 8 10 9 7 5 3 1

First published in Great Britain in 2013 by
Arrow Books
Random House, 20 Vauxhall Bridge Road,
London SW1V 2SA

www.randomhouse.co.uk

Addresses for companies within The Random House Group Limited can
be found at: www.randomhouse.co.uk/offices.htm

The Random House Group Limited Reg. No. 954009

A CIP catalogue record for this book
is available from the British Library

ISBN 9780099585275

The Random House Group Limited supports the Forest Stewardship
Council® (FSC®), the leading international forest-certification organisation.
Our books carrying the FSC label are printed on FSC®-certified paper.
FSC is the only forest-certification scheme supported by the leading
environmental organisations, including Greenpeace.
Our paper procurement policy can be found at:
www.randomhouse.co.uk/environment

MIX
Paper from
responsible sources
FSC® C016897

Typeset by SX Composing DTP, Rayleigh, Essex
Printed and bound by CPI Group (UK) Ltd, Croydon, CR0 4YY

Acknowledgements

This book could not have been written without the help of Molly Paterson, who so very kindly shared her memories with me of her time in the Women's Timber Corps. Thank you, Molly, for the little details which added authenticity to the work of my character Sarah, and I hope you spot your name in the book!

Having spent time in Singapore, Malaya, Thailand and Sri Lanka, I know how humid it gets – and because I was born in Australia and came to live in England as a schoolgirl, I have vivid memories of how difficult it is to settle into a new way of life in a very different country. I have used my own experiences in this book, but thanks must also go to those lovely people whose memories of living in the Far East at that time were extremely helpful, and who gave me vivid descriptions of life on board the refugee ships that made those hazardous journeys to safety.

To J. Warner, I appreciate the time you took to explain the workings of the Auxiliary Units of the British Resistance Organisation, and to P. Nash, thank you for all the long e-mails regarding tip-and-runs, airfields and RAF history. Thanks too to Kath Cater, mother-in-law extraordinaire, for telling me about your milk deliveries during the war.

Again I must thank my brilliant agent, Teresa Chris, for her continued encouragement and support, and Georgina Hawtrey-Woore for her enthusiasm and advice – and of course my husband for taking over the running of the house and the evening meals. Without any of them I would be lost.

Chapter One

Malaya, December 1941

Despite the isolation of the rubber plantation, and the simplicity of the large, tin-roofed wooden bungalow that jutted from the hillside on stilts above the canopy of trees, the Fuller family always dressed for dinner, even when dining alone.

But tonight they had a guest – a very special guest – and nineteen-year-old Sarah Fuller had taken extra care with her appearance. Instead of the usual cotton blouse, skirt, and sensible shoes Philip Tarrant saw her in every day at her father's plantation office, she had changed into a shantung silk dress that skimmed her slender figure and was the colour of rich cream; her clear complexion was enhanced by the string of pearls around her neck, and she'd pinned a frangipani flower into her freshly washed fair hair.

Philip was twenty-four and looked very handsome in his white shirt and tuxedo. As their eyes frequently met over the candlelit table, they shared moments of silent intimacy which brought a flush to Sarah's cheeks that had little to do with the humidity and heat of the tropical night.

Tall and darkly attractive, Philip was the son of the wealthy plantation owner. He'd left Malaya as a schoolboy and had returned eighteen months ago, moving into his family's magnificent white colonial house that stood hidden amid the trees further up the hill, so he could take over the reins of the plantation from his widowed, ailing father who had relocated upcountry into the much cooler Cameron Highlands.

Philip was considered to be a great catch among the ambitious, social-climbing matrons of the Malaysian peninsula who had daughters to marry off, but it appeared he only had eyes for Sarah – and she still found that fact rather miraculous.

After all, she was only the plantation manager's daughter, an ordinary secretary who, unlike most of her peers, had never left Malaya because her father didn't approve of English boarding schools and long family separations. In the echelons of what passed as high society amongst the white expats here in Malaya, she was regarded with a certain reserve that had hardened somewhat since Philip had shown interest in her.

Sarah tore her gaze away from him and tried to concentrate on the delicious food their Chinese cook, Wa Ling, had spent most of the day preparing. She fully understood the infinitesimal layers of the social hierarchy that ruled this colonial outpost – and knew without a doubt that if this delicate relationship with Philip should founder, there would be a degree of smugness amongst those who'd openly sneered that such a match couldn't last.

But for now she was happy to bask in the love that shone from his eyes whenever he looked at her, warmed by the sound of his voice and his nearness as they worked together in the estate office, bent over maps of the vast plantation and discussing the shipping contracts and warehouse capacities, along with her father, who had managed the business almost single-handedly for many years.

She set aside these warm thoughts and listened for a moment to the idle chatter that was going round the table. Her mother, Sybil, wasn't as animated as usual, and although her advanced condition was masked by a voluminous chiffon dress, Sarah knew she was finding it uncomfortable to be so pregnant in this heat. But Sybil Fuller was not a woman to be beaten by such things, and she still looked serene and beautiful, her pale hair and delicate features enhanced by the candles' glow as she kept a watchful eye on Jane, her youngest daughter.

Sarah felt the usual pang of sorrow when she looked at her sister. Jane was seventeen, and quite beautiful when she wasn't in one of her funny moods. Sometimes it was difficult for those not in the know to realise that Jane was different to other girls her age, but since the riding accident four years ago in which she'd suffered a devastating head injury, the doctor had said she would forever be a child of twelve. Yet there remained vestiges of the young woman she might have become in her astonishing ability to solve mathematical problems that were far beyond Sarah's capability – and in this talent lay the spark of hope that she might one day fulfil at least part of her true potential. Jane's tragic accident had cast a shadow over them all, but, with love and determination, the family had seen to it that she continued with her schooling and remained an intrinsic part of their hectic lives – regardless of what other, less charitable people might say.

Sarah noted that Philip was listening with rapt attention as Jane explained how she'd finally managed to solve a mathematical conundrum that had eluded her for several days. Realising he was fully occupied, she turned her gaze to her father.

Jock Fuller was an imposing figure in his dinner jacket and bow tie, but Sarah knew he felt much more at home in his daily attire of baggy shorts or old jodhpurs and faded shirt, the brim of his battered, sweat-stained hat pulled low as he strode through the trees on his regular inspections of the tappers and coolies.

Jock was stocky and broad-shouldered, with a head of thick hair that was yet to turn silver and a dashing handlebar moustache that almost hid his wide, well-defined lips. At forty-five his eyes were still a bright blue which, in moments of displeasure or anger, could turn steely. His face was weathered from many years in the sun, but for a patch of pale flesh high on his brow where his hat brim always rested, and his big square hand looked incongruous as it held the delicate crystal glass to his lips, the gold cygnet ring winking in the flickering light. But Sarah knew that hand could be gentle, that the tough, no-nonsense exterior hid a loving heart and a strong sense of fair play.

She let the various conversations drift about her as she regarded, with pleasure, the large square room she'd known all her life. The long dining table was at the centre of the room and could seat twenty when all the leaves had been added. The wooden walls were mostly bare, but for a large framed print of the King and Queen which had pride of place above the highly polished teak chiffonier that housed the family crystal and best silver. Two huge Chinese jars stood sentry on either side of the door into the drawing room, and a large potted fern had been placed to hide a particularly stubborn patch of damp in one corner. Damp and mould were the enemy in this tropical paradise, and nothing could escape them.

Curtains of white voile brushed softly against the hardwood floorboards at the French windows which had been flung open to garner the slightest breeze that might drift in through the screened veranda from the forest canopy. Candlelight flickered in the downdraught of the ceiling fans, and glinted on the silver and crystal that had been so carefully placed by the soft-footed servants on the snowy white linen tablecloth. There were small bowls of colourful flowers down the centre of the table, and the china was delicate and gold-rimmed.

It was at moments like these that Sarah felt an inner glow of utter contentment. She loved this house, these people around her and the scents and sounds of the country she would always call home. The world beyond the peninsula held no lure for her, for her heart was here – and like her father, she had no intention of ever leaving it.

Sarah sipped the cool wine as the dirty dishes were replaced with crystal bowls of lychees smothered in a light syrup and soft ice cream. She smiled at her younger sister who was beginning to fidget beside her. 'Just wait until everyone is served, Jane,' she murmured.

Jane slumped back in her chair and pulled a face. 'It's boring having dinner with the grown-ups,' she muttered. 'I much prefer eating with Amah.'

Sarah grinned and tweaked the long, fair plait which fell over Jane's shoulder. 'I'm sure you do,' she replied. 'Amah spoils you. But you're a big girl now, and it's important you learn how to conduct yourself at the dinner table.'

Jane puffed out a long sigh, then glanced at their mother, who was dipping her spoon into the dessert, and followed suit, the ice cream dripping onto her chin in her haste and threatening to mark her pretty white dress.

Sarah quickly handed her a linen napkin to mop up the spill, and Jane shot her a mischievous grin as if she knew she was behaving badly, and could get away with it.

The meal was finally over and, whilst the servants quietly cleared the table, Jane wandered off in search of Amah, and the others slowly moved into the drawing room. No one hurried in the tropics, especially during the monsoon season, when the temperature rose along with the humidity, and the rains did nothing to alleviate the stifling heat.

The drawing room had glass doors leading to the back veranda, which overlooked the forested hills that towered behind the bungalow and kept this part of the house permanently in dark green shadow. It was furnished with deep-cushioned rattan chairs, teak tables and cabinets holding delicate ornaments, and there was a collection of native spears arranged on one wall, and several large, exquisitely carved Malay figures stood among the strategically placed potted ferns. Jock had pinned an enormous map of the world on another wall, beneath which was a long, narrow table he'd since buried beneath layers of papers, magazines and mouldering books. A Christmas tree stood in one corner of the room, festooned with tinsel and glossy baubles, a rather ancient and ragged angel staring woefully down at them from the topmost branch. There were no presents beneath it yet, for it was still very early December.

As the servants brought in the coffee and handed the cups round, Sarah rather hoped that she and Philip could slip out to the veranda and share a few quiet moments together, but it seemed her father had other ideas, for Jock had settled his sturdy bulk into his favourite rattan chair by the wireless and was urging Philip to sit beside him so they could discuss the war in Europe over brandy and cigars.

Philip shot her a glance of apology, but there was nothing for it. Jock was clearly delighted to have the younger man's undivided attention and was soon in full flow, expounding his theories on what should be done to stop Hitler in his tracks. It seemed he was determined to monopolise Philip – and the evening's conversation.

Sarah's disappointment grew as she sipped her coffee and her father droned on and on. She'd heard it all before, and soon he would tune in the wireless for the BBC World Service news, after which he would discuss it minutely long into the night.

Sybil Fuller was clearly of the same opinion, and she gave an exasperated sigh as she set her coffee cup rather firmly on the low table. 'Really, Jock,' she said, 'I do think we should change the subject. It's not suitable for after-dinner conversation, and all this talk of war is unsettling and not doing me *or* the baby any good.'

Jock regarded her from beneath his dark brows with a mixture of affection and impatience. 'Unsettling or not, my dear,' he said gruffly, 'it is our duty to keep up with the news from home.'

Sarah smiled at this. Pops always called England 'home', but in fact he hadn't ever stepped on English soil because he'd been born in Scotland and had left for Malaya as a baby in his mother's arms to rejoin his father. Malaya and rubber were his passion, his life – and he could no more exist in England than one of the exotic birds that inhabited the surrounding jungle.

Sybil flapped her hand at him. 'Hitler already has

most of Europe in his greedy grasp. What's to stop him from using the Japs to—?'

'We are in a privileged position here,' interrupted Jock as he settled further into the cushions, stretched out his long legs and puffed on his cigar. 'The Japanese might have signed allegiance with Hitler back in nineteen-forty, but so far the war is confined to Europe – and I believe it will remain so.'

'Then why are we building air-raid shelters everywhere?' retorted Sybil, who seemed determined to pick an argument.

'Merely precautionary devices to deter scare-mongering,' he said with a sniff. 'Air raids on Malaya by Japan are out of the question. Their nearest base is over six hundred miles away in Indochina, and they don't possess the necessary long-range aircraft. If they should dare to attack by sea, they will be picked up by our first-class radar system and met by the barrage of big guns we have all along the coast. Impenetrable jungle and mangrove swamps effectively cut us off from inland incursion, and the British Forces will defend us to the hilt. Singapore and Malaya are impregnable fortresses designed to protect Britain's possessions in the Far East – and our rubber is vital to the war effort.'

'I still don't like it,' murmured Sybil.

Jock nodded to the silent houseboy who'd been sitting on a rush mat by the door, and waited while he replenished the brandy glasses. 'You have no need to worry, my dear,' he said comfortably as he swirled the brandy. 'Neither that scrawny house painter, Hitler, nor the yellow-bellied Japs would dare bring trouble to these shores. They know well enough what we British are made of and we'd soon send them kicking and screaming back to where they came from.'

Seeming to lose her appetite for debate, Sybil gave a deep sigh, rolled her eyes and said no more, but Sarah knew what was really bothering her mother, and it had very little to do with air-raid shelters and the war.

Sybil was forty-two and had been quite put out by her surprise pregnancy, and although she'd come to terms with her condition, and was now looking forward to the birth, she wasn't coping with the heat and humidity very well at all. She was a loving, sweet mother, but at heart, she was a born socialite – spoiled and pampered by Jock, adored by her daughters and much admired by their friends for her beauty and wit, and her ability to light up any room she entered. Used to robust health and a full social calendar, she was finding this lack of energy trying, and her enforced confinement to the isolation of the plantation was making her edgy.

Born into the wealth and privilege of a well-connected family of Australian sugar exporters and refiners, she'd come to Malaya with her parents when she was twenty for a holiday. She'd met Jock at a party and had married him against her parents' wishes the day after she turned twenty-one and came into her late grandmother's money. Jock had only been an apprentice manager of this rubber plantation then, and not the rich, ambitious tea planter or ship owner they'd been hoping for for their daughter. Sarah knew she still loved him – that their marriage was strong and passionate – but she also understood that her mother needed to escape the strictures of family and duty now and then for the bright lights of Singapore.

Unlike Jock, who preferred the tranquillity and order of the plantation, Sybil loved Singapore and all it had to offer. Before her pregnancy, she would often get their driver to take her and Jane down to the bungalow they owned close to Raffles Place so she could entertain, and be entertained by, her many friends – to take tiffin at Raffles, and attend tennis parties, cricket matches and picnics before dancing the night away at the popular Singapore Club. But it had been several months since Jock had put his foot down and forbidden her to travel, and Sybil was growing restless.

'I think I'll take my coffee outside,' Sarah murmured as the two men crossed the room to the large map that Jock had almost covered in different coloured pins. 'Why don't you join me? It might be cooler there.'

Sybil took her hand and struggled out of the deep chair as Jock continued to pontificate and jab at the map. 'What a good idea,' she said softly. 'There's enough hot air in here to launch an entire fleet of barrage balloons.'

They both giggled as they walked arm-in-arm out onto the back veranda where more ceiling fans stirred the heat-laden air. The Malay houseboys had lit the oil lamps which swung from the rafters, and they scurried to bring the *Mems* more cushions and coffee before being shooed away by Sybil, who then settled into a chair, lit a cigarette and finally appeared to relax.

Sarah remained standing by the railing, unable to settle after the talk of war had stirred her fears that the peninsula could come under attack. She'd seen the fortifications along the coast – the ugly barbed wire, the Bofors guns, pillboxes and civilian air-raid shelters – and had heard about the daily arrival of troopships in Singapore harbour. And despite the evidence to the contrary and her father's reassurances, she shared her mother's doubts as to just how safe they really were from an enemy attack.

Unwilling to dwell on such dark thoughts, she peered through the sturdy mesh screens that protected the wrap-round veranda from flies and mosquitoes to the black stillness of the mountains and the jungle that sprawled over them and down to the very edges of the plantation. The orange flames in the oil lamps flickered in the breeze which still carried vestiges of the day's heat in its dank, musty breath, and this smell of the jungle almost smothered the delicate scents of the orchids, jasmine and frangipani that grew in wild abundance amid the trees. Moths battered against the screens, mosquitoes whined, and tiny pinpricks of light from the fireflies blinked in the darkness as the deep bass hooting of macaque monkeys echoed into the night.

Other jungle sounds drifted up to her as she stood there – the lonely howl of a wild dog, which always sent shivers up her spine; the scream of something small at the instant before death; and the constant click and tick of millions of insects and crickets. She'd been born to these sounds and scents and they were as familiar to her as her own face in the mirror – surely nothing as ugly as war would come and destroy them?

Sybil must have sensed her daughter's thoughts. 'Your father's right, darling,' she murmured. 'I was only trying to rile him for want of anything else to do. Naughty, I know, but there are times . . .' She stubbed out her cigarette with unwarranted vigour. 'We'll be quite safe here, you'll see. The only real danger is that we might all die of boredom.'

'If you want something to do, then we could play cards,' Sarah suggested reluctantly, 'or finish the jigsaw puzzle we started last week.'

Sybil didn't seem too enamoured by the idea either, for she pulled a face, gave a vast yawn and swung her feet off the footstool. 'I'm going to tuck Jane in and then I'm off to bed.'

Sarah felt a stab of concern. 'It's still quite early. Are you feeling unwell?'

Sybil pushed out of her chair and came to stand by Sarah, her good humour restored. 'I'm absolutely fine,' she replied. 'But I've had enough for one day.' She patted Sarah's cheek and smiled. 'I'll rescue Philip from your father and send him out to you. Lord knows, he probably needs to escape by now, and you young things should have a quiet minute or two together.'

Sarah blushed and dipped her chin. 'That would be

lovely, but you know how Pops is. He'll insist on them listening to the news.'

'I really don't understand why,' Sybil replied with a sigh. 'It's nothing but gloom and doom at the best of times.' She kissed Sarah's cheek and turned away, just as the elderly Amah emerged from the shadows further down the veranda, her bare feet silent on the varnished boards, her simple sarong outlining her tiny figure.

'Come, *Mem*, it is time to rest,' she murmured as she took Sybil's arm. 'I have sweet oils to massage your legs and back. You will sleep well tonight.'

'First I must say goodnight to Jock and our guest, and look in on Jane,' Sybil replied.

Sarah watched them move back into the house. The little Malay woman had been looking after Sybil since before Sarah was born, and they all loved and relied upon her. No one knew how old she was, but her lined face and snow-white hair belied the almost youthful grace with which she carried herself and the elegance of her hands as she used them to illustrate a point. They knew very little about her despite the years she had been with them, but it was rumoured that she had family down in Singapore.

Sarah took a cigarette from the silver box on the low table and lit it, not ready yet to go back indoors. There was still a chance that Philip would join her. But as she stood there, enfolded in the damp velvet of the tropical night, she heard the static coming from the large wireless and knew that her mother's rescue mission had failed. There would be no escape for either of them now, for her father was a stickler for listening to the news and insisted that everyone still up and about should join him. But perhaps tonight he wouldn't notice her absence while he had Philip there.

His voice boomed out. 'Sarah? Sarah, I know you're out there. The news is about to begin.'

She reluctantly stubbed out the half-smoked cigarette and stepped back indoors. 'It's much cooler outside,' she coaxed. 'I thought Philip and I could—'

'Not now, dear,' he said, raising his hand for silence as the chimes of Big Ben announced the news.

Sarah sank into a nearby chair and smiled at Philip, who was looking rather battered by the lecture he'd just had on the war. Poor Philip, he'd so longed to enlist, but his responsibilities at the plantation meant he was in a reserved occupation and could only join the part-time local defence volunteer unit alongside her father. Yet she knew he was well informed through his business contacts with the military and government officials, and probably knew more about the war than Jock did – but of course he was far too polite to argue, or to point out that many of Jock's views were somewhat old-fashioned and short-sighted.

With her father sitting forward in his chair, fully engrossed as he stared at the wireless, Sarah and Philip were able to gaze at one another longingly as they kept half an ear open to what the newsreader was saying.

The news was just as gloomy as her mother had predicted. Rationing in Great Britain was tighter than ever; the military service call-up had been extended to include men and unencumbered women between the ages of eighteen and fifty-one; although an air raid on the east of England was reported to have done little damage. Slightly more encouraging was the news that the Russians were striking a major counter-offensive against the Germans in Moscow, and were actually making some headway.

As the news came to an end, Philip got to his feet. 'I must take my leave, sir,' he said firmly. 'I'm meeting Harris at the warehouses in Singapore early in the morning, and there are some papers I need to go through before we can send the shipment off.'

'I was rather hoping we could discuss the Japanese question,' rumbled Jock, 'but I suppose it can wait.' He must have noted the look that flickered between Sarah and Philip, for he suddenly broke into a broad smile. 'I think I'll turn in,' he said. 'Sarah can see you off.'

Philip shook his hand, and when Jock had stumped out of the room, he turned to Sarah with a loving smile and laced his fingers through hers. They walked together into the heat of the night, and the music of an orchestra of crickets.

Sarah silently moved into his embrace and gave herself up to his kiss, her body melting into his as the sensations began to overwhelm her. She had never known such intense emotion, and although she was finding it increasingly hard to resist the urgency to explore the sensations further, she knew she must.

'Oh, Sarah,' he breathed into her hair some time

later. 'I've waited all evening to kiss you.' He drew back, still holding her to him, as he looked into her upturned face. 'I love you, my darling girl, and can't imagine life without you.' He became hesitant all of a sudden and drew back further.

'Whatever's the matter?' she asked as his expression grew solemn and he reached for the inside of his tuxedo jacket.

'I hope that what I'm about to do will not startle you, Sarah,' he said in a rush. 'Do you think – when all this madness is over – that you might – might consider . . .?'

Her heart was pounding so hard she was certain he must hear it. 'What are you trying to say?' she coaxed softly.

He dropped to one knee. 'Will you marry me, Sarah?' he asked breathlessly. 'Will you make me the happiest man in the world by becoming my wife?'

She could barely breathe as she looked down at him. This was the moment she'd dreamed about, the words she'd thought she'd never hear, and tears of joy almost blinded her. 'Oh, Philip,' she breathed. 'Yes. Of course I will.'

He sprang to his feet, crushed her to him and smothered her face in kisses. And then he was opening a jewellery box and fumbling with the diamond ring that nestled within the velvet lining. 'This was my mother's,' he said softly as he placed it on Sarah's finger, 'and I give it to you with all my heart.'

'I will treasure it always,' she breathed, noting how perfectly it fitted, and how simply beautiful the solitaire diamond was as it caught the light from the flickering lanterns. She looked back at him with rapture. 'I want to tell the world,' she said. 'I want to wake up the whole house and shout it from the rooftops.'

'Darling girl, so do I.' Philip drew her back into his arms. 'But I've yet to ask your father's permission,' he admitted. 'Do you think he'll mind awfully that I've rather jumped the gun?'

Sarah shook her head and giggled, but any further words she might have uttered were smothered by his passionate kiss, and the rest of the troubled world seemed to fade away as they became lost in each other's arms.

Chapter Two

They had agreed that Sarah should wear her ring on a slender gold chain around her neck until Philip had had the chance to ask her father's permission. When Sarah eventually drifted off to sleep, she dreamed about her wedding day. Her dress was of the finest silk with an overlay of the same delicate lace that made up the long veil. Sybil's diamonds sparkled in her ears and at her throat, and, as her father led her down the imposing aisle of St Andrew's Cathedral, there, waiting at the altar, was Philip.

But somewhere beneath the rousing organ music was another noise – one that shouldn't have been there at all – and it seemed to be getting louder.

The image of her special day disintegrated, the sound penetrating the soft cocoon of happiness that enfolded her until that too drifted away. She opened her eyes and frowned into the darkness beyond the gauzy drifts of mosquito netting as she tried to identify what could have woken her.

And then she heard it again. It was unmistakeably the sound of a fast-approaching truck, its headlights flashing between the slats of the bamboo shutters as it followed the meandering, steep track through the plantation up to the house. 'What on earth?' she muttered as she sat up and glanced at the bedside clock. It was barely three-thirty in the morning – certainly not the time for people to come calling unless it was an emergency.

Flinging back the mosquito net, she grabbed her Chinese silk wrapper from the chair, padded barefoot across to the window and quietly unlatched the shutters. She could tell it had been raining, for there was a heavy scent of wet earth and jungle in the air. Although the moon was bright between the skeins of thin cloud, the shadows were dense beneath the tree canopy, and she couldn't see beneath the broad veranda to where the truck had slithered to a halt. A sudden fear chilled her. Something must be very wrong.

She could barely draw breath as she heard the soft knock on the front door and the hushed voice of the senior houseboy turning sharp as he conversed with this unexpected visitor. Edging away from the window, Sarah crept to the door. Opening it a crack, she listened to the scurrying bare feet of the houseboy and his timid knock on Jock's bedroom door. 'So sorry wake you, *Tuan*,' he said in a hoarse whisper before he closed the door.

Sarah couldn't make out what the boy was saying from her listening post, but she heard her mother's sleepy voice asking what was happening, and her father's soft command to go back to sleep – but it was the heavy tread of booted feet pacing back and forth in the drawing room that made her mouth dry and her pulse race, for whoever their caller was, he was clearly on edge.

Sarah dodged out of sight as her father emerged from the next room resplendent in silk dressing gown and leather slippers. 'This had better be important,' he growled as he strode down the narrow hall and walked into the drawing room.

'It is, sir. I assure you.'

Sarah would have recognised Philip's voice anywhere – but the sense of dark urgency in his tone only served to stoke her fear. Galvanised into action, she quickly dragged on underwear and a cotton frock. Not bothering to brush her hair or find a pair of shoes, she tucked the gold chain and her engagement ring out of sight beneath the collar of her dress, hurried out of her room and headed towards the sound of their muted voices.

Philip was dressed in the makeshift uniform of the local defence volunteers, which consisted of khaki-coloured knee-length shorts and short-sleeved shirt, long socks and boots, and a slouch hat, the brim pinned up on one side with the unit's insignia. The two men were standing almost head to head as Philip's low voice urgently relayed the purpose of his visit. Their faces were grim, the tension in the room almost tangible.

'What is it? What's going on?' Sybil appeared at Sarah's side in her dressing gown, closely followed by the Amah and a wide-eyed Jane.

Both men turned towards them, but it was Jock

who responded to their sense of alarm. 'This does not concern you,' he said gruffly. 'Go back to bed.'

'I will do no such thing,' retorted Sybil as she walked further into the room. 'What is the meaning of this, Philip?'

Jock's expression was one of exasperation as he realised his wife was determined to stay. 'Amah, take Jane back to her room and keep her there,' he ordered with a sigh. Catching sight of the curious servants who'd come to see what had caused such an early disturbance, he shooed them away with orders to bring tea.

As a protesting Jane was led rather forcibly away by a determined Amah, Jock's gimlet gaze settled on Sarah momentarily and then he shrugged his shoulders. 'You and your mother had better sit down. Philip's news is rather disturbing.'

At Sybil's sharp intake of breath, Jock took her hand to steady her as she sank into a chair.

Trying to gauge the severity of his news from his expression, Sarah could only see a tautness in Philip's jaw, and a strange light of excitement in his dark eyes that made her feel decidedly uneasy. She perched on the edge of the chair by her mother, unable to quell the dread that lay coldly in the pit of her stomach.

Philip took a deep breath and, after a curt nod from Jock, began to speak. 'Just over three and a half hours ago, the British India troops patrolling the beaches at Kota Bharu on the north-eastern shore of Malaya spotted three Japanese ships drop anchor just off the coast. These ships were escorted by a fleet of light cruisers, destroyers, minesweepers and sub chasers. They began to bombard the coastline at about half-past midnight, and immediately launched their landing craft.'

Sarah heard her mother gasp, but her own heartbeat was so rapid, her fear so sharp, she found she couldn't move to console her as she stared in horror at Philip.

'The seas were rough and a good many of the enemy landing craft capsized. The beaches were, of course, heavily fortified with landmines, barbed wire and pillboxes, but despite a spirited and heroic defence by the Eighth Infantry Brigade, the Indian Ninth, and the Thirteenth and Seventeenth Battalion Dogra Regiment – and the addition of four howitzers and heavy artillery – they came in overwhelming numbers and managed to land on the beach.'

He took a shallow, unsteady breath. 'The latest news is that another Japanese landing has taken place in Siam at Singora, but the details are sketchy. At Kota Bharu there is hand-to-hand fighting on the estuaries that lead straight to the Allied airfields. Needless to say, the RAF and the RAAF are giving sterling air support to force the enemy into retreat.'

'Thank God,' breathed Sybil. 'But how did they manage to get through our sea defences and radar posts so easily? Surely someone should have spotted a large fleet of warships offshore?'

Philip cleared his throat, his gaze fixed on his boots. 'They were seen yesterday,' he admitted softly, 'but the commanding officer of the British Forces in the Far East feared that the Japanese were merely trying to provoke a British reaction, and thus provide an excuse to go to war – so he delayed any operations overnight to see what would happen.'

They sat in stunned silence, unable to voice their whirling thoughts and emotions as the servant poured tea and tried to look as if he wasn't listening.

'I'm afraid there's more bad news,' said Jock as he put his hand softly on Sybil's shoulder. 'An hour after the Japs tried to land in Malaya, their air force made a dawn lightning strike on the American Pacific Fleet which was lying at anchor in Pearl Harbor on the Hawaiian island of Oahu. Ships have been sunk and hundreds killed. There's little doubt Roosevelt will soon declare war on Japan.'

With a sense that her world was slowly unravelling, Sarah looked to Philip and her father for reassurance, but their grim expressions made fear crawl in cold fingers along her spine.

'But surely,' said Sybil, 'if the Americans finally enter the war then the Pacific will be safe from further Japanese attack?' Her voice was unsteady as she clung to Jock's strong arm, her expression full of hope. 'We'll be all right, won't we, Jock?'

'Our forces are the very best in the world,' he replied firmly. 'Allied to the might of America, we'll soon have these Japs on the run. They don't have the stomach for real fighting – that was proved during their war with China – so we'll be quite safe.'

'Absolutely, sir,' said Philip. 'Our new defences in Singapore are so strong that I doubt any of us will get the chance to actually see any real action – more's the pity.' He took Sarah's hand. 'Your father and I must go to Kuala Lumpur. The local Defence League has sent out a call for every member to attend an emergency meeting. I'll try to telephone you later today.'

She stood, shocked by how badly she was trembling. 'But you won't be going north to fight, or anything, will you, Philip?'

'I shouldn't think so,' he said with rather more disappointment than Sarah wanted to hear. 'I'm only a volunteer, after all, and our chaps upcountry will soon have the blighters back in the sea.'

'I'll get dressed and follow on,' said Jock as he drained his cup of fragrant tea and then strode out of the room.

Philip drew Sarah into his embrace. 'We may be away for some time,' he murmured. 'But don't worry. I'll look after Jock.'

'See that you do,' said Sybil, her voice unsteady. 'The silly man's likely to shoot himself in the foot with all the excitement.' She blinked away her unshed tears and hurried out of the room.

Philip's hand was strong and warm as he led Sarah towards the front door, but despite his calm veneer, Sarah could almost feel the excitement building inside him – and that terrified her, for she'd seen it reflected in her father's eyes – and excitement led to carelessness and even the euphoric belief that they were invincible.

Once outside, he took her swiftly into his arms again and kissed her. 'Try not to fret, my darling. We British know how to fight, and every man on this peninsula is ready to do his bit to protect all we hold dear.'

'That's exactly what I'm afraid of,' she admitted, her words muffled by his shirt.

He drew back and tucked the loose strands of hair behind her ears as he looked down into her eyes. 'But it won't ever come to that, Sarah. The Japs are just sabre-rattling and trying to scare us. We aren't Pearl Harbor – we're very well prepared.'

This didn't sound at all reassuring in the circumstances, and she couldn't help but voice her doubts. 'But if they've got through our radar and reached the beaches, then surely—'

'They won't get much further,' he said flatly.

'Are you sure?'

'Positive.'

They fell silent as they stood there above the forest canopy, their gazes locked, the words she really wanted to say imprisoned by a dreadful sense that if articulated, they might tempt fate and bring about disaster.

His eyes were very dark as he traced his fingers tenderly over her cheek. 'I have to go,' he murmured regretfully. 'It's a long drive to KL.'

Sarah nodded, unable to speak through the lump that had lodged in her throat.

Philip seemed to understand, for he cupped her

cheek and softly kissed her lips. 'I'll be back tonight to talk to your father, and then we can celebrate, my darling. Please try not to worry.' Before she could reply, he'd turned to run down the wooden stairs to the clearing where he'd parked his truck.

Sarah stepped out onto the rain-washed veranda and cupped the precious diamond ring in her hand as he climbed behind the wheel. She struggled not to show her fear as she returned his cheerful wave.

The truck engine roared in the pre-dawn stillness, causing birds to fly from their roosts in alarm, and the monkeys to screech. And then he was gone, the headlight beams lost amid the trees, the sound of the engine dwindling to silence.

Sarah was still standing on the veranda when Jock came hurrying out several minutes later with Sybil distractedly following in his wake, her long fair hair drifting over her shoulders and her dressing gown fluttering round her ankles.

She caught a glimpse of her father's sturdy brown knees between the voluminous shorts and long socks, and the slouch hat was rammed low over his eyes. 'Look after your mother and sister,' he said gruffly. 'I doubt I'll be back before tonight, so make sure those bills of lading are in order, and see to it that the tappers and coolies don't take our absence as an excuse to idle about.'

He kissed her forehead, gave her a swift hug and stumped down the wooden steps to the truck parked beneath the overhanging veranda. With barely a wave, he drove away.

Sarah took her mother's slender hand as they followed the flash of the headlights through the trees. Once they were gone, they put their arms about each other's waist and continued to stand there as the pre-dawn chorus of birdsong filled the already heat-laden damp air. It was only four o'clock in the morning, but already it felt as if the day had lasted for ever.

Their private thoughts were interrupted by Jane, who came running out in her nightdress, her face alight with excitement. 'Are you going to marry Philip? Is that why he came so early to talk to Pops? Can I be a bridesmaid?' She tossed back her tangle of long fair hair. 'It's all terribly romantic, isn't it – and he's so handsome. You are lucky, Sarah.'

Sybil drew her to her side. 'That's quite enough, Jane,' she admonished softly. 'You're far too young to have an opinion on such things – and I don't think Sarah is feeling frightfully lucky right at this moment.'

Jane looked at them both and frowned. 'Then why did Philip come to see Pops in the middle of the night? And why were they wearing that uniform? Are they soldiers now?'

Sarah and Sybil exchanged glances over Jane's head. 'Not really, darling,' Sybil murmured. 'But he and your father have to dress like that when they go to KL on special business.' She smoothed back the untidy hair and kissed her cheek. 'I shouldn't worry your pretty head about such things when I'm sure Wa Ling can be persuaded to cook us all pancakes for breakfast.'

Jane regarded her mother and sister thoughtfully, and Sarah suddenly wondered if Jane had a much clearer understanding of what was going on than they realised.

Sybil's smile was tinged with sadness as she cupped Jane's chin. 'Go and get dressed, and let Amah brush your hair,' she murmured.

As Jane pouted and reluctantly left the veranda, Sybil's smile faded. 'Your father and I agreed that it's better if we don't tell her too much,' she said softly. 'She wouldn't understand, and we don't want her upset by all this talk of war.'

Sarah shook her head. 'I think Jane knows far more than we give her credit for,' she replied. 'We forget sometimes that although she has childlike ways, she also possesses a keen curiosity and hears a lot of things that perhaps she shouldn't.' She blushed. 'And, judging by her questions just now, I suspect she overheard Philip proposing to me last night.'

Sybil reached for her hand, her smile warm and delighted. 'Oh, my dear. I'm so pleased. Is there a ring? Can I see it?'

Sarah drew the slender chain from beneath the bodice of her dress and held out the ring so her mother could coo over it. 'He was planning to ask Pops' permission today, but with everything else going on it looks as if we'll have to put our plans on hold for a while.'

'Not at all,' said Sybil, her eyes alight with pleasure and excitement. 'Goodness me, it's taken him long enough to pop the question. We can't have him dilly-dallying now just because of a few little yellow men causing trouble upcountry.'

Sarah gave Sybil a gentle hug, the mound of the baby between them making it rather awkward. 'Perhaps, when Philip and Pops get back, we could all go down to Singapore City and celebrate the occasion at Raffles?' she said, in an effort to keep the mood light. 'We could do some shopping and have a bit of a holiday before Christmas.'

Sybil caressed the mound of her stomach where it pushed against her dressing gown. 'I'd like that, but I'm not sure your father will agree. Baby's not due until late February, but he's such an old fusspot he's refused to let me go anywhere. Besides, he won't want to leave the plantation, and with things as they are, I actually think I'd rather stay here.'

Sarah was startled by this uncharacteristic declaration from her mother. 'I never thought I'd hear you turn down a trip to Singapore.'

Sybil laughed and slipped her hand into the crook of Sarah's arm. 'The mere thought of travelling all that way in this heat is too exhausting. But don't you dare tell your father I said that,' she added quickly. Her smile softened and her voice was mellow. 'Bless him. He clucks about me like a mother hen as it is. And he's got enough to worry about without me adding to his woes.'

They walked slowly along the veranda until they came to Sybil's bedroom. 'I'm thrilled about Philip's proposal,' she said as she turned in the doorway. 'That's one in the eye for those old cats at the country club,' she added with a saucy wink, 'and I can't wait to tell them all just how enormous that diamond is.'

Sarah kissed her mother fondly and left her to prepare for the rest of the day while she went in search of a houseboy to ask Wa Ling for the pancakes. But the happiness she should have felt over her engagement was obscured by doubt and a growing fear. For with the Japanese threatening the north-eastern shores and Philip and her father itching to get stuck into the fighting, she could no more concentrate on weddings and shopping than fly to the moon. She just wanted them home, and life to return to normal – but she sensed that things were about to change, and that nothing would be quite the same after today.

Twenty minutes later they were seated at one end of the dining table as the servants brought pots of tea and coffee, fresh milk and chafing dishes filled with delicate pancakes. Sarah and her mother did their best to appreciate the food, but neither of them was hungry, and they left Jane to do justice to Wa Ling's efforts as they sipped their morning drinks. The talk was desultory, not only because of the rude awakening at such an early hour and the worry over Pops and Philip, but because – unlike Sarah, who was often up before dawn – Sybil had never really come to terms with being up and about much before ten, and usually had her breakfast on a tray in her bedroom.

Sarah sipped the hot, strong black coffee and tried to pull her thoughts into order. There were many things to be done in the office today, and her father expected her to keep a clear head. A shipment was due to be delivered to Singapore harbour, and she would have to check that the lorries were loaded properly, and the drivers had the appropriate documents. There were also papers to read through, and the bills of lading to organise before she even started on typing the letters and checking the weekly accounts. At least the tappers and coolies knew what was expected of them, and the Chinese foreman would see they kept to the daily routine.

Sybil interrupted her thoughts by clattering her teacup in its saucer and pushing it away. 'As you'll be busy for most of the day,' she said, 'and I can't sit about here worrying over your father, I thought Jane and I could have a bit of a morning siesta to catch up on our sleep, and then go down to the country club so she could have a swim in the pool. I did promise Elsa Bristow I'd make up a four at bridge this afternoon, and there are always plenty of young people about to keep Jane company.'

Jane dabbed her mouth with a linen napkin and carefully placed it beside her empty plate. 'I'd prefer to go and help Sally Bristow with her horses,' she said tentatively.

'You know how I feel about you and horses,' said

Sybil. 'You're to stay away from them, do you hear me?'

'But I don't see why I can't—'

'That's enough,' snapped Sybil uncharacteristically. 'I will not have you anywhere near horses or stables – and if you continue to argue with me, you won't go to the country club either.'

Jane bowed her head and gave a deep sigh. 'Can I wear my new bathing costume then?'

'Of course you may. Now run along and finish the homework your tutor set.'

Jane regarded her mother with a woeful expression. 'Do I have to?'

'Yes,' said Sybil firmly. 'Mr Dawson will be here tomorrow and he expects to see what progress you're making on that essay.' Sybil smiled to coax Jane out of her sulk. 'I know it's still frightfully early, but as you're awake and full of breakfast, it's the ideal time to get things done before it gets too hot.'

Jane was clearly not persuaded.

'When you've finished,' continued Sybil, 'you can nap for a couple of hours, and then we'll go to the club and have lunch there after your swim. And do remind Amah to pack a parasol. She always insists upon sitting right by the pool out of the shade so she can keep an eye on you, and I don't want her getting sunstroke again.'

Still sulky, Jane nodded and slowly headed for the small study at the back of the house where her homework awaited her on the rather scratched and scruffy desk that Sarah had once used.

Sybil ran her fingers lightly over her hair, which her maid had styled into a smooth, neat chignon, and then brushed non-existent crumbs from the light-weight dress that covered her burgeoning stomach. 'I don't like to bully her, but she's making excellent progress considering her difficulties, and it's so important she's properly educated. Her handwriting could still do with some improvement, as could her grammar.'

Sarah finished her coffee. 'Having said that, she certainly hasn't lost her extraordinary ability with figures,' she replied. 'In fact, I was wondering if she'd like to come to the office for a couple of hours a week and help with the book-keeping.'

Sybil frowned. 'Do you think giving her that kind of responsibility is wise?'

'I certainly think we should give her the chance to spread her wings a bit. She's getting bored, Mother, and I'm sure Philip would agree to pay her a small wage. That way she'll feel she's doing something worthwhile, and will have a bit of her own money to spend.'

Sybil sighed deeply. 'Maybe,' she murmured, 'but I'd square it with your father first. You know how he hates surprises – especially when it concerns his precious office.'

Sarah was about to reply when she thought she heard a roll of distant thunder. The monsoon storms had been a regular feature all week, and it sounded as if there was another on the way. But as the rumble continued and developed into something else, she felt a prickle of unease. 'Do you hear that, Mother?'

'It sounds as if we're about to have yet another downpour,' Sybil replied as she got to her feet. 'I think I'll go and have a lie-down before the sun comes up and the humidity gets any worse.'

Sarah pushed away from the table and stood by the open doors. 'That isn't thunder,' she murmured as the hairs on the back of her neck began to prickle.

'No, you're right.' Sybil turned towards the sound and frowned in concentration. 'It's more like the noise of lots of planes – big planes. And it's getting nearer.'

Sarah and Sybil stepped out onto the veranda and scoured the sky for the source of that deep rumble.

It was almost half-past four in the morning and the full moon was casting bright light over the forest canopy. The sky was black, laced with tendrils of cloud – and high above them against that darkness winked the pinprick lights of many aircraft.

'Are they ours?' breathed Sybil.

'I can't tell. They're too far away to see any insignia, and I'm not very well up on aircraft recognition. But I hope to God they are, because there's no mistaking the fact that those are bombers.'

Sarah became aware of the house servants creeping onto the veranda, and the coolies and their families emerging from their bamboo huts to stand in the clearing and stare up at the sky. Then she felt Jane's hand slip into hers.

'They look pretty,' she said. 'Are they going to the RAF base in Singapore?'

'I really don't know,' Sarah replied carefully, her gaze still fixed on the many lights and the shark-like shadows that were now crossing the moon. There was something stealthy and sinister about them that made her skin crawl, and, as she watched, she saw the formation change, with some of the bombers taking up a much lower flight path. There was little doubt in her mind now that they were Japanese, and the Singapore airfields at Seletar and Tengah lay directly in their sights.

The sense of dread was tangible as all eyes remained fixed on those dark harbingers of death. Sarah and her mother exchanged fearful glances as Jane leaned against the veranda railing and watched the bombers slowly move out of sight.

Sarah saw how pale her mother was suddenly, and decided it was time to get Jane indoors and the servants back to their duties. 'The show's over,' she said as the last bomber disappeared into the distance. The coolies and servants melted away instantly, and she turned to Jane. 'Have you finished your homework?'

Jane looked mulish. 'It's boring,' she muttered. 'And I'm sick of being treated like a baby.'

Sarah's reply was forestalled by a muffled boom that came from the far south and resonated through the forest canopy.

Jane clutched the railing, her eyes wide with alarm. 'What was that?'

'Fireworks,' said Sybil quickly as another boom echoed the first and was swiftly followed by several more.

Jane frowned. 'That sounded very loud,' she replied, 'and I can't see any rockets or sparkles going up.'

'That's because they're too far away,' replied Sybil purposefully. 'Go and do your homework, Jane, otherwise there will be no lunch at the club, and no swimming.'

Jane eyed her mother and sister for a long, tense moment, then turned on her heel and went indoors.

Sarah had seen the look in Jane's eyes and the scornful curl to her lip, and it confirmed her suspicion that Jane hadn't been fooled – that she understood all too well that something bad had happened. 'We'll have to tell her the truth, Mother,' she murmured. 'She's not stupid and she knows something's up.'

'Not yet,' replied Sybil. 'Not until your father agrees.'

Sarah realised her mother was simply playing for time in the hope that the night's events would prove to be nothing more than a hiccup in the orderliness of their lives, but as she turned back to the railing, her mouth dried and her fears increased. The glimmer of distant searchlight beams flickered through the red haze that was slowly building on the southern horizon. The unthinkable had happened. Singapore was under attack.

Chapter Three

Cliffehaven, England, December 1941

Beach View Boarding House was almost silent but for the usual creaks and groans of old timbers and pipes settling, and the snores she could hear coming from Jim and Ron in the two basement rooms. Peggy Reilly eased her back into the mound of pillows she'd propped against the headboard of the big double bed, and sleepily held her baby to her breast. It was barely three in the morning and Daisy was not yet twelve hours old.

She gave a wry smile as she thought of her husband, Jim, who would no doubt tell her tomorrow that he hadn't slept a wink on that bunk bed – that his father's snoring had kept him awake, and the smell of damp dog and abandoned ferret cages was irritating his sinuses – but by the sound of things, he was doing all right down there and a couple of nights of discomfort wouldn't kill him.

She settled more comfortably into the pillows, enjoying the unaccustomed space of the entire double bed and the peace of not having a restless Jim muttering in her ear or prodding her in the back with his elbows.

She smiled down at the tiny baby in her arms and softly touched her cheek. 'It's nice to be just you and me for a bit, isn't it, Daisy?' she whispered.

The baby continued to suckle, her tiny fists bunched beneath her chin, the long dark lashes feathering her peachy cheek. Peggy lovingly ran her finger through the downy shock of dark hair as her thoughts turned back to Jim and Ron.

Jim had been banished from the bedroom by the young midwife, Alison Chenoweth, so he had gone downstairs to the room next to his father's. It had once been the domain of their two young sons, Bob and Charlie, but since they'd been evacuated to Somerset, it had become a useful space for Ron to throw all his clutter and store the bicycles.

Peggy had heard the arguments as Jim tried to clear a space amid the collection of wellington boots, poacher's coats, old ferret cages and numerous bits of fishing tackle, and had also heard the slam of the back door as Ron had stomped off to the pub in high dudgeon with his dog Harvey. The situation couldn't be allowed to go on for long – Irish tempers flared far too easily – but at least peace had been restored now they were both asleep.

In the soft light of the candle that flickered in a saucer on the bedside cabinet, Daisy continued to suckle, unaware of everything but her hunger. Peggy smiled as she held her close. She'd forgotten how delicious babies could be, and how the great waves of love almost overwhelmed her every time she looked at her. Nonetheless, the reality of being a new mother again at forty-four was a bit of a shock, and although she'd thought she was prepared – after all, she'd had four other children and was also a grandmother – she was rather disconcerted by how weak and sore she felt. But, looking down at the tiny person at her breast, she knew it was all worth it.

Daisy would be her last baby – the doctor had insisted upon that after the complication of her breech birth – and she was determined to enjoy every single moment of this precious and surprising gift. They grew so quickly, changed from helpless babes to demanding toddlers, and even more demanding young people struggling to find their place in the world, and she knew she had to hold onto this time and treasure it.

The minutes ticked by, the sound of snoring continued, and Peggy's eyelids fluttered, heavy with sleep. It had been a long, exhausting and exciting day, and the arrival of little Daisy had thrown the household routine into chaos. There had been a stream of visitors to coo over Daisy, and for a while Peggy had felt like a queen, sitting up in bed in the new and obviously expensive pink silk and lace bedjacket her sister Doris had brought. But the euphoria that had followed the protracted and painful labour had dwindled into an overwhelming weariness, and she'd been rather relieved when Alison Chenoweth had firmly sent everyone away.

She looked down as Daisy stopped feeding. She was fast asleep. 'Long may it last,' she whispered as she rubbed the tiny back to bring up any wind, and bundled her against the cold in the soft blanket Mrs Finch had spent the last six months knitting.

The old cot which had seen much use over the years stood at the foot of the bed, well away from the draughts that whistled through the rattling frame of the sash window and made the blackout curtains sway. Peggy wrapped the bedjacket more firmly round her shoulders, eased out of bed and shivered as her bare feet touched the cold lino. There was another icy draught coming under the bedroom door from the hall.

She carefully tucked Daisy into the cot and made a mental note to get Jim or his father to find something to block the draughts out, but she suspected it would be up to her as usual. The pair of them meant well, and could certainly talk a good story about how capable they were at mending and making things – but they always seemed to have something more important to do than things about the house.

Once Daisy was warmly settled, Peggy drew Jim's thick dressing gown over the bedjacket and winceyette nightdress and stuffed her feet into her slippers. She picked up the tall glass of milk from the bedside table and took a long drink before blowing out the candle and drawing back the curtains. She still felt rather wobbly and light-headed, but at least she was upright. It wouldn't be long before she was back in harness again.

Peggy stared out of the window to the sky where

thick clouds scudded across the moon. There had been no bombing raids all week, and although it was a relief not to have to camp out in the freezing cold, damp Anderson shelter with everyone crammed in like sardines, there was still a tension in the air which increased every time a plane flew over.

Beach View Boarding House was three streets back from the seafront, and one of the many four-storey Victorian terraced houses that lined the steep hill. It had been in the family for years, but after war had been declared the visitors had stopped coming, and now the empty rooms were being used as billets.

There was usually a houseful of family and lodgers, but since Julie, her last evacuee, had returned to London, there was only Fran, Suzy and Rita billeted on the attic floor, and the elderly, bird-like little Mrs Finch, who was her permanent lodger, on the first floor next to the bathroom. Her youngest daughter Cissy was a secretary on the nearby RAF base, but rarely managed to get home on leave any more, whilst Anne, her eldest, was down in Somerset with her own baby, keeping her little brothers company.

Anne's husband, Martin Black, was a Spitfire pilot with over twenty sorties under his belt. Although he'd recently been promoted to Air Commodore in charge of setting up new airfields, he was clearly frustrated by this new posting where he spent his days in an office dealing with paperwork and pen-pushers. To Anne and Peggy's great dismay, they realised he was champing at the bit to climb back into a plane, and with so many young men being killed, it was almost a foregone conclusion that he'd soon get his wish.

She tried to keep these worrying thoughts at bay as she looked down from her window at the long, narrow garden which sparkled with frost in the moonlight. The back gate opened onto a twitten that ran between the terraces and led eventually to the open grasslands and farms that lay to the north of Cliffehaven. The flint wall had been damaged long ago in an air raid, the makeshift repairs leaving it looking rather woebegone, but Ron's vegetable garden was already sprouting a few green shoots beneath the thick cover of straw he'd put over it to protect it from the frost.

Peggy regarded the ugly hump of the Anderson shelter at the bottom of the garden, the sagging washing lines that were strung between the neighbouring fences, the outside lav, the shed and the chicken coop. The first few birds had been gifts from a group of Australian soldiers who'd come to tea almost two years before. Over the ensuing months Ron and Jim had somehow managed to increase the flock – though no one questioned their method, all too aware they might not approve of the answer – and now there was a cockerel in charge of a harem of ten hens. This cockerel made the most fearful racket every morning, but the number of eggs his hens laid more than made up for that.

Peggy let the curtain drop back over the window and returned to bed, keeping Jim's dressing gown on for a while longer until the sheets warmed again. She lay in the darkness and listened to the soft snuffle of her sleeping baby, the comforting scent of Jim's shaving soap drifting from the dressing gown. Her eyelids grew heavy and, with a long sigh of contentment, she fell into a deep and dreamless sleep.

Mrs Cordelia Finch was feeling rather sprightly this morning, despite the fact that there was ice on the inside of the windowpanes, the milk on the doorstep was almost frozen solid, and her hearing aid was making the most annoying buzzing sound. At seventy-something – she'd lost track and no longer cared how old she was as long as she continued to enjoy reasonable health and kept her wits – she was still capable of taking over the reins from Peggy and getting downstairs in the morning to cook breakfast. In fact, it was the knowledge that she could still be useful that was making her feel so chipper.

As she clutched the cold milk bottles and rather damp newspapers, she resisted the longing to pop in and see Peggy and the darling baby, for she could hear the murmur of Jim's voice behind the closed door and didn't like to intrude.

Leaving the hall, she hobbled into the kitchen and abandoned her walking stick in a corner. With the milk and newspapers safely on the table, she slipped her arms into Peggy's voluminous wrap-round apron and tied the strings at her tiny waist. Her arthritic hands fumbled a bit as they always did in the cold weather, but once she'd stirred the fire back into life in the

Kitchener range, the heat would soon ease the knots in her joints.

A small shovel of precious anthracite and a couple of logs from the pile Ron always left beside the scuttle soon had the fire blazing, and she set the kettle on the hob and the teapot to warm while she laid the table. All this activity made her feel a bit giddy, and she had to sit down for a moment to catch her breath.

The buzzing from her hearing aid was becoming a real nuisance and she switched the blessed thing off, once more mourning the loss several months before of the lovely new device Peggy had bought her. It had been so careless of her to trample it into a million pieces – but then she *had* been alone in the pitch darkness of the Anderson shelter, disorientated and afraid as she'd woken to the vibration of the overhead bombers.

She clucked impatiently at her wandering thoughts and turned her attention to more practical things – like making that pot of tea, and getting on with preparing the breakfast.

As she stood in the warmth of the range in Peggy's kitchen and stirred the large saucepan of porridge, she contentedly hummed a little tune and regarded her surroundings. She had come to live at Beach View several years ago – long before this nasty war had spoiled things – and this room was the warm, beating heart of the boarding house that was now her home.

No one could deny it was shabby, for the chairs were mismatched, the table scarred, the lino worn into holes by the stone sink and in the doorway to the basement, but somehow it didn't matter. This was the room where everyone met to eat and talk, to knit and sew, listen to the wireless or catch up on local gossip, and Cordelia loved it. She felt safe here, warmed by the knowledge that Peggy's family loved her and that even the young girls who were billeted here accepted her as an intrinsic part of their lives.

She sipped her tea and carried on stirring the porridge, her thoughts drifting back to the distant past when she'd been the youngest of four siblings growing up in the big house by the beach in Havelock Road.

Her parents were already middle-aged when she'd been born. The family was comfortably off as her father was a solicitor who had his own practice, and Cordelia had been blessed with a happy, fulfilled childhood. Her eldest brother was already married by the time her first birthday came round, and although she possessed some faded sepia photographs of those early days, she couldn't remember ever meeting him, for he'd resigned his practice partnership with their father before she was two, and had gone in search of a more adventurous life in the tropics. The second brother was much closer in age and had been her hero, for he always had time for her and was tall and handsome, with kind eyes and a rather fine moustache. He'd been killed in the trenches in 1917, and she remembered she'd been inconsolable for months.

Cordelia stirred the porridge a little more vigorously as she thought of her sister Amelia. They had never got on, for Amelia was five years older and very bossy, and it had taken some courage and will power to stand up to her. Amelia had become even worse in adulthood, and despite being a spinster, took it upon herself to tell Cordelia how to run her home, look after her husband, and raise her sons. Amelia was now living alone in a bungalow on the north-western edges of Cliffehaven, running a branch of the WI and on the committees of half a dozen good causes – no doubt enjoying her position of power, and telling everyone what to do.

'Good luck to them,' she muttered. 'I'm glad I don't have to listen to her any more.'

The porridge was bubbling nicely and she carefully slid the saucepan away from the direct heat and covered it with a lid. With a second cup of tea at her elbow, she sank into the kitchen chair and glanced at the newspaper headlines.

The battle for Moscow was still raging, as was the tank battle in Tobruk; the Japs had invaded Siam and there was heavy fighting in Malaya. America and Britain had declared war on Japan – and Germany and Italy had declared war on America. She set the papers aside, for they'd done very little to restore the bright mood that had waned after all those memories had come flooding back.

In fact, as she sat there in the quiet kitchen and heard the thin wail of the newly born Daisy drift in from the other room, the past returned even more forcefully. She had lost her precious daughter hours after her birth, but her sons had thrived, only to fly the nest decades ago to seek their fortunes in Canada.

She rarely heard from them now, just the odd card at Christmas and perhaps a hastily written aerogramme which told her very little. There were grandchildren she'd never seen, and, no doubt, great-grandchildren too – but they probably didn't know she existed.

Cordelia realised she was feeling a bit sorry for herself and determinedly snapped out of it. Disappointments were all a part of life's rich tapestry, and there was absolutely no point in dwelling on them now. She'd been lucky in so many ways, with a strong and happy marriage that had survived their moving into her childhood home in Havelock Road to look after her elderly parents in their last years.

When her husband died, she'd been left alone in that big house, and had at first managed quite well. But she hadn't been used to seeing to repairs and bills and the day-to-day problems that her husband had always taken care of, and, with her hearing getting worse, and age and arthritis hampering her, things began to slide out of control. Her husband's estate had not been as large as he'd planned – something to do with rather unwise investments – and she'd finally resorted to living in just two of the downstairs rooms without even the help of a daily woman. But then a pipe had burst in the attic water tank during one very cold winter and brought the ceiling down, and it had all become too much to bear.

Peggy Reilly had heard about her plight from the plumber and had called round immediately to offer help and practical advice. Cordelia sighed contentedly.

Dear Peggy, she was such a treasure. That visit had seen her move into Beach View while the repairs were done, and it hadn't taken a great deal of persuasion from Peggy to make the arrangement permanent. The newly refurbished house had been sold, the money carefully invested, and Cordelia was content to live out the last of her years at the heart of this warm and loving family.

'Silly old fool,' she muttered as she clattered her teacup in the saucer and blinked away the sentimental tears. 'Sitting here blubbing when you have so much to be thankful for – you should be ashamed of yourself.'

'To be sure, is it talking to yourself now, Cordelia Finch?'

She glared at Ron, who'd come into the kitchen in his muddy boots, the equally filthy dog, Harvey, scrambling in behind him. His sudden entrance and bellowing voice had startled her. 'At least I can have a sensible conversation that way,' she retorted, 'which is more than I've ever had with you.'

He waggled his greying brows, his blue eyes twinkling with humour in the weathered face as he rolled up the ratty sleeves of his disreputable old sweater and hitched up his sagging and much-patched trousers. 'Is that right now? And what great things are ye debating? The price of bananas? The amount of sugar you'll not be letting me have in me tea?'

She fiddled with her hearing aid as she regarded the boots and the panting dog that seemed to be grinning at her, and tried to look cross – though it was hard to achieve when the pair of them eyed her with such cheekiness. Like his dog, Ron was a charmer, an old Irish rogue in his mid-sixties with more blarney than was good for anyone. But he did make her laugh. 'Get those boots off,' she ordered, 'and do something about Harvey. He stinks to high heaven.'

'He's been rolling in the compost again, heathen eejit,' Ron muttered as he toed off his boots, flung them back down the stairs in the vague direction of the basement scullery and grabbed Harvey by the scruff. 'Will ye be following the boots, ye great lump,' he growled.

The Bedlington-cross eyed him mournfully as he was dragged towards the concrete steps. Harvey was a big dog, with a shaggy brindle coat, floppy ears and long legs. In possession of an entire catalogue of expressions which he used to great effect when he knew he was in trouble, he was as scruffy and unruly as his owner.

They were both a pain in the neck, but Cordelia could forgive them anything, for Harvey and Ron had proved their courage many a time during the air raids as Harvey sniffed out survivors beneath the debris, and Ron helped to rescue them.

'I don't know what Peggy will say if she sees this floor,' she muttered as Ron shut the door on Harvey, who proceeded to howl as if he'd been abandoned in the pit of hell, and not in the basement right next to his bowl of food.

'Peggy will not be seeing any floor for a while yet,'

said Jim cheerfully as he appeared in the doorway carrying a pile of dirty nappies. 'She's to rest and be looked after, so she is. Treated like a queen.' He wrinkled his nose. 'Where do I put these?'

'There's a bucket under the sink,' Cordelia replied as she pointed to the faded gingham curtains that hid all the cleaning paraphernalia. 'Let them soak in there.'

She watched as he delved beneath the old stone sink. Jim was another rogue, with a glint in his eye and enough blarney to make you blush. A handsome man in his forties, Jim could charm the birds off the trees, and sell sand to the Arabs. He could also turn his hand to some dodgy dealing, which often led to trouble between him and Peggy – but it was clear that he adored Peggy and his family, and for Cordelia that was enough to redeem him.

Cordelia brought her wandering thoughts back into order as she heard the three lodgers coming down the stairs to knock on Peggy's door. Fran and Suzy were nurses at Cliffehaven hospital and little Rita drove a fire engine. They were all young, with good appetites, and would need this filling hot breakfast to start the day, for it was bitterly cold out there.

'Let the dog back in before he upsets the baby with his racket,' she said wearily. 'But clean him up a bit first.'

Ron winked at her and she did her best to glare with disapproval at such cheek – but she could feel her face burn, for he always made her want to giggle like a silly schoolgirl when he flirted like that.

Ron went to sort out his dog and Jim went outside to see if there were enough eggs to perhaps keep a few as barter for extra margarine or flour.

Cordelia carefully avoided the mud on the linoleum as she returned to stirring the porridge. It was lovely to be in charge of a kitchen again, and with a new baby in the house, and all the sweet young things dashing in and out, it chased away the gloom of memories and war and made her feel much more like her old self.

'To be sure, that is the sweetest wee cub I ever did see,' said Fran as she came into the kitchen, starched apron crackling over her neat uniform as she helped herself to tea. She tossed back the mane of fiery hair from her face and dreamily stared into the teacup. 'All that dark hair and those long eyelashes – makes me feel all warm and broody.'

'I'd have thought that being one of twelve would have put you off babies,' said Suzy as she followed her to the table and reached for the teapot.

Fran shrugged. 'Well now,' she replied. 'Maybe it does make a girl stop and t'ink, and I've had the endless lectures from Father O'Brian which are enough to put a girl off men and babies for life – but when they're that wee and that perfect . . .' She sighed and sipped her tea.

'I suspect we're all feeling a bit clucky at the moment,' said Rita as she came clumping into the kitchen in her usual attire of sturdy boots, thick, manly trousers and moth-eaten WW1 flying jacket. 'But it will wear off soon enough when it's bawling its head off at two in the morning.'

'And what side of the bed did you get out of this morning, Miss Grumpy?' teased Fran, her Irish lilt in direct contrast to Rita's local, rather flat accent.

Rita's brown eyes twinkled as she tried to bring order to the riot of dark curls that sprung round her face and fell to the sheepskin collar of her leather jacket. 'The same side I get out every morning. But there was an emergency call-out to a chimney fire just before I got off duty, and I've only had three hours' sleep.'

Suzy's fair hair glinted beneath the starched cap in the weak sun that came through the dirty windowpane as she helped Cordelia ladle the porridge into bowls while Fran set out a tray to take into Peggy. 'You'd be better off going back to bed,' she said, her vowels rounded and smoothed by her careful upbringing in Surrey.

Rita shrugged. 'I'm up now, so I thought I'd catch up on the arrangements for the motorcycle race next week, and then do a bit of work on the Norton. She's misfiring again.'

'You and that bike,' sighed Cordelia, who secretly envied the freedom and opportunities young girls had these days. 'It isn't at all ladylike to be haring about on that ugly great thing, and it's dangerous.'

'Only if you don't know what you're doing,' said Rita with a fond smile. 'Don't worry about me, Grandma Finch. I'm as tough as old boots.'

Cordelia glanced down at Rita's thick, laced boots

and gave a sigh of exasperation. She was such a pretty little thing – why on earth she had to dress like a boy, was beyond her.

Having organised Peggy's tray to her liking and sent Fran off with it, Cordelia sat down to her own breakfast. As the girls chattered, Harvey lay supine in front of the range, and Ron discussed the situation in Malaya with Jim, she felt a warm glow of happiness. This was her home, and these were the people she'd come to love the most – and at this very moment she wouldn't have exchanged it for a pot of gold.

Chapter Four

Malaya

The plantation office was a simple wooden structure raised above the ground on sturdy concrete pillars to keep the white ants at bay. Nestled deep in the tree-covered valley and powered by one of the many generators on the estate, it was close to the vast storage sheds and the workshops where the trucks were maintained.

The windows and door were heavily screened against the flies and mosquitoes which buzzed and whined with monotonous persistence against the backdrop of jungle sounds. Sarah's part of the office was sparsely furnished, for apart from the mouldering desk and rather rickety typist's chair there was just a line of rusting metal filing cabinets against one wall, and a fly-spotted framed print of the King hanging from another. An ancient, rusting fan hung from the rafters beneath the corrugated iron roof, each slow, barely useful rotation accompanied by a most annoying squeak which seemed impervious to any amount of lubrication.

Sarah had been on tenterhooks all day, and although

she had a great deal of office administration to deal with, she found that even the most mundane tasks required added concentration. And yet there were moments when she simply stared into space, lost in thought as the monsoon rain hammered on the tin roof and the shadows deepened beneath the regimented rows of rubber trees.

She had been unable to relax enough to take her usual midday siesta, and as the hours had ticked slowly away and the telephone remained stubbornly silent, she became increasingly worried about her father and Philip. Up until today, the local Defence League had been a bit of a joke, with old men and boys playing at soldiers and going off to camp in the jungle or shooting their guns on the nearby range. No one had honestly believed that they might actually have to fight. But the call to the headquarters in KL meant that the attempted Jap invasion was being taken with the utmost seriousness – and that was extremely unsettling.

By mid-afternoon she could stand it no longer and had gone up to the house in the hope that the local radio station might shed some light on what was happening. But it seemed the station was no longer transmitting – which only made her worry more.

It was now late afternoon and the rain had finally stopped, but the temperature had soared and the air was torpid with heat and the smell of rotting jungle vegetation. Sarah placed the cover on her typewriter and pushed back from the scarred desk, which was one of a pair that her grandfather had imported from England many years before. She needed a shower and a change of clothes, for her blouse stuck unpleasantly to her back and her hair was limp with perspiration – but she remained sitting there, reluctant to leave in case she missed her father and Philip, who were bound to call in here before going up to the house.

She lit a cigarette and restlessly twisted back and forth on the creaking chair as she gazed through the screened windows into the rapidly dwindling light. The Chinese and Malay coolies were splashing barefooted through the mud as they returned with the day's second harvest of latex, stowed in jars which they carried in straw baskets dangling from the ends of the long poles across their shoulders. The Malay women wore plain sarongs, but in their drab shirts and short, baggy trousers it was hard to tell if the Chinese were male or female for, like their Malayan counterparts, their heads and shoulders were hidden by the wide conical hats that kept off the worst of the rainwater that still dripped from the trees.

Like her father, Sarah had always marvelled at the resilience and stamina of the hard-working coolies who were such an important part of the plantation – and she followed their progress through the trees until they were out of sight.

The latex would be stored and processed in the huge barns that lay just beyond the estate office, and then sent by truck down to Singapore, where it would be loaded onto cargo ships bound for England, America and Australia. The war in Europe had seen a sharp rise in the demand for rubber, but the convoys of supply ships had to run the gauntlet of German U-boats and aerial attacks. Now that the Japanese had made their intentions clear, the journey would be even more hazardous.

Sarah stubbed out her cigarette and looked at her watch. It was almost six, and time to get home before her mother and Jane returned from the country club. She adjusted the combs in her hair so it didn't straggle and stick to her hot face, gathered together the pile of letters she'd typed ready for Jock's signature, and went into his office.

This room was very much her father's, for it was redolent with pipe-smoke – a pleasure that Sybil had banned from the house long ago. It too had been sparsely furnished, with the cluttered desk taking up most of the space. The large chair behind it was sagging, the horsehair stuffing poking through where the leather had succumbed to Jock's weight. In one corner stood a coat-tree, adorned with one of Jock's old sweat-stained hats and a moth-eaten black umbrella, and in another was a small bamboo cabinet which held glasses, soda siphons, and bottles of gin and whisky to offer visitors – or for Jock to enjoy the odd nip when he felt the need for restoration after a hard morning's work.

Sarah tidied away the documents strewn across the desk, emptied the ashtray, placed his pipe back in the rack with the others and put the magnifying glass back in the desk drawer. Jock would never admit it, but his eyesight wasn't as good as it once was, and he swore that the print was getting smaller on the contracts he had to read.

Leaving the stack of letters neatly on a fresh blotter, she left the office and let the screen door clatter behind her as she went down the wooden steps to the clearing where she'd parked the Austin Twelve. Her father had had it imported shortly before war had been declared and it was Sarah's most treasured possession, for it gave her the independence to get about when she wanted and meant she didn't have to rely on their driver, who was usually ferrying her mother somewhere.

The black coachwork was dull with dust and rain splatters, and the interior was stifling even though there had been very little sun that day. She climbed in, opened the windows and turned the key, noting the sweetness of the purring engine. The rains had turned the narrow track into a quagmire, the ruts and potholes filled with murky water so it was difficult to see how deep they were. Sarah drove slowly, not wanting to damage her precious car as it slid and slithered up the steep hill to the house.

The scene around her was as peaceful and lush as always, and as she reached the flattened clearing in front of the house she stepped from the car and took a deep, refreshing breath of the cooler air. The colours of the birds and wildflowers seemed more vibrant against the dark, glossy green of the wet trees, and despite the humidity and the low rain-filled clouds that were drifting ever nearer, it was pleasant to be out of the stifling heat of the valley.

Sarah had showered and changed by the time Sybil and Jane returned from the club, and in answer to her mother's silent, questioning look, Sarah shook her head.

'We will change for dinner as usual,' said Sybil with a brittleness that betrayed her worry. 'I'm sure they'll be back soon, and there's absolutely no reason to allow standards to slip.' With that she went off to her room to prepare for the evening.

Dinner was an almost silent meal, and even Jane seemed to catch their mood, for after chattering about her day at the club, she finally fell silent and then asked to leave the table before pudding was served.

Sarah and her mother moved into the drawing room for coffee and they sat in silence as they stared out of the French doors at the rain that thundered on the roof and drenched the veranda. There was no need to talk, for their thoughts were the same, their fears growing as the time ticked away and the soft-footed servants exchanged worried glances.

When the grandfather clock in the hall struck midnight, Sybil sent the servants to bed, but there would be no sleep for her and Sarah until the men returned. They continued to sit there, unable to voice their fears as the clock struck one and then two and three.

The drum of the rain muffled all other sounds and they both almost jumped out of their skins when Jock slammed the front door and came stomping into the room, looking like a drowned and very disgruntled bear.

Sarah kept her gaze fixed on the doorway as her mother hurried to greet him and the ever-alert houseboy scurried about bringing towels, a glass of whisky and a dry shirt. 'Where's Philip?' she asked in alarm.

'Still down in Singapore,' muttered Jock as he vigorously rubbed his hair dry, handed the towel back to the Malay servant and drank the whisky down in one. 'That's better,' he said with a deep sigh. 'It's been one hell of a day and I reckon I earned that.'

He softly kissed Sybil's cheek and scolded her for waiting up for him, then held the glass out to be refilled. He rejected the dry shirt and offer of food and plumped down into the couch.

'You do look rather dishevelled, dear,' said Sybil with admirable understatement as she eyed the sweat-stains on his shirt and the mud on his socks and boots. 'What *have* you been up to?'

'Helping to strengthen the beach defences and build extra gun emplacements and pillboxes in KL. Then we were sent down to Singapore to lend a hand with the clearing up after that treacherous Jap raid.'

'How bad was it?' asked Sybil, her eyes dark with anxiety.

Jock took a gulp of the whisky. 'A number of bombs fell on Raffles Place,' he muttered. 'The bungalow's gone, I'm afraid.'

'A bungalow can be rebuilt,' said Sybil impatiently. 'What about casualties? Are our friends all right?'

'Most of the damage was done at the airfields, the Sembawang Naval Base, and Keppel Harbour. Philip's yacht was blown to bits, along with most of the other boats in the Marina, and rumour has it that sixty-one died and over seven hundred were injured – most of the casualties seem to have been troops from the Gurkha Rifles and the Indian Infantry.'

Sarah couldn't stand it any longer and broke in before her mother could ask another question. 'Why is Philip still in Singapore?'

'One of our warehouses took a direct hit, and he's had to stay to sort things out. He sends his apologies for not ringing, but the phone lines are all down. He'll be back sometime tomorrow.' His face creased into a warm smile. 'In the midst of the mayhem he found time to ask me if he could marry you.'

Sarah held her breath and clutched the ring at her neck.

Jock laughed. 'Well, I couldn't refuse, could I? Not when you'd already agreed and had the ring to prove it.'

'Oh, Pops, thank you,' she said in relief as she went to hug him.

'He's a fine young man, Sarah,' he said gruffly. 'I'm delighted for you both.' Clearly rather embarrassed by his daughter's show of emotion, he reached again for the whisky and took a restorative gulp.

Sarah hugged her mother, drew the ring from the

chain, and put it on her finger where it sparked like flames in the candlelight.

'I wish I was young again,' Jock sighed as he stared morosely out of the open doors to the rain that was still drumming on the veranda. 'Seeing all those chaps setting off like that . . . I tell you, Sybil, I'd be right with them if I could, and that's a fact.'

Sybil stared at him in puzzlement. 'What do you mean? What young men? Where are they going?'

Jock continued to watch the rain for a moment. 'We older men want to muck in as well, you know,' he grumbled, 'but it seems we don't have that choice – not if we have the responsibility of running plantations.'

'Thank God for that,' breathed Sybil.

He glared out at the rain. 'They're going to need every able man up there, and I feel utterly bloody useless.'

'Jock, you're frightening us, and so far you haven't made one bit of sense,' said Sybil rather sharply. 'Will you please tell us what has been happening in Singapore?'

'I suppose you have a right to know, but what I'm about to tell you is top secret, and not to be repeated.'

'Do get on with it, Jock,' snapped Sybil. 'Can't you see we're both on tenterhooks?'

Jock glanced at his watch and then finished the whisky. He carefully placed the empty glass on the nearby table as if he needed those few seconds to mull over what he should say. 'The battleships *Repulse* and *Prince of Wales* will have left Singapore about half an hour ago with an escort of four destroyers to engage the enemy in the north.'

Sarah and her mother could only stare at him in horror as the full import of what he said began to sink in, but it was Sarah who voiced their fears. 'Is it really so bad up there that we have to send battleships?'

Jock must have heard the fear in her voice and seen it mirrored in Sybil's face, for he rose to take them into his embrace. 'It's just a precaution,' he murmured. 'Lieutenant General Percival has ninety thousand British, Indian and Australian troops under his command, and with the Allied air forces and the Royal Navy giving support, we'll soon have those yellow devils routed.'

Sarah and her mother leaned into his embrace and tried to find comfort in his words. But in the sudden heavy silence that followed the abrupt end of the rainstorm, Sarah thought she could feel an ominous tension in the air. It was as if the jungles of Malaya were holding their breath.

Chapter Five

Cliffehaven

England was in the grip of a cold, wet winter, with gale-force winds that howled across the rooftops, rattled the windows and generally made life difficult. It was only just four in the afternoon, but already it was dark outside, and Peggy snuggled further under the blankets, the feather-filled eiderdown tucked up to her chin.

There was something quite primal in the pleasure of being snug and warm while the wind moaned outside and the rain beat on the window. On days like this she was relieved not to have to be out there, standing in the endless queues at the local shops, dashing here and there doing things for her neighbours or battling the wind to reach the WVS centre at the Town Hall where she helped pack emergency rations of food and clothing for the homeless.

And yet, as she lay there, she had to admit she was getting rather bored with it all. She missed her kitchen, and the evenings by the fire – missed the chatter and warmth of being at the heart of the family. It was all very well to have people popping in at all times of the day, but as much as she loved seeing them, she preferred to be up and doing and in charge of things.

With this thought, she grabbed Jim's dressing gown and pulled it on before clambering out of bed and stuffing her feet into her slippers. She was feeling much more herself after nearly four days of doing nothing, but despite Alison Chenoweth's thorough bed-baths, she felt grubby and her hair was sticking to her head in a most unbecoming way. With Daisy asleep and not due for another feed until six, she would have a bath – and to hell with the water rationing.

She found the lovely unused bar of lavender soap she'd been saving for a special occasion, and then rummaged in the wardrobe and drawers in search of some warm and comfortable clothes. Another quick glance to make sure Daisy didn't look about to stir, and she opened the door.

The house was quiet, and she suspected Mrs Finch was upstairs with her hearing aid switched off, having her afternoon nap. If Jim caught her sneaking up to have a bath there'd be hell to pay, but as he was at work in the projection room of the Odeon Cinema, what he didn't know couldn't hurt him. But she still dithered in the doorway, wondering where Ron and the girls might be.

'This is ridiculous,' she muttered. 'I'm a grown woman, and if I want a bath, I'll jolly well have one.' She closed the bedroom door quietly and crossed the hall to the flight of stairs that went right up to the attic rooms, and, grasping the bannister, she started up.

By the time she'd reached the first floor landing her legs felt decidedly wobbly and she was out of breath, which was silly – a week ago she'd been running up and down these stairs like a spring chicken. Well, she admitted silently, not exactly running – one couldn't run when nine months pregnant and as big as a barrage balloon.

She stood there for a moment to get her breath back, and then, fearing that Mrs Finch might suddenly come out of her room, hurriedly made use of the lavatory, and then took two towels from the airing cupboard and headed into the bathroom. She locked the door and sank onto the wooden chair that stood by the bath. She felt a bit light-headed, and suddenly wondered if this had actually been such a good idea.

The icy cold of the room cleared her head, and she drew Jim's dressing gown more tightly round her as she closed the blackout curtain on the dark, gloomy day and switched on the light. She found the matches and, standing well back, turned on the gas boiler and held the match to the pilot light. There was a loud bang and two tongues of flame shot out of the vent – but Peggy was inured to this and simply waited for the boiler to settle down.

Once this was achieved she waited a few more moments before turning the taps. As the steam began to rise and form condensation on the white tiles, Peggy placed the precious bar of lavender soap in the dish at the end of the bath and rummaged in the cabinet for her shampoo.

Eyeing the almost empty bottle with a rueful smile, she realised one or all of the girls had been using it. That was the problem with so many females in the house – shampoo, lipstick, stockings, and even face powder were fair game when left lying about. But she didn't mind. The girls worked hard and times were tough, and it wasn't as if she'd not been guilty herself of borrowing the odd dash of lipstick and bit of talc now and again.

Peggy eyed the regulatory two inches of water in the bottom of the bath and decided that having missed out on three proper baths she was due an extra few inches. Minutes later she tested the water, added some cold and then hurriedly slipped out of her nightwear.

The icy cold of the bathroom goosed her flesh and she quickly slid beneath the lovely hot water until it lapped about her ears. Closing her eyes, she lay there, revelling in the luxury. Every extra hour of work and every penny saved for this bathroom had been worth it, she decided.

After some moments she realised she was in danger of falling asleep, so she reluctantly roused herself and reached for the soap. Once she was sweet-smelling again, she clambered out of the rapidly cooling water, wrapped herself in a large bath towel and used the tin jug that always stood by the bath to wash her hair.

Still feeling slightly light-headed from her exertions, she dragged on her underwear and red flannel vest and quickly pulled on the old tweed skirt and warm sweater. She was sitting on the chair rubbing her hair dry when she heard the low moan of the first call of the air-raid siren.

Leaping to her feet, and regretting it instantly, she dropped the towel on the floor, steadied herself for a moment then unbolted the door. She stumbled to Mrs Finch's room, which was right next door, and went in without knocking.

Mrs Finch was snoring happily as she lay fully dressed beneath the eiderdown, her discarded hearing aid dangling from the bedside table.

Peggy gently shook her awake.

'Whasamatter?' she mumbled as she emerged from her deep sleep.

'Air raid,' mouthed Peggy as she handed her the hearing aid, grabbed her gas-mask box and helped her off the bed.

The dear old thing was a bit unsteady on her feet, but then Peggy wasn't much better, and they both swayed a bit as Peggy handed her the walking stick and tucked her hand into the crook of her arm. The sirens were louder now, reaching their highest pitch, and Peggy was frantic to get Cordelia downstairs so she could reach Daisy, who was now crying.

'You go,' ordered Mrs Finch. 'I can manage perfectly well.'

Peggy was torn between the needs of her frightened baby and those of this frail old lady she'd come to love.

Mrs Finch pushed past her and started down the stairs. Clutching the bannisters, she swayed on each step with heart-stopping regularity, and Peggy rushed to help her down to the hall. 'Get the air-raid box from the kitchen,' she shouted over the screams of the baby and the wailing sirens, 'but don't go down the cellar steps. I'll be with you in a minute.'

'I know what to do, dear. See to Daisy.'

Peggy tore into the bedroom and plucked the thoroughly agitated Daisy from her cot. Wrapping her firmly in several small blankets, Peggy kicked off her slippers and dug her feet into her everyday shoes, grabbed her gas-mask box and fresh nappies and rushed into the kitchen.

Mrs Finch had donned her overcoat and was sitting halfway down the concrete steps that led to the basement, the air-raid box of essentials clasped to her chest, her walking stick and gas-mask box lying on the scullery floor next to a packet of biscuits. 'Oh dear,' she quavered. 'I'm quite all right – but I think I've broken the biscuits.'

Peggy held the fractious baby in one arm, and helped Mrs Finch to her feet. 'You're more precious than any biscuits,' she muttered as she took the air-raid box and left it on the top step.

Once they'd reached the scullery and the walking stick and gas mask had been retrieved, Peggy steadied Mrs Finch as they hurriedly negotiated the rough path to the Anderson shelter. At least it had stopped raining, but the sirens were still wailing, Daisy was still screaming and the searchlights had begun to flicker into life against the dark sky.

The Anderson shelter was bitterly cold and stank of

damp, rust, and mouse droppings. A bench had been fixed on both sides and a deckchair had been wedged into a corner so that Mrs Finch could be comfortable. There was an oil lamp hanging from the tin roof, and a primus stove for cooking tucked away under the bench beside the special gas-mask cot for Daisy.

A kerosene heater stood by the entrance so the fumes could escape through the many gaps in the door. On the back wall, Ron had fixed a wooden shelf, which held a battered saucepan, an equally battered kettle and teapot, as well as chipped mugs, mismatched cutlery and some tin plates. It wasn't exactly welcoming, and hardly a home-from-home, but it had been their refuge now since the first air raid in 1940, and they'd become inured to its dubious attractions.

Peggy helped Mrs Finch into the deckchair and, with Daisy still screaming and flailing in her arms, attempted to light the lamp and the heater. Daisy suddenly became fascinated by the flickering light and forgot her fear, and Peggy handed her to Mrs Finch who'd at last had a chance to switch on her hearing aid.

'I need to go back and get the rest of the stuff,' she said clearly.

Mrs Finch nodded and held Daisy close as Peggy dashed out of the shelter. Retrieving the precious digestive biscuits as she ran up the scullery steps, she put them back in the box, yanked on her overcoat and grabbed the pillows and spare blankets which were always to hand for just such an emergency.

Heavily laden and out of breath, Peggy stumbled outside again. The sound of approaching bombers was interspersed with the sharp rat-a-tat-tat of the ack-ack guns as red tracers stitched through the sky and the searchlight beams swung back and forth in search of the enemy.

She didn't stand about to watch, but ducked her head and almost fell into the shelter. Slamming the door, she dropped everything on the bench and collapsed beside it as she tried to catch her breath. She really did feel awful, with a head full of cotton wool, legs like jelly and a dull ache at the pit of her stomach.

'I don't wish to state the obvious, dear, but you've been overdoing things,' said Mrs Finch as she gently rocked a now pacified Daisy back and forth in her arms. 'Why are you even out of bed, let alone dressed?'

Peggy's heart was racing and she felt sick and faint. Dropping her head to her knees, she fought to stay conscious. 'I'll be all right in a minute,' she insisted.

Mrs Finch didn't reply, but her silence spoke volumes.

Peggy waited for her pulse to return to normal, and as it did the nausea faded along with the feeling that she was about to faint. She slowly lifted her head and reached for the large fresh-water container she always kept in the shelter. The tin mugs weren't very clean after sitting out here for days, but she didn't care, and she poured the cold water and drank greedily. The second cup restored her to something approaching normality, and she smiled to reassure Mrs Finch that she was indeed all right.

It was impossible to talk, for the bombers were right overhead now, probably heading for the large naval dockyard further down the coast. It had already taken a fierce hammering over the past year, and she couldn't help but wonder if there was much left to bomb. Of course there was always the chance they would dump the last of their deadly load on Cliffehaven before they scuttled back across the Channel – and these 'tip and runs' had caused a great deal of damage to the town.

Peggy was about to hold out her arms for Daisy so she could put her in the special cot, when she saw how Mrs Finch's old face was alight with love as she looked down at the baby she cradled – and how the arthritic fingers so tenderly touched her cheek and held her close. Daisy's wide, unfocussed blue eyes looked up at her, and it seemed as if she understood the muttered words of endearment and was soothed by them.

Peggy felt an almost overwhelming need to cry at this heart-warming scene, and she had to swallow a lump in her throat and blink back tears as she tidied the blankets and rifled in the box for the milk and tea.

The deep inside pockets of Ron's ankle-length poacher's coat held a hare and a brace of rabbit. He'd been tramping the hills for most of the day, glad to be out of the house despite the appalling weather, and had hoped to snare a couple of ducks from Lord Cliffe's lake. Unfortunately, some stupid bugger had put up a big wire fence which seemed to stretch the entire length of the estate and effectively shut him out.

This fence had really got his back up, for the Cliffe estate was one of his hunting grounds now the gamekeepers and groundsmen had gone off to war, and with Lord Cliffe spending more time in London, it had become Ron's personal larder. He'd walked the length of the fence and then peered through the gloom at the big notice that had been nailed to one of the sturdy posts and grimaced in disgust. The Forestry Commission had taken the place over – and trespassers would be arrested and heavily fined.

Not that this particular threat worried him; he was always trespassing, and so far had eluded those trying to catch him. But it did worry him that the wire seemed very strong and the fence was much too high for a man of his age to negotiate. With a large household to feed it would just make life more difficult.

He'd stood there in deep contemplation as Harvey ran back and forth in search of anything hidden beneath the tough, wind-blown grass and spiny gorse. The lake had provided ducks and quails along with their eggs. There were salmon in the streams that ran through the estate forest, and pheasant and partridge, even the occasional deer. Alf the butcher and Fred the fishmonger paid well for anything he managed to get, and although the risks involved were high, it was worth it just for the excitement.

Deciding to bring his wire-cutters next time, he'd eventually turned his back on the fence and headed morosely for home. It was already dark, and although it had at last stopped raining, the wind still tore across the hills like a fury, chilling Ron to the bone despite his woolly hat, three sweaters and thick coat. Yet his mind wasn't really on his discomfort or even on the problems posed by the new fence – it was occupied with thoughts of Rosie and the strange way she'd been acting just lately.

Rosie was the landlady of the Anchor pub, and the best-looking woman in Cliffehaven as far as Ron was concerned. Blessed with an hourglass figure, long, slender legs and eyes a man could drown in, she exerted a powerful attraction, and Ron had been besotted with her from the moment she'd arrived. But Rosie had played hard to get, and although there was no doubting that she liked him, she'd kept him at arm's length for years.

There had always been a bit of a mystery about Rosie, for no one knew anything much about her, other than that she'd come from outside of town to take over the Anchor, and that there didn't appear to be a husband in the picture despite the fact she wore a wedding ring. Lively and attractive in her early fifties, she'd set many a heart fluttering amongst her male customers, but she'd kept them at arm's length too, run an orderly house and seen to it that there was never a breath of scandal attached to her.

Ron had begun to help change the barrels and bring the crates up from the cellar when the pub was shut, and little by little she'd rewarded his perseverance by spending her few precious free hours with him. Their flirting had become a game which they both enjoyed, and although Rosie was a good deal younger than him, it seemed she didn't mind being courted by a rather scruffy old Irishman. And then one summer night he'd taken her to a charity ball at the Grand Hotel on the seafront, and after he'd walked her home, she'd kissed him and told him she loved him.

Ron dug his hands into his deep pockets, his heart warmed by the memory of how sweetly soft her lips were, and how perfectly she'd fitted into his embrace. But then she'd confessed she had a husband and that, because he was locked away in a mental hospital, divorce was out of the question. His love and admiration had grown as she'd opened her heart to him that night, and although he'd longed to take her to bed and kiss away her cares, he'd respected her wish not to betray her sick husband further with such intimacy.

In the months that followed, Rosie had told him snippets of her life story, but when she'd revealed that shifty, two-faced Tommy Findlay was her brother, he'd been undeniably shocked. However, he had to accept there wasn't anything he could do about it. Tommy had never done anything to him personally, but Ron knew he was light-fingered and sly. He detested the man for his smarmy ways and underhand dealings with the women who fell for his dubious charms, and wouldn't have trusted him to tell him which way the wind was blowing. But as Rosie happened to share

Ron's opinion of her brother, he'd decided that as long as Tommy stayed out of Cliffehaven and away from Rosie and the Anchor, they could just forget about him.

As summer had slowly waned into autumn and then winter their friendship had deepened to something very precious and Ron had thought Rosie felt the same way. But four weeks ago there had been a subtle change in her – so subtle he'd hardly noticed at first. Then he began to realise that she didn't seem to want to talk to him as much as he sat at the bar during opening hours, and would cut short their afternoon teas in her rooms above the pub with some excuse about washing her hair or doing shopping. Yet the real eye-opener was when she'd asked one of the other men to help with the barrels and crates, and he'd known for certain that something was very wrong between them.

He'd watched her more closely after that and detected a brittleness in her laughter, a darkening in her eyes as she studiously avoided his gaze, and a certain impatience that manifested itself in a shrug or a tut. It was as if she was trying to distance herself from him and, with each small rejection, his heart ached just that bit more.

He'd tried asking her what the matter was, but she'd merely shrugged away his concern and told him not to fuss – in fact, she'd made him feel as if he was being a nuisance, and that had really hurt. So he'd stayed away for a while in the hope that his absence might bring her round. But there had been no telephone call, no little note through the letter box at Beach View, and as the days had turned into weeks, he'd begun to wonder what he'd done to make her behave in such a way. It was simply so out of character.

Now Ron was a plain-speaking man who didn't like being kept in the dark, and he'd had enough of pussyfooting about. He loved the bones of her, and if something was troubling her then it was his duty to sort it out – regardless of the pain it might cause him.

'It's the Anchor for me tonight, Harvey,' he said purposefully as they plodded homeward. 'Ye'll have to be content with sitting by the fire with the women. Me and Rosie have things to discuss and ye'll only be in the way.'

Harvey grinned back up at him, his ears flapping in the wind as he trotted alongside him.

'Ach,' said Ron. 'You don't care, do you? They say 'tis a dog's life, but if all I had to worry about was me belly and a warm bed at night, to be sure I'd change places with you in a flash.'

Harvey gave a single bark and ran off.

'Eejit beast,' Ron muttered affectionately.

He followed the dog, his heavy boots treading confidently over the hills he'd tramped since he was a lad fresh off the boat from Ireland. He loved it up here, even in the cold, for the only sound he could hear was the distant thunder of the breakers crashing against the cliffs and the sough of the wind in the grass and the trees. The sky above him was black, the moon veiled in scudding clouds – and if he ignored the gun and searchlight emplacements that now dotted the hills, he could believe he was treading in the footsteps of the ancient people who'd once lived and hunted here.

As he reached the top of the chalk cliffs that sheltered the northern end of Cliffehaven beach, the tranquillity was suddenly shattered by the wail of sirens. Ron stood there and watched the searchlights fizz into life as one by one the sirens began to gather strength all through the town.

Harvey hated them and he raced back to Ron and pressed his shivering length against his legs as he set up a piteous howling.

'Shut up,' Ron muttered as he stroked the soft head.

Harvey took absolutely no notice, his howls rising in volume as the sirens reached their highest pitch.

Ron knew he would carry on like this until the sirens stopped, so ignored him and peered into the darkness across the wind-ruffled waters of the Channel. Pinpricks of light revealed about four enemy bombers which were still out of range of the guns. This was obviously one of those short, sharp raids meant to keep them all on their toes.

Ron grabbed Harvey's collar and dragged him towards the tumbledown remains of an old barn. It was unlikely they would bother with one man and his dog, but the gun emplacements and searchlights were obvious targets, and Ron didn't fancy getting blown up before he had the chance to talk to Rosie.

The flint barn and farmhouse had long been abandoned, the family relocated to a farm in Scotland so the army could use their home for target practice. Now there were just the few remnants of walls standing to mark at least a hundred years of one family's endeavour.

Ron wrapped his coat tightly round him and pulled the woolly hat further down over his ears as the rumble of the enemy planes drew nearer and the ack-ack guns began to rattle beneath the booms of the Bofors.

Harvey was quite happy to wait out the raid now the sirens had fallen silent, and he sat with his nose on his paws next to Ron, his eyebrows twitching as they watched the bombers head west of Cliffehaven and out of reach of the guns on the cliffs.

From his shelter high above the town, Ron could see Cliffehaven spread out beneath him. The horseshoe bay was guarded to the east by chalk cliffs, and to the west by steep hills that tumbled down right to the shingle beach. The town sprawled back from the sea and up the lower slopes of the hills. It had grown since the war had begun, with factories and warehouses to the north, and hastily built emergency housing beginning to take over the bombsite behind the station. Although he couldn't see much in the dark, he knew there were gaps now where whole streets of houses had once been, that some of the big hotels on the seafront had been turned to rubble, and that the station buildings were little more than shattered shells.

Ron puffed contentedly on his pipe and waited for the all-clear to sound as he looked down on the town he'd lived in most of his life. Like his father before him, he'd been a fisherman, and when his sons were old enough, he'd continued the tradition by teaching them the trade. But Jim hadn't liked the life, and he'd turned his back on fishing to become a projectionist at the local cinema – which to Ron's mind was eminently sensible. Fishing was a tough, ill-paid occupation that was hostage to the weather and sea conditions – and given half the chance, Ron would have found something else to do. But fishing was all he knew, and when he'd retired several years ago, he'd passed on the small fleet of boats to Frank, his eldest, who, in turn, would pass it on to his only surviving son.

Ron felt the usual pang of sorrow as he thought about Frank's other two boys who'd been killed on a minesweeper. The First World War had been bad enough, killing almost an entire generation of young men, and here they were less than thirty years later, fighting another one. Now, with the Japs and Americans involved, the whole world was once again teetering on the very edge of disaster.

He was snapped from these dark thoughts as the sirens began to wail another warning and Harvey joined in. From his vantage point Ron could see three of the bombers heading out to sea – but as he watched, he stiffened and got to his feet. The fourth bomber was flying low over Cliffehaven, its intentions all too clear.

The three Reilly men had seen enough death and destruction in the first war to last them a lifetime, so Jim and his brother Frank were relieved that age and Frank's reserve occupation as a trawler-man meant they didn't have to take up soldiering again in this one. Like their father, Ron, they'd signed up for the Home Guard and ARP, which added more responsibility to their daily lives, but on the whole, they felt they were at least doing their bit in the effort to beat back the Hun.

However, things were changing, and Jim knew that he and his brother might find themselves in the thick of it again. The age of conscription had suddenly been raised to fifty-one, and reserve occupations such as fishing were no longer a guarantee against call-up. The British fishing fleets had dwindled almost to nothing as the RNR commandeered the trawlers and their crews to assist the minesweepers in clearing the seaways. The few that remained fished off Iceland, the Irish Sea and the west coast of Scotland, but they had to contend with U-boat attacks, mines and ever-decreasing fishing waters, which meant their catches were small.

Frank was barely making a living off Cliffehaven with his two small boats and elderly crew, and had had to resort to working in the new armament factory to make ends meet. He'd confessed to Jim that he knew this couldn't last, and was simply marking time until his call-up papers came in the post.

Ever the optimist, Jim wasn't worrying about being called up. He was the only professional projectionist in Cliffehaven and the cinema was one of the few sources of entertainment to keep up morale, and he reckoned he had a pretty good case to argue should anyone try to get him back into uniform.

As he sat in the warm fug of the Odeon Cinema

projection room and kept an eye on the film running through the reels, he thought he was probably one of the luckiest men alive. Daisy was a perfect baby, Peggy was the best wife any man could wish for, and so far this war had proved to be quite an adventure. Like his father, he enjoyed a challenge, and getting round the strictures of rationing and shortages had provided a bit of excitement between the long and rather tedious hours of fire-watching and warden's duties. It was almost like the old days when he and Ron used to go across the Channel in the fishing boat and do a bit of smuggling.

The sound of the wailing sirens snapped him out of these pleasant thoughts, and he peered through the narrow window into the auditorium. The manager was off this afternoon but his second-in-command, Gertrude Raynor, had fastened back the doors and was beginning to turn on all the lights.

There was the usual chorus of boos and hisses as the sirens reached their ear-splitting screech, and Jim brought the film to a halt. As the curtains closed across the screen and the elderly usherettes herded the audience out of the cinema, he switched off the lights in the projection room, grabbed his coat, checked the padlock on the cupboard where he kept his stash of illicit whisky and cigarettes, and hurried down the back stairs. He was quite glad of the break, for he'd been on his own all afternoon, and needed the lavatory.

He had hoped to work his way through the hurrying audience to the Gents without being seen – but as he reached the foyer, he saw that most of them had already left. About to sneak towards the back of the cinema, he was brought to a sudden halt by an imperious voice.

'And where do you think you're going? Don't you know there's a raid on?'

Jim spun round to face Gertrude Raynor, who wielded her power as under-manager with a singular lack of humour and a bark like a sergeant major. 'To be sure, I'd have to be deaf not to hear that racket,' he shouted over the wailing sirens. 'But the call of nature is rather more urgent.'

Gertrude sniffed her disapproval and folded her arms beneath the pendulous bosom that strained the buttons on her dark blue jacket. 'It's against the rules to be in the cinema during a raid,' she retorted. 'There are lavatories in the public shelter.'

Jim doubted he'd make it that far. 'I'll be over there in a minute,' he said, backing away from her towards the Gents.

'See that you are,' she boomed, rattling the large bunch of keys. 'I'm locking up, so you'll have to use the back door.'

Jim didn't waste time answering her and, as he rushed into the Gents, he heard the slam of the front door. The old witch probably enjoyed locking him in. No wonder her poor husband had been one of the first men in Cliffehaven to enlist – probably couldn't wait to escape that harrowing voice.

Having seen to his needs, he remained seated in the stall, trousers round his ankles, overcoat hanging on the back of the door, relishing the peace and quiet as the sirens stopped their wailing. It didn't sound as if it was a big raid, and he suspected they were heading further down the coast anyway – so he'd take advantage of this short break to read his paper and have a cigarette.

He unfolded his newspaper and settled down to scan the sports pages. This was far more pleasant than sitting in that overcrowded shelter where one had to use a bucket behind a hessian screen if caught short – and it smelled nicer too.

Jim became vaguely aware that the sirens were going off again, but he was more concerned with the football results, for it looked as if Tottenham were already in trouble and the season had only just got going.

And then it was as if a mighty fist had punched him in the back and sent him flying in a whirlwind of dust and brick and bits of pipe. The air was sucked from his lungs as he was flung through this maelstrom, spinning and weightless, unable to breathe. Then he hit something hard and unforgiving, and knew no more.

Chapter Six

Ron and Harvey were already running as the bomber tipped the last of its load on Cliffehaven High Street and streaked across the Channel with a Spitfire on its tail. The resulting explosions made the earth tremble beneath them, and Ron could see a red glow already blossoming against the dark sky as he raced down the hill.

His mouth was dry and his lungs were wheezing like an old set of organ pipes as he tried to ignore the stitch in his side. Harvey seemed to know they weren't heading for home, for he was running ahead as Ron thudded along the twitten, past the house and the Anderson shelter where, no doubt, everyone was waiting for the all-clear. Ron could barely breathe now, but he didn't dare stop – not until he'd reached the High Street and seen for himself that Jim was all right.

The clamour of fire-engine and ambulance bells almost muffled the sound of the all-clear as Ron staggered along Camden Road, past the deserted row of little shops and the equally deserted Anchor. He didn't spare a glance for the bomb site where the school and a block of flats used to be, or for the large, ugly clothing factory that took up a whole block just down from Cliffehaven hospital. But he did notice that the fire-station doors had been flung open and the engines were gone.

His heart thudded painfully, the dread growing as he dredged up the last of his energy and pushed on. Reaching the end of Camden Road, he finally stumbled to a halt, rested his hands on his knees and fought for breath as he looked up the High Street.

His worst fears had been realised, and he felt sick, for the Odeon Cinema and the shops on either side had been reduced to blazing rubble. Noxious black smoke swirled and roiled as flames belched from severed gas pipes and feasted on the upholstered seats that lay scattered across the street. Above the shouts of the fire crews and the ARP wardens could be heard the steady roar of the fire, the crackling of burning timbers, the groans of shifting beams and the splintering of glass.

Ron slowly climbed the hill, dread weighing heavy round his heart as he came to a standstill and, with Harvey quietly sitting at heel, he watched the emergency crews set to work. The heat from the flames was intense, the remains of the roof were shifting dangerously and the upper circle balcony was poised to crash down at any moment. The danger of a secondary explosion meant that no one could do anything much until the gas was turned off from the mains. It would be a while before Harvey could be sent to search for survivors.

Ron caught sight of John Hicks, the Fire Chief, who was shouting orders and directing his crews to aim the jets of water where they were most needed. John was a young man in his thirties who'd lost a leg during the rescue mission to get the Allied soldiers off the Dunkirk beaches, but that hadn't stopped him from continuing the job he was so good at.

As John turned towards him and paused for a moment to lean on his walking stick and clear the smoke and soot from his eyes, Ron approached him. 'Is there anyone in there?' he shouted above the noise.

'We don't think so,' John replied, wincing as he changed his stance, his tin leg clearly giving him trouble. 'I've sent young Rita down to the shelter to check against our list of cinema and shop staff, and to ask if anyone has noticed someone is missing. Public places are always difficult, as we simply can't know the numbers involved.'

Ron felt a little easier in his mind. Jim wasn't a fool and would be down the shelter. He thanked John and stood back as the gas engineers arrived to turn off the mains.

It was a highly organised routine which had been perfected during the many raids they'd suffered over the last three years. Ambulances stood by as water jets were aimed at the flames; wardens began to close off the road, and the gasmen struggled to open the heavy manholes to turn off the gas. The civilian fire-watch teams were already making a start on clearing the rubble from the road as the heavy-lifting crews arrived with their bolt-cutters, lorries and winches.

Bit by bit they had the flames under control, and

now the gas was off, the heavy-lifting crews brought down the balcony and shored up the roof so the firemen could clamber over the rubble and reach the flames at the heart of the buildings.

Ron rolled up his sleeves and was about to get stuck in to help clear away the debris that was hampering the firemen when he heard Harvey give a sharp bark.

Harvey's ears were up, his eyes alert as he sniffed the air.

Ron held onto his collar. 'What is it?'

Harvey began to whine and dance on his front feet. And then, with one mighty thrust, he'd torn from Ron's grip and was bounding over the still-smouldering rubble to become lost in the thick smoke.

'Harvey's scented something,' he shouted at John as he pointed towards the blinding smoke and began to clamber over the charred velvet curtains, seared plush seats and bits of ornate plaster mouldings.

Ignoring the yells to stop, Ron pulled his woolly hat down almost to the bridge of his nose, and yanked up the neck of his sweater to cover his mouth. The smoke was choking him and making his eyes water, and he was almost knocked off his feet as a jet of water from a fireman's hose drenched him.

Stumbling, half-blinded and soaked, Ron followed the sound of Harvey's insistent barking. He circum-navigated the shattered lavatories and urinals and clambered over the doors and the cast-iron cisterns that lay scattered amid the debris. The yard at the back of the cinema was awash with water pouring from the broken pipes in the lavatories. Ron looked around, but he couldn't see Harvey.

'Where are you, you eejit beast?' he managed through a hacking cough.

Harvey's front paws and great head appeared over the low wall that ran along the back of the yard. He barked once as if to tell Ron to get a move on, then he was gone again.

Ron sloshed through the cold, filthy water and swallowed the fear of what he might find when he looked over the wall. Then dread and anxiety fled and the relief burst from him in a great roar of laughter.

'To be sure 'tis no laughing matter, Da,' said Jim furiously. 'Fer God's sake don't let the others see me like this.'

Ron knew it wasn't really funny – that he shouldn't be laughing at his poor son – but the relief was such that he was almost hysterical. He couldn't speak; his stomach ached with it, and he had to hold onto the wall for support as his legs threatened to give way on him.

'Everything all right here, Ron?' asked Rita, who was almost unrecognisable in her waterproof coat and trousers and sturdy helmet.

Ron nodded, but was still helpless with laughter as he put out a hand to stop Rita from getting any nearer to the wall. ''Tis fine, to be sure,' he spluttered. 'Me and Harvey will see to it.'

Rita frowned. 'See to what, Ron?' She tried to dodge

past him and peep over the wall. 'What's going on over there?'

'Nothing,' he said quickly as he steered her away. 'To be sure, Rita, girl, you'll not be wanting to take care of this.'

'Well, if you're sure, Ron,' she muttered. 'But it's all a bit irregular.'

That almost set Ron off again, and he had to bite his lip. 'Irregular – aye – that it is,' he rasped. 'But 'tis best you leave it to me.'

Rita shot him a look that told him this wouldn't be the end of it, and then turned to make her way through the rubble to report to John.

'Has she gone?' The hoarse whisper came from the other side of the wall.

Ron hoisted himself onto the wall and sat astride it. 'Aye, but she'll be at me to tell her what happened here.'

Jim was quite a sight as he huddled, knees clasped to his chest against the wall, the dog anxiously pawing and snuffling him. His face was black with soot, his hair was singed, there was a lump on his forehead the size of an egg, and his humour had clearly deserted him. Naked as the day he'd been born, he had only the remnants of his tattered shirt to protect his modesty.

He nudged Harvey away and glared up at Ron, daring him to start laughing again. 'You're to say nothing to anyone about this, Da, or I'll murder you, so I will.'

Ron made a concerted effort to keep a straight face

as he dropped down into the deserted strip of land that backed onto the cinema, and took charge of the anxious dog. 'How the divil did you end up like this?' he asked in amazement.

'I got blown off the lav,' Jim replied grimly.

Ron fought to quell the laughter but he was unable to stop it. He collapsed against the wall and slid to the ground as the tears rolled down his cheeks. 'Ach,' he gasped, 'to be sure, Jim Reilly, you'll not be suffering from the constipation for a while.'

'It's not bloody funny,' Jim snapped. 'How would you feel if you were blown to high heaven and left stark naked in the middle of the High Street? I only just managed to get over the wall before John Hicks and his lot arrived.'

'I can't say I've ever been in such a position,' Ron replied as he blew his nose and dried his eyes. 'Though there was the time I got shot in the arse by the Germans, and I—'

'Will you give it a rest, Da? I'm freezing to death here, with a headache the size of a house – and you're going on about your effing shrapnel.'

Ron didn't take offence. He was used to people not wanting to hear how he was a martyr to the moving shrapnel that was still lodged somewhere near his spine. 'Aye, I can see you're cold,' he murmured as he took off his heavy coat, shook some of the water off it, and wrapped it round his son's shoulders.

Jim wrinkled his nose as he slid his arms into the sleeves and drew the coat over his nakedness. 'Ach, what the hell have you got in this thing? It stinks to high heaven.'

''Tis better to stink than to be bare-arsed,' Ron replied nonchalantly as the moon appeared from behind the scudding clouds. It was only then that he noticed the cuts and bruises on his son's body and was immediately remorseful. 'I'm sorry I laughed, son,' he murmured. 'Are ye bad hurt?'

'I thought you'd never ask,' said Jim with a glower. 'Me back's as sore as hell, and I think the hairs on me arse have been singed. But for all that, there's nothing broken.'

Ron was glad to hear it, and would have said something sympathetic if he hadn't heard voices and the crunch of boots approaching the wall from the other side. 'We'd better get going before they find us,' he said. 'Can you walk?'

Jim nodded and got to his feet. Holding the coat tightly wrapped around him, he kept in the darker shadows by the wall as he set off with Harvey over the scrubland.

Ron followed closely behind him, hearing him hiss and curse as his bare feet found brambles, hidden bits of flint and abandoned shards of pottery. 'Ride on me back, son,' he muttered as they reached the deeper shadows of the trees.

'Ach, Da, I'm too heavy.'

'Just do as you're told for once, Jim Reilly, or ye'll be crippled, so you will.'

Jim clambered reluctantly onto his father's back,

and Ron staggered a bit under his weight. 'What the hell have you been eating, boy?' he panted as he set off.

'I told you I was too heavy,' Jim protested.

'To be sure, 'tis all that hot air you're blowing. If you stopped talking it would be easier, so it would.'

They mumbled and grumbled at each other as they headed for home, yet the weight of his son on his back, and the feel of his arms about his neck, was no burden to Ron, but a gift from God – for it was only by a miracle that his son had been saved today.

Peggy and Mrs Finch had heard the explosions coming one after the other and guessed that the tip-and-run had hit the High Street. Peggy was momentarily worried about Jim and then decided she was being silly, for he would have gone to the shelter like everyone else. He was, no doubt, sitting down there with his cigarette and paper, enjoying a few moments of respite until he had to return to work.

Peggy still didn't feel quite up to the mark, but she hoped that once she could get indoors and sit by the fire, she'd perk up a bit. She had definitely done too much on her first day out of bed, but then, she reasoned, anything was better than lying about doing absolutely nothing, and she had to get back into the swing of things sometime.

When the all-clear sounded, Peggy helped Mrs Finch out of the nest of pillows which had been tightly packed around her to stop her falling out of the deckchair when she nodded off. With the baby in one arm and a steadying hand beneath Mrs Finch's elbow, they slowly walked back up the garden path and took it in turn to use the outside lav. Two hours in a cold, dank shelter with little to do but drink tea had its effects, and although neither woman liked using this dark, odious lav, it was very handy at times like these.

They finally made it to the kitchen and Peggy checked the blackout curtains were closed before she switched on the light. 'If you could hold Daisy a minute, I'll stoke the fire and warm up the room,' she said.

Mrs Finch frowned as she took Daisy into her arms. 'You'll leave the broom where it is,' she said firmly. 'I only swept in here this morning.'

Peggy grinned. The hearing aid was obviously not working again. She cheerfully stoked the fire, filled the kettle and put it on the hob. The air raid hadn't affected the water or the electricity, which was a blessing – but it was better to put the evening meal together while she could, for there were constant power and water cuts now, and one never knew when they were going to happen, or for how long.

Shedding her overcoat, she looked in the big vegetable basket on the larder floor and found two cauliflowers, a couple of sprouting onions, a rather wrinkled pair of parsnips, a small turnip and several large, but whiskery potatoes. Taking her wrap-round pinny from the hook on the back of the door, she set about enthusiastically preparing a vegetable stew. A stock cube and a dash of Lea & Perrins would give it a kick and make up for the lack of meat.

Peggy was quite enjoying herself – it was good to be doing something useful again, and her kitchen was warming up nicely. She had just finished putting all the vegetables in the big pot when Daisy decided she was hungry and began to squirm and whimper.

'I won't be a minute,' Peggy murmured as she hastily thickened the stock cube gravy with the smallest teaspoon of flour, and added it to the vegetables. Once the heavy pot was in the range's slow oven, she wiped her hands on her apron, tossed it aside, and reached for Daisy.

'I'll feed and change her in the other room,' she said.

Cordelia clucked with impatience. 'You can do all that in here, in the warm,' she said. 'We're both women, for heaven's sake.'

Peggy giggled, but she had to silently admit to feeling a bit embarrassed about breastfeeding Daisy in front of the older woman. So, after she'd changed Daisy's sodden nappy, she draped one of the baby blankets over her shoulder, thereby covering her exposed breast as Daisy latched onto her nipple.

Cordelia bumbled about making a pot of tea, and once they both had a cup by their elbow, started to rummage through her enormous knitting bag. 'I thought I'd make Ron a new jumper from the ones you threw out in the summer,' she said. 'He's looking decidedly ragged these days – more like an old tramp than a respectable family man.'

Peggy smiled at the memory of Cordelia's previous disastrous attempts. 'He scrubs up well, though,' she reminded her. 'When he's in his suit, and he's had his hair cut and eyebrows trimmed, he still looks quite handsome.'

Cordelia giggled. 'It's getting him to sit still long enough so that Fran can trim his brows that's the problem, but I suspect he quite likes a fuss being made of him – and I'm sure Rosie appreciates it too.'

They lapsed into companionable silence as the fire crackled in the range and the aroma of stewing vegetables began to seep into the room. Daisy finished feeding and fell asleep in Peggy's arms, and she was content to keep her there and enjoy these precious moments of quiet before everyone came home. There would be ructions, she knew, for she'd been under strict instructions to stay in bed at least ten days after Daisy's birth. No doubt Fran and Suzy would get into a huddle with Alison and she'd be for the high jump – but, she decided, she would do things her way.

The front door was suddenly opened to let a howling gale into the house before it was slammed shut again. Peggy looked up as she heard Ron and Jim's voices in the hall and waited in some trepidation for them to enter the kitchen.

Ron and Harvey sauntered in as if they didn't have a care in the world. While Harvey sniffed the baby – he liked babies – and then collapsed with a grunt of pleasure in front of the fire, Ron pulled off his woolly hat and rubbed his hands through his thick, greying hair. 'I suppose the air raid had you out of bed, eh, Peggy?'

'You could say that,' she replied as she eyed him with deep suspicion. He was up to something, she knew the signs. 'I thought I heard Jim come in with you?'

'Aye, that he did, Peg, but he's takin' a wee rest. You see,' he said with a hint of a snigger, 'he's had a bit of an afternoon, so he has.'

Peggy rose from the chair and deposited Daisy carefully in the old family pram, covered her with a blanket and then turned to face Ron again. She folded her arms. 'What have you two been up to?' she asked darkly. 'And don't bother lying to me, Ronan Reilly, I can always tell when you're hiding something.'

''Twas not me had the adventure,' protested Ron. He stuffed the woolly hat into his trouser pockets and reached for the teapot. 'He's feeling a wee bit sorry for himself,' he said, clearly trying not to laugh. 'Perhaps it would be best if you asked him what's happened.'

She frowned as he refused to look at her. 'Have you both been drinking?' she asked, her tone ominously even – a warning to anyone who knew her that she was not to be messed with.

'Not at all,' he replied, his eyes wide and innocent as he looked at her over the teacup.

Peggy turned on her heel and marched into the hall. 'I don't know what you and Ron have been up to, Jim Reilly,' she said as she reached for the door handle, 'but I aim to get to the bottom . . .'

Words failed her as the door swung open to reveal a naked and rather battered Jim examining his backside in her dressing-table mirror.

'To be sure, Peg, me darling, I've burned me arse something terrible. Can you see how bad it is?'

Peggy shut the door, eyed his blackened face and cuts and bruises, and then examined the reddened buttocks and singed hair. 'What the hell have you been doing, Jim?'

He eyed her mournfully and told her about the bomb blowing him off the lavatory seat.

Peggy tried very hard to keep a straight face as she murmured words of sympathy and took another look at his reddened bottom. 'Well, you'll find sitting down a bit painful for a while,' she managed. 'I'll get you some cream to put on it.' Her voice wavered as the giggles threatened.

Jim turned away in disgust, grabbed her hand-mirror, and tried to examine his nether regions more closely. 'To be sure I'd've expected some sympathy from me wife,' he muttered. 'Why is it that everyone thinks it's funny when a man's been almost blown to bits and has a sore arse to prove it?'

'It's not funny at all,' she spluttered as she fought to hold back the laughter.

Jim glowered as he put down the hand-mirror, and then a twinkle came into his eyes and the corners of his mouth twitched. 'It was a hell of a shock,' he admitted. 'One minute I was reading me paper and the next I was flying. I came to without a stitch on.'

He began to chuckle. 'I felt a right fool – and when I heard the fire engines coming I clambered over the wall and hid.'

Peggy saw him wince as he pulled on his dressing gown and carefully sat on the bed beside her. Sober now, she reached for his hand. 'I'm just so relieved you weren't killed,' she murmured.

He put his arm round her and held her close as he kissed the top of her head. 'I can see the funny side of it now,' he admitted, 'and once I've had a long soak in the bath I'll be fine. But you know what this means, don't you, Peg?'

She looked back at him and shook her head.

'With the cinema gone and me stash of fags and whisky blown sky high, I'm out of money as well as a job. Unless I can find something worthwhile, the army will soon send me my call-up papers.'

Peggy snuggled closer to his side, her head on his shoulder as her thoughts whirled and the worries increased. 'Let's not think about that now,' she said eventually. 'You're alive, that's all that matters.'

Cordelia had listened while Ron regaled everyone over supper with how Harvey had sniffed out Jim cowering naked behind the wall, but, unlike the others, she really didn't think it was at all funny. Poor Jim was lucky to be alive, and she could only imagine the awful humiliation he must have suffered to be found like that – and to have his father actually joke about it. She was just thankful that only his pride had been hurt and that his injuries hadn't been more serious.

Jim had done his best to make light of it all during supper, but Cordelia could tell that he was worried about his future – as was Peggy. The last thing dear Peggy needed was for him to be called up, what with the baby, the air raids, and this big house to run.

Feeling tired and a little out of sorts, Cordelia had left the kitchen shortly after the nine o'clock news, and made her way up to her bedroom. It had been a long, rather fraught day, and although it had been heartening to hear the news that the Russians actually had the Germans in retreat from Moscow, the situation in the Far East was very worrying.

Once she'd prepared for bed, Cordelia rummaged in the bottom of her wardrobe and drew out the cardboard box she'd placed there the day she'd arrived at Beach View. Snug in her dressing gown and slippers, she sat in the chair by the gas fire in her room and, after a momentary hesitation, lifted the lid.

Her gaze fell on the bundle of letters tied together with a blue ribbon. The ink was faded, and the paper had become brittle as she'd read and re-read them during the years when her darling husband had been fighting in the trenches. She set them aside, not needing to read them again, for she knew them almost by heart, and his return home had wiped away the fear and made it all seem rather unreal.

The second bundle of letters was much thinner, and she'd tied a narrow black ribbon around them. These few letters had been sent by her brother, Clive – again from the trenches. She had no wish to go through them, for they invoked such sad memories of a brother she'd adored and lost.

Cordelia set them to one side and sifted through the sepia photographs, pausing now and again to study the faces, and the fleeting moments in their lives that had been captured in perpetuity. Most of them were stiffly formal studio shots, and she gave a wry smile as she regarded the one of her parents.

Her mother was seated in an ornate chair, her long skirts carefully draped at her feet, her wide-brimmed hat tilted fetchingly as Cordelia's father stood behind her, one hand on her shoulder, the other grasping his jacket lapel. They looked terribly grand and prosperous, and her father's moustache fairly bristled with pride as he stared almost defiantly at the camera.

She set the photograph aside and continued to delve through the mementos. There were little hand-made birthday cards and crayon drawings given to her by her sons when they were still small, and a few short letters and hastily scrawled postcards that had been sent from Canada which hardly gave her any flavour of what their lives were like now. With a deep sigh, she continued to sort through the rest, and finally found what she was looking for.

Her oldest brother had been a good letter-writer, and she'd found these few amongst her parents' things after they'd died. The sequence wasn't complete, for many of them had been lost or destroyed over the years, but they still told an interesting story, and she could remember, as a child, asking her father for the stamps to add to her collection.

Charles Fuller had married seventeen-year-old Morag Campbell after meeting her in her parents' hotel whilst on a walking tour in Scotland. At twenty-five he'd decided he no longer wanted to be a small-town solicitor like his father and, as Morag was quite an adventurous sort of girl, they had upped sticks and sailed off to Malaya, where he became a well-paid legal advisor to the rich tea and rubber planters and the British expatriates.

But it appeared that life wasn't perfect for this ambitious couple, for Morag had suffered several miscarriages, and they both despaired of ever having a child. When she eventually became pregnant again, Charles was already in his mid-forties and immersed in his flourishing legal practice, so she had left him in Malaya and gone home to Scotland in the hope that this time she would go full-term.

Their son, John Angus Charles Fuller, was delivered safely in the cottage hospital overlooking Loch Leven, and eight months later he travelled with his mother back to Kuala Lumpur. Charles' later letters were full of his son 'Jock', and there were grainy photographs of the little family taking tea beneath palm trees, sitting on beaches beneath vast white umbrellas, and attending race meetings in their finery. Life, it seemed, was complete, and they lived like royalty in a big house that overlooked the Strait of Malacca, waited upon by numerous native servants.

Cordelia flicked through the photographs. Charles had grown fat in his later years, but Morag retained her girlish figure, and their son thrived to become a stocky, well-built, handsome young man. But Morag's sudden death from some dreadful tropical fever had changed everything.

There was only one more letter from that time, and it had arrived long after both their parents were dead. It was a rather sad postscript to the hopes and dreams that Charles and Morag had shared in the tropical heat of Malaya, for Charles had written that Jock had no yearning to be a lawyer, and had taken a lowly post as an apprentice rubber plantation manager. Charles had consequently lost heart in the practice and was planning to retire to a bungalow in Singapore.

Cordelia had written back, but she'd received no reply – and a few short years later the postman had delivered a black-edged envelope to the family home in Havelock Road. The card inside had been a formal notice of Charles' death. There had been no letter to accompany this announcement, no address to which she could reply – and no explanation as to how he'd died. But from the tone of Charles' last letter, she could only surmise that he'd found it impossible to carry on without his beloved Morag.

Cordelia sat with the card in her hand as the gas fire popped and hissed in the grate. There had been so few clues in those letters, and as Charles had died some years ago, there was no way of knowing if his son, Jock, was still in Malaya.

She looked at the envelope and the rather gaudy stamp attached to it. He'd still been there in 1924, and by her reckoning, must now be in his mid-forties. Did he have a family? Was he still working on a rubber plantation? Or had he since left Malaya for some other exotic-sounding place?

She put the card back into the envelope, replaced everything in the box and closed the lid. It was all very confusing, and she felt rather foolish to be suddenly concerned about Charles' son. Her brother had been a stranger, his son merely a smiling face in a photograph – but no matter how distant or estranged he might be, Jock was family, and she could only pray that he was somewhere safe, far from the Japanese invaders.

The girls had gone out, Mrs Finch and Peggy were in bed, and Jim had followed Rita's advice and gone down to the fire station to see if there were any jobs to be had.

Ron had scrubbed himself clean in the scullery sink before donning his best suit, shirt and tie. Now he placed the dark blue scarf around his neck, eyed his reflection in the mirror above the dresser in the kitchen and winked. 'To be sure, you still have it, Ronan Reilly. Handsome divil that you are.'

Ron had taken extra care this evening, for he knew it was important that Rosie could see that he meant business. With his hair brushed, chin shaved and best shoes shined to a gleam, he was almost ready to leave for the Anchor. There was just one more thing to complete the look, but it would mean borrowing it from Jim, and as he'd spent the evening ribbing him, he doubted his son would lend him anything.

He eyed Harvey, who was watching him from the rug in front of the range – no doubt expecting a last walk. 'Not tonight,' murmured Ron. 'You're to stay and look after everyone.'

Harvey thumped his tail, gave a great yawn and sprawled happily back in the glow from the range.

Ron closed the kitchen door behind him and hurried down the concrete steps to the cellar. The scullery was by the back door which led into the garden, and consisted of the large copper boiler, a stone sink and a heavy mangle. The rest of the cellar had been divided into two bedrooms, and he walked past his own to the second where Jim would stay until Peggy let him back into their bed.

Glancing over his shoulder, and alert for the sound of Jim's footsteps on the kitchen floor above him, Ron opened the door and turned on the light.

It was a fairly large room with a window that looked out onto a very narrow strip of earth which ran between the house and the front garden wall and under the short flight of steps that led from the pavement to the front door. This was where his grandsons Bob and Charlie had slept before they'd been evacuated to Somerset. Ron missed their noisy chatter, but he wasn't here to go down memory lane – he was here for a specific reason.

Looking round the cluttered room, he eventually found what he was searching for. The grey fedora wasn't new, but Jim had kept it in excellent condition, and Ron carefully placed it on his head before hastily leaving the cellar and hurrying down the garden path to the gate. There would be ructions if Jim spotted it was missing, but he had the feeling his son was feeling too sorry for himself to even notice.

It was a cold night, and he was glad of the warm scarf as he strode along the twitten and crossed the street which ran up the hill from the seafront. All was quiet as he walked confidently down Camden Road in the pitch dark, yet he had to admit silently that he was feeling a little nervous. What if Rosie refused to talk to him? Or what if she did talk, and the things she said meant that it was over between them? It didn't bear thinking about.

Ron hesitated outside the Anchor's sturdy door, his hand hovering over the heavy iron latch. He could hear someone playing the out-of-tune piano and the accompanying chorus of off-key singers as they massacred Vera Lynn's lovely song, 'We'll Meet Again'. Almost too afraid to face Rosie, he was on the point of turning away, but then he berated himself for being such a fool. He'd survived the trenches and getting shot in the arse by the Huns – what harm could a five-foot-two blonde do him?

He lifted the latch and went down the single step

and into the fug of cigarette smoke, spilled beer and the press of too many people in a small room with low ceilings. He raised his hat to two young girls as he pushed past them and through the crush to the equally crowded bar, where he eagerly sought the first sight of his darling Rosie.

But there was no sign of her – just the two middle-aged women she'd taken on part-time. He stood there waiting for one of them to finish serving so he could ask if Rosie was upstairs, or if she was unwell – it was most unusual for her not to be in the bar at this time of night. Then the thought struck him that she might be out – with someone else – and he felt a terrible clench about his heart.

Ron anxiously willed Brenda to hurry up and finish serving the man further along so he could talk to her. Then he heard the latch on the door behind the bar and looked eagerly towards it, expecting to see the lovely Rosie come sashaying in, in her frilly blouse and neat black skirt and high-heeled shoes.

But it wasn't Rosie who came into the bar, and Ron stiffened with shock.

'Well, well,' said Tommy Findlay with a smirk. 'It's my old mate, Ron. What can I get you? Pot of bitter, isn't it?'

Ron eyed the expensive sports jacket and neatly pressed twill trousers, the oiled hair and flaring moustache, and the bright blue eyes that missed nothing. 'What are *you* doing here?' he growled.

Tommy winked as he pulled on the beer pump.

'That would be telling, Ron, and if you don't mind me saying, it's not really any of your business, is it?' He set the pewter pot on the bar. 'That's eightpence ha'penny to you, Ron.'

Ron eyed the smeary pot and the short measure with a grimace. 'I'll have a full measure in a clean pot for me money,' he rumbled. 'Where's Rosie?'

Tommy grudgingly poured the beer into a cleaner pot and topped it up before placing it too firmly back on the bar. 'Rosie's away for a while,' he said, the smirk returning. 'I don't reckon she'll be back before Christmas, so if you don't approve of the beer or the way it's served, I suggest you drink in another pub.'

'Where's she gone?' Ron asked anxiously.

Tommy wiped the spill with a cloth and leaned forward, his voice low beneath the hubbub of surrounding chatter. 'She's where she should have been instead of down here serving the likes of you,' he said, his blue eyes like narrow shards of flint. 'The pub will probably be sold, 'cos she won't be able to look after her husband and this place.'

Ron stared at him in confusion. 'But her husband's in St Mary's hospital,' he breathed.

'Not any more,' replied Tommy with a malign grin. 'Never mind, Ron. I'll send your regards next time I write to her.'

Ron turned his back on him and pushed through the crush until he reached the pavement. Gulping in the cold air, he had to lean against a lamp post for a few minutes before he could find the strength to walk. 'Oh,

Rosie,' he breathed. 'My darling Rosie. Why did you not tell me? I would have understood.'

As the bell clanged for last orders, Ron pushed away from the lamp post and staggered back to Beach View. She had gone – without a word or a backward glance. Had she ever really loved him, or had he simply been an old fool to believe that she ever could? He would probably never get the chance to ask her now.

Chapter Seven

Malaya

Two weeks had passed since the Japanese had first landed in Malaya, and the horrifying news that both the *Prince of Wales* and the *Repulse* had been sunk by Japanese torpedo bombers had left everyone reeling. This disaster was followed by the appalling realisation that now that they had no battleships to safeguard the peninsula, and their air force had been all but wiped out in the enemy air raids, Malaya had only the land-based Army to beat back the invaders. And those Allied forces were mostly fresh-faced recruits with no experience of war, let alone fighting in swamps and jungles.

The Japanese invaders seemed to be unstoppable as they continued their onslaught through the peninsula with a shocking speed and ferocity that didn't allow the Allied forces to regroup. It soon became clear that their mode of transport, the humble bicycle, was ideal for manoeuvrability through the jungles and swamps, and by the twenty-second of December, the three main arteries of the invasion had reached Kuala Kangsar in the west, Kuala Dungun in the east and, from Kota

Bharu, they had headed deep into the very heartland of the peninsula, towards Kuala Lipis.

With all the big guns pointed out to sea, this land invasion had the Allied forces in disarray and retreat. As stories of Japanese brutality, and the torture and murder of the injured and those who'd surrendered or helped the Allies, filtered down through the peninsula, the trickle of terrified refugees racing for the safety of Singapore became a flood.

Sarah was in the estate office with her father, who now always wore a pistol in his belt and had a rifle close to hand. Since Philip had driven north to bring his father down from the Cameron Highlands and away from the fighting, Sarah had found it hard to concentrate on anything, and the sight of that pistol didn't make it any easier.

She eyed the pile of paperwork that had yet to be dealt with, and the long list of coolies, servants and tappers which had been heavily scored through. 'Another twenty disappeared last night,' she said, 'and I suspect it won't be long before the rest follow.'

'One can't really blame them, especially if the rumours of torture and murder are true – which I suspect they are.' He pushed back from his desk, blew the dust from a glass and filled it with whisky. 'I think it's time for us to think about leaving for Singapore as well.'

'But we can't go before Philip gets back,' she protested.

'Knowing your mother, it will take at least a week to

pack, and by that time he'll probably be back anyway.' He took a hefty gulp of whisky and stared through the wire screens to the dappled light beneath the rows of rubber trees. 'I've already made arrangements to take over the Bristows' bungalow – Elsa and her daughters sailed for Sydney last week, and the Brigadier has sold the horses to the military and moved into army accommodation for the duration. Once we're there, then I'll see about getting you all on a boat to England.'

She stared at him. 'But you've said constantly that Singapore is an impregnable fortress – surely you don't think the Japs . . .?'

'I don't know anything any more,' he said with a deep sigh. 'But with the situation the way it is, I'd prefer to have you and your mother and sister safely shipped out of here.'

'But Mother can't travel all that way – not in her condition.'

'She's tougher than you think,' he muttered. 'And I'm sure there will be doctors on board should she need one.'

Sarah bit her lip. 'The ships leaving Singapore are troopships, Pops, not luxury cruise liners. I really don't think Mother—'

'Your mother will do as I tell her, and so will you,' he barked. 'I can't possibly risk you staying here.'

Sarah eyed him warily. It was rare for him to snap at her – but then she could understand that he was deeply worried, not only for the safety of his family, but for the future of Malaya and his lifetime's work.

'I didn't realise we had any relatives still in Scotland,' she said.

'We don't,' he said brusquely. 'My mother was an only child, and apart from a couple of very distant cousins who I've never met or corresponded with, there's no one to take you in.'

'So, why England and not Australia? At least there we'd be with our grandparents.'

'The Japs are too close to Australia and I have two aunts in England,' he explained, slumping into his chair. 'Amelia and Cordelia – they were a lot younger than Dad, so hopefully they're still alive.'

'And what if they aren't?' she dared ask.

Jock gave an impatient grunt before finishing his whisky. 'Questions, questions,' he grumbled. 'It may never come to that, but if it does, I will send a telegram to the last addresses I had for them, asking for an immediate reply. Should there be no response, then I will have to think of something else – but you will leave here, Sarah, I'm determined about that.'

Sarah shivered as a sudden thought chilled her. 'You'll be coming with us, though, won't you, Pops?'

'To Singapore, yes, but I have responsibilities here, so I won't be able to be with you all the time – and certainly won't be travelling to England. One must do one's duty at a time like this, Sarah. Mine is to help defend Malaya, and yours is to watch over your mother and sister should you have to leave.'

Sarah could see the logic in his plans, but the thought of travelling so far to a strange country with a pregnant mother and an immature sister, made Sarah's pulse flutter. 'But,' she ventured carefully, 'England is being bombed, and Hitler is threatening to invade. How can it possibly be any safer there?'

Jock reached for the jar of pipe tobacco that always stood on his desk. But his hand was shaking, and he almost knocked it over. 'Damn and blast it,' he muttered, his voice breaking with raw emotion. 'I don't know, Sarah. I can't answer all your questions.' He sat there, tears glistening in his eyes, his jaw working as he fought to keep calm. 'I just know that I have to make sure you're all out of harm's way,' he finally managed.

Sarah felt a great swell of love for him as she rounded the desk and put her arms about his neck. She adored her father, and to see him like this was agony, for it was clear that he was torn between the need to keep everyone safe, and the knowledge that they might be parted for months before the situation here was resolved.

She rested her cheek against his and felt the bristles where he'd forgotten to shave that morning. 'I'll look after them, Pops,' she murmured.

He patted her hand and nodded before he turned to filling his pipe. 'I know you will,' he said eventually.

'Let's go up to the house and have some tea,' she suggested. 'With so many plans to make, we need to discuss things as a family.'

'I still have a great many things to deal with here before I can sit about drinking tea,' he said gruffly. 'And I have already spoken to your mother, and she agrees with me that Jane shouldn't be told too much. We don't wish to frighten her, so we've decided to tell her that Sybil needs to be near her doctor in Singapore until the birth.'

'Jane and I had a long talk yesterday,' Sarah said quietly, 'and she knows there's a war on, and that the Japanese are fighting our soldiers in the north. She can see for herself that the country club is almost deserted, that the school has closed down and a good many of her friends have gone down to Singapore or taken boats to Australia or England.'

Jock's fist hit the desk, making everything shudder. 'You had no right to talk to her about any of it without my express permission,' he barked, his eyes now sparking with fury.

Sarah flinched, but knew she had to make her father understand that he was making a terrible mistake by not being honest with Jane. 'She asked me question after question – and they were very telling. She knows far more than you think, Pops, because she hears things, sees things, and can put two and two together. I can't see how not being honest with her would help. She needs to know what's happening, Pops,' she said firmly, 'especially if we have to leave for England.'

He looked at her squarely for a long moment, and then his shoulders slumped in defeat. 'It seems you know her better than I,' he said. 'Perhaps your mother and I have made the mistake of thinking of her as a child, and treating her as such. But we are only trying to protect her.'

'I know, Pops,' she replied softly. 'But surely she's better protected if she knows exactly what's happening and can be prepared?'

'You're right,' he conceded. He looked back at her then and smiled. 'Thank you, Sarah – for everything.'

'Let's lock the office and have that tea,' she coaxed. 'Then we can all sit down and make plans.'

Jane hadn't been at all fazed about the reason for their move south. In fact she'd been delighted that she wouldn't have any more schoolwork, and had got quite excited at the prospect of seeing some of her friends again. She had her bedroom in disarray as she pulled things from her wardrobe and chests of drawers for Amah to pack, and badgered her mother and sister constantly with questions about England.

Neither of them had been any help, as they'd never been there, but Sarah managed to find an old school primer which had pictures of country cottages with thatched roofs, of narrow lanes and rolling hills, and sheep and cattle grazing amid patchwork fields. There were pictures of the Houses of Parliament and Big Ben, one of Buckingham Palace, and others of Westminster Cathedral, Piccadilly Circus and St Paul's. But as there was very little information alongside these black-and -white photographs, Sarah couldn't answer many of Jane's questions – and Jane had made it quite clear that she felt rather short-changed.

As there had only been one minor air raid on Singapore since the beginning of the month, and the

Argyll and Sutherland Highlanders seemed to be holding back the Japanese north of Kuala Kangsar, it was decided they would celebrate Christmas at home and start their journey south the day after Boxing Day.

Christmas was a strange affair, for the Chinese cook had fled along with his countrymen, and they were left only with Pan the Burmese driver, an elderly houseboy and gardener, and Amah, who'd vowed to stay with them for as long as she was needed.

There was quite a bit of laughter as Sybil and Sarah struggled to decipher recipes from a book and cook dinner in the bamboo-roofed kitchen which was set apart from the house. Neither had even boiled an egg before, and they didn't know the first thing, but with Amah giving advice and Jane chattering non-stop as she chopped fresh vegetables from the garden, it turned into quite a jolly affair.

After a supper of stir-fried vegetables with noodles and a slightly charred spit-roasted chicken, there were presents to be opened and admired, and glasses of imported champagne to raise in a toast to the King and to the end of the war. But underlying the laughter was the fear for Philip who had not yet returned – and the dread of the unknown, for the future looked very bleak.

They had planned to leave two days before, but it was agreed it would be best to wait, for Sybil had gone down with flu-like symptoms, and she wasn't well enough to travel. Luckily it was only a forty-eight-hour bug, and on the third day Sybil declared that she was absolutely fine and didn't want to waste any more time.

It was now the twenty-ninth of December, and Sarah closed and locked the shutters over her window before turning to regard the room she'd slept in since she'd left Amah's nursery. The linen and soft furnishings had been carefully laundered and packed away in a large cedar box. The wardrobe and chest of drawers were empty, and her silver-backed brushes and dressing-table set had been stowed away with her clothes in one of the trunks that her father had strapped into the back of the plantation lorry. Apart from the ornately carved bed, the room was bare of everything familiar, and Sarah felt a pang of sorrow.

She picked up her broad-brimmed hat, tucked her handbag under her arm and took advantage of having the house to herself for a while to walk through the silent rooms.

As Jock would be returning here on his own to keep an eye on things, the dining-room furniture had been covered in dust sheets, and the expensive glass, silver and china all packed away in yet another trunk along with Sybil's collection of delicate ornaments. There were no more family photographs on display and the gaps on the shelves showed where favourite books had been taken away to be packed. The Christmas tree was gone, the tinsel and baubles boxed and stowed in a cupboard for next year. But the patches of damp were visible now, for the gardener had shifted all the house plants out to the veranda where they could be watered by the monsoon rains and the humid mists that floated down from the nearby mountains.

Sarah's footsteps disturbed the silence, but each empty room echoed with memories, images of happy times, of laughter and tears and love. She blinked back the tears as she moved out onto the veranda. Breathing in the smell of the jungle, she listened to the sounds she'd heard since birth and tried to absorb them so she could carry them with her until she returned.

She would have to be strong – have to justify her father's faith in her to look after her mother and sister, no matter what they might have to face. But oh, how she ached to see Philip, to be in his arms again knowing he'd made it safely through with his father.

She turned on her heel as the treacherous tears threatened again, locked the doors and headed to the front of the house. Without hope she was already defeated – and she had to keep believing that they would all come through this nightmare and return to this home that they all loved so dearly.

On reaching the front veranda, Sarah looked down to the clearing. Sybil was organising their smaller cases in the boot of the big car, while Jock and the two elderly servants strapped down the trunks and boxes and spare petrol cans in the flatbed of the plantation truck. Sarah's own car was parked beneath the veranda, for it wouldn't be needed in Singapore.

Amah stood with a small bag at her feet, her bright blue sari stirring in the warm wind and her silvery hair glinting in the early sun. She was trying to coax a mutinous Jane into leaving her favourite bright green lizard behind. 'You must leave Azirah here,' she said quietly but firmly. 'She would not like it in Singapore, and you will be taking her away from her family.'

Jane held fast to the little cage. 'But she's my pet, and I don't want her getting killed.'

'Better to be killed with her family, than all alone in Singapore,' said Amah. 'Let us find them a nice cool spot to hide.'

Sarah came down the steps and watched as the gentle Malay woman coaxed Jane into opening the cage and releasing the lizard and her babies. The lizard family shot off into the undergrowth and out of sight, and Jane burst into tears.

'Come on, Jane,' Sarah called. 'You can help me cover my car with the tarpaulin so it doesn't get too dirty while we're away.'

Jane sniffed and brushed away her tears. 'I know I'm being silly,' she said, 'but saying goodbye to Azirah sort of makes everything a bit too final.' She glanced across at her parents, who were still packing their things away, and then longingly up to the house.

'It's difficult for all of us,' soothed Sarah, 'and I think we've all shed a tear or two today, so you're not alone.'

They hauled the tarpaulin over Sarah's beloved car and she gave the bonnet a pat and turned away. Like Jane, she'd said enough emotional goodbyes for one day.

'Right,' said Jock. 'Everything's stowed away and tied down. We'd better get going.' He nodded to the gardener and houseboy who'd been helping him, and they clambered into the back of the lorry with their bundles, pulled down their conical straw hats and settled as best they could amid the luggage for the long journey.

Sarah climbed into the back seat of the large car and sat next to Sybil, who was already looking a little wan as she fanned her hot face. 'Are you all right?' she asked.

Sybil nodded. 'I've brought a flask of iced tea and some dry crackers in case I feel queasy, and Pan has promised to drive carefully so we aren't thrown about.'

Pan waited for Jane and Amah to climb into the front beside him, the expression on his round brown face inscrutable as he started the engine.

The truck led the way down the track, and as Pan followed the trail of dust, Sarah glanced over her shoulder to catch one last glimpse of the house. And then the car followed the bend in the track and it was lost from sight.

They had finally left the relative shade of the plantation and were following another, wider track which would take them to the main road which went directly south to Johore Bahru and the causeway to Singapore.

Sarah could already feel the perspiration gather in the small of her back as the plush leather seats warmed up, but this was a small inconvenience compared to the heartache of leaving her home and the fear for Philip. She glanced at her mother, who was sleeping peacefully in the breeze coming through the open window. Sybil still looked very pale, with dark shadows under her eyes, but she'd eaten a good breakfast – cooked by Amah – and seemed quite comfortable.

The truck led the way and they kept some distance from it so the dust stirred up by the wheels didn't come in through the open windows. It had been a relatively smooth journey so far, with only a few coolies and Malay families plodding down the track laden with children, carrying poles heavy with filled baskets, and carts piled with household furniture, elderly relatives and more small children.

But as they reached the main road leading south, the truck came to a grinding halt and Jock climbed down. He stood beside the lorry and took off his hat to scratch his head in bewilderment. Sybil slept on, so Sarah and the others went to see what the matter was.

Sarah gaped in amazement, for the stream of humanity filled the road and straggled into the jungle that ran alongside it. The faces of those fleeing the north were Chinese, Indian, Malay, Burmese and Siamese, with every combination mixed in as well. Barefooted children carried cooking pots and bundles of firewood; donkeys pulled carts heavy with furniture, wizened grandparents and grizzling toddlers; and rickshaws were laden with caged chickens and more elderly people. Coolies' poles were sagging from the weight of the things they carried in their baskets; women were bent almost double beneath rolls of bedding and sacks of rice; and cyclists weaved in and out of this melee with their wives and children perched precariously on the handlebars and crossbars as the drivers of cars and lorries hooted impatiently. It was an orderly rush to safety, but the fear in every face was clear.

'Edge in where you can,' Jock ordered Pan, 'and watch out for the children. We don't want to run them over.'

They slowly moved off again, edging inch by inch into the never-ending, dense stream of displaced humankind. Within seconds there were cheeky-faced urchins clinging to the running board and clambering over the bonnet, and Pan scowled as he hooted the horn and tried to wave them away – but they simply ignored him and continued to enjoy the brief respite from their long trek.

Sybil woke and found she was staring into the face of a particularly sweet little girl with the biggest brown eyes and glossiest black hair. 'Oh,' she breathed, 'how pretty. Do we have anything we can give her?'

'I wouldn't, *Mem*,' said Pan flatly. 'Give to one, and you'll be swarmed by them with their hands out.'

Sybil sighed as she regarded the endless, plodding river of the dispossessed. 'Such a shame we can't give them all a ride. They look very tired, and these children are far too young to be making such a terribly long journey.'

Sarah took her hand as the car inched along behind the truck, the children continued to clamber over both vehicles, and the adults trudged stoically alongside them. They had been travelling for almost three hours, a cloud of dust hovered above them all, and it was stifling in the car now they'd had to close all the windows.

'We will have to stop soon, *Mem*,' said Pan. 'The engine is getting very hot and must have more water.'

'Pull over somewhere in the shade if you can find any,' said Sybil, 'and then you can rest while the engine cools down.' She turned to Sarah. 'Thank goodness for that,' she murmured. 'The baby is playing havoc with my bladder.'

Pan tooted the horn and indicated his intentions to Jock, and half an hour later they'd managed to edge out of the crush and find a bit of shade under the trees of the encroaching jungle. Having rested for an hour and topped up with water, oil and fuel, they set off again.

It was getting dark now, and they had taken eight hours to do a journey which would normally only take two. They were all hot, tired and uncomfortable, especially Sybil. 'The baby's pressing on my bladder again, Sarah,' she whispered. 'I can't hold out for much longer.'

'Pan, would you pull over? *Mem* needs to get out for a minute.'

Pan flashed the headlights to tell Jock he was stopping and gradually pulled to the side of the road. Sarah helped her mother out of the car and Amah hurried to her side, clearly guessing the reason for the stop. 'I take *Mem*,' she said firmly. 'You take Jane – Pan go over there,' she ordered, pointing further down the road.

Sarah and Jane found bushes to hide behind. 'I never imagined we'd be doing this sort of thing,' said Jane moments later. 'And I can't believe how many people there are on their way to Singapore – wherever will they all live when they get there?'

Sarah was about to reply when she heard a noise that made her blood run cold. 'Get down,' she ordered, grabbing her sister's hand.

'What is it? What's happening?' cried Jane as she was yanked to the ground.

'Keep very still,' Sarah urged as the noise of the planes came closer and closer.

There were screams from the street and the scurrying and trampling of panic as the refugees scrambled to find shelter. People flung themselves beneath the trees, hauling their children and belongings with them, babies cried and small children wailed in fear, but all sound was lost in the gigantic roar of Japanese planes.

The bullets came hard and fast as the plane engines screamed overhead, their downdraught blowing people off their feet and scattering possessions. They hit indiscriminately, catching women, children, men, animals and the elderly as they fled from the terror. The bullets whined and spat, hitting trees and earth with a dull thud, kicking up dirt and dust and showering those hiding beneath the trees with falling branches and leaves. The metallic strikes zinged and whined against cars and lorries, shattering windscreens, and the agonised bray of injured mules, cattle, goats and donkeys added to the horror of it all.

Sarah held Jane close, shielding her with her body as they tried to flatten themselves into the ground and away from the onslaught. As the shriek of the enemy planes finally faded into the distance, the wails of anguish rang out, echoing again and again through the jungle and all along the road.

'Have they gone?' asked Jane fearfully as she got to her knees.

'I think we should stay here,' Sarah replied as she desperately looked round for sight of their mother and Amah.

'But they're all leaving.' Jane pointed to the stream of people who were trying to gather up their children and possessions to search for their missing loved ones.

Sarah didn't know what to do. Should she risk going back into the open when the Japs might be on their way back to strike again? Or had they done their worst? 'Let's wait until Pops calls for us. He'll know when it's safe.'

'Sybil,' shouted Jock from further down the road. 'Sybil, are you and the girls all right?'

'We're fine,' shouted Jane. 'So are we,' called Sybil.

'Stay where you are,' he ordered. 'I'm coming to get you.'

Jane scrambled to her feet and ran towards his voice before Sarah could stop her. 'I'm here, Daddy. Me and Sarah . . .'

Sarah reached her before Jock and quickly pulled her away from the terrible sight that had frozen her to the spot. But one glance had been enough, and Sarah knew they would have nightmares for a long while after today.

Pan's bloody body lay slumped on the road, his protective arm still covering the remains of the little girl who had so enchanted Sybil, and close by lay a dead mule and three more children. A woman was sitting in the road cradling her dead baby as she rocked back and forth and howled with grief. The limp, shattered body of an elderly man was being lifted reverently from beneath a fallen cart while the bewildered, terrified survivors gathered their belongings and their children and slowly continued their journey as if in a trance.

'They're all dead, aren't they?' Jane's face was ashen, the tears rolling silently and unheeded down her cheeks. 'The Japs killed Pan and those little children. How could someone do that?'

'Because we're at war,' said Sarah, her voice shaking with rage and despair. 'And people get killed in war – even though they've played no part in it.'

Jock came and put his arm round both of them, his face drawn. 'Take Jane to the truck and give her some tea out of the flask. I need to find your mother.'

'I'm here,' said Sybil, who had blood trickling down her cheek, 'and don't fuss, Jock, I scratched my face on something sharp in the grass. Amah and I are fine but for the mosquito bites.'

'Stay here then, and wait while I help to move the

bodies and clean up back at the car. 'You'll have to drive it, Sarah. Think you can manage?'

She nodded and kept a tight hold on her sister and mother as Jock strode back to the road, calling for the cowering gardener and houseboy to come and help him. She felt sick with fear, for they were nowhere near Singapore yet, and once they'd left the jungle behind for the open road and the causeway, they would be sitting targets for a brutal enemy who clearly regarded helpless women and children as fair game.

Chapter Eight

Cliffehaven

It had been a quiet Christmas in Cliffehaven, for the strict rationing had meant they'd had to scrape together what they could to put a half-decent meal on the table on Christmas Day. Presents had been necessarily small and practical as there wasn't enough money to splash out on luxuries – and even Peggy's snooty sister, Doris, had confessed that the bath salts she'd brought for Peggy had been an unwanted gift she'd had in her bathroom cabinet for some time.

It was on occasions such as this that Peggy felt the absence of her other children most keenly. The house didn't feel the same without Bob and Charlie charging about at four in the morning to show everyone what Santa had brought – or Cissy and Anne singing away as they stirred the Christmas pudding and helped put up the decorations in the dining room. This room had been deserted in favour of the kitchen since the boys had gone down to Somerset, and was now a depository for bits of furniture and things that might come in useful, but it had been decided that the paper chains would remain there until the boys' return, and they looked rather dusty and forlorn now.

Still, Peggy was content to have a quiet time of it, for Daisy woke her frequently in the night, and, as the weeks had gone on, she'd begun to wonder if she'd ever have a full night's sleep again. It wasn't just Daisy keeping her awake, for there was also the worry over Jim and Ron – and even Mrs Finch – not to mention her deep concern about her son-in-law, Martin, who had finally managed to persuade his superiors to let him leave his desk job, take a sideways career path, and lead a squadron again.

Peggy had managed to get through on the telephone to Somerset to talk to Anne and the boys. There had been little time to say anything much, except to ask after everyone's health, tell them she loved them, and say hello to her granddaughter, Rose Margaret, who was far too young to understand the mechanics of telephone calls. It seemed that Anne was stoically bearing up to this latest development in her husband's RAF career, even though she didn't like it one bit. As for the boys, they were as bright as always and full of news about their chores on the farm – and then the pips had gone, and she'd replaced the receiver and burst into tears.

Bob was almost fifteen, and already deeply involved in the running of the farm. He'd sounded so grown-up, his voice quite deep since it had broken, and even Charlie seemed to have become more thoughtful. It wasn't fair. Her children were growing up without her, and although they were happy and well, she resented the fact that another woman was getting the benefit of watching them grow and mature. If she could have faced Hitler that day, she'd have told him straight what she thought of him, and punched him on the nose.

As the new year of 1942 began and the weather turned even chillier, with a sharp wind blowing off the sea and frosty, star-filled nights, the residents of Beach View Boarding House huddled round the range, grateful for the logs and the small amount of coal that Ron and Jim had managed to procure. No one questioned where the extra coal had come from; they were just thankful to be warm.

At least the news was a bit more cheerful, for Rommel was being beaten back in Libya, and the Russians had sent the Germans into a humiliating defeat after their attempts to capture Moscow. On the home front, there had been a terrible mining disaster in Staffordshire in which fifty poor men had been trapped, but at least the Germans seemed to have given up their bombing raids for a while – no doubt too busy dealing with the numerous RAF raids on Germany. And the Yanks were due to arrive in the spring, which was bound to cheer everyone up.

Peggy tucked Daisy into the old pram which had done such sterling service over the years, and hoped she'd stay asleep long enough for her to catch up on the washing. It was a brisk, bright day, and ideal drying weather, and although Peggy would have liked nothing better than to put her feet up, she knew she couldn't avoid the chore any longer.

The copper boiler in the basement had been lit, and the first load of washing was already flapping on the line when Peggy saw Ron and Harvey come down the garden path. Neither of them looked very happy with life, and Peggy knew it was time to ask Ron what the matter was.

He edged past her as she began feeding the second batch of washing through the heavy mangle. 'To be sure, I'll do that for yer, Peg,' he said as he knocked the mud from his gumboots and promptly trampled it into her clean tiles as he reached for the handle.

They worked together in silence as Harvey gobbled down his food and slumped with a sigh of pleasure on Ron's bed. Peggy had given up trying to keep the dog out of Ron's room. There were more important things to worry about – like what was eating Ron.

She decided not to shilly-shally and to ask him straight out. 'What's been worrying you, Ron?' she asked as she folded a damp sheet into the basket at her feet. 'And don't deny it,' she said as he shook his head. 'You've been grumpy for weeks.'

'Aye, well, me shrapnel's playing up in this cold weather,' he said dismissively. 'To be sure I'm a martyr to it.' He winced and put his hand on his lower back as if to emphasise the point.

Peggy wasn't fooled. 'I'm sorry to hear your back's playing up, Ron,' she said softly, 'but I get the feeling there's something else bothering you.' She noted the way he chewed his lip and sensed that he wanted to tell her, but needed a bit of time to pull his thoughts together.

As the rollers squeezed the water from the last sheet and Peggy carefully folded it into the basket, Ron dug his hands in his pockets and looked down at his feet. 'Rosie's left the pub,' he said flatly.

Peggy stared at him in amazement. 'Good heavens,' she breathed. 'But why?'

Ron told her what Tommy had said. 'To be sure that wee girl has broken me heart, Peg,' he confessed. 'I never thought she'd just up sticks and leave without a word.'

Peggy patted his slumped shoulder. 'Poor Ron,' she murmured. 'No wonder you've been so quiet these past weeks.' And then she became brisk. 'But I wouldn't believe a word Tommy Findlay said,' she added purposefully. 'There has to be more to this than meets the eye, Ron. Rosie isn't the sort of woman to play fast and loose with anyone she cares about – and she does care for you, Ronan,' she said more softly. 'It's obvious in the way she is when you're together.'

'D'ye think so?' There was a spark of hope in his eyes.

Peggy nodded. 'I wouldn't mind betting that Tommy's only telling you half the story. Rosie's husband is a very sick and dangerous man, Ron, and he'll never be released from secure care.' She smiled warmly at the older man who'd become father and friend over the years. 'Don't let Tommy Findlay cause trouble between you – just be patient. Rosie will come back as soon as she's able, and then you'll know the truth.'

'I could wring Findlay's neck, so I could,' he growled as he hauled the basket up and carried it outside to the washing line.

'We've all felt like that at some point,' muttered Peggy as she grabbed a pillowcase and flapped the creases out of it with such vigour it cracked like a whip. 'He's a nasty piece of work, and I'm amazed someone hasn't done away with him years ago.'

Ron grinned and left her to peg out the rest of the washing, while he went to check on his vegetable patch.

Peggy stood and looked in satisfaction at the three lines of flapping washing, then picked up the basket and went back indoors. She was glad Ron was feeling more cheerful, but that still left the worry over Jim having to work in the armaments factory alongside his brother. It was well paid, but that was because it was a dirty, dangerous job, and they both clearly hated it.

The fourth cause of her worry was sitting in the chair by the kitchen range.

Cordelia Finch was wrestling with wool and needles, tutting and clucking with annoyance as she tried to pick up dropped stitches. She looked up as Peggy came into the kitchen and gave a sigh of exasperation. 'Can you try and sort this out, dear?' she said. 'I seem to be at sixes and sevens today.'

Peggy was only too glad to have an excuse to sit down. 'I'll make a pot of tea first,' she said.

'Yes, I've got a thirst too,' Cordelia replied, fiddling with her hearing aid. 'Perhaps we could make a pot of tea?'

Peggy smiled fondly and made the tea, and then settled by the fire to try and make sense of Mrs Finch's knitting. 'You seem a bit distracted, Cordelia,' she said some time later. 'Is something bothering you?'

'Well, it's all a bit silly really,' she began. 'You see, I don't even know if there's anybody there to actually worry about. But if there is, then it's all rather serious.'

Peggy frowned. 'Who are you talking about, Cordelia?'

'My brother's son. You see, I don't know if he's still there – or even if he has a family. So it's a bit foolish of me to worry about them, isn't it, when they might not even exist in the first place? But I do, Peggy. I really do.'

'I'm sorry, Cordelia, but you aren't making a bit of sense.' Peggy put down the knitting and reached for the gnarled hands which were clasped tightly in Cordelia's lap. 'Start at the beginning and tell me about your brother,' she encouraged.

As Cordelia began to talk of the brother she'd never known, Peggy slowly began to understand why the older woman had been so distracted of late. She kept hold of Cordelia's hands as she talked, and when she'd finished, she gave them a heartening, gentle squeeze. 'I agree that the news in the Far East is extremely worrying,' she said, 'what with Hong Kong and Malaya being overrun by the Japs, and the Philippines under constant threat of invasion. But your nephew could be anywhere after all this time, and I really do think you should try and stop fretting.'

Cordelia dabbed her eyes and blew her nose. 'I know I should,' she admitted, 'but he is family. And if he has a family of his own, and is still in Malaya . . .' She gave a deep sigh. 'I feel so helpless, Peggy.'

'Do you think your sister might have an address for him?'

Cordelia sniffed and folded her hands more tightly into her lap. 'I very much doubt it,' she said. 'Amelia doesn't approve of people who go to live abroad.'

Peggy didn't really know how to answer this, so didn't try. She sipped her tea and thought about Cordelia's problem, wondering how on earth she could help. And then she had a bright idea. 'My nephew, Doris's son Anthony, works for the MOD. He might know someone who could find out if the Fullers still live in Malaya.'

The sweet little face brightened immediately. 'Do you really think he might? Oh, that would be so helpful – as long as it isn't too much trouble.'

'I'll speak to Doris this afternoon and ask her to ask him. I can't promise anything, Cordelia, but he's a very nice young man, and I know he'll do all he can to help if it's at all possible.'

'That would be lovely,' said Cordelia. 'Thank you, Peggy, you are a dear.'

Peggy picked up the knitting again and frowned

over the dropped stitches. She didn't feel particularly 'dear' at the moment, for she'd never got on with her eldest sister, and every conversation or meeting was a minefield. Doris could wind her up tighter than a clockwork train – and Doris clearly knew it. To have to ask her for anything was not going to be easy.

Lunch consisted of spam sandwiches and the last of the stewed apple with a drop of cream from the top of the milk as a treat. Cordelia headed for her bedroom shortly afterwards to take her afternoon nap, and, with the washing all lovely and dry and smelling sweetly of fresh air, Peggy folded it carefully away to be ironed after tea.

Having changed and fed Daisy, she tucked her beneath the blankets in the deep, coach-built pram, fastened the rainproof cover and put up the hood. Negotiating the front steps was always a bit of a struggle, but Daisy didn't seem to mind being bumped from one to the next, and soon they were heading down the hill towards the seafront.

The wind was stronger down here, and Peggy was glad of the rather ancient and moulting fox pelt she'd clipped round her neck. The warm winter coat Jim had bought her for her birthday last year fitted now she'd lost her fat tummy, and her feet were snug in the fur-lined boots he and Ron had given her for Christmas. She tugged the woolly hat over her dark, wavy hair to cover her ears, not caring if she looked silly, and made her way along what was left of the promenade.

Cliffehaven had changed since the start of the war. What remained of the pier had been totally destroyed by an enemy bomber crashing into it, and two of the big hotels had been demolished in an air raid. Coils of barbed wire ran along the boundary between promenade and beach, and there were signs everywhere warning of landmines hidden in the shingle. The once gentle bay now looked ugly, with tank-traps at the low-water mark, gun emplacements on the promenade, and the scars of bullets marking the once-elegant shelters that were dotted along the seafront. The shelters had been there since Victorian times, but the stone seats were chipped, the beautiful glass windows broken, and the pretty finials and curlicues that had once graced the roofs were mostly reduced to splinters.

As seagulls hovered and shrieked, Peggy breathed in the smell of salt and seaweed, determinedly ignoring the stench of the clumps of ugly oil that littered the shingle and told the tale of too many ships and planes meeting their end in the Channel waters. It was a lovely day despite the cold, her baby was beautiful and she felt refreshed.

Havelock Road was at the very end of the long promenade, the rather grand houses set in large gardens which overlooked the sea. It was a quiet, leafy area, and regarded by most as the posh end of town – which it was, Peggy conceded. There was a small park which had a lake surrounded by weeping willow trees, and formal rose-beds leading to shady corners where benches had been placed. The iron railings had long since gone to be turned into Spitfires and anything else that might be needed in the war effort, but it was still a pleasant place to visit – if one had time to sit about doing nothing.

Despite Doris's best efforts, Peggy had never been jealous of her or her house – or the way she seemed able to spend money like water. Doris was married to the rather boring Ted Williams, who was manager of the Home and Colonial store in the High Street, and who enjoyed having a flutter on the stock market. Peggy would pick Jim over him any day, for at least her Jim had a bit of life about him, whereas Ted had been middle-aged before he'd turned twenty-five, and just went to work or played endless rounds of golf. Doris wheeled him out now and again when she needed an escort for one of her interminable charity functions, but to Peggy, it seemed they were like strangers who just happened to live in the same house.

Their son Anthony was a studious, rather shy Oxford graduate of thirty-one who'd taught physics and mathematics at a private school before the war. He'd been approached by someone from the MOD when the school had closed down, and instead of evacuating with his pupils, he'd stayed in Cliffehaven.

What he did was secret, but Peggy knew he spent most of his time in the underground bunkers that lay beneath nearby Castle Hill Fort. The Fort, which predated the first Napoleonic war, was fenced off now, with soldiers guarding it night and day, so whatever he did had to be extremely important – as Doris never tired of telling her.

Peggy pushed the pram along the pavement and noted the weeds that had begun to push through the cracks. There were also potholes in the road, some of the kerbstones were broken, and the gutters were muddy and littered with dead leaves. The council workers had far more important things to do these days than pander to the needs of the rich and self-important – but Peggy reckoned the residents of Havelock Road would soon be making their complaints to the Mayor.

She came to a shocked halt as she reached Mrs Finch's old home. The house had once been a fine example of Victorian architecture, but now it, and its neighbour, had been reduced to ruins, and Peggy was glad that Cordelia couldn't see it. The rooms were open to the elements, the side wall had gone completely, and the chimney had crashed through the roof and smashed into the core of the house, taking floors and windows and bits of furniture with it. Rubble was strewn across the two gardens and a tree had fallen down, its topmost branches left to rest against the remains of what had once been a bedroom.

Peggy felt a pang of sadness, not only for Cordelia, but for the lovely house, and the Galloway family who had lived there, and she just hoped that no one had been killed. With a deep breath to quell her emotions, she gripped the pram handle and carried on walking. She would ask Doris what had happened to the Galloways and their neighbours.

She finally came to her sister's house, and paused for a moment to get up the nerve to knock on the door. Doris and Ted lived at the very end of Havelock Road, in a large detached house which was almost hidden by a spreading chestnut tree, high hedge and an equally high flint and brick wall. There were no iron gates at the two entrances any more, but the shingle driveway that curved past the front door had been weeded and recently raked. The garage had been added on twenty years ago, and it stood to one side of the house, the wooden double doors firmly padlocked, the squares of glass in the tops gleaming as if they'd just been cleaned.

'Doris certainly likes everything neat and tidy,' murmured Peggy to her sleeping baby. 'But I bet she got someone else to clean those windows and rake the drive.' She pushed the pram over the shingle – which wasn't easy, for it was quite dense – and headed for the front door, which was set back beneath a neat porch.

She rapped the iron knocker, heard the sound echo through the house, and began to fret. Perhaps it would have been better to telephone first, she thought. It was silly to walk all this way and then find Doris wasn't at home.

She rapped again and then stood on the porch with its clean doormat and eyed the deep bay windows which looked out onto the front garden. Regimented rows of daffodils and crocuses sprouted between the snowdrops and dormant perennials, and the grass had been trimmed at the edges. Not a weed had dared to mar the dark flower beds, nor a leaf left to lie on the lush grass beneath the tree.

The sound of a bolt being drawn brought her attention back to the front door. Steeling herself, she plastered on a smile.

Doris stood in the doorway dressed in a silk blouse, tweed skirt and two-tone high-heeled shoes. Her make-up was immaculate, her hair freshly washed and set – but her expression was unwelcoming. 'Good grief,' she said. 'What on earth are *you* doing here?'

'Daisy and I needed some fresh air,' said Peggy, 'and I wanted to ask you something.'

Doris looked a bit shifty as she remained in the doorway and effectively barred Peggy's entrance. 'You should have telephoned first,' she said as she fiddled with the string of pearls round her neck. 'It's not awfully convenient at the moment.'

Peggy stood her ground. 'Why? Who have you got in there? One of your old titled cronies? Don't worry, I won't show you up, but I do need to use your lav. It's a long walk from Beach View and this cold weather . . .'

'For goodness' sake,' Doris hissed. 'Have you no shame, Margaret? Whatever would the neighbours think if they heard you talking about such things on the doorstep?'

Peggy hated being called Margaret, and Doris knew it. 'I really couldn't care less,' she replied. 'Now, are you going to let me in or not?'

Doris shifted from one well-shod foot to another

and ran her manicured hands down her tweed skirt. 'It's a little awkward,' she said.

Peggy couldn't resist teasing her. 'Have you got your lover in there? Or are you and Ted in the middle of something naughty?'

Doris reared back her head, chin quivering as her eyes became flinty. 'Don't be vulgar, Margaret. I simply have Anthony visiting, and we have private matters to discuss before he has to return to his extremely important work with the MOD.'

Peggy chuckled. Even in high dudgeon, Doris couldn't resist bragging. 'That's perfect,' she spluttered. 'Anthony is just the person I need to talk to.'

'Why?'

'You'll find out when you remember your manners and let me in,' she retorted.

Doris looked extremely put out about the whole thing, but years of social climbing and caring about what the neighbours might think won her over and she stepped back and held the door open so Peggy could struggle alone to get the pram into the hall.

'I hope she doesn't start crying,' she said with a sniff. 'I've suffered the most fearful headache these past few days and simply couldn't bear it.'

'She'll sleep for another hour yet,' replied Peggy, her fingers crossed behind her back as she kicked the brake into place. 'Is there any chance of a cuppa after I've used your lav? Only I'm parched.'

'Lavatory, Margaret. Don't be so common.' She turned on her heel. 'We're in the drawing room,' she said over her shoulder. 'The tea is already made. I'll get the girl to bring another cup.'

Peggy's sympathies were with the young woman who came in to clean, and wondered vaguely why she didn't find a better paid job in a factory. Anything had to be easier than running after Doris all day for a pittance.

Peggy used the downstairs cloakroom, which was terribly posh with lovely tiles, a big iron radiator which warmed expensive fluffy towels, and even a slab of perfumed soap to wash one's hands. She could have stayed in there all day.

The drawing room was filled with sunlight. The panoramic sea view – seen through the tape criss-crossed over the deep bay window – was quite magnificent, and Peggy always felt as if she was on a luxury cruise liner when she paid one of her rare visits here.

Anthony stood as she entered the room. He was tall and a little too slender, but he had a pleasant smile, nice brown eyes behind dark-framed spectacles, and a shock of rather unruly brown hair. Dressed in casual corduroy trousers, brogues and a sweater, he looked every inch the Oxford graduate. 'Hello, Aunt Peg. You look well. How's Daisy?'

Peggy gave him a hug and kissed his cheek. 'Daisy's asleep, and I feel ready for a cup of tea after that long walk. It's quite brisk out there, you know.' She pulled off the woolly hat, slipped off her coat and fox pelt and carefully sat down on the expensively covered couch.

It didn't do to dent the plumped cushions or mark the silky upholstery – not in Doris's drawing room.

Afternoon tea was laid out on a trolley, and her mouth watered as she saw there were sandwiches, biscuits and even a slab of what looked like real ginger cake. The tea was poured into wafer-thin china cups so delicate that Peggy was always terrified of breaking one. But the tea was hot and strong – no doubt one of Ted's perks for being the manager of the Home and Colonial – and boosted her no end.

Two sandwiches and a slice of cake slipped down very easily as she made small talk with Doris and congratulated Anthony on his presence of mind in bringing the cake.

He smiled shyly at her and pushed his glasses up his nose. 'I managed to persuade the fortress cook to let me have it,' he said. 'She seems to think I need feeding up.'

'You said you wanted to talk to Anthony,' said Doris as she fitted a cigarette into a long ebony holder and lit it with her gold lighter.

Peggy turned to her nephew and told him about Cordelia's dilemma. 'I know it's a bit of a long shot,' she finished. 'But you were the only person I could think of who might be able to help.'

He ran his fingers through his hair as he thought about it. 'I might know a man who might know someone who could help,' he murmured, 'but it could take some time. The situation in Malaya is tense, to say the least, and the civilians are leaving in droves. Even if her nephew *was* there before the war, he could be anywhere by now.'

'I realise that, but Cordelia is fretting, and just knowing that someone's looking for him will ease her mind no end.'

'I really don't know why you feel you have to get involved in other people's affairs,' sniffed Doris. 'After all, Cordelia Finch is only a lodger.'

'She's far more than that,' said Peggy, reaching for her woolly hat. 'By the way, Doris, what happened to the Galloway family and their neighbours? I see the houses are gone.'

'They took a direct hit on the same day the cinema was flattened, but luckily both families had already left Cliffehaven. Joanna Galloway is in Cornwall with her children, and the Sandersons are in Wales with their granddaughter.' She looked rather pointedly at her watch.

Peggy took the hint and picked up her coat. Doris had yet to ask about how Jim was after being blasted out of the cinema, but at least the Galloways and their neighbours were safe.

'Thanks, Anthony. I'll wait to hear from you.' She smiled up at him as he stood to help her with her coat – Anthony always did have lovely manners. 'Why don't you pop in to us on your next day off? I know Jim and Ron would love to see you.'

'That would be nice, thank you, Aunt Peg.' He gave her a slow, sweet smile as he handed her the ratty bit of fur.

'That's fit only for the dustbin,' said Doris with a shudder. 'I do hope it hasn't got any nasty things living in it.'

Peggy wrapped it firmly round her neck, pulled the woolly hat low over her ears, and buttoned her coat. 'Thanks for the cuppa, Doris,' she said, and headed for the door.

Anthony took a peek at the sleeping Daisy and then helped Peggy get the pram through the front door and over the shingle driveway. 'I'll do my best, Aunt Peg,' he said, 'but these are difficult times, with millions of people on the move. Either way, I'll pop in and see Mrs Finch if you think that would help.'

Peggy grinned. 'She'd love to see you again. But I can't promise ginger cake and fine china.'

He smiled back with a mischievous glint in his eye. 'It's the company that counts,' he replied, 'and I've always felt at home in Beach View.'

Peggy gave him a quick hug and headed for home. She was very fond of Anthony, and just wished he could find some lovely girl to marry. But the stumbling block was Doris, of course, for no girl would ever be good enough – and no girl had yet proved she felt strongly enough about Anthony to stand up to her.

Chapter Nine

Malaya

There had been no further attacks from the Japanese planes as the endless stream of refugees slowly approached the long causeway which would take them to Singapore Island. But it was soon clear that Singapore itself was a prime target, and after the first of the nightly bombing raids, the two Malay servants disappeared into the swarming melee of the native slums and were never seen again.

Sarah had always liked the Bristows' bungalow, and as she'd helped Amah and Jane unpack the essentials from the trunks and boxes they had brought with them, she'd felt quite at home. But there was always the fear for Philip, and it overshadowed her days and haunted her nights. The Japanese were swarming all through the peninsula – had he become trapped? Was he still safe, or had he been shot and killed like so many others? It had now been confirmed that the Japanese weren't taking prisoners, and the knowledge made her sick at heart.

The Singapore she had known and loved had changed since her last visit. Alarmingly, it proved to be ill-prepared and far from safe, despite the vast number of troops that were arriving daily, and the reinforced defences round the island. The sirens would shriek every night as the bombers roared overhead and the crump of exploding bombs rocked the very foundations of the house. Food was scarce; air-raid shelters weren't completed; blackout was erratic; water had to be boiled; and the family had taken to sleeping on mattresses beneath Brigadier Bristow's billiard table. If it hadn't been for Amah's knowledge of the native markets, they would have starved.

Jock had not returned to the rubber plantation as he'd planned, for not only would it be foolhardy in the extreme to risk such a journey; he'd come to realise that his family was in terrible danger, and that he had to find some way to get them out of Singapore. The Japanese were closing in rapidly on Kuala Lumpur, and despite their vast numbers, the British and Allied armies had little air or sea support and couldn't hold them back.

Sarah's anxiety over Philip's whereabouts was tempered with worry over her parents. Sybil was looking decidedly off-colour, despite her denials. The scratch on her face was taking its time to heal – although it didn't seem to have become infected, which was always the danger in the tropics – and she was still suffering from the mosquito bites which formed ugly red lumps on her arms and neck and itched constantly, even though Amah smothered them in her special creams.

By the end of their first week in Singapore, Jock was on the point of exhaustion. He spent his days desperately trying to find a passage for his wife and daughters on one of the ships. He stood in endless queues, badgered officials, tried to pull strings and call in favours – but it seemed the entire white population of Malaya and Singapore were just as determined to get their wives and children out, and there just weren't enough ships.

Sarah and Jane were playing a board game in the sitting room when they heard the truck pull into the front drive. They looked up expectantly as Jock opened the door, threw his hat on the hall table and strode into the room.

'Good news,' he announced, slinging his crumpled jacket over the back of a chair and unfastening the holster at his waist. 'I've got you all a passage on the *Monarch of the Glen*. You leave on the dawn tide for England, the day after tomorrow.'

As Jane congratulated him for being so clever, Sarah was overwhelmed with mixed emotions. 'But you're coming with us, aren't you? It's pretty clear by now that you can't go back to the plantation.'

Jock locked the pistol in a drawer, poured the last of the Brigadier's whisky into a glass and swallowed it down. 'I must stay here and help defend Singapore. It's my duty – and I'm damned if I'll run away like a rat leaving a sinking ship.'

'But, Daddy, you aren't a soldier,' said Jane, 'and *we* need you.'

He eyed his daughters fondly. 'I need to know that you and your mother are safely on your way to England,' he said. 'But I also need to do my bit here. Once I don't have you to worry about, I can focus more clearly.'

'Your father is right,' said Sybil as she came into the room. 'We must all be brave and do as he wishes.' She gave Jock a wan smile and sank gracefully into a nearby chair. 'We're leaving the day after tomorrow, you say? Then you'd better tell us what the arrangements are, so we can be prepared.'

'Are you feeling all right, Sybil?' he asked in alarm. 'You look very flushed.'

'I am a bit hot, and I have a slight headache,' she said, dismissing both with a wave of her hand. 'But I'm sure it's just the tension of these past few weeks. Don't fuss, Jock.'

He eyed her suspiciously, but she smiled back at him brightly enough, so he turned and reached into his jacket pocket for a sheaf of papers. 'We must be on the docks at four in the morning with all your identification documents, and ready to board by five. You will be allowed to take one suitcase each.'

Sybil gasped. 'But I can't possibly get everything I'll need in one case.'

'Darling, you'll just have to be careful with your packing,' said Jock quietly. 'You won't need tea dresses and ballgowns, or a hundred pairs of shoes and gloves.'

'But what about the family silver, and my Meissen

figurines? I can't just leave them here in Elsa's bungalow.'

'I'll make arrangements for them to be stored safely somewhere,' he soothed. 'But I would advise you take your jewellery – you might need it to sell if I can't get money to you.'

Appalled, Sybil stared back at him. 'Most of it was my grandmother's,' she said, 'and I would *never* sell it.' She rose from the chair, clearly flustered. 'Really, Jock,' she muttered, 'you're upsetting me with all this talk of running out of money.'

He caught her hand and held it to his lips. 'I'm being cautious, Sybil,' he murmured. 'None of us knows how long we'll be parted – and you'll need money in England to see you and the girls through.' He put his arm round her thickened waist. 'I've arranged with our bank here to telegraph its counterpart in Cliffehaven and then start to transfer money into my father's old account which he'd set up years ago. I've also sent telegrams to Cordelia and Amelia, warning them of your impending arrival.'

Sybil nodded. 'We'll also need cash for the journey,' she murmured. 'Do you think we'll be going ashore anywhere on the way? Only we're going to need warm clothes in England, for none of us owns anything warmer than a thin cardigan.'

'I really don't know,' he admitted, 'but I'll see if I can exchange some Malay dollars into pounds sterling.'

Sybil dabbed her hot face with a scrap of hand-kerchief, and rubbed the reddened lumps on her arm.

'I must tell Amah what's happening and prepare her for the journey. I do hope—'

'I'm sorry, Sybil,' Jock said as he stilled her hand. 'Amah isn't allowed to go with you.'

'But she must,' Jane protested. 'She's part of the family, and we can't leave her here.'

'I'm sorry, my darlings,' he replied, 'but Amah isn't a British subject. She will not be allowed to sail with you.' As the three of them began to argue with him rather forcefully, he held up his hands for silence. 'I will see that she is safe and well provided for,' he said firmly. 'Amah is as important to me as she is to you, and I promise I will look after her.'

'I have family in Singapore,' said the tiny woman in the doorway. 'They will shelter me. Thank you, *Tuan*.' She put her hands together and bowed low. 'If you would excuse, please, I must help *Mems* to pack.'

That night and the following day were spent packing – and her mother was right, for no matter how careful she was, Sarah still couldn't get all she wanted into the large leather case. She looked in despair at all the pretty frocks and hand-sewn nightwear and blouses she had to leave behind and then sadly had to accept she needed the space for more precious things.

The silver-backed dressing-table set was wrapped in with her underwear; two pairs of light sandals were wedged in the corners of the case, and the photographs had been painstakingly taken from the heavy family albums and placed between the pages of *The*

Jungle Book, which had remained a great favourite since childhood. The framed photograph of her and Philip standing on the veranda the night they had celebrated their engagement had been tenderly placed within the folds of a hand-painted silk evening wrap. She possessed only a pearl necklace and studs in the way of jewellery, and these she would tuck in their velvet box and carry in her handbag when she wasn't wearing them.

Sybil had come up with the bright idea that they should all wear as many clothes as possible to add to the amount of things they could take, and Sarah had three dresses, two lightweight cardigans, and a jacket, on hangers waiting for the following morning. She would also wear a hat and put spare gloves and some silk scarves in the jacket pocket.

Some of the clothing she would wear tomorrow held a secret, for Amah had set them all to sewing Sybil's precious jewellery into the linings. At times like this it wasn't wise to have such valuable things simply locked in a suitcase.

It was five in the afternoon on their last day in Singapore, and every time she heard a car engine, Sarah looked out of the bungalow window anxiously in the hope it might be Philip. To see him again, to know he was safe, was all she wanted. But their ship would leave in fourteen hours, and once it had sailed, it could be months before she discovered what had happened to him.

'I know there's no point in me telling you not to

worry about Philip,' said Jock as he watched her pace the room. 'But the minute I hear anything I'll send you a telegraph. I promise.'

They both turned in surprise as Amah, usually so calm and quiet, came running into the room with a cry of distress. 'It is *Mem*,' she sobbed. 'You must call doctor.'

They rushed into the big bedroom and found Sybil writhing on the bed, her hands clutching her head, her clothes soaked in perspiration as angry red spots flared on her neck and chest.

Jock scooped her up in his arms. 'Get the car, Sarah. She needs to go to hospital.'

With Amah and Jane running after them, Jock and Sarah raced out of the bungalow. Sarah's hands fumbled with the key as Jane and Amah climbed in beside her, and Jock clambered into the back with an extremely distressed Sybil still clasped in his arms.

'Put your foot down, Sarah,' Jock commanded.

The journey through the city to the General Hospital on the Outram Road was as fraught as always, with bicycles, rickshaws, cattle, goats, chickens and natives jostling for space alongside trucks, dilapidated taxis, and armoured cars.

Sarah drove as fast as she could, swerving recklessly to avoid small children who darted out from the crowd, and speeding when she could past the native foodstalls and open sewers, dodging potholes, skinny cats and stray dogs.

The sirens began to wail before they even had sight

of the hospital, and Sarah automatically slowed down.

'Ignore them,' ordered Jock. 'Put your foot down and keep your hand on the horn. There isn't a moment to waste.'

Sarah kept one hand on the horn, gripped the steering wheel and pressed her foot almost to the floor. Her way was now hampered by people rushing for shelter, but after a few hair-raising near misses, she managed to get to the huge hospital complex. She brought the car to a screeching halt outside the front entrance, and Jock was halfway out of the door before she could switch off the engine.

The bombers screamed overhead as she reached for Jane and Amah's hands and they raced towards the front door. A hail of bullets spat across the hospital driveway, missing them by inches, and they almost fell through the doors and into the reception area.

There was no sign of Jock, and Sarah was shaking so much she could barely speak as she haltingly asked the cowering receptionist where he'd gone. The girl pointed and ducked down behind her desk as a bomb exploded in the distance, and Sarah grabbed the others and began to run.

Having never been inside the hospital, Sarah soon discovered that the place was built like a maze, with endless corridors and confusing twists and turns. Amah was struggling to keep up, and she waved them on, but as they turned yet another corner and stumbled into the European wing, they saw Jock pacing back and forth in front of a closed door.

They were all out of breath and Sarah had a stitch in her side, but the look on her father's face squeezed her heart. 'How is she?' she panted. 'What's the matter with her?'

Jock didn't stop pacing. 'The doctor's with her now,' he muttered. 'He thinks she's got dengue fever.'

Sarah held Jane's hand tightly as she tried to digest this awful news. Dengue fever could be fatal if it was one of the stronger strains of the virus – and with her mother's pregnancy it would only complicate things. There were so many questions she wanted to ask, but with Jane and Amah there, she didn't dare.

They all turned as Dr Cook came through the screens, and he gave them a reassuring smile. 'It is as I suspected,' he said, 'but there's no cause for alarm. Mrs Fuller has one of the milder forms of the virus and it will not harm the baby. We've set up intravenous drips to rehydrate her and combat the effects of the fever.'

Jock plumped down into a nearby chair and covered his face with his hands. 'Thank God,' he breathed. 'I thought I was going to lose her.'

Dr Cook patted his shoulder. 'She needs to rest and sleep now, but I'm hopeful that in three or four days she will be quite well again and ready to go home.'

'But she and our daughters are booked on the *Monarch of the Glen*, which leaves early tomorrow,' said Jock as he ran his hands distractedly through his hair. 'Can't you get her well enough to travel before then?'

Dr Cook shook his head. 'That is a terrible dilemma, Mr Fuller, but it would be most unwise to move her until the fever has run its course. The medical facilities on board a troopship will be basic to say the least – and the risk to mother and baby would simply be too great.'

Jock got to his feet and turned to his anxious daughters, his face lined with anguish. 'You will have to go without her,' he said hoarsely. 'But I promise I will stay with her until I can get her on another ship.' He gathered them to him and looked once again at the doctor. 'May they see her for a moment to say goodbye?'

'Of course. But don't expect too much from her. The fever is making her a little confused.'

Sarah was trembling as she led Jane through the screens. Sybil looked very vulnerable and small in the hospital bed, and her hand felt dry and hot as Sarah gently held it.

'We've come to tell you we love you, Mummy,' said Jane with admirable calm as she sat on the other side of the bed. 'But Daddy says we have to go on the ship to England in the morning, so we want you to get better quickly so you can come later.'

'Darling girls,' murmured Sybil. 'So sweet of you to come. Has Amah made the tea yet? I must dress for dinner.' Her eyelids fluttered and she sank into oblivion.

Sarah was close to tears and so was Jane, but they sat holding their mother's hands as she slept, each treasuring these last few moments until they could all be together again.

There was very little sleep for any of them that night, for not only were they worried about Sybil, they had yet another enemy air raid to contend with – and the terrifying news that Kuala Lumpur had been taken by the Japanese. Jock had given Sarah a piece of paper with the addresses of the two great aunts, and she had tucked it carefully into her handbag. The sudden new responsibility for making sure that she and Jane reached their destination safely made it even harder for her to settle to sleep.

Bleary-eyed at three in the morning, they dragged on their layers of clothing in the darkness, picked up their cases and headed for the car. They stilled as they heard a series of deep booms in the distance. 'What was that?' asked Sarah sharply. 'I didn't hear the air-raid warning.'

Jock shook his head. 'The military are blowing up the causeway to stop the Jap advance into Singapore,' he said. 'Now get in the car. We can't afford to miss the ship.'

Amah sat between Sarah and Jane, patting their hands, kissing their fingers, and murmuring to them as she'd done when they were babies. It was a small comfort, but it simply emphasised the reality of their leaving, and by the time they reached the port, both Sarah and her sister were fighting back the tears.

The quayside was in chaos, for the night's bombing

had hit a warehouse, the Nee Soon Barracks, and two of the oil refinery towers. Black smoke was drifting in the humid air as fire and ambulance bells jangled and sergeant majors bellowed out orders to their men. Women and children in their hundreds were milling about clutching their permitted single suitcase, while husbands and fathers tried to quell their fears and remain stoic in the face of this enforced parting.

Native porters carried great bundles of supplies from the ships as the stevedores orchestrated the unloading of armoured cars and tanks, their voices ringing out above the roar of engines and the general mayhem. And as Sarah and the others climbed out of the car they saw troops of young, fresh-faced soldiers pouring down the gangplanks of a nearby merchant ship to be marched off to the nearest assembly point.

As the sampans and Chinese junks bustled back and forth between the many inlets and estuaries, they were dwarfed by the huge ships that lay at anchor in the harbour or were tethered to the wharfs. The *Monarch of the Glen* had once been a luxury cruise liner, but it had been stripped of all the refinements when it had been seconded to the Royal Navy to carry troops and supplies to the Far East. Standing tall at the pier, its three funnels belched smoke into the already sulphurous air as the seamen swarmed over the decks like ants.

Sarah and Jane kept their hands tucked firmly round Jock's arms as they headed out of the administration shed and slowly pushed their way through the jostling, milling crowd towards the iron gangway that led to the ship's lower deck. Amah was waiting for them, her sweet face shadowed with sorrow.

'I will say goodbye now,' she said. 'And wait for *Tuan* in the car.'

As Sarah hugged her she felt the slender frailty of her, and breathed in the familiar and much loved scent of the oils she used on her skin and hair. 'We'll come back soon,' she promised. 'Just please take care of Mummy for us.'

Amah nodded and cupped her cheek. 'Of course,' she murmured, 'and when this war is over you will all come home to Amah again.'

Sarah couldn't watch as Jane tearfully said her own goodbyes, and she felt the knot of fear tighten in her stomach as the reality of what was happening began to sink in. She blinked away the tears, determined not to weaken – but she didn't want to leave the only home she'd ever known – didn't want to abandon her sick mother in the hospital, or Philip, wherever he might be – or Amah, who'd loved and cherished her all her life.

She watched the tiny figure walk away and become lost in the milling crowd, and then turned to her father and buried her face in his jacket. 'I'm frightened, Daddy,' she admitted.

He drew her head into his hands. 'I'm frightened too,' he said, 'but the Fullers are made of strong stuff, and we'll see this thing through.' He kissed her forehead. 'Be brave, my beautiful girl – and remember that your mother and I love you very much.'

'I don't want to go,' sobbed Jane as she flung herself

against Jock. 'Please don't make me go, Daddy.'

He gave a groan of despair and held Jane close. 'You'll be safe with Sarah,' he crooned. 'Please don't cry, Jane. I hate to see you cry.'

The shrill command of the ship's siren stilled them all, and beneath that screaming warning they could hear the distant hum that could only mean the impending arrival of enemy aircraft.

'Get on board quickly,' said Jock, wresting Jane's clutching hands from around his neck and nudging them both forward.

As Sarah grabbed Jane's hand, she was almost knocked flying by a distraught woman carrying a young baby. Managing to just about keep on her feet, but losing her hat in the process, she took a tight hold on Jane and her suitcase as the crowd surged in panic towards the gangway.

The Japanese planes screamed overhead, dropping bombs which exploded in the sea, missing the ships by a hair's breadth. The guns from the anchored ships and the batteries in the port blasted out, and the quayside shuddered beneath their feet.

People were screaming now, pushing, shoving, fighting to get on board the ship. Some fell in the murky water of the harbour while others attempted to scramble up the ropes which tethered the *Monarch* to the pier. Hats and suitcases fell into the water, and sailors reached to help the terrified women who stumbled up the iron steps with their children clinging to their skirts. And on the dockside, the military policemen wrestled several men away who'd been trying to get on board.

'The planes are turning,' someone shouted. 'They're coming back.'

Sarah didn't need to urge Jane to hurry, for they were being swept along in the mad rush to get on deck. And as they gained the top of the gangway, they felt the shudder of the ship's guns reverberate in the deck beneath them as salvo after salvo was fired at the enemy. Crouching on the deck in terror, they huddled together as the bullets zipped past them and the roar of the planes competed with the thud and boom of the big guns.

More guns continued to blaze around the harbour and from the other ships that were anchored nearby, and a great cheer went up as one of the fleeing enemy planes took a direct hit and plummeted into the water in a ball of flames.

Once the enemy planes had gone, and it was deemed safe, everyone slowly got to their feet and stood in dazed silence, seemingly incapable of doing anything in the aftermath of that surprise attack.

Sarah finally pulled herself together and led the way to the next deck and found a gap for her and Jane by the railings. They were high above the quay and the people below swarmed like insects as yet more women and children came on board – and in the distance she could see the remains of the oil refinery tanks that were still burning, and the skeletons of ruined buildings.

'I can't see Daddy,' said Jane, her voice high-pitched with fear. 'Where is he?'

Sarah couldn't see him either. There were too many people moving about and the smoke from all the fires was too thick. And then she spotted the lone figure waving at the end of the pier where the stevedores were already untying the ropes from the capstans and flinging them towards the sailors on board several decks below.

'There!' she said excitedly. 'Down there!'

They waved to him, the tears streaming down their faces as they called down to him, and he waved back. But they couldn't hear what he was saying, for the three sharp blasts from the ship's hooter drowned out everything.

The ship gave an almighty lurch and began to pull away from the wharf.

Sarah and Jane leaned precariously over the rails to keep him in sight for as long as they could – and then Sarah saw a truck come hurtling down the pier, scattering dock workers and sailors before screeching to a halt beside Jock.

The driver leaped out and stared up, following Jock's pointing finger until his gaze found Sarah's.

'Philip,' she screamed as the tears flowed and she waved frantically. 'Oh, Philip, thank God you're safe. I love you, darling,' she sobbed. 'I love you so much.'

She watched through her tears as he shouted something back, but it was impossible to hear anything, and the ship was moving further and further from the dock. She kept waving until the *Monarch of the Glen* swung towards the harbour entrance and they were both lost from sight.

God keep you all safe, Sarah prayed silently as she and Jane clung to one another tearfully and watched the shores of their homeland slip out of sight. It could be months, maybe years, before she saw Philip or her parents again, but they would always be in her heart, no matter how far apart they were.

Chapter Ten

Cliffehaven

Almost two weeks had passed since Peggy had spoken to Anthony, and so far they hadn't heard back from him. Peggy kept a close eye on Cordelia, for as the situation in the Far East worsened, she seemed to lose her spirits, and it was important to keep her busy and uplifted while they waited for news from Anthony.

It wasn't quite six in the morning and Jim was still snoring in bed, enjoying the luxury of his one day off from the hated factory. Peggy had dressed in the dark as the north wind howled around the house and rattled the windows, and then quickly bathed and fed Daisy in the kitchen before tucking her warmly into the pram. It was far too cold to put her outside, but perhaps if the wind dropped and the sun came out, she could take her for a bit of a walk later so they could both get some fresh air.

The house was quiet and she tiptoed across the hall to fetch the newspaper from the letter box and the milk from the doorstep. It was bitterly cold still, and she shivered as she closed the door and went back to the warmth of the kitchen to drink a cup of very weak tea and scan the newspaper headlines. Apart from the Russian victory over the Germans, there was very little to be cheerful about.

Soap was to be rationed, dried fruit would be in very short supply now that Greece had fallen, and North Africa was in turmoil. Australia was bracing itself for invasion as the Japanese continued their onslaught in Malaya, Hong Kong and the Philippines. Several British ships had been sunk in the Channel, Hitler was still threatening to invade, and the heroes of Bomber Command were suffering even heavier losses than their comrades in the other squadrons.

Peggy reached into her apron pocket for her packet of Park Drive and lit one. The sooner the Americans managed to replace the ships and planes they'd lost at Pearl Harbor, the sooner they could help the beleaguered Allies in the Pacific. It was all very distressing.

'To be sure you'll not be wanting to read all that,' said Ron as he stumped up the steps with Harvey at his heels. ''Tis depressing, so it is, and there's nothing you can do about it but carry on as usual.' He carefully placed the little basket of eggs on the table beside her and reached into the pocket of his coat. 'Alf sends his regards,' he said with a wink as he laid the package next to the eggs.

Peggy carefully unfolded the newspaper and gasped. 'Bacon?' she breathed. 'And so much of it! How on earth—?'

'Ask no questions, and I'll tell ye no lies,' he

interrupted, tapping the side of his nose.

She eyed him sharply as she puffed on her cigarette. 'Have you been poaching again?'

He took off his coat and slung it over the back of a chair. 'Now, Peg,' he replied, 'how on earth would I be doing such a thing when the Cliffe estate has a fence around it the height of a mountain?'

'Wire-cutters,' she replied dryly. 'I saw you put them in your pocket the other day and wondered what you were up to.'

His blue eyes twinkled. 'To be sure, Peggy girl, it is suspicious you are. Can you not trust a poor auld man who only has the welfare of his family at heart?'

Peggy giggled. 'You're a rogue, and I would trust you with my life, Ronan Reilly, but you and Alf will get caught one day and end up in prison.'

Breakfast was a banquet that morning, the smell of sizzling bacon wafting through the house to lure everyone out of their beds and into the kitchen. Harvey left his post by the side of the pram and sat hopefully at Ron's knee – but there were no scraps this morning.

They ate the freshly laid eggs with their dark yellow yolks and the crisp bacon and fried bread in an almost reverent silence, mopping up the remains with fingers of more bread and finally pushing their plates away with sighs of pleasure and regret that the meal was over.

Peggy took pity on Harvey and gave him some extra dog biscuits. Then she and the three girls washed the dishes and tidied the kitchen while Cordelia made a fresh pot of tea, and the men went off to prepare for a bitterly cold day at sea. They were meeting Frank in Tamarisk Bay, which was just around the headland to the east of Cliffehaven, and were taking one of the fishing boats out to try and catch their supper.

'You be careful out there,' said Peggy as she wrapped a thick woollen scarf round Jim's neck and pulled a woolly hat over his ears.

'Ach, will you stop fussing,' he said before sweeping her into his arms and giving her a resounding kiss. 'We'll be back before you know it with enough fish for Mrs Finch to make one of her special pies.'

Peggy became flustered as she always did when Jim kissed her like that. 'Be off with you,' she said, playfully swiping him with the tea towel, 'and send my love to Pauline. Tell her I'll try and get over there as soon as the weather takes a turn for the better.'

Jim rolled his eyes and pulled on his gloves. 'To be sure Frank's wife could always come here,' he muttered as he peeked into the pram and adjusted the blanket under his daughter's chin. 'It isn't as if you don't have enough to do without traipsing all the way to Tamarisk Bay.'

Peggy nudged him away from the pram before he could wake Daisy. 'Leave her be, Jim,' she said wearily. 'You'll have plenty of time to play with her when you come home.'

Ron and Jim clumped down the steps, Harvey barking excitedly at their heels as they strode along the path and through the back gate. It was a long walk over the hills to the next bay, and Peggy hoped their trip was worth all the trouble. But then it was good for Ron to spend a day with his sons – and good for Jim and Frank, who'd finally settled their differences and were beginning to be real brothers again.

As Fran left to go on duty at the hospital and Rita departed on her noisy motorbike for the fire station, Peggy and Cordelia settled down to their cups of tea while they made a shopping list. The queues outside the shops started early, and most of the time Peggy didn't even know what she was actually queuing for – but a line of women waiting outside in the cold or wet meant something was on offer, and if it wasn't needed, it could always be swapped for something else later on.

Suzy came back downstairs some time later, looking very smart in a tweed skirt, blouse and cardigan. 'I've decided to treat myself to a shampoo and set,' she told them as she pulled on her coat and headscarf. 'And then I'm going to meet Sally Hicks at the little tea room opposite the hospital and have a coffee and teacake to celebrate.'

'My goodness,' said Cordelia, 'you are spoiling yourself today. What's the occasion?'

Suzy shrugged. 'Nothing really,' she replied as she tugged on her gloves. 'We've been so busy at the hospital that I never seem to be out of uniform. I just want to feel like a girl again, that's all. And Sally feels the same now she's got the baby.'

Peggy smiled. Sally and her crippled brother Ernie

had come from the East End slums of London to be her first evacuees, and they had become an intrinsic part of the Reilly family. So much so, that when Sally's aunt had taken Ernie into her home in Somerset for the duration, she had also taken the two Reilly boys, and had even agreed to Anne going down there with Rose Margaret. Sally had married the Fire Chief, John Hicks, and six months ago she'd presented him with a healthy son.

'It won't be much of an outing if Sal's taking Daniel with her. She can bring him round here if she likes. I'll look after him.'

Suzy smiled. 'Bless you, Peg, but John's doing baby-sitting duties today. Though I don't think he quite realises what a handful his Danny can be.'

Peggy chuckled. Danny was a large, robust baby who was into everything now he could crawl, and had a fierce temper when thwarted. 'It won't do John any harm,' she said comfortably. 'Go and have fun, Suzy. You and Sal deserve it.'

Half an hour later Peggy was standing in a queue outside the grocer's. There were equally long lines outside the butcher's and baker's as well, and as the wind tugged at their headscarves and chilled their faces, the women exchanged the latest gossip, cooed over babies and moaned about the rationing and the weather. Queuing had become quite a social occasion, and today the talk was all about the Americans who were due to arrive in England within the next two months.

It was almost an hour before Peggy arrived at the counter to purchase her ration of the newly delivered packets of tea, but during that time she'd managed to swap some of her powdered milk tokens for tins of spam, and her egg tokens for sugar. The butter, milk and cheese ration was quite generous as she had special catering coupons as well as the extra ones the government gave her as a nursing mother, so all in all, she felt quite privileged.

With her string shopping bag tucked away beneath the pram, she strolled along Camden Road and joined the queue at the bakery. White bread was becoming more and more scarce, but the rather tough brown loaves were better than nothing, and when she saw some little iced buns she splashed out and bought seven so that everyone could have a treat after their tea.

Feeling quite heroic after all this effort, she wheeled the pram further down the road and stood in line outside the butcher's. Alf was behind the counter as always. He was a big, red-faced man with a loud laugh and a generous heart, and would often add scraps of mince or a pork chop to the parcel of someone he thought deserved it.

She eventually got to the counter and smiled up at him. 'I just need nine sausages and a packet of lard today, Alf. We had a lovely breakfast this morning, so they won't need much tonight.'

'I thought Ron and 'is boys was going fishing for their supper?' he said.

'They are,' she replied, 'but there's no guarantee they'll actually catch anything.'

He winked at her and selected the sausages off one of the tin trays that were lined up beneath the glass counter. He glanced into the pram as he wrapped them and the packet of lard in newspaper. 'Daisy's coming on a treat, ain't she?' he said, his Cockney accent still as strong as ever, even after thirty years of living in Cliffehaven. 'Reminds me of me own nipper when she were that age. Proper little madam, I can tell you, but she's turned out all right. Joined the flaming navy of all things,' he said proudly as he handed over the parcel with another wink. 'Mind 'ow ya go, Peg, and give me regards to Ron.'

'You mind how you go, Alf,' she said with a meaningful look as she handed over the food stamps and money.

She could still hear him laughing as she wheeled the pram outside and headed back to Beach View. She'd had enough fresh air, her feet were like blocks of ice despite the fur-lined boots, and Daisy was waking up, no doubt with a dirty nappy and a raging hunger.

As she walked back along Camden Road she had to stop repeatedly to talk to the friends and neighbours who wanted to look at Daisy and exchange a few pleasantries. Peggy was soon chilled to the bone, and as she'd heard all the gossip and was growing a bit tired of saying the same thing over and over, she didn't stop again, just waved hello and kept on walking. But as she passed the Anchor pub she saw something that made her slow down.

Tommy Findlay was having a heated exchange with Eileen Harris, who worked for the local council. Eileen was clearly no pushover and was giving Tommy a right earful, and Peggy would have loved to stop to listen in, but unfortunately she was far too visible to the pair of them. She walked very slowly, hoping to catch the gist of their argument, but as she was on the other side of the road, the wind kept whipping their words away.

Tommy looked up and caught sight of her, and Peggy ducked her head and walked quickly on. She had no wish to get involved, for she didn't think much of either of them and thought they deserved one another. She carried on at a fast pace until she'd reached the junction.

Eileen Harris was the sister of Julie, who'd been billeted with Peggy for a few months the previous year. Julie had been a lovely girl, but she'd gone back to London just before Christmas to continue her midwifery, and Peggy still missed her. There had been a falling out between the sisters initially, but they'd made it up before Julie had left. Peggy had had to keep her mouth shut when Julie had believed Eileen's lies, for family ties were important and Julie needed someone to call her own after her parents had been killed in the Blitz. But Eileen was a bitch, a selfish, lying cow, and if Tommy's sudden appearance in Cliffehaven had upset her, then it served her right.

Peggy's jag of fury was short-lived as she headed for the twitten and pushed the pram along the muddy path to the back gate. Daisy was crying now and waving her arms about. It was time to forget about Eileen and Tommy and the trouble they'd caused all those years ago, and to see to her daughter's needs.

Daisy was now nine weeks old, with a good appetite and a very loud cry when she wanted something. She waved her arms and legs about, kicking off the blanket and wailing as Peggy grabbed the string bag of shopping, lifted her out and carried her up the steps to the kitchen.

'Good heavens,' said Cordelia, who was sitting by the fire as she sewed a button back on Ron's shirt. 'Someone's not happy.'

Peggy dropped the shopping on the draining board, placed the screaming baby safely in the other armchair and pulled off her outer layers. 'We're both cold and hungry,' she said above the yells. 'The queues were endless as usual, and it's freezing out there.' She warmed her hands by the fire and looked at the clock on the mantel. It was quite shocking how quickly the day had gone, for it was almost two o'clock. No wonder Daisy was starving.

She quickly folded a towel and placed it on the table. Having fetched a clean nappy, baby powder and a tub of petroleum jelly from the cupboard in her bedroom, she changed Daisy's nappy. 'There's a fresh packet of tea in there,' she said as she sat down and pulled off Daisy's woollen hat and mittens. 'I could do with a cup and no mistake – but the buns are for tonight.'

As Cordelia bustled about making the tea and a

sandwich for Peggy's lunch, Peggy fed her daughter. Warming nicely by the fire, she leaned back in the chair, eyes closed as the blissful silence descended, and she began to relax at last.

Cordelia put the cup of tea close to Peggy's elbow, then she finished sewing the button on, folded the shirt and set it aside. There were still more buttons to replace and patches to be sewn in Ron's disreputable clothes, but her eyes were getting tired now.

She took off her half-moon glasses and pinched the bridge of her nose. She seemed to feel tired all the time just lately, but as she looked fondly at Peggy, she realised she wasn't the only one. Poor Peggy was clearly exhausted, and trying to do far too much as usual, and Cordelia felt cross with herself for being so selfish. If only she could do more to help, she fretted – but age and arthritis meant she was slow and clumsy, and standing in queues in this freezing weather was beyond her. It was an absolute nuisance being old, but then the alternative of being six feet under in the local graveyard didn't appeal to her at all.

She was about to pick up the next shirt to mend when there was a knock at the front door. 'You stay there, Peggy,' she said quickly. 'I'll go.'

It took her a while to get to the front door, even with her walking stick, for she'd been sitting for too long and her knees had stiffened up. The nice-looking young man who towered over her on the doorstep looked familiar, but Cordelia couldn't quite place him. 'Yes?' she asked.

'Hello, Mrs Finch,' he said as he took off his hat. 'It's me, Anthony Williams. Doris's son.'

'What a lovely surprise,' she said and stepped back so he could come into the hall. Slamming the door on the howling gale that was tearing up from the seafront, she looked up at him eagerly. 'Do you have any news of my nephew?'

'I do, as it happens, but can we go into the kitchen? My feet are like ice after that long bike ride from Castle Hill.'

Cordelia dithered, as it wasn't proper to let the young man into the kitchen while Peggy was feeding Daisy – but she couldn't possibly keep him in the hall, or take him into the dining room, which was little more than a glory hole now.

And then Peggy rescued her by calling out for them to come into the warm. 'I'm quite decent,' she said with a laugh as they walked in. 'And Daisy has stopped bawling, so we can all enjoy a sensible conversation without having to raise our voices.'

Cordelia sat and watched as Anthony approached the playpen in the corner where Daisy lay beneath her pink blanket, surrounded by her soft toys, rattles and rag books. He tickled her tummy, and she kicked her legs and giggled, and Anthony smiled down at her.

Such a sweet smile, thought Cordelia. How on earth the truly awful Doris could have produced such a handsome, gentle son, she had no idea.

Anthony unwound his college scarf from his neck and shrugged off his thick coat. 'With that curly dark hair and those brown eyes, she looks just like you, Aunt Peg,' he said with a soft smile. 'How are you coping?'

'All things considering, we're managing very well,' she replied, 'but that's enough about me and Daisy. I can see that Cordelia is bursting to hear what you've discovered, so sit down and tell her while I freshen the pot of tea.'

Cordelia looked into his dark brown eyes and felt a spark of hope as he smiled at her. 'You've found him, haven't you?' she asked.

'In a roundabout way,' he said as he pushed his glasses up his nose. 'But it was someone else who did all the hard work. You see, a friend put me onto a chap he knew, and he did the research. Jock Fuller was still living on a rubber plantation in Malaya when the hostilities broke out with Japan. He has a wife, Sybil, and two daughters. Sarah is nineteen and Jane is seventeen.'

Cordelia experienced a sharp pang of distress. 'Are they safe? Did they manage to get away from the Japanese?'

He smiled as he reached into his trouser pocket and pulled out a brown envelope. 'I happened to be at home when the postman came. He knew you'd moved in here some time ago, but as we're Peggy's family, he thought it would be kinder for one of us to deliver it.'

He looked a bit bashful. 'Telegrams are horrid things to get in these troubled times, so I took the liberty of opening it. I do apologise, but it's good news, Mrs Finch, I assure you.'

Cordelia put on her glasses and looked at the brown envelope which had been addressed to her old home in Havelock Road. With trembling fingers, she pulled out the telegram.

'WIFE AND DAUGHTERS LEAVING SINGAPORE MONARCH OF THE GLEN * ETA CLIFFEHAVEN MARCH * KEEP SAFE FOR DURATION * URGENT REPLY SINGAPORE CLUB * JOCK FULLER * END.'

'Oh, my goodness,' she breathed, her eyes brightening with excitement. 'How wonderful that they've escaped! And to think I didn't even know if they existed. Two daughters, how lovely. Oh goodness me, I'm feeling rather tearful. How silly.' And then reality set in. 'But what about Jock? Surely he isn't staying in Singapore?'

'I'm sorry, Mrs Finch, but it certainly looks as if he means to, for he's asked you to reply care of the Singapore Club.'

'Oh dear,' she said, her voice trembling. 'I do hope he doesn't get caught up in the fighting – but at least he was able to get his family out of harm's way.' Then a thought struck her. 'But where on earth can they stay?' she fretted.

'Well, here, of course,' said Peggy.

'But you have enough to do without three more people to feed,' protested Cordelia. 'I simply can't expect you to have them here.'

'My dearest Cordelia, they are your family – and as such they are mine too. They will stay here for as long as they need. The girls can have the big double bedroom at the front, and the mother can go in the single next to them.'

Cordelia burst into tears. 'Oh, Peggy, you're so very kind. What on earth would I do without you?'

'Hello, what's going on?'

Anthony shot to his feet as Suzy walked into the room, all rosy and sparkling-eyed from her walk in the cold, and despite her emotional outburst, Cordelia couldn't help but notice the awestruck look on his face as the girl took off her headscarf and unbuttoned her coat.

She blew her nose and tried to regain control of her emotions. 'Anthony has found my family,' she managed through the lump in her throat, 'and they've escaped Singapore and will be here next month. Isn't that wonderful?'

Suzy gave her a hug. 'It certainly is, Grandma Finch,' she said softly. 'I'm so happy for you.' She turned to Anthony, who still looked rather stunned. 'What a wonderful thing you've done for our darling Grandma Finch,' she said, blushing prettily at the intensity of his adoring gaze. 'How can we ever thank you enough?'

He cleared his throat and fiddled with his glasses. 'I didn't do anything, not really,' he managed.

'I rather think you did,' she murmured, 'and it was most awfully kind of you.'

Cordelia watched in fascination as the two young

people regarded one another. She could almost feel the magic that was happening between them, and knew that she was witnessing love at first sight. *Oh, what a happy, happy day*, she thought as the tears flowed down her face again.

Peggy had noticed it too, and she dabbed at her own eyes before handing Cordelia a clean handkerchief. Suzy looked particularly pretty today, with her freshly washed and set hair, and her glowing eyes. There was a luminosity in her face that she suspected had very little to do with the long, cold walk home, and she was reminded of her daughter's wedding day, when Anne's face had glowed as she'd walked up the aisle towards Martin.

She turned away and couldn't help a wry smile as she poured everyone another cup of tea. She'd always been on the lookout for a nice girl for Anthony, but she'd never even considered Suzy – and yet now it seemed obvious they were a perfect match. Suzy was a well-brought-up girl from a good family who'd seen to it that she'd had the best private education they could afford. Nature had blessed her not only with a sharp mind, but with golden hair, creamy skin and big blue eyes – and the longest, shapeliest legs Peggy had ever seen.

But for all her beauty and grace and her devotion to her nursing, Suzy could be as quietly stubborn and strong-willed as a mule – and when she felt passionate about something she stuck to her guns and fought for it with a restrained but implacable determination.

Doris had once declared that she thought Suzy was a bit soft and too easily led by the more flamboyant Fran, and that nursing was probably all she was good for. It would be interesting to see how she'd react if anything came of this instant attraction. One thing Peggy knew for sure: if Anthony was the man for Suzy, then Doris would soon discover that this seemingly quiet, reserved young woman was a formidable opponent.

She handed round the teacups and halved two of the iced buns. 'We must celebrate Cordelia's news properly,' she declared, 'and then once we've finished our tea, I'll go down to the post office before it shuts and send that telegram to Jock.'

'I'll go,' said Anthony. 'You have a lot to do here, and it's only a short detour on my way home.' He refused to take any money from Cordelia to pay for the telegram, and then turned hesitantly to Suzy. 'Could you bear to stand the cold again and come with me?' he asked softly. 'Then once we've sent it, perhaps we could go for a drink and a bite of supper?'

'That would be lovely,' she replied, 'but I can't be out too late. I'm on duty again at six tomorrow morning.'

'That's settled then,' said Peggy briskly. 'But I'd advise you not to go to the Anchor. The beer's terrible and the new manager gives short measures.'

Anthony and Suzy eyed her with amazement at this outburst.

'Just take my advice,' she said rather more moderately. 'The Ship is a much nicer pub and it's only just down from the post office.'

The clock struck four as the two of them left the house, quietly happy with each other as they pulled up their collars and ducked their heads against the wind.

'That's going to put the cat amongst the pigeons,' said Cordelia with a twinkle in her eye. 'Doris and Suzy are chalk and cheese. I'd love to be a fly on the wall when Doris realises her son has found someone she won't be able to bully.'

Peggy gave her a hug. 'It's been quite a day, hasn't it? I'm delighted that you'll have some real family to fuss over at last. You'll be able to play the Great Aunt to the hilt.'

'You're my family, Peggy,' Cordelia said, her expression earnest. 'And although Jock's daughters are related to me by blood, they are strangers and can never mean as much to me as you do.'

'Oh, Cordelia,' Peggy said as the tears threatened once more.

'Don't you dare start crying again, Peggy Reilly, or you'll set me off too.' She struggled out of her chair and grabbed her walking stick. 'I think I'll go upstairs and write Jock a long letter now I know where to send it. Call me if you need anything, won't you?'

Peggy nodded and followed her up the stairs to make sure she didn't take a tumble, and once she was settled by her gas fire with her writing box, went back to the kitchen.

She was peeling the rather whiskery old potatoes that Ron had stored down in the cellar when she heard the telephone ringing in the hall. With a humph of exasperation, she wiped her hands on her apron and went to answer it. Telephones were a luxury, and if she and Jim hadn't been running a boarding house before the war, they would never have paid for one – but now it was essential, and she couldn't imagine what life would be like without it. Still, sometimes it was just a blasted nuisance.

'Beach View Boarding House,' she said automatically.

'I want to speak to Cordelia Finch,' said the rather bossy voice at the other end of the line.

'Mrs Finch is not available at the moment,' said Peggy cautiously. 'Could I take your name and number and get her to call you back?'

'You may not. This is her sister, Miss Fuller. You will tell Cordelia that I've had a telegram from someone purporting to be my nephew – demanding that I take in his wife and daughters who are on their way from Singapore of all places.'

'Cordelia has had the same telegram, Miss Fuller.'

'Then I hope she has refused to take them in. I don't hold with these people going to live abroad – and then turning up the moment things turn sour, bringing their horrid diseases and habits with them, and expecting everyone to down tools and give instant assistance.'

Peggy was lost for words at the vitriol that was coming down the line. 'They are your brother's grand-children,' she managed finally. 'Surely you—'

'My brother turned his back on England and his family many years ago, and therefore lost the right to expect anything. I will not be replying to the telegram.'

'We are glad to give them shelter, Miss Fuller,' said Peggy flatly, 'and with an attitude like yours it's a good thing they won't have to stay with you.'

She put the receiver back before the other woman could reply and marched back into the kitchen positively trembling with fury. What a nasty, vindictive old witch – how she could be related to sweet Cordelia was a complete mystery.

She left the potatoes in the sink, plumped down at the table and lit a cigarette. There were times when people really shocked her, and this was one of them. How could anyone be so cold and unfeeling – especially when it was family? She puffed furiously on the cigarette until she'd calmed down enough to go back to peeling the spuds.

She wouldn't tell Cordelia about her sister's call, she decided. It would only upset her, and from what Cordelia had told her about Amelia, the two of them had never got on anyway, and rarely communicated, so there would be no harm done.

Chapter Eleven

Cordelia had spent the rest of the afternoon writing her letter to Jock. There were so many things she needed to tell him, and so many questions burning to be asked. By the time she'd finished, she wondered if perhaps she'd rambled on too much, and if he would be able to read her writing, for it was a bit wobbly and ill-formed. She eased the stiffness in her fingers and held them out to warm in front of the gas fire, her thoughts as meandering as her letter.

If Jock was staying in Singapore then he was in great danger, for the news had said that the Japs had taken Kuala Lumpur and were swiftly advancing towards the island. She could only hope that Churchill's boast that Singapore was a fortress held true. It was unthinkable that such a strategic and important island could fall into enemy hands. But then Jock had wisely seen to it that his wife and daughters had escaped, and this brought her a thrill of pleasure. It would be lovely to get to know them – to be able to help as much as she could to ease them into the way of life here. They would find it very strange, she realised, and extremely cold after being in the tropics, but she and Peggy would see to it that they were warmly welcomed and made to feel at home.

With that happy thought, Cordelia found a stamp, sealed the letter, turned off the gas fire and went very carefully down the stairs. She was finding them a little difficult of late, for her balance was a bit off, and she held tightly to the bannisters and her walking stick and took each stair one at a time. On reaching the hall, she fiddled with her hearing aid, and with a smile of pleasure, could hear that Ron and Jim had returned from their fishing trip.

The kitchen was in chaos as the two men had taken over the sink to gut and wash their catch, their voices ringing out as they told Peggy what an adventure they'd had. Harvey had rolled in something nasty and stank to high heaven, and Peggy was dragging him out of her kitchen and slamming the cellar door on him.

His piteous howls were ignored, and Peggy rolled her eyes at Cordelia as the howls rose in volume and the men's tales took on even greater colour. Cordelia grinned as she sat at the table and watched the men skilfully wield their wickedly sharp knives. There was always something interesting going on at Beach View and it quite perked her up.

'To be sure, and Jim thought he saw a submarine,' said Ron gleefully as he rinsed the gutted sea bass under the tap and dropped it in a bucket of water. 'He was all for turning tail and running for home.' Ron chuckled. 'But it was only the bottom of an old boat that had turned turtle.'

'Aye, well, it could have been,' muttered Jim, 'but if it wasn't for my good eyesight, we'd all be in the brig now and under charge.'

'Why?' asked Peggy sharply.

'The coastguard spotted us – but luckily they were too far away to recognise the number on Frank's boat, and we managed to get round the headland and ashore before they could catch us.' Jim grinned. 'You should have seen us, Peg. I reckon we broke the record for beaching the boat and getting the catch indoors – even the auld man here managed to run up that shingle to Frank's place like a two-year-old at Kempton races.'

'I'll give you auld man,' grumbled Ron as he wiped his fishy hands down his trousers and left silvery scales to gleam on the worn corduroy. 'To be sure I'm fitter than you, Jim, after all the years you've been sitting on your arse in that cinema.'

Peggy got out of her chair and, arms akimbo, cleared her throat rather loudly to grab their attention. Her expression was dark, her voice flat with anger. 'Do you mean to tell me that you went out without permission? And risked prison and a large fine just to catch four fish?'

'It was eight, actually,' replied Ron with airy disregard for Peggy's crossness. 'Frank had his share too.' He grinned at her. 'It was worth it, Peg. These pollock will fetch a good price from Fred the Fish, and the bass are big enough to feed everyone tonight.' He gave her a winning smile as he popped the fish heads into a separate pot for soup. 'Are you not partial to a bit of fish, Peggy?'

'I'm partial to having my husband kept out of prison,' she retorted. 'There'll be no more fishing unless I see the official permit first.'

'Ach, Peg, you worry too much,' said Jim as he reached for her.

Peggy drew back sharply. 'You're not coming any-where near me until you've washed away the stink of fish, Jim Reilly. As for you, Ron, you should know better.' She glared at them. '*And* you can clean up the mess you've made of my sink and the lino. There's water and fish scales everywhere.'

'But I told Fred the Fish we'd meet him as soon as we got back. He'll be waiting,' protested Jim.

'Then he can wait a bit longer,' snapped Peggy. 'No one leaves this kitchen until it's spotless. Do you hear me?'

'To be sure, Peg, they can probably hear you halfway down the street,' muttered Ron.

Peggy flicked a tea towel at him and he laughingly dodged out of the way. 'You're a hard woman, so you are, Peggy Reilly, but we'll have this kitchen like new before you can blink.'

'That's what you said when you promised me new lino last year,' she retorted. 'And do something about that dog. He's making enough noise to wake the dead.'

Cordelia watched the cleaning-up operation with amusement. This was what she loved about Beach View. There could be heated rows and lots of shouting, but under it all was the rock-solid love that bound them into a formidable team that could take on the world. She knew that once Peggy's kitchen had been restored to her satisfaction, and Harvey and the men were scrubbed clean, things would calm down and they would laugh about it over their illicit fish supper.

Cordelia waited until they'd cleaned everything and scrubbed down the dog as well as their hands, then gave her letter to Ron to put in the postbox on the way to the fishmonger's. Then she unhooked the wrap-round apron Peggy had given her for Christmas and slipped it on, tying the strings round her waist and adjusting the folds over her non-existent bosom. Fish pie with lashings of potato topping was her speciality, and if they were going to eat before it got too late, she needed to get on.

Fran and Rita came in just after the pie had been put in the oven, so there was plenty of time for them to wash and change before tea. Jim was on fire-watch tonight, and Ron was doing warden duties with the Home Guard, so they ate as soon as it was ready, and then left to go out into the bitter night, their share of the iced buns wrapped in paper to have later with their flasks of hot tea.

Suzy's absence had been commented upon, and Peggy had simply said she was out with a friend for the evening she didn't want the girl bombarded with questions, or to make too much of things at such an early stage. Fran was a bit put out that she hadn't been invited along, for they usually went everywhere together, but as she was tired from a long shift at the hospital and looking forward to an evening of leisure, she didn't probe further.

She and Rita were helping Peggy with the washing-up while Cordelia freshened the pot of tea. The wireless was on most of the time now, for there was always something to listen to, and quite often there would be news bulletins throughout the day.

Cordelia checked the time and sat down in her chair by the range. Daisy had been changed and fed, and was gurgling happily to herself as she lay beneath the blankets in her old pram, and Cordelia smiled fondly as a hand or a leg waved about. It was lovely to have a baby in the house again.

With the washing-up done and the tea poured, Peggy sat down while Fran and Rita made a fuss of Daisy and set her giggling. 'Don't get her too excited,' said Peggy softly. 'Or she won't settle, and with Jim out until dawn, I'm looking forward to a good night's sleep.'

Daisy continued to bat the rattle that hung from the pram's hood, and wave her arms and legs about, as the solemn voice of Bruce Belfrage announced that there would be a direct broadcast from the Prime Minister, Mr Churchill.

The women glanced at one another fearfully, knowing something very serious was afoot if Mr Churchill was going to speak to the nation.

'*When I broadcast directly to my fellow countrymen*

last August,' he began in that familiar gravelly voice, *'it seemed to be our duty to do everything in our power to help the Russians meet the prodigious onslaught launched against them. We had no means whatsoever of providing effective war against Japan compared with those days of nineteen-forty, when the whole world, except ourselves, thought we were down and out.'*

Cordelia and the others listened as Mr Churchill continued to talk about the magnificent Russian efforts to beat back Hitler's armies, which he declared would end Hitler's dominance in Europe. But it was a strangely defensive speech, for he talked about the terrible difficulty he had over fighting Germany and Italy on the home front, supporting Russia in what he termed as 'our darkest hour', and sustaining a defence of the Pacific and the Far East single-handedly. He carried on in the same vein for a while and then he paused for a long moment, and everyone held their breath.

'I speak under the shadow of a heavy, far-reaching military defeat,' he said solemnly. *'Singapore has fallen. All the Malayan Peninsula has been overrun.'*

There were sharp intakes of breath, and Cordelia felt tears of anguish prick as Churchill continued to rally the Allies into showing continued courage and fortitude in the face of this new enemy.

'We must remember that we are no longer alone,' he finished. *'We are in the midst of a great company. Three-quarters of the human race are moving with us. The whole future of mankind may depend on our action and conduct.*

So far we have not failed, and we shall not fail. Now let us move forward steadfastly together into the storm and through the storm.'

Peggy had found it difficult to sleep, for the news that Singapore was now in the hands of the Japanese was a terrible blow – and the knowledge that the heavily protected island had fallen so swiftly simply brought it home to all of them how very vulnerable they all were.

She'd tossed and turned and eventually got up and dressed in the dark. Having made a cup of tea, she sat at the kitchen table and smoked a cigarette while she fretted about the future. Hitler had been threatening to invade for months, and now the eyes of the world were on the Far East and the Americans had yet to arrive in England, it seemed to Peggy that it was the optimum time for him to carry out that threat.

She thought about Jim and his brother Frank, waiting for the dreaded call-up papers to arrive. For once, Peggy felt helpless. It was all very well for Winston Churchill to ask them all to make sacrifices, when they were already scraping the barrel when it came to food, heating, clothing, and even the most mundane of everyday necessities – just how much more could everyone be squeezed when morale was already at such a low ebb?

These were dark days indeed, and although it was important to appear cheerful and to shrug off the inconveniences, Peggy was beginning to waver beneath the weight of all the responsibilities of keeping her family in good spirits. Poor Cordelia was worried sick about her nephew, and she couldn't think how she could ease that anxiety, for they could have no idea of whether he'd been killed in the fighting or had been taken prisoner. There were terrible rumours coming out of the Far East of brutal treatment handed out to prisoners by the Japanese, and she just hoped that Jock had managed to escape.

She stubbed out the cigarette and went to fetch Daisy, who was beginning to stir. It wouldn't help anyone if she became gloomy, and it was up to her to keep up morale and think about the positive things, she decided as she bathed Daisy in the kitchen sink. Having dressed her in the sweet knitted layette, she carried Daisy to the fireside chair and fed her, glad of her comforting warmth and weight in her arms as the household continued to slumber and her fretfulness ebbed.

Churchill was right about keeping strong and steadfast, for little Daisy and the rest of her family had to be protected from the terror that was exploding across the world – and if that meant making sacrifices, then she would soldier on willingly.

Having come to this conclusion, Peggy finished feeding Daisy and put her in the playpen so she could stretch and kick and watch her while she finished the ironing.

'Good morning, Peggy,' said a bright-eyed Suzy as she came into the room half an hour later. 'You're up early.'

'So are you, considering how late it was when you came in,' replied Peggy with a soft smile as she stirred the porridge.

Suzy blushed. 'The time just seemed to fly,' she said as she poured a cup of tea. 'We have so much in common; I don't think we stopped talking all evening.' She smiled back at Peggy. 'He even knows my brother,' she said in a kind of wonder. 'They were both up at Oxford and in the same debating team.'

Peggy couldn't help but smile. Suzy looked radiant this morning, despite the early hour, and just talking about Anthony had brought a sparkle to her eyes. 'It's a small world, isn't it?' she said quietly as she scooped out a good helping of rather watery porridge and placed the bowl in front of her.

Suzy nodded and tucked into the porridge, her fair hair gleaming beneath the starched nurse's cap, the blue of the uniform enhancing her eyes. 'Anthony says the world has got even smaller now Singapore has fallen. I do so hope that Grandma Finch's relations make it safely on that long journey.' She finished the porridge. 'Anthony says they'll have to go via Africa, then across the North Atlantic to the west coast of Scotland.' She shivered daintily. 'The thought of all those U-boats lying in wait, and the rough seas – I don't know if I'd be that brave.'

'I'm sure you would if your life depended upon it,' murmured Peggy.

'That's what Anthony said.' She looked at her watch, quickly finished her cup of tea and reached for her thick woollen cloak. 'I must dash or I'll be late, and then Matron will be down on me like a ton of bricks. Tell Fran I'll meet her in the canteen at lunch-break.'

Peggy grinned as the girl rushed out of the house. With all her Anthony this and Anthony that, anyone would think Suzy was in love. But at least her happiness was catching, and that small interlude had cheered Peggy no end.

Ron and Jim returned just as Cordelia, Fran and Rita had sat down to their breakfast. The men looked exhausted after their long night on duty, but Jim was due to start his shift at the factory in less than three hours, so she quickly put the porridge in front of them and went to fetch the newspapers from the letter box.

Silence fell as they read the headlines and the following articles. Churchill's speech had been much commented upon by the columnists, and there was a good deal of condemnation of the Government for not having had the foresight to ensure that the Far East was adequately covered by air and sea.

'Come on, Cordelia,' said Peggy after breakfast was over and everyone had gone their separate ways. 'Cover your hair with this scarf. I know they're not due for several weeks yet, but we need to prepare rooms for your family, and I need help to get them straight as they've been empty for so long.'

Cordelia eyed her knowingly but didn't argue. With the scarves knotted over their hair, they were soon on their way upstairs armed with fresh linen, the Hoover and a basket full of cleaning materials and dusters.

The large room at the front looked out over the nearby rooftops to a narrow glimpse of the sea, which glittered in the early spring sunshine. With two single beds, a gas fire, wardrobe and chest of drawers, it would accommodate the two young girls very well. The room next door was a single, with a window overlooking the back garden – it was always a bit dark in there, and Peggy had tried to combat the gloom with white-painted walls and cheerful yellow curtains and bedspread.

The morning was spent scrubbing, airing, polishing and making beds. Now the windows gleamed, the beds looked welcoming and the furniture smelled lovely with beeswax. 'I'll get Jim to bring up the two spare armchairs from the dining room,' said Peggy as she flicked the duster needlessly over the spotless windowsill. 'The girls might need a bit of time to settle in, and they can sit in here if it all gets a bit much downstairs.'

'I don't know about you, Peggy, but I could do with a cuppa,' replied Cordelia.

'Then I suggest we put on our coats and hats and walk to the little café opposite the hospital in Camden Road and treat ourselves to tea and scones. I think we've earned it, don't you?'

Cordelia smiled. 'You don't have to spend money trying to cheer me up, Peggy dear, but that sounds a lovely idea. I could do with some fresh air, and it's so much easier to walk when I have the pram to hold onto.'

Cordelia put on her hat and coat and waited patiently in the chair by the range until Daisy had been changed and fed and was warmly tucked into her pram.

They set off at a slow pace, with Cordelia pushing the pram and Peggy keeping a steadying hand on it to steer it straight. The wind was quite blustery as it tore up from the sea and the gulls were wheeling and screaming overhead – but there were shoots of snowdrops and early daffodils pushing through the grass verges, and the sun was bright, cheering them up no end.

They stopped frequently to exchange pleasantries and discuss the fall of Singapore, and it was almost half an hour before they reached the little teashop that was squeezed between the ironmonger's and the chemist in Camden Road. It wasn't as grand as the teashop on the top floor of Plummers, the High Street department store, but it was cosy and warm with a far more relaxed atmosphere. There wasn't room for the pram, so Peggy parked it by the window where she could keep an eye on Daisy, who was asleep.

They were greeted by a dozen or so familiar faces and the wonderful smell of fresh baking. Finding a table close to the window, they settled down and ordered a pot of coffee, which would be a huge treat, and scones and jam, which was an even bigger treat. Peggy and Cordelia knew most of the other diners, and the conversation flowed back and forth easily as they waited for their food.

And then Doris walked past, glanced into the

window and headed straight inside. 'I'm surprised you can afford this sort of thing,' she said with a sniff as she arrived at their table.

'Hello, Doris,' said Peggy with brittle breeziness. 'I'm very well, thanks for asking. How are you?'

'Rather put out, if you must know,' she said waspishly. She pulled off her leather gloves and, after a momentary hesitation, brushed non-existent crumbs from a chair and sat down at the next table. 'That's why I was on my way to see you.'

Peggy eyed her warily, wondering what she'd done now to upset her sister.

'Anthony told me he was going to visit you yesterday afternoon, and although he'd promised to be home in time for a glass of sherry with may friend, Lady Charlmondley, he didn't get in until after midnight.' She glanced around the room, then continued, in strangled vowels, 'Lady Aurelia was most understanding, but then she and I are very close friends.' This was said just loudly enough for everyone to hear.

Peggy didn't dare catch Cordelia's eye and she had to bite her lip to stop giggling. 'Well, he is over thirty,' she managed finally, 'and probably found something more interesting to do after he left us than sit about drinking dubious sherry with a couple of old women.'

A few hastily muffled titters went round the room and Doris reddened. 'It would never occur to may Anthony to think in such a disrespectful way,' she declared. 'Ay have brought him up to behave with impeccable manners. Something must have happened to distract him.'

Suzy had certainly done that, thought Peggy. 'I'm sure you and Aurelia managed quite well without him,' she said as the waitress brought their order.

'That is not the point, Margaret. May Anthony has never let me down before unless it was something unavoidable like his important work for the MOD. Ay mean to get to the bottom of this, you mark may words.'

The waitress finished clattering china and cutlery and turned towards Doris, notepad and pencil at the ready.

'Ay'll have coffee, toasted teacake and jam,' said Doris.

'Sorry love,' said the middle-aged waitress, who didn't seem to realise that no one called Doris love – especially not underlings like waitresses, 'but that's the last of the coffee, and there ain't no teacakes to be 'ad. I can do yer a bit of toast, if you like.'

Doris eyed her with disdain, pulled her gloves back on and stood up. 'Then Ay will take my custom elsewhere,' she said haughtily, and without a goodbye to Peggy or Cordelia, swept out of the teashop.

'She's a one, ain't she?' said the waitress with a frown. 'Did I say summink to upset 'er?'

Peggy smiled back at her. 'Doris is easily upset,' she said lightly. 'I wouldn't take it personally.'

They settled down to enjoy the delicious coffee and scones, and once the pot was empty and the final crumbs had been gleaned from the plate, Peggy sat back and lit a cigarette. It would be lovely to have the time and money to do this once a week, she thought as she relaxed in the warm ambience. But then she wasn't Doris, and counted herself lucky that such a treat was possible maybe a couple of times a year.

Half an hour later they reluctantly left the warm fug of the tea room and began the short walk home. The sun was much lower in the sky now and almost obliterated by the thick, dark clouds that were gathering. The seagulls were still screeching from the rooftops and lamp posts, but the wind had changed direction, and was now coming from the north, threatening snow.

Cordelia held grimly to the pram handle as they slowly made their way back to Beach View, and Peggy had to put a steadying arm round her waist to stop her from being blown over.

They reached the back gate all in one piece only to be almost knocked down by Harvey, who came tearing out of the basement to greet them. Leaping up, his great paws reached their shoulders as he tried to lick their faces.

'Get down, Harvey, for goodness' sake,' snapped Peggy as she shoved him away. 'You'll have us both in the vegetable patch in a minute.'

Harvey was just too pleased to see them to take any notice, and he rested his front paws on the side of the pram and proceeded to wash Daisy's face.

Daisy gurgled and batted at his long nose, and

Peggy grabbed his collar. 'Ron,' she shouted. 'Will you come and get your dog?'

Ron appeared in the doorway, his expression rather more solemn than usual as he carefully made his way down the garden path. He grabbed Harvey and hauled him off the pram. 'Sorry, Peg,' he muttered with a slur. 'I'll clean those paw marks off for you later.'

Peggy eyed him sharply as she caught the smell of whisky on his breath. 'You've been drinking,' she said flatly and pushed the pram into the basement. 'It's a bit early, isn't it?'

'Jim and Frank are here,' he said. 'We've been drowning our sorrows, so we have,' he said with a lopsided grin.

'Oh God, what now?'

He said nothing as he shooed Harvey upstairs and then helped her lift the pram into the kitchen.

One glance told Peggy something was up, for Jim and Frank were sitting at the table with a half-empty bottle of whisky between them. She made no comment as she pulled off her coat, helped Cordelia out of hers and settled her in her usual chair by the range.

Peggy's pulse was racing and she began to regret the rich afternoon treat as her stomach clenched in dread. All three men liked a drink, but not this early in the day – and not when they were supposed to be at work. Something was very wrong. 'What's happened?' she asked sharply.

Frank was a mountain of a man and he seemed to

fill the small kitchen chair beside the much slimmer Jim, but they both had the dark hair and blue eyes of the Reillys, and now they both wore the same sour expressions. 'We've had our call-up papers,' he said. 'Arrived at the factory with the second post.'

Peggy sat down hard on the chair beside Jim. 'I thought you'd be deferred call-up now you're both working at the munitions factory?'

'Aye, so did we, but with women doing the job equally as well, the powers-that-be decided we'd be of more use elsewhere.' Jim slopped more whisky into their glasses, his expression morose.

'But you did your bit in the last war,' protested Peggy. 'Where are they sending you?'

'We have to report to Southfields barracks in Yorkshire,' said Frank, his voice slurred from the amount of whisky he'd been drinking. 'It seems the Army can't do without us again – our experience is much needed to reinforce the war effort.'

'But Frank, you only have a couple of years before you turn fifty. Surely you won't be expected to—?'

'We'll both be at the mercy of the Army, Peg,' interrupted Jim. 'After a short retraining course in Yorkshire, we'll be given our orders – and then we'll know more about what we'll be doing.'

Peggy poured some whisky into a clean glass, her hand trembling so badly that she spilled some on the oilcloth that covered the old table. 'When do you have to leave?' she said, the words barely audible through the lump in her throat.

'Three days' time,' he replied, reaching for her hand.

'But you can't,' she gasped. 'Daisy and I need you here – and it's too soon – much too soon.'

'Ach,' he said, making light of the situation. 'That's the Army for you, Peg. They say jump, and you ask how high.'

'It's not fair,' she whispered. 'You've already done your bit. Surely they won't send you off to fight?'

'It's not something either of us relish,' said Jim with brittle joviality, 'but whatever they decide to do with us, this war will soon be over with me and Frank on the case, and I'll be under your feet again before you know it.'

Peggy swallowed the whisky and felt it burn all the way down her throat and into her chest as she held tightly to Jim's hand. Churchill had talked of sacrifice and courage – of remaining strong and stoic in the face of conflict. She had thought she had nothing else to give, but this was the sacrifice she had never believed she'd have to make. It was the same sacrifice that a million women had made before her, and yet the man she'd loved for so long was facing an even harder challenge, and in that moment of awful clarity, she realised she must dredge up all her courage and fortitude and keep smiling through.

Despite the amount of whisky he'd drunk, Jim remained stone-cold sober, and after Frank had left the house to stagger back home across the hills, he'd telephoned Somerset, and had managed to speak to his sons and daughter for a few precious minutes before the pips went and he was cut off.

There were tears in his eyes as he replaced the receiver, and Peggy took him in her arms and held him until he was more himself again.

'Bob and Charlie were full of questions,' he said as they returned to the kitchen. Peggy noticed thankfully that Daisy had drifted back to sleep again. 'But our Anne was trying hard not to cry – I could hear it in her voice.'

'There'll be plenty of tears, Jim, but it's only because we love you so much,' she murmured. 'Oh Jim,' she sighed. 'What on earth am I going to do without you?'

He pulled her onto his lap as he sat by the range. 'You'll do as you've always done,' he said softly. 'You'll work like a trooper and battle away, worrying over everyone and everything until you're so tired you'll fall into a deep sleep and not have time to think.'

He ran his finger down the line of her cheek and grinned. 'You'll not have me snoring in your ear, or getting under your feet – and I'll not be run ragged trying to do all the jobs you set for me.'

'I've yet to see you break out in a sweat to do any of the jobs around here,' she said with mock severity. 'I'm still waiting for the bedroom windows to be fixed so they don't let in the draught and rattle all night.'

His dark eyes twinkled as he held her close. 'Perhaps we ought to go and check on those bedroom windows – just to see if there's anything I can do to stop them from rattling.'

She knew that look in his eye and giggled. 'Oh, I think that's a very good idea,' she murmured.

He gathered her into his arms and carried her out through the hall and into the bedroom, nudging the door closed behind him.

Chapter Twelve

The *Monarch of the Glen*

The *Monarch of the Glen* had been stripped to the bare minimum so she could carry thousands of troops and their equipment to the world's trouble spots. There were 1,500 women and children on board after she'd left Singapore, and it soon became clear that the Captain and his crew had done their best to accommodate them despite the lack of comfortable facilities.

The first few hours on board had been tearful and rather frightening after that Japanese air attack, and, like the others, Sarah and Jane were disorientated and heartsick at leaving their loved ones behind. The crew were kind but firm as they ordered everyone to put on their life jackets and make a bundle of essentials in case they had to quickly board a lifeboat. They were herded down below deck where hundreds of mattresses had been laid on the floor, and told that this was where they would have to stay until the danger of enemy attack was past.

It was dark and poorly ventilated below deck, with the noise of hundreds of frightened children and bewildered women drowning out the steady thud of the ship's great engines. But this precautionary measure proved wise, for within hours of sailing they'd heard the shrill blast of the ship's air-raid siren. The Japanese bombers had returned to finish what they'd started back in Singapore harbour.

Sarah and Jane had clung together as they felt the ship zigzag to avoid their attackers. Bombs exploded all around them and the ship's guns boomed out, making the hull of the ship resonate with the noise. There were muffled gasps of fear, the wail of a baby and the terrified cries of toddlers, but everyone kept a tight hold on their terror, knowing it would spread like a forest fire and consume them all if it was released.

The attack seemed to last for hours as they sat there in the darkness, but the all-clear finally sounded and there was an audible sigh of relief as the ship continued on her way.

Two more days and nights passed down in the bowels of the ship, and like the other women, Sarah and Jane tried to make the best of things, and not dwell on the possibility that they could be shadowed by an enemy submarine, or that the Japs would attack them again. Pushing the mattresses together, Sarah sorted through their cases and used their jackets to make the emergency bundles they would have to carry everywhere. The dresses with their few pieces of jewellery sewn into the hems were carefully rolled alongside the small box of first-aid supplies Amah had insisted they take, and they added cardigans and spare sun hats, and the precious book which contained all the family photographs. Tying the bundles with thick string, Sarah warned Jane that she must never let her bundle out of sight.

The mood below deck was anxious and rather depressed, but when morning came on the third day they were released from the cloying darkness of their prison, and they poured gratefully onto the decks and breathed in the sea breeze, lifting their faces to the warm sun as hundreds of children raced about the decks in the sheer joy of being free again.

Sarah held Jane's hand as they stood next to their bundles and life jackets and looked out at the ocean which stretched to every horizon. 'I want to go home,' whispered Jane.

'So do I,' murmured Sarah, as she put her arm round her sister's shoulder. 'But we can't, not until the Japanese have been beaten.'

'Do you think our house and the plantation are still there? I miss my bedroom, and Amah and my lizard,' Jane said, her voice wavering as she tried to quell her tears. 'But most of all I miss Mummy and Daddy. Do you think Mummy's better now? Will she be on a ship too?'

Sarah couldn't answer her questions. She was still feeling bewildered by the speed and urgency of their departure – afraid for the home she'd lost and the way of life which had been so cruelly snatched away from her. She didn't know what was happening back in Singapore, if her mother had recovered and had had the baby – or if her father and Philip were at this very moment engaged in battle against the invaders – and it was this not knowing that increased her anxiety.

'We must be brave, Jane,' she said as her sister rested her head on her shoulder. 'Pops is trusting us to do the best we can, and once we're in England we'll be able to write to him, and he'll send us news of Mother.'

She gave Jane a handkerchief to dry her eyes. 'Singapore will not have to fight alone for long,' she soothed. 'The Allies will soon come to their aid, and then the Japanese will be sent packing once and for all.'

Sarah and Jane had been billeted down in the hold along with the other single women and older children – the cabins had been allocated to mothers with babies and toddlers. But as they explored the ship, they discovered that the conditions in the cabins weren't that much more comfortable. Strangers had to share the small spaces, often with several children, and the portholes had been painted black and were tightly locked. It was hardly surprising that everyone preferred being on deck during the day.

Clearly discipline and order had to be maintained, and the women were given what appeared to be an endless list of rules. Like most of the others, Sarah and Jane realised that many of these rules were there to protect them and happily complied. But the hundreds of children on board saw only new challenges, and the rule about never climbing on the railings was frequently disobeyed.

The punishment was swift and effective, meted out by a huge bosun who constantly patrolled the decks. Plucking off the offenders, he administered a good spanking, popped a sweet in the squalling mouths and sent them on their way. The railings were swiftly abandoned as climbing frames.

A sort of order began to emerge as the days passed. Meals were taken on benches in the vast dining room where long trestle tables stretched from one end of the room to the other. The food was nutritious, if a bit predictable, and consisted of stews that were served from huge tureens and accompanied by rice. But there was always fruit to be had, on the strict understanding that not a banana skin, bit of peel or apple core – indeed, absolutely nothing – should be tossed overboard. An enemy plane could spot the floating jetsam and pinpoint their position for their submarines.

With so many children on board the noise was deafening, and it was soon decided to rope off an area of the deck for them so they wouldn't disturb everyone else. It was also decided that they should have two hours of schooling a day, and Sarah and Jane volunteered to help the teachers, who were rather swamped by the sheer number of pupils. Jane did sums with the little ones, while Sarah helped with reading and writing, but it was all very pleasant, for they sat beneath large awnings on deck as the cool breeze drifted from the sea.

Shipboard life was peaceful and ordered, and Sarah enjoyed being kept busy as she helped in the dining room, taught the children and organised deck games with Jane and some of the older girls. And then, just as she was starting to feel more relaxed about things, the women were gathered together in the dining room one evening, and told by the grim-faced Captain that Singapore had fallen and that the Japanese were now advancing on Java, Sumatra, Borneo and Indonesia.

A deep despondency fell over everyone, and it seemed that the blackout on board was more profound than ever that night, and down in the hull there was the sound of muffled sobbing as the women wept over the unknown fate of their men.

Sarah had comforted Jane by telling her that their parents would have escaped in time, but once Jane was asleep, Sarah shed her tears into her pillow. She so wanted to believe that her mother had managed to get on a ship out of Singapore before the fall – and that Philip and her father had somehow managed to avoid capture. There were junks and sampans everywhere, yachts and motor boats at anchor in the Marina that surely could be put to use as a means of escape. Thousands of small islands surrounded Singapore – perhaps they'd managed to evade the Japs and were even now sailing towards safety.

She knew in her heart that it was wishful thinking, but she refused to listen to that small voice of reason and doggedly remained hopeful – for if she gave in to doubt, she would be lost.

Determined to keep their spirits up, she and Jane volunteered for even the most menial of tasks, and at the end of each long, hot day they would fall asleep almost the moment their heads touched their pillows, exhausted from their toil and lulled by the steady thrum of the ship's great engines.

There were women they knew from Kuala Lumpur and Singapore on board, and it seemed the will to survive and overcome adversity with as little fuss and complaint as possible had infected them too, and soon everyone was putting on a brave face and making the best of things.

The routine on board rarely changed, with school in the morning, daily boat-drill and the occasional talk given by someone who had an interesting tale to tell. As friendships were made and the women organised themselves, the atmosphere lightened and it felt as if they were on a cruise. Everyone seemed to have their special place to sit on the decks on their emergency bundles rather than their life jackets, as they could be quickly damaged in the hot sun. And as the ship drew ever closer to Ceylon, there was an air of excitement which was quite infectious, for few of them had ever been there.

Chapter Thirteen

Cliffehaven

The precious time had slipped away and now it was Jim's last day at home. Peggy was trying her best to remain positive and cheerful – and to indelibly print the images of those treasured few hours in her mind so she could relive them whilst he was away.

But the reminders of his leaving were everywhere – in the Home Guard uniform she was pressing; in the highly polished boots that waited on a square of newspaper by the door; in the kitbag and rifle that stood in the corner of their bedroom – and in the empty spaces on their dressing table where his brushes and nail-kit had always been.

Jim and Ron seemed to be dealing with this dreaded departure in their own inimitable way. They had left the house very early and returned with sacks of coal hidden beneath a large square of lino they'd draped over the wheelbarrow. They'd cut logs, stacked them next to the shed and covered them with a tarpaulin to keep the rain off, and then laid the new lino in the kitchen. Jim had actually fixed the rattling window and made a draught excluder with an old stocking that he'd stuffed with newspaper, and then nailed on the bottom of the bedroom door.

Then he'd spent an hour just sitting with Daisy in his lap, watching her every move, as if he too was trying to absorb these memories to carry with him – and as Peggy watched in amazement, he did something she'd never seen him do before. He changed Daisy's nappy and then warmed the bottle of milk she always had in the mornings now, and fed her. Once she was asleep, he'd tucked her into the pram, and then carried it down the steps so that he and Peggy could take their youngest daughter for an amble down to the seafront.

'I'm going to miss this old place,' he said as they sat on a stone bench and stared out at the sea. 'Funny, isn't it?' he mused. 'You don't really appreciate things until you're about to lose them.' He put his arm round Peggy's shoulder and drew her close. 'I've not been the best husband in the world, but I do adore you, Peggy Reilly.'

She could feel the tears prick as she rested her head on his broad shoulder. 'You're the best husband I've ever had,' she said lightly, 'and I adore you too.'

He tipped back his head and roared with laughter. 'And how many husbands is it that you've had, Peggy?'

She grinned up at him. 'Just the one – but that is more than enough. You're a handful, Jim, and always have been, but I wouldn't change you for the world.'

They sat for a while longer and watched the waves roll like molten glass over the shingle as the gulls swooped and hovered on the wind and clouds gathered on the horizon. Peggy shivered, not from the cold, but from sudden dread of what the future might hold for them both.

'Are you cold?' asked Jim as he pulled up her collar and kissed her nose.

'I am a bit,' she said. 'We'd better get back before it starts to rain. Look at those clouds coming in.'

Jim pushed the pram up the steep hill and carried it back indoors. Peggy went into the kitchen to make a pot of tea and was surprised not to see Cordelia in her usual chair by the fire. And, as she made a couple of corned beef sandwiches for their lunch, she realised the house seemed too quiet altogether.

Jim seemed to notice it too. 'I've never known the place so quiet,' he muttered as he lit a cigarette. He shot her a crafty smile. 'Perhaps we should take advantage of being alone for once – I need to check those repairs on the bedroom window.'

She slapped him playfully with a tea towel and would have taken him up on his offer if the kitchen hadn't been invaded at that moment by Cordelia, Fran, Suzy, Rita and Ron, who were all looking suspiciously pleased with themselves. 'What are you all up to?' Peggy asked.

'Well, now,' said Fran, 'as this is to be Jim's last night at home, we thought you deserved a special treat.'

'So we've got you tickets for the theatre matinee of Noël Coward's *Blythe Spirit*,' said Cordelia breathlessly.

'And we've arranged for you to have a drink in the interval,' added Suzy.

'But you're not to be stopping off anywhere on the way home,' warned Ron. 'We have a special treat for you here after the show – and you can't be late.'

Peggy blinked away her tears as Jim tried to embrace everybody at once. Cordelia didn't seem to mind being crushed and kissed, and she went pink as she giggled and slapped his arm playfully. Ron hugged his son, his eyes suspiciously bright, and Harvey tried to join in this wonderful new game and ended up with his nose being sharply slapped as it probed up Fran's skirt.

Order was finally restored and Rita looked at the clock on the mantelpiece. 'The show starts in three hours,' she said, with a teasing light in her eye. 'If you want to look handsome and debonair, Uncle Jim, then you've just about enough time.'

'Ach, you cheeky wee girl,' laughed Jim. 'I'll show you – see if I don't.' He grabbed Peggy's hand. 'Come on. Let's get our glad rags on and leave them to whatever it is they're planning. It's clear they want us out of here.'

Peggy and Jim emerged from their bedroom almost an hour later to discover that the house was deserted – and that even Daisy had been whisked away. 'But what about her afternoon feed?' Peggy fretted.

'They'll give her a bottle, never you mind. She's getting used to it, so she is, and with two nurses to look after her, she'll not want for a thing.'

Peggy knew he was right, but it would feel strange not having Daisy with her – they hadn't spent more than the odd hour apart since she'd been born.

Jim looked down at her appreciatively. 'That colour blue really suits you, Peg. You're a good-looking woman, so y'are, and I could eat you up.' He closed in on her and threatened to muss her hair and smudge her lipstick. 'As they all seem to have gone out, why don't we risk a quick one before we leave?' he murmured.

She playfully pushed him away. 'You're impossible, Jim Reilly,' she said with a laugh. 'I've not dressed in my best two-piece suit and hat for you to take it all off again.' She giggled at his woebegone expression. 'Now, pass me my overcoat and find your hat, and then we can be off.'

Peggy tucked her hand in his arm as they headed down Camden Road. Her heart was so full of love for him that it almost overrode the fear that curled inside her. Jim was such a handsome man – tall, straight and broad-shouldered in his best suit and smart overcoat, his fedora placed just so over his right brow, his dark eyes repeatedly looking down at her as if she was the most beautiful woman in the world. He made her feel special, treasured and cherished, and the thought that it could be many months, perhaps even years, before they would walk down this street together again made her want to cry.

Jim seemed to read her thoughts and he tucked her hand even more firmly into his arm and squeezed it. 'This is our day,' he said softly as they reached the bottom of the High Street, 'and nothing is allowed to spoil it. D'ye hear?'

She nodded, unable to speak for the lump in her throat.

'Good girl,' he murmured. 'Now, we've time for a wee drink in the Ship before the show starts. Come on, Mrs Reilly, best foot forward.'

The one drink turned into two as friends crowded round them to wish Jim well, and Peggy had to drag him out so they wouldn't be late for the show. They just made it before curtain up, finding their seats in the stalls as the lights dimmed.

Peggy watched Jim's profile repeatedly as the comedy slowly unfolded. She loved the way his eyes crinkled at the corners when he laughed, and was glad he was enjoying himself. It was rare for them to go to the theatre together, and it was a real treat – a very special and thoughtful gift from the others.

They enjoyed the drinks that were waiting for them in the bar at half-time, and held hands like two young lovers as the play continued. And when it was over, they stood with the rest of the audience and clapped enthusiastically.

'That was fun,' said Jim as he settled his hat back on his head and gave her his arm once more. 'I never thought I'd like that sort of thing, but it's as good as Laurel and Hardy any day.'

It was bitterly cold and they walked quickly through the blackout towards home, their footsteps echoing in the almost deserted street. Beach View looked as if it was all in darkness too, but then the blackout curtains would keep out even the smallest chink of light.

Jim put the key in the lock and frowned as they stepped into the hall. 'Where is everyone?' he asked. 'And why are all the lights off?'

And then the lights came on and people poured down the stairs and out of the kitchen and dining room. 'Surprise!' they yelled in unison.

Peggy and Jim were stunned as they were surrounded by their friends and relations. There was Frank and Pauline, Anthony, little Sally and her husband John Hicks with their son Danny, Alison Chenoweth, Suzy, Fran, Rita and Cordelia, as well as Fred the Fish and Alf the butcher with their wives. And then, bounding down the steps in a flurry of frills and petticoats and straight into her father's arms, came their daughter, Cissy.

'Oh, me darlin' girl, 'tis pleased I am to see you,' Jim murmured as he held her tight.

'Well, I couldn't just let you go off, could I?' she said, tossing back her fair hair and widening her big blue eyes in the theatrical way she'd always had. 'And I've brought Martin along too, but he's busy with Grandpa Ron at the minute.'

Peggy hugged her beautiful, vivacious daughter and noted she was getting too thin. 'Aren't they feeding you properly at the airfield?' she asked.

Cissy laughed. 'Of course they are, but I do so much running about after my Air Commodore that it doesn't have time to stick to my bones.'

Peggy frowned, for Cissy had always been rather flighty. 'Your Air Commodore? Not another conquest, surely?'

Cissy giggled. 'He's old enough to be my father,' she assured her mother. 'But he's my boss now. I've been assigned to drive him everywhere and take notes when he has important meetings – and he's the sort of man who's on the go all the time. I have a really hard job keeping up with him.'

Conversation soon became almost impossible as everyone tried to talk at once, and Peggy began to wonder where Daisy was, and how on earth they would get everyone into the kitchen without it turning into a game of sardines.

And then the dining-room door was flung open and Ron and her son-in-law stepped into the hall. Ron was in his best suit and looked quite respectable for once, but Martin looked absolutely splendid in his RAF uniform.

He twirled his handlebar moustache and called for order. 'If our honoured guests, Mr and Mrs Reilly, would please step this way,' he said in his plummy tones, 'there is a special surprise awaiting them.'

Peggy and Jim looked at one another and grinned excitedly before linking hands and stepping through the door. They gasped in delight, for the room had been transformed.

The excess furniture had been cleared, the floor swept, and the tables put together to form a T. There was a fire burning brightly in the hearth, and the curtains had been rehung to hide the ugly plywood which had been nailed over the broken windows. The dust had been cleaned from the old paper chains, and a tiny Christmas tree stood in the corner, glittering with tinsel and baubles. White linen cloths covered the tables, candles flickered in jam jars down its length, and each place setting had a paper napkin tucked into a wine glass.

'Oh, Martin, Ron,' Peggy breathed, the tears almost blinding her. 'How very, very lovely.'

'To be sure, you've worked wonders,' breathed Jim as he took it all in. 'That has to be the hardest day's work you've done in a long time, Da,' he teased.

There was a muffled giggle from the other side of the room and a curtain twitched as someone hushed the giggler.

Peggy's eyes widened. She'd know that giggle anywhere.

She ran across the room and flung back the curtain to be immediately swamped by Anne and her two boys. 'Oh, Bob, Charlie, Anne. Oh, my darlings.' She burst into tears as she tried to kiss all three at once. 'How you've both grown,' she managed as she held them close. 'Bob, you're taller than me, and Charlie, you've put on weight – and Anne, oh, Anne.'

'Let the dog see the rabbit,' boomed Jim as he swept the boys into his embrace and whirled them round. 'To be sure you're too big to be lifted any more,' he panted as he set them down moments later. He looked at his boys with such love and pride that Peggy simply couldn't stem the tears.

'But how did you manage to get travel permits at such short notice?' she asked Anne as she accepted a handkerchief and tried to dry her eyes.

'We've got Martin to thank for that,' she replied as her husband came to join them. 'He pulled lots of strings and wouldn't take no for an answer.'

Peggy looked up at the handsome flying officer and stood on tiptoe to kiss his cheek. 'I can never thank you enough,' she murmured. 'You've made this evening very special by bringing our family home to us.'

He looked rather embarrassed. 'Not at all,' he said. 'It was a purely selfish gesture, as it meant I get to see my wife and daughter for a bit too.' He grinned as the two boys raced off to the kitchen to get Harvey, who'd been locked downstairs. 'And it's good to see those scallywags back where they belong – even if it is only for a few days.'

Peggy was so emotional she could barely speak. The love they had all shown her and Jim was beyond price, and as Jim took her in his arms, she knew this day, this night, this moment would stay with her for ever.

Daisy was wheeled in from the kitchen so she could be a part of it all, and Anne's daughter, Rose Margaret, toddled in with Cissy, all pretty in a pink frilly party dress. Neither Peggy nor Jim could believe how much she'd grown, for the last time they'd seen her, she'd been a baby in her mother's arms. It was the same for the boys, and Peggy couldn't take in how tall and grown-up they looked – especially Bob, who was now wearing long trousers and had a suspicion of dark fluff on his top lip and chin.

There was a great deal of chatter and laughter as everyone got reacquainted and Ron went round with the sherry bottle. Cordelia sat in the one armchair and became quite pink in the face as Ron topped up her glass. Daisy and Rose were cooed over, Harvey got under everyone's feet and Charlie managed to skid into the Christmas tree and bring it crashing down on top of himself.

Order was quickly restored and everyone finally took their places at the table. Peggy and Jim had pride of place at the top of the T, with Frank and Pauline beside them. Martin and Ron organised everyone else to their satisfaction and then went off to bring in the food which Anne, Cissy, Pauline and Cordelia had slaved over for half the afternoon.

There were tiny portions of delicious salmon to begin with, courtesy of Fred the Fish and his lovely wife Joan. A huge joint of beef was next – a gift from Alf and his wife, Lil – and this was accompanied by roast potatoes, tinned peas and Yorkshire pudding. To follow was a delicious chocolate cake, courtesy of Castle Hill kitchens and the cook who was trying to put flesh on Anthony's bones.

Martin had raided the officers' mess to provide wine and cordials, and Cissy had somehow managed to get hold of a very rare and precious box of liqueur chocolates to eat with the equally precious packet of coffee that Ron had somehow managed to acquire.

As the boys got to know their tiny sister Daisy, and Rose Margaret sat clapping her hands in the high chair, Harvey trotted back and forth between them all to make sure they knew he was there and of course in need of scraps. He soon worked out that the best place to sit was next to Rose's high chair, for she seemed to enjoy throwing her food at him.

As Jim talked to the boys and made a fuss over his granddaughter, Peggy watched them all with a swell of love that threatened to overwhelm her. Anne looked beautiful, with her shining dark hair and eyes and her flawless skin – and for a moment Peggy wondered if she was expecting again. There was something radiant about her – but then that could just be love and the homecoming.

Cissy was much calmer than she'd been before she'd joined the WAAF, but she still liked to hold centre stage with her outrageous stories and her flirting eyes. And as for her boys – Bob was so tall and broad, the image of his father already, although he had yet to turn fifteen – and Charlie, darling little Charlie, with his mischievous grin and his freckles, how he'd filled out in the long, long year since she'd seen him.

Peggy turned to Sal, who was struggling to keep Danny from climbing all over Harvey. 'Your auntie Vi has done a marvellous job with my boys,' she said softly. 'They look so well and happy.'

'She's done a good job on all of them,' said Sal as she retrieved Danny from Harvey's back and wrestled to make him sit on her lap. 'We was – were hoping to have Ernie with us and all tonight, but 'e's got a bit of a cold on 'is chest, and Vi thought it best to keep him down there. We've promised to send him a special parcel so he won't feel 'e's missed out.'

Peggy squeezed her fingers. Sal's East End accent was still noticeable, but it was all part of her charm. 'Don't forget where I am, love,' she said. 'There's always tea in the pot if you fancy a natter like the old days.'

Sal grinned. 'I'll remember that when I ain't – haven't got a pile of dressmaking to do and Danny's on 'is best behaviour.' She put the little boy back on the floor where he immediately made a beeline for Harvey again. 'He's a right little tearaway,' she sighed happily. 'Just like 'is dad.'

John Hicks laughed. 'I heard that. And as your punishment, you'll have the first dance with me once Ron gets that gramophone going.'

'Gawd,' she replied, raising her eyes to the heavens and giggling happily. 'There go me toes.'

As the last morsel of chocolate cake was devoured along with the coffee, the table was pushed back against the wall and the chairs dotted about the room. Ron, Frank and Jim argued over the best way to get the old gramophone going, and as soon as the first notes of 'Little Brown Jug' drifted into the room, nearly everyone took to the floor.

Peggy was happy to sit and watch as the youngsters enjoyed themselves, and it seemed Daisy liked the music too, for she was kicking her legs and laughing as she sat in Peggy's lap. Rose Margaret was wiggling her bottom and laughing like a drain as Cissy and Alison danced with her, and Anthony and Suzy were smiling into one another's eyes as they moved about the floor.

'That's a bit of a surprise,' murmured Anne as she sat next to Peggy. 'I hope Suzy knows what she's letting herself in for.'

'I think Suzy will be quite capable of dealing with your aunt Doris,' she replied. 'By the way, why isn't she here tonight?'

Anne blushed. 'We didn't invite her,' she confessed. 'I'm sorry, Mam, but she always puts a damper on things and we didn't think you'd mind.'

Peggy patted her hand. 'Not at all,' she reassured her, 'and not having Doris around means those two can have fun without any fear of her spoiling it.' She gave a sigh of happiness that was also tinged with sadness, for no gathering was really complete without her other sister Doreen. 'I wish your aunt Doreen could have come. She always liked a good knees-up.'

'We did telephone her office in London, but she's away with her boss on business. The girl on the switchboard said she'd be sure to give her the news about Dad, so I expect she'll ring when she can.'

The evening progressed and got rather raucous as the bottles of wine and whisky and beer flowed, and inhibitions – what there were of them – were forgotten in the cause of making sure Jim and Frank had the best send-off they could provide. Ron danced the waltz with a flustered, giggling Mrs Finch, while Cissy did the jitterbug with her father. Fred the Fish proved to be an expert at the Lambeth Walk, and Frank managed to get Pauline round the floor without crushing her toes.

Anne and Peggy put their young ones to bed, and then joined in the fun. Jim swept Peggy into a quickstep which left her breathless, and Ron grabbed hold of Alf's wife Lil and showed everyone that dancing wasn't just for the young. Bob steered his sister Cissy round as if he was doing penance for some heinous sin, while Charlie quite happily allowed the vivacious midwife, Alison, to clasp him close while she taught him how to waltz.

The clock on the mantelpiece struck midnight and Ron called for silence. 'Fill your glasses,' he ordered. 'I wish to make a toast.'

'Ach, bejesus, Da, not one of your endless speeches,' protested Frank, who was very unsteady on his feet.

'I'll talk for as long as I want,' said Ron, as Martin and Anthony went round the room topping up glasses. 'To be sure, 't'will be the last time for a wee while that I'll get the chance, so it is, and I mean to have me say.' He rather spoiled the effect by tripping over the dog and almost landing in Cordelia Finch's lap.

'Get on with it, Da,' laughed Jim. 'You're wasting good dancing and drinking time.'

'Aye, well, I'll have me say anyway,' he said, glaring at his son from beneath his bushy brows. 'I'm proud of both of you, so I am. You're fine men, so y'are, strong and straight and true, and we love the bones of you. Take our love with you, know that you'll always be in our hearts wherever fate and the Army takes you, and may God bring you both safely home.'

There wasn't a dry eye in the room as everyone raised their glasses and murmured, 'God bring you both safe home.' Silence fell as they all drank.

Ron placed the stylus on the record and the sweet voice of Vera Lynn floated into the room: 'There'll be Bluebirds over the White Cliffs of Dover'.

Jim took Peggy in his arms as Frank reached for Pauline, and the four of them danced while everyone stood and watched with tears in their eyes. And then, two by two, they all joined in until the song was over.

As silence fell once more, they formed a circle and sang 'Auld Lang Syne', with as much gusto as they could manage, and then ended up in a group hug.

It was sometime later, after their guests had gone home and everyone was asleep upstairs, that Jim turned to Peggy in their large bed and drew her close. 'I'm a lucky man,' he murmured into her hair. 'And I'll carry tonight with me for every second until I come home.'

Peggy closed her eyes as she pressed her cheek against his broad chest, and prayed that he would come home – soon – and all in one piece.

Chapter Fourteen

Peggy lay awake in Jim's arms long after he'd fallen asleep, the rise and fall of his chest and the steady beat of his heart against her cheek soothing her. She didn't want the night to end, didn't want to waste even a second in sleep, for this was the last time – possibly in years – that she would have him all to herself.

And yet, all too soon, the cockerel crowed as the sun lightened the sky and Jim began to stir. She could hear Daisy whimpering in her cot at the end of the bed, and the soft footfalls of someone coming down the stairs. The house was waking, the dreaded day had begun.

Jim watched as she changed Daisy's nappy and brought her back into the bed to feed her. When Daisy had finished, he took her in his large hands and held her against his naked chest, rocking her gently back and forth as he told her softly how much he loved her.

Peggy dragged on her dressing gown and let them have this special moment to themselves while she prepared for this awful day. Having managed to get into the bathroom before Cissy, who usually took an age in there, she had a good wash, brushed her teeth and hair and was downstairs within a few minutes. The house was stirring despite the late night they'd all had, and there were voices in the kitchen, and the delicious smell of frying bacon was drifting into the hall and up the stairs.

Peggy quickly went into her bedroom to get dressed and found that Jim was already up and in his dressing gown. Daisy was back in the cot, wide awake and laughing up at him as he pulled faces at her.

'I'll not be putting that uniform on until the last minute,' he informed her as she struggled to pull up her corset. 'The train doesn't leave until midday, and I aim to lounge about like a man of leisure for as long as I can.' He eyed her quizzically. 'What the divil are you wearing that thing for? You've not an ounce of spare flesh to hold in.'

Peggy was a bit red in the face and hot from her struggles. 'It isn't decent not to wear a corset,' she panted. 'Things wobble about, and at my age it's unbecoming.'

He gave a great roar of laughter that startled Daisy and made her whimper. 'Lord love you, Peggy Reilly,' he said as he placated his tiny daughter, 'd'ye not know that it's the wobbly bits I love best?'

'Well, I don't,' she said, as she hunted about for a pair of stockings that didn't have too many darns in them. 'If you've nothing else better to do, take Daisy into the kitchen and put her in her pram while I finish getting dressed.'

'But I like watching you get dressed,' he teased as he waggled his dark eyebrows.

She blushed to the roots of her hair and shooed him

out of the room. With the door firmly closed behind him, she leaned against it for a moment, battled the awful urge to collapse into a complete soggy heap on the bed, and got on with dressing. There would be time for tears when he was gone – but until that train had left the station she would plaster on a smile and damned well keep it there.

Breakfast was bedlam, for Frank and Pauline had stayed overnight, as had Anne, Martin and Cissy. With the five girls, Ron and Cordelia Finch all trying to help cook the breakfast, amuse Rose Margaret, stoke the fire and wash the dishes from the previous night, they kept tripping over one another. Harvey had taken refuge beneath the table, Charlie and Bob were outside with their father inspecting the chickens and collecting eggs, and Martin had tucked himself away in a corner to read the newspaper while he smoked his pipe.

Peggy put Daisy's pram and playpen in the hall to make room, and as it would be impossible for fourteen people to sit round the kitchen table, got Cissy to help her prepare the one in the dining room. 'How are things at the airfield?' Peggy asked.

'Pretty ghastly,' replied Cissy with unusual solemnity. 'We've lost so many of our poor brave boys – boys we've known since the start, boys we cared for. It's so hard to see them leave, and then to count the planes back in again, knowing that only a few have made it home.' She gave a tremulous sigh. 'The new intakes are getting younger and younger, some of them not much older than our Bob.'

'Oh, Cissy. How can you bear it?'

She tried to make light of it with a shrug. 'One just knuckles down and tries not to think too much,' she replied. 'But it's awfully hard when it's someone you rather cared for.' Her hand trembled as she set a knife and fork on the table. 'James bought it last week,' she said softly. 'His plane was shot down and the chaps that saw it said there was no sign of a parachute before it crashed.'

'Oh, darling.' Peggy put her arms round her daughter as she remembered the lovely young man she'd brought home last summer.

Cissy drew back from her embrace and blinked away her tears as she rather forcefully blew her nose. 'I'm fine, really I am, and it's selfish of me to burden you with my troubles when you've got Dad and Uncle Frank to worry about.'

'We're all rather in the same boat,' said Anne as she came into the room with the clean cups and saucers. 'I never stop worrying over Martin and my heart's in my mouth every time the telephone rings. But we all have to learn to keep smiling through and make the best of it if we're to win this war.'

Peggy embraced both her daughters and hurried back to the kitchen before she let the side down by bursting into tears. The noise and kerfuffle would drown out the treacherous doubts and fears that assailed her, and if she kept busy she wouldn't have time to think. She would get through today – would soldier on no matter what. If Anne and Cissy could do it then so could she, and to hell with Hitler.

Breakfast was leisurely as well as noisy, and everyone enjoyed the bacon and sausages that Vi had sent with Anne from Somerset, along with the lovely yellow butter which they smeared on their toast with some of Pauline's homemade marmalade. Copious cups of tea were drunk as Bob and Charlie told their father about their jobs on Vi's farm, their village school and Bob's dream to own a farm himself one day.

Anne regaled them with stories about her voluntary work with the local WI, who'd turned out to be a jolly bunch of young farmers' wives who possessed a very earthy sense of humour, which manifested itself in rather risqué ideas for fundraising – like selling kisses, and doing bathing-belle fashion parades in wellington boots.

Rita, Fran and Suzy had to leave for work, so they said their goodbyes and hurried off, their eyes suspiciously bright despite the smiles. Moments later, Jim and Frank left the dining room to go and get ready for their journey. The party was over, the laughter now muted. It was almost time to say their own goodbyes.

Peggy and Pauline sat close to one another. They didn't need to say anything, for their thoughts were attuned – but Peggy knew her sister-in-law was remembering when she'd had to say goodbye to her three sons at the beginning of the war, and her heart went out to her, for she must be finding it almost impossible not to think of the two who had not come back. She silently took her hand and squeezed her fingers, and Pauline nodded in understanding, her bright little smile as forced as Peggy's.

It was clear that both men had also decided to put a brave face on things, for they came into the dining room in their Home Guard uniform and shining boots, and stamped to attention, snapping off a very smart salute.

Harvey barked at this unusual behaviour, and Charlie pulled him close and soothed him, his own little face quite pale as he regarded his father and uncle who looked so very different all of a sudden.

'Right, you 'orrible lot,' roared Frank, who'd once been a sergeant major, 'prepare for parade. You have fifteen minutes and the last man in the hall not fully dressed and ready will be on charge.' He leaned towards a rather flustered Cordelia. 'That does not include you, Private Finch,' he said in more temperate tones. 'You are excused any charge this morning, but you must be prepared in time to travel in my truck.'

They played their parts to the hilt, scampering about finding coats and hats and lost shoes, while Harvey thought this was a wonderful game and charged about getting in the way. He found one of Peggy's good shoes and ran off with it, the two boys in hot pursuit. When it was returned, she couldn't be cross with him, although there were teeth-marks in the leather and she had to clean off his slobber.

Daisy had her nappy changed and Peggy dressed her in her prettiest pink layette before wrapping her warmly in a blanket. Anne had made a special effort with Rose as well, and she was dressed in her best woollen dress, with a hat and matching coat which had a velvet collar. Pristine white socks and sweet little shoes finished off the outfit, and she gave everyone a twirl just to show them how pretty she was.

Peggy's smile was genuine as she looked at her granddaughter and realised there was a great deal of Cissy about her. Anne would have trouble with that young madam when she was older, and no mistake.

One by one they arrived in the hall and stood to attention as Alf the butcher arrived in his delivery van to help get them all to the station. Cordelia let Jim help her downstairs, and kept hold of his hand a little longer than necessary as if to silently convey her deep affection for him. Cissy was last – as usual – making a breathless entrance into the hall all of a fluster as she tried to button her coat and straighten her hat.

'Private Reilly, you're late on parade,' roared Frank as Jim did his best not to laugh. 'It's spud bashing for you.'

She smiled up at him sweetly. 'You said the last *man* in the hall – and I'm obviously not a man – so you can shout all you like, Uncle Frank, because I don't peel potatoes – not with these nails.' She flashed ten perfectly manicured fingers at him, the red varnish gleaming against her pale skin.

'You always did have an answer to everything,' Frank said with a grin. 'Come on then, let's get to the station.'

Jim made a fuss of Harvey and shut him in the kitchen so he couldn't follow them, but the dog's howls could be heard right down the street, and Peggy thought they echoed the aching anguish they were all trying so very hard to disguise.

Frank had obviously made an effort to clean his truck but it still stank of fish, and yet it didn't seem to matter as Peggy and Pauline crammed in the front seat with Daisy and sat next to Jim and Frank, leaving the boys to ride in the flatbed with their grandfather. Cordelia opted to travel in Alf's slightly sweeter smelling van, and Anne, Cissy and Martin clambered in after her with Rose.

Frank tooted the horn, waved his arm out of the window and they set off. As they drove in convoy down Camden Road, Peggy slipped her free hand into Jim's and held on tight, her smile fixed as she acknowledged the calls of good luck from their friends and neighbours. She could see that Pauline was doing the same, but sharing this awful burden didn't make it any easier to bear.

All too soon, they arrived at what was left of the station and reluctantly clambered down to the pavement. The old booking hall had been obliterated in a raid two years ago, and there was a sort of Nissen hut in its place from which the station master emerged. He gave a smart salute as Jim and Frank hoisted their kitbags and rifles over their shoulders and did their best to look jaunty.

The train was already in, and men in uniforms from

all the different services, or in their best suits, were leaning out of the windows or standing about amidst their kitbags and suitcases to say a last goodbye to their loved ones. There were a lot of familiar faces – boys not much older than Bob whom Peggy had known since they were babies; men who'd worked on the fishing boats, in the shops or for the council; and others who'd been tellers in the bank, postmen, deliverymen and street-sweepers – all putting on a brave swagger as their women determinedly kept smiling.

Peggy found that she couldn't breathe, and her legs were shaking so much she could barely stand. Anne seemed to realise how distressed she was, for she quickly passed Rose to Martin and took Daisy from her. 'I'll look after her, Mam,' she murmured. 'You're not going to faint, are you?'

Peggy shot her a grateful smile and shook her head. 'I'm fine,' she lied as she held tightly to Jim's arm. Struggling to breathe, she walked with him down the platform. They found the correct carriage, and Jim gently prised her fingers from his arm and went with his brother into the carriage to stow their belongings in the luggage rack above their seats. Then, after a long pause in which they no doubt girded themselves for what was to come, they jumped down from the train and began to say their goodbyes.

Peggy had eyes only for Jim as he ruffled his sons' hair and gave them a fierce hug. He kissed Anne, Cissy and Pauline, and shook Martin's hand, and then kissed Cordelia, who was losing her battle with her tears.

And then he wrapped his arms about his father. 'Take care of them for me, Da,' he murmured.

'Aye, I'll do that, son – and you take care of yourself,' he managed as his eyes reddened and his jaw worked.

As Frank towered over Ron and held him in a bear hug, Jim kissed Rose Margaret and then touched the sleeping Daisy's cheek before turning to Peggy. 'I'll be back before you know it,' he said gruffly. 'Give me a kiss, me darling girl, so I may carry it with me.'

Peggy clung to him fiercely as he kissed her. She could hear the guard's whistle blowing, the slam of doors like a salvo of gunfire echoing down the long platform, and the hiss of the steam that was billowing all around them. But all she could feel was the sweetness of his kiss and the tender familiarity of his hands cupping her face – and she never wanted it to end.

He pulled slowly and reluctantly away from her as the guard blew his whistle impatiently and began to shout from the other end of the platform. 'Keep smiling, Peg,' he whispered. 'I want to take your smile with me, not your tears. I love you.'

And then he was gone, Frank climbing into the carriage after him and slamming the door. As one, she and Pauline took a step towards the train, and as the window was pulled down and the brothers leaned out, they reached for their outstretched hands for one last touch – one final word of love.

The train chuffed and puffed and the wheels began to turn, slowly at first and then faster and faster. They could no longer hold onto their hands, could no longer run fast enough or hear their voices above the clanking of the wheels and the shrill whistle as the smoke and steam billowed over them.

And then it was the end of the platform, and they could only stand and watch as the train curved around the bend – watch until it had become nothing more than a speck in the distance. And then it was gone, leaving only an awful, empty silence behind.

Pauline had gone straight home after dropping the others off at Beach View, and although they'd tried to persuade her to stay another night, she'd insisted she needed time to herself.

Cordelia had quietly followed everyone into the kitchen on their return from the station, and had sat in her usual chair by the range as Cissy made a pot of tea and Anne tried to coax little Rose Margaret out of her hat and coat. She was a beautiful child, Cordelia mused, with her mother's big brown eyes and dark curls, but was clearly rather a handful.

She turned her attention to Peggy, who was as pale as wax despite the determined jut of her chin. It was a good thing she had Daisy to occupy her, she thought, but the hardest part would come tonight, when she was in that big bed all alone. And Cordelia knew how that felt, for she'd spent almost three years on her own while her husband was in the trenches, and not a night had passed without her being fully aware of the empty space beside her.

Cordelia accepted a cup of tea from Cissy and

returned her sweet, sad smile. There didn't seem to be anything to say, no words that could bring any real comfort, so it was best to remain silent and give support when it was needed. She sighed. And it would be needed during the next few dark days, for Anne would soon be returning to Somerset with Rose and the boys, Martin only had a forty-eight-hour pass which ended at six this evening, and Cissy would be back on duty tomorrow.

She looked up and saw that Ron was watching Peggy too, and realised that it would be up to them as the oldest to provide the backbone to this family until Peggy was strong enough to take up the reins again – and the thought was rather daunting.

The silence was shattered by the roar of planes flying low as they headed for the Channel, and everyone looked up and followed the sound until it had faded into the distance. The war went on, the world turned and nothing changed, despite the small human trials and tragedies that were unfolding behind the closed doors of every town and hamlet. And this knowledge seemed to bolster them, for they began, finally, to talk.

Ron slurped down the last of his tea. 'Right, you boys,' he said gruffly. 'It's time to stretch our legs and give Harvey a good run. Find some old gumboots and wrap up warm, it's cold up on top.'

The boys looked to Peggy and she nodded with a wan smile. They gave her a hug and raced down the basement steps to change.

Ron winked at Peggy. 'I'll bring 'em back in time for their tea, so you've no need to fret.'

'I never worry when they're with you, Ron,' she replied as she lit yet another cigarette.

Cordelia washed up her cup and saucer and left them to dry on the drainer as Anne tried to soothe Rose out of her tantrum at being left behind. Cissy heated a bottle of formula milk and then lifted Daisy out of her pram and pulled a chair up close to her mother.

Cordelia eyed the little family scene around the old range and decided it was time to leave them. They needed to share these close moments – needed time to come to terms with the awful void that Jim's departure had left behind. She reached for her walking stick, took the discarded newspapers from the kitchen table and headed for her bedroom.

Ron strode across the grasslands, his cheeks stinging with the cold as Charlie and Harvey raced ahead. This was what he needed, he realised; the cold wind and the scent of the sea in his nostrils would soon rip away the gloom and invigorate him. He glanced at Bob, who was striding alongside him. He was the image of Jim at that age, and in a way that also helped to restore his spirits.

'Have you brought your nets, Granddad?' Bob asked as they breached the hill and stood looking out at the sea.

'Aye, they're in me pocket – but it's a bit too windy for the rabbits today. They'll be snug in their burrows until nightfall.' He grinned at the boy, still unable to believe how tall he'd become. 'Now, if we had the ferrets that would be a different matter entirely.'

Bob dug his hands in his pockets as the wind tore at his dark hair. 'Have you thought of getting some again? Only a lot of the farmers down in Somerset still use them, and they don't seem at all concerned about the odd air raid.'

'Aye,' Ron replied thoughtfully, 'but your mother wouldn't like it. She always complained of the smell, so she did.'

'But they don't smell,' Bob protested, 'not if you keep them clean.' He grinned and nudged Ron's arm. 'Go on, Granddad, you know you've been itching to get another Delilah and Cleopatra, and now you've got the cellar to yourself, Mum can't really complain if you keep them down there like before.'

The idea was tempting, and Ron did know someone whose ferrets had just had kits. 'I'll think about it,' he muttered. 'Come on, I want to show you something.'

They walked along companionably, the boy keeping pace with his grandfather as the younger Charlie raced back and forth with Harvey. Ron was strongly reminded of how he used to come up here with Jim and Frank when they were boys. How long ago it seemed – and how much had happened since. Determined not to spoil the moment by getting down-hearted, Ron led them towards the high fence that now surrounded the Cliffe estate.

'That's put paid to your poaching,' teased Bob as he regarded the sturdy wire.

Ron just grinned as he fingered the wire-cutters in the deep pocket of his coat. Peggy would never forgive him if he took the boys poaching, and he had no intention of upsetting her – especially today. 'The Forestry Commission has taken it over,' he explained, 'and rumour has it that the Women's Land Army are taking charge and are about to set up a new corps to solve the labour shortage now there's such a high demand for timber.'

'We've got a lot of Land Army girls down in Somerset,' said Bob, 'and I've heard them talking about it. They seem to reckon they'll have an easier time of it cutting down trees instead of ploughing and harvesting, but I doubt they will.'

'Girls are silly,' announced Charlie as he dug his hands into his coat pocket and kicked the fence for no apparent reason. 'They giggle and talk about lipstick and boys and moan about their hands and nails. Me and Ernie prefer working with the German POWs – they're much more sensible.'

Ron raised his eyebrows. 'You have German prisoners of war in Somerset? Is that safe with so many women on their own?'

Bob shrugged. 'Dunno, but they have to stay in camp at night like the Ities, and there's always soldiers keeping an eye on them. Auntie Vi said we should feel sorry for them 'cos they're a long way from home, and it's not their fault Hitler is such a beast. She says that if we treat them fairly, then our men will be too if they get into the same situation.' He screwed up his face as he looked at Ron. 'What do you think, Granddad?'

'I think it's time we got out of the wind and had that flask of tea and packet of biscuits I have in me pocket,' he said gruffly. 'Come on, last one to the old farmhouse is a rotten egg.'

Bob seemed to forget he was all grown up and raced after his brother and the dog, and Ron jogged along for a while and then slowed to a steady walk, deep in thought. Vi was sort of right in her thinking, but he suspected she was simply trying to keep a fair judgement on things for the boys' sake. The reality of prisoner of war camps in the first war had been far from cosy, going by the tales some of his mates had to tell afterwards – and with the Japs coming into this war with a history of brutal abuse and a total disregard for the Geneva Conventions, he doubted there would be much fair play to be had for the poor divils caught out in the Far East.

He dismissed these dark thoughts and smiled as he saw the two boys urging him to hurry. This was what mattered now, for they would soon be leaving for Somerset again, and he might not get the chance to be with them for another year or so. It was not the time to dwell on such things as war and prison and death and dying – but on family and home and the love that bound one person to another.

He quickened his pace and finally reached the tumbledown walls of the old farmhouse. Sitting on a hummock of grass, he poured tea into the tin mugs and handed them round.

As the boys drank their tea and munched on their biscuits, Ron lit his pipe and prepared to tell them the story about how he came to have moving shrapnel in his back. It wouldn't be the whole story, neither would it be particularly true – but he'd told it so many times before that he could embellish it so it made them laugh – and he loved hearing them laugh.

With the gas fire lit against the chill of the early spring day, Cordelia settled down in her chair. But instead of putting on her glasses and reading the papers, she stared into the flames for a long while, her thoughts returning to the other times when she'd had to say goodbye. There had been too many over the years, and she understood too well how bereft Peggy must be feeling now. Yet she knew that feeling would pass, that Peggy's spirit would be revived as she slowly picked up the pieces and returned to the everyday needs of her home and family.

Cordelia reached for her glasses and lifted up the rather creased and grubby *Daily Mail*, deciding to give it a quick glance before she settled down to read the *Telegraph*, which she'd always preferred. She skimmed through most of the paper and found nothing much different to the news bulletins she heard on the wireless every night. The *Telegraph* had the same news, of course, but there was an interesting piece on Lord Beaverbrook, who was now the Minister of Supply, and further comment by the Editor on Churchill's recent speech and the awful events unfolding in the Far East.

There was also a report and long analysis on the successful 'Channel Dash' made by the Germans from Brest in Brittany, through the Straits of Dover and into the North Sea to reach their base in Germany. It was the first time since the Spanish Armada that enemy ships had sailed along the Channel, and it was shocking how easily they'd managed to avoid the heroic and determined efforts to sink them by the Royal Navy and the RAF.

It seemed that there was bad news everywhere, and she was about to set the paper aside when a small headline at the very bottom of the back page caught her eye.

JAPAN CLAIMS SINKING OF
REFUGEE SHIP

A radio broadcast was sent out yesterday from the Japanese, who claim that their Imperial Air Force has sunk the refugee ship, the HMSS Monarch of the Glen *which was carrying women and children to safety from Singapore. This cannot be confirmed, and could be a treacherous and cruel piece of propaganda. But the* Monarch of the Glen *has not been sighted since leaving Singapore and has not arrived at her first port of call as scheduled.*

Cordelia let the newspaper flutter unheeded to the

floor as the terrible sense of loss overwhelmed her. The family she'd never known she had was gone; the plans and dreams she'd happily envisaged were lost – scattered like smoke on the wind.

The anguish that had been building all day swelled until she couldn't fight it any longer, and she buried her face in her hands and wept.

Chapter Fifteen

A week had passed since Jim and Frank had left for Yorkshire, and now that Anne and the boys were back in Somerset with Rose Margaret, and Cissy had returned to her duties at the airfield, Peggy was struggling to cope. The house was suddenly too empty and quiet, the nights alone in that big bed too long.

She cooked and cleaned, cared for Daisy, took long walks with the pram, queued at the shops and struggled with the laundry, but her thoughts were constantly with Jim, wondering how he was getting on, and where the Army would send him and Frank. With the world in such turmoil, they could be sent anywhere – for even Darwin and Broome in Australia had suffered several devastating air raids, and Java, Rangoon and Hong Kong had been overrun by the Japanese.

Peggy finished hanging out the washing and stood for a moment by the pram where Daisy was gurgling happily in the spring sunshine. It was the beginning of March, and Ron's vegetable patch was coming on a treat, the chickens were still laying a good number of eggs, and she could see the first green buds sprouting on next door's lilac tree. Spring was definitely around the corner, for there were only a few pale clouds drifting in a leisurely fashion across the blue sky, and the breeze felt several degrees warmer than of late.

She adjusted the blanket over Daisy, tipped the hood so the sun didn't fall directly onto her face and adjusted the fly netting. It was time to get back in harness, she decided; time to stop moping about feeling sorry for herself when so many other women were rolling up their sleeves and getting on with things.

She picked up the laundry basket, hung it back on the hook in the scullery and was about to go up the stairs to the kitchen when she saw Ron at the back gate. He was looking decidedly furtive, his gaze darting towards the back door and the kitchen window as Harvey whined at his heels.

Peggy drew back into the shadows of the scullery and watched, intrigued, as he closed the gate behind him and almost tiptoed down the path with his hand firmly grasping Harvey's collar.

'What are you up to?' she asked as he stepped over the threshold.

His eyes widened and he tried very hard to cover his surprise and guilt at having been caught out. 'Hello, Peg,' he blustered as he let Harvey free and eased past her. 'Nice day for the washing.'

Peggy folded her arms, a smile twitching at the corners of her mouth. 'A nice day for mischief too,' she said wryly. 'Why so furtive, Ron?'

'Me?' he asked in wide-eyed innocence. 'Furtive? To be sure, Peggy girl, 'tis suspicious you are.'

Peggy laughed for the first time in a week. 'I think I have a right to be, you old scallywag.' She saw how Harvey was whining and sniffing at the pockets of his old poacher's coat. 'What have you got hidden in there this time? One of Lord Cliffe's game birds? Or is it a fresh salmon from his lake?'

'I've not been poaching,' he protested stoutly. 'To be sure, Peg, that estate is too well guarded now and a man would be a fool to even try.'

'I'm sure that hasn't deterred you one bit.' She plucked at the coat and Harvey barked and wagged his tail.

'A fat lot of good y'are at keepin' secrets,' he muttered to the dog. His gaze didn't quite reach Peggy's as he shuffled from one foot to the other. 'Now you're to promise not to fly off the handle, Peg,' he said hastily. 'Only it was Bob's idea and as they were going spare for the price of a bit of pipe tobacco, I thought . . . Well, I thought it would do no harm,' he finished in a rush.

She couldn't be cross with him. He'd been so lovely to her over the past week, even though it was clear he too was feeling the emptiness of the house. 'You'd better show me what you've got then,' she said with a smile.

He reached into one of the deepest pockets and very gently drew out two young ferrets which looked at Peggy with bright inquisitive eyes and twitching whiskers.

Peggy stepped back, remembering how sharp ferret teeth could be.

'This is Flora,' said Ron as he held up the chocolate-brown one which had tan-coloured ears and face markings. 'And this is Dora.' Dora was black all over except for a ring of white round each eye which made her look a bit like a small panda.

Peggy eyed them both as they squirmed in Ron's large hands. She didn't like ferrets; they were too much like weasels – and therefore, to her mind, no better than vermin. She certainly didn't appreciate them in the house, and Ron's previous ferrets had been banished to the cellar.

But as they looked back at her with their big brown eyes, she could see how appealing they were, and as she tentatively reached out to stroke them, she discovered their fur was beautifully soft. 'They look very young,' she murmured. 'Are you sure they've been weaned?'

'They're seven weeks old,' he replied, 'and the jill stopped feeding them over a week ago.' He dangled them over his arm and slowly stroked their furry bellies. 'I've had them neutered and de-scented, so you've no worries about the smell this time.'

He looked at her with such hope that she could only relent. 'All right,' she said, 'but they don't come upstairs and they are to go nowhere near Daisy. Is that understood, Ron?'

'Aye,' he said cheerfully. 'You'll not have a moment's worry over them, Peg.'

She doubted that very much, but kept her thoughts to herself. 'And what exactly will you feed them with?

There is a war on, you know, and eggs and milk are too precious to give to ferrets.'

'You'll not be worrying your head about a thing,' he said hastily. 'Ferrets don't eat much and I've made an arrangement with a pal of mine to get cheap cat food. They can have a drop of my milk and cheese ration and the odd scrap from the table.'

Peggy didn't like the sound of this at all, but Ron had missed having ferrets about ever since he'd set his last two free at the beginning of the war, so she couldn't deny him this little pleasure. 'As long as you remember it comes out of your ration and not anyone else's,' she murmured.

'Thanks, Peg,' he said and grinned at her as he tucked them back into his pocket. 'I've missed not having Cleo and Delilah about, and when Bob and I got to talking the other week . . .' He gave a shrug. 'They'll keep me mind off Rosie, and perhaps help to bring in more rabbits for the dinner table.'

Peggy patted his arm. 'I'll leave you to settle them in then,' she said softly.

She climbed the steps to the kitchen and found Cordelia at the sink scraping carrots. 'They look nice,' she said as she put the kettle on the hob. 'Did you have to queue very long to get them?'

'No dear, I couldn't get any rice,' she replied rather distractedly. 'But then I didn't realise you wanted any.'

Peggy smiled as she set out the mismatched cups and saucers. Cordelia really did need a new hearing aid, but after forking out for the last one only to have it trampled on days later, she was loath to risk it again.

She watched Cordelia continue to scrape the carrots, realising suddenly that the elderly woman had been distracted ever since Jim had left. She hadn't really taken much notice until today, and she felt awful about how selfish and uncaring she'd been.

'Is something the matter?' she asked.

'I can't do them in batter, dear,' she replied. 'They wouldn't taste nice at all – and besides, we don't have any flour.'

Peggy signed to her to turn up her hearing aid, for this conversation was going nowhere and she needed to get to the bottom of whatever it was that Cordelia was fretting over.

Cordelia dried her hands on her wrap-round apron, fiddled with her hearing aid and smiled rather sheepishly. 'I forgot that I'd turned it right down,' she admitted.

'Is something worrying you, Cordelia?' asked Peggy clearly. 'You seem a bit distracted of late.'

The elderly woman patted Peggy's arm and shook her head. 'I've just been feeling my age a bit,' she said, 'and of course I miss Jim about the place – but really, Peggy dear, there's nothing for you to worry about.'

Peggy wanted to believe her, but she had the feeling Cordelia wasn't being entirely truthful. However, she let it pass in the hope that the older woman would confide in her when she felt ready to do so. 'We must get those rooms ready again for your family,' she said in the hope of cheering her up. 'They must be about due to arrive in Scotland.'

Cordelia turned her back and fished a carrot out of the bowl of water and began to slice it on the breadboard. 'I'm sure they'll send us a telegram when they get here,' she replied, 'there's no need to rush.'

Peggy frowned. Cordelia had been so eager for them to come to Beach View, and had happily tried to follow their long journey on one of Bob's old atlases and discussed all the things she could do with them once they'd arrived.

She touched Cordelia's shoulder. 'You don't seem as excited at the prospect of having them here,' she said clearly. 'Are you beginning to have doubts?'

The paring knife flashed dangerously close to the little fingers as the carrots were chopped. 'Of course I'm not, dear,' she said firmly, 'but with everything else that's going on, one can't depend on anything any more. I'd prefer to wait and see if they make it safely here before you go to all the trouble of preparing rooms again.'

Peggy could see her logic, but didn't really understand her reticence after her initial joy at discovering she had two great-nieces to fuss over. She made the tea and called down to Ron, who seemed to be shifting things about in the cellar – no doubt unearthing the old ferret cages that had become buried beneath all the rubbish he kept down there.

Once the three of them were seated at the table and Harvey had had his dog biscuit and saucer of tea, she told them of her own plans. 'I've decided to go back and work part-time with the WVS,' she said. 'They need every spare pair of hands they can get, and I feel I've rather let the side down by not going back after Daisy was born.'

'Aye,' muttered Ron around the stem of his pipe. 'You'll enjoy getting out of the house for a wee while. D'ye want me to look out for Daisy?'

Peggy shook her head. 'She can come with me. There's always a spare corner at the Town Hall. But I might need you to babysit if I have to go and man a tea wagon or attend some emergency.'

Ron and Cordelia nodded. 'We'll both keep an eye on her,' said Cordelia. 'It will do you good to have some time to yourself for a change.'

Peggy smiled at her naïvety. There would be precious little time to be had once she was back to sorting through old clothes, making up parcels to send to the troops abroad, or packets of sandwiches for the servicemen who were passing through on their way to the docks further along the coast, or dealing with the homeless and dispossessed. The work of the WVS was constant and time-consuming, but very satisfying, and what she was really looking forward to was being so tired at the end of each day that she didn't have the chance to think about things.

Cordelia was an honest, straightforward woman, and she'd found it extremely hard to keep acting as if nothing had happened when all the time her thoughts were with all those poor women and children on that ship. But Peggy and the rest of the family had their own sorrows, and the last thing they needed was for her to lose control and spill out her anguish.

She'd lain in bed night after night thinking about the sinking of the *Monarch of the Glen*, and had trawled every newspaper since in search of further news, but there had been nothing – not even a hint that it might have just been a cruel hoax by the Japanese. Yet there had been tales of terrible atrocities in Hong Kong, and Cordelia suspected that targeting a ship full of women and children was not something this particular enemy would deem reprehensible.

They had eaten a sandwich for lunch and then Peggy had taken Daisy down to the Town Hall so she could sign up for duty again and get back into the swing of things. Cordelia had waited until she was out of sight before she carefully made her way down the cellar steps.

Harvey greeted her by thumping his tail on the cellar floor, but his attention was fixed on Ron, who was fiddling about with straw and bits of newspaper.

Ron finished layering the straw and paper-strips on the floor of the large wire-fronted box which he'd set up beneath the scullery sink, and looked up in surprise as Cordelia reached the bottom step.

'Hello,' he said cheerfully. 'Do you want me to get one of the deckchairs out? It's a lovely afternoon, so it is, and quite sheltered in the corner next to the fence.'

'Not at the moment, but thank you,' she said as she

eyed the box. 'Isn't that where you used to keep Cleo and Delilah?'

'Aye, it is that,' he said with a gleeful grin. 'And soon there will be new residents.'

'Oh, Ron,' she sighed as she sat down on the bottom step. 'You know how Peggy feels about ferrets. She's not going to like it.'

Ron laughed. 'She's agreed to let me have them as long as they stay down here. Would you like to see them?'

She wasn't at all sure she would, but as Ron was looking so eager, and she needed his advice, she decided to be brave. 'As long as they don't bite,' she murmured. 'I still remember Cleo sinking her teeth into my thumb. It was painful for weeks.'

'These ones are just babies,' he replied as he reached into his coat. 'As long as you keep your hands away from their mouths, you'll be fine.' He drew the two kits out and held them against his chest for her inspection. 'Flora and Dora,' he said by way of introduction.

'They're very sweet,' she said and smiled. 'Can I stroke them?' At his nod, she reached out and touched the soft fur, remembering how Cleo and Delilah would go into an almost ecstatic trance when they had their tummies rubbed.

'They seem to like you,' said Ron, 'but I think that's enough for now. It's time we put them into their box so they can settle in and get used to their new home.'

Cordelia saw how tenderly he placed them on the fresh straw and newspaper, and how he'd hooked the water and food bowls to the wire mesh so they wouldn't spill over their bedding. She continued to watch as they completely ignored a whining, curious Harvey who had his nose pressed to the wiring, and sniffed every corner, exploring their surroundings before tucking into their food and water. 'They look as if they'll settle nicely,' she murmured.

'Aye, they will that,' he said as he pulled Harvey away, got off the floor and brushed his hands down his disreputable trousers. He eyed her keenly as she continued to sit on the cold stone step. 'Were you wanting to talk to me about something, Cordelia?' he asked.

'I do need to talk to someone,' she admitted, 'but I'm not sure if even *you* can help me with this particular and rather worrying dilemma.'

'You can tell me all about it once you're off that step and all nice and comfy in the sunshine.' He took her hand and steadied her as she got to her feet. 'I'll get the deckchairs out of the shed, and we can sit and put the world to rights in the garden.'

Minutes later the deckchairs had been cleaned of cobwebs and dead spiders, and they were sitting in the sheltered corner by the neighbouring fence, Harvey happily snoring at their feet.

Cordelia told him about the piece in the newspaper, the sleepless nights she'd had ever since, and her unwillingness to burden Peggy or the family when they had their own worries over Jim and Frank. 'I know it's not really fair to lay it at your door,' she admitted, 'but I so badly needed to tell someone, and I trust you to give me an honest opinion.'

Ron puffed on his pipe for a while and then gave a deep sigh. 'There's no doubt that some of those refugee ships were attacked – especially in the last hours before Singapore fell – but from what I understand, the survivors were picked up by other ships in their convoy.'

'That's what I've been hoping,' she replied, 'but the newspaper report didn't say anything about the *Monarch of the Glen* being in a convoy – only that she was late arriving at her first port of call.' She wrung her hands in her lap. 'It's simply too awful to think of all those women and innocent children being lost at sea.'

'And there's no further news in the papers? No follow-up to the story?'

Cordelia shook her head. 'I've looked through both the papers we have here every morning, and even gone through all the ones at the tobacconist's each day – he wasn't too happy about it, but let me look as long as I didn't crease the pages.'

'There's probably a news blackout on it,' said Ron. 'That sort of thing is bad for morale, and I'm surprised it got past the censors in the first place. There again, it could just be a vicious bit of propaganda.'

'Do you really think so?'

He chuckled. 'The Germans claimed they'd sunk HMS *Firle Park* a few weeks ago – turns out she wasn't a ship at all, but a military headquarters somewhere in the middle of the Sussex countryside.'

'But the *Monarch is* a real ship,' she said tremulously. 'Is there any way we could find out if she made that first port of call – or if she's been spotted since? Do you think Anthony might know someone we could talk to?'

Ron chewed the stem of his pipe as he considered this and then, realising it had gone out, took a while to relight it. Once he'd got a good burn going, he leaned back and stared into the distance. 'He might,' he said thoughtfully, 'but what we need is someone with contacts in the Navy.'

Cordelia felt a spark of hope, for Ron knew just about everyone in Cliffehaven and, she suspected, an even wider circle of acquaintances much further afield.

He tamped down on the tobacco in his pipe with a grubby thumb. 'I'll have a word with Rear Admiral Price. He's a nice chap, still has contacts at Admiralty House – and he owes me a couple of favours.'

'Oh, Ron, thank you,' she breathed. 'I knew you'd be able to help.'

He patted her hand. 'Don't get your hopes up too high, Cordelia,' he said gruffly. 'He might only have bad news.'

Cordelia blinked away the tears. 'At least I'll know,' she murmured. 'It's the uncertainty of everything that's so hard to bear.'

Peggy had been welcomed back with open arms, and had got stuck into packing parcels for the boys abroad immediately. She was thoroughly enjoying herself as she stood in line behind one of the long trestle tables and packed socks, cigarettes, packets of biscuits, small tins of golden syrup and a dozen and one little things to make life a bit more cheerful for the servicemen who were stuck in some inhospitable corner of the world.

She glanced across the room frequently to keep an eye on Daisy, whose pram was parked alongside eight others. It seemed that she wasn't the only woman who needed to escape the kitchen and nursery, and it was fun to catch up on the scandal, and to exchange ideas of how to dress up a scrag-end to make it edible.

'Stand by your beds,' muttered her friend Gladys. 'Officer approaching.'

'Oh Gawd,' breathed Peggy as her sister entered the hall. She ducked her head in the hope she wouldn't be spotted. 'Tell me when she's gone,' she whispered.

'No such luck, Peg. She's making a beeline for you.'

Peggy took a deep breath, kept her head down and carried on packing her box before passing it to the next table where it would be sealed. She could see Doris now, resplendent in the WVS uniform of dark green skirt and jacket and rather silly hat. The suit fitted far too well to have been taken from stores, and Peggy suspected she'd had it tailor-made, and hoped that little Sally Hicks had not been bullied into taking less than the usual charge for such detailed work.

'Margaret. I didn't expect to see you here.'

Peggy pulled another box in front of her and reached

for a pair of socks. 'Hello, Doris,' she said. 'I thought it was time to get stuck in again.'

'Well done,' said Doris, as she shifted the long strap of her tan leather handbag over her shoulder. 'It's rather fortunate that I've bumped into you, actually,' she said quietly. 'I wonder if you could leave that for a moment? There's something I'd like to discuss with you.'

Peggy looked at her in alarm. This was most unlike the usual rather hectoring Doris, and now she looked at her properly, she could see there were dark shadows beneath her eyes, which couldn't quite be masked by the heavy layer of face powder. 'Of course,' she stammered. 'Let's go in the canteen and have a cup of tea.'

Doris curled her lip. 'If we must, but I was rather hoping we could go to Plummers.'

'I've got Daisy with me and I can't be long; there're too many comfort boxes to pack and not enough hands to do them.' Not waiting for Doris to reply, Peggy led the way through the crush to the canteen which had been set up in the smaller of the two council meeting rooms.

Doris took a sip of tea and raised her severely plucked brows in surprise. 'Good heavens,' she breathed. 'It's proper tea and every bit as good as Plummers'.'

'What did you want to talk about, Doris? Only I don't have much time.'

Doris regarded her evenly. 'I was quite hurt not to be invited to your party the other week,' she said. 'It comes to something when one learns of such things from your butcher.'

'That was none of my doing,' said Peggy hastily. 'Martin organised it as a surprise.'

Doris's nostrils narrowed and her eyes hardened. 'I also understand that my son was there – fraternising with that Suzy.'

'You make it sound as if she's the enemy,' said Peggy as she blew on the hot tea. 'Suzy and Anthony weren't "fraternising", as you put it, they were having a bit of fun at a family party.' She knew immediately that she'd said the wrong thing.

'A family party to which I had not been invited,' said Doris coldly. 'But as Suzy and Fran and Rita were there, along with the butcher and fishmonger – and probably Uncle Tom Cobley and all – one can only surmise that you have a strange idea of the meaning of the word family.'

'I'm so sorry, Doris,' she said with genuine regret. 'But I didn't do it on purpose.'

Doris eyed her for a long moment before she reached into her handbag for her cigarette case and gold lighter. She blew smoke and returned her steely gaze to her sister. 'But then you didn't make any attempt to make reparation either. You could have telephoned. I was at home all that evening.'

Peggy didn't know what to say. She was genuinely ashamed of not wanting her sister there, and for not phoning her – but then Doris wasn't exactly easy to have around, especially at a party where Jim and Ron got merry and started fooling about. 'I've already apologised,' she said quietly. 'Please believe me when I say it won't happen again.'

Doris smoked her cigarette, her eyes narrowed against the smoke as she watched the women working behind the canteen counter. 'It seems my family is determined to cause me hurt,' she said. 'Edward spends his weekends on the golf course and his evenings at the club; you don't invite me to family parties; and Anthony seems to prefer spending his precious few hours of leave with that Suzy person instead of with me at home.'

She curled her lip as she stubbed out the cigarette in the tin ashtray. 'Suzy,' she muttered in disgust. 'One would have thought she had grown out of such a ridiculously childish name. But then I've always said she's a wishy-washy kind of girl with only half a brain, and far too easily led on by that Irish flibbertigibbet, Frances.'

Peggy realised that her sister was harbouring all sorts of hurts, and for the first time in her life actually felt rather sorry for her. 'Anthony and Suzy get on rather well, and she's much brighter than you give her credit for,' she said reasonably. 'She's a ward sister now, and often works in the theatre alongside the surgeons. Don't dismiss her, Doris,' she warned. 'Suzy is quite a tough character, and it's clear that Anthony's smitten.'

'She isn't at all the sort of girl I want for my Anthony,' Doris retorted, 'and I have made that very plain to him.'

'That's a shame,' Peggy said carefully, 'because the more you try to keep them apart the more determined they will be to stay together.' She leaned across the table and stilled Doris's fingers, which were rapping out a tattoo on the table. 'I know you're ambitious for your son; we're all ambitious for our children – but there comes a time when we have to let them go so they can find their own way in the world.'

'Just like you did with Cissy,' hissed Doris nastily. 'I understand she's no better than she should be, carrying on with all those men at the airfield.'

Peggy pushed back from the table. 'Don't take your anger out on me, Doris,' she said evenly, 'or get spiteful about my children. See to your own – and ask yourself why Ted prefers the company at the golf club instead of coming home.'

She left the table before her sister could reply and headed for the other room, rather ashamed at how catty she'd been – but then Doris had no right to say such things about Cissy. Her daughter might flirt a bit, but she certainly wasn't a tart as Doris had suggested.

Still cross with herself and Doris, she checked on Daisy, who was fast asleep despite all the noise, and went back to her place at the packing table where she snatched up an empty box and began to fill it.

'Blimey,' said Gladys with a knowing expression, 'if looks could kill, I wouldn't want to be in your sister's shoes.'

Peggy had a sudden, dark suspicion that there

was far more to her sister's unhappiness than she was letting on, and she wondered if it was something to do with Ted. 'Neither would I,' she murmured thoughtfully.

Chapter Sixteen

Another week had passed since Jim and Frank had left for training camp, and it was fervently hoped they would be granted a short leave. Ron was still finding it hard to come to terms with the fact that his two sons could soon be in the thick of it somewhere. What with the Japs rampaging through the whole of the Far East and even managing to attack Australia, and Hitler doing his best to annihilate Europe, there seemed little chance that his boys would be stuck somewhere safe in England for the duration.

He left Beach View dressed in his Home Guard uniform, the Fairbairn-Sykes fighting knife well hidden in the depths of his canvas bag of supplies which he carried over his shoulder to see him through the long night. Instead of heading for the platoon's headquarters in the centre of town, he struck out along the back alleyway and headed for the hills. This twice-weekly walk was always undertaken in the dark, his destination one of utmost secrecy, and his absence at the Home Guard meeting would be explained if necessary by his commanding officer, who had also been recruited into the GHQ Special Reserve Battalion 203.

Very few people knew about these specialised battalions, or of the covert activity they'd been preparing for over the past two years. Like the others, Ron had signed the Official Secrets Act shortly after he'd first been approached by Colonel Gubbins.

After the fall of France in May 1940, Gubbins was ordered by Churchill to create a force of civilian volunteers, recruited primarily from the ablest members of the Home Guard. The ideal candidates were farmers, foresters, gamekeepers and poachers whose knowledge of their particular area was indisputable, and who could be trained in the necessary skills for guerrilla warfare and the silent kill. Their task was to operate from secret underground bases, and if Britain was invaded, to be the front line of defence and carry out attacks and sabotage against enemy targets such as supply dumps, railway lines, convoys and enemy-controlled airfields – and to harry and disrupt supplies and lines of communication. Each man was equipped with a revolver and Sten gun, as well as the fighting knife and a silenced .22 sniper rifle.

Keeping to the shadows of the trees and away from the skyline, Ron skirted the gun emplacements and fire-watch positions that were dotted over the hills, and walked down into the valley, past the ugly wire fencing that encompassed the Cliffe estate and further into the dense woodlands where the gorse grew in thick clumps beneath the gnarled old trees and brambles deterred walkers. He trod carefully through the clinging goose grass and ivy, making sure he left no trace of his passage as he followed the path that only he could see.

The operational base was constructed of preformed corrugated iron segments, sunk into the ground with concrete pipe access and a maze of escape tunnels. Well hidden beneath a tangle of brambles, wild honeysuckle and rose, goose grass and sprawling gorse, it had been built deep into the ground so the roof was simply a low mound beneath this natural camouflage, the air vents disguised as old bits of drainage piping. The Royal Engineers who built the bases were told they were to be for emergency food storage.

Ron edged around it until he came to the trapdoor that was cunningly set in the earth and hidden by yet more greenery. He rapped three times on the door so the man inside didn't shoot him, pulled the hidden lever and went down the moss-covered concrete steps. Another lever drew the trapdoor shut above him.

'The owl is flying tonight,' he said.

'Then the sun must be out,' came the reply.

Ron grinned. Some of these passwords were ridiculous. He switched on his torch and made his way along a short, narrow concrete tunnel. After a right-angled turn, this led into a large, dimly lit cavern which had been fitted out with wooden bunks, heating, ventilation and enough rations of food and water for fourteen days, should the invasion come. Another tunnel led to a second bunker about a mile away, and this held hundreds of cases of ammunition, plastic explosives, timing devices, detonators and grenades. This secret arsenal had been prepared by the end of 1940, and would remain there until Hitler was defeated.

'Evening, Maurice,' he said cheerfully to the Rear Admiral, who was drinking tea from a tin mug as he sat in a deckchair beneath the hurricane lamp. 'You've beaten me to it tonight.'

Maurice Price was a tall, well-built, vigorous man in his late sixties, with a weathered face and a shock of thick white hair. 'I thought I'd get settled in early,' he said in his educated voice. 'My wife was threatening to find me yet another job around the house.'

Ron grinned. 'Aye, the women will do that to you, to be sure. 'Tis better to keep one step ahead.' He put down his canvas bag and pulled out his thermos flask and wickedly honed knife before settling into the second deckchair, which was close to one of the air vents. 'Any orders tonight?' he asked, glancing at the army radio set up in the corner.

Maurice shook his head. 'We'll hear soon enough if there's a flap on,' he said comfortably. He passed Ron a packet of bourbon biscuits, which were a rare treat. 'I found them in Harrods when I went up to town,' he explained.

Ron munched a chocolate biscuit, savouring each crunchy, creamy bite before washing it down with the strong tea. 'What's it like up there?'

'The shops are almost empty, the prices are high and there's hardly anyone about – except in the Criterion Brasserie, where one had to wait for ages to get served

– but they did do a very good breakfast. Poor old London's suffering,' he added with a sigh. 'So much of it is rubble, and it's difficult to find one's way around now so many of the landmarks are gone.'

Ron nodded. He could just imagine it, though he hadn't been to London in years. 'St Paul's is still standing though,' he said, remembering a photograph in the newspaper after the Blitz. 'Hitler didn't get that.'

They sat in silence for a long moment, sipping their tea. If the Germans did carry out their threat to invade, then Ron and Maurice and a thousand other men like them would be the front line of defence. Although the majority had learned their skills in the first war and were now retired, they'd been passed fit and perfectly able to do the job after a rigorous two weeks at a special training camp in Wiltshire. Ron and his comrades had learned to smile at the jibes about Dad's Army, even though it galled them – for the image that derisive description brought actually served to disguise the real force that lay beneath.

'While I was in London, I managed to talk to someone about the *Monarch of the Glen*,' said Maurice eventually. 'It seems she *was* attacked just after leaving Singapore, but escaped unscathed.'

'That's a relief,' said Ron. 'So why was she late to her first port of call?'

Maurice shrugged. 'Perhaps she had to take evasive action; no one knows. But she reached Ceylon only a day late, and arrived in South Africa on time. She's quite a fast ship, you know, which is why she'd been seconded to carry troops and supplies quickly to the troublespots.'

Ron grinned. 'That's good news they're on their way. Cordelia will be delighted.'

'Ah, well,' said Maurice as he reached for his pipe. 'There's no guarantee of that, actually.' He glanced at the huge sign which forbade them to smoke and, with a sigh, stuck his unlit pipe between his teeth. 'The people in South Africa tried to persuade the women with young children to stay there for the duration, and so far there hasn't been a list of those who took up the option. Cordelia's relatives could well be among them.'

Ron followed suit with his pipe and sank lower into the deckchair. 'At least they're still alive,' he muttered.

'Absolutely,' Maurice agreed. 'The chap I spoke to at Admiralty House said that with communications as they are, it's almost impossible to get exact passenger lists and keep tabs on all the women and children fleeing the Far East. But he could tell me that the *Monarch* joined a convoy of merchant ships to come up the Atlantic, and a good many of the women with particularly young children had been transferred to an even swifter ship, the *Laetitia*. I believe the *Laetitia* has already reached Glasgow, and the rest of the convoy is due to arrive any day.'

'Thanks, Maurice. You've helped no end, and no doubt Cordelia will feel much easier about things now.'

'Glad to help, old chap.' He grinned as he pulled a

bottle out of his kitbag. 'How about a drop of rum to liven up the tea while we play a hand of cards to pass away the time?'

Chapter Seventeen

The *Monarch of the Glen*

Sarah and the other women had heard the Japanese radio announcement of the sinking of their ship, and realised immediately what a devastating effect such a statement would have on their menfolk back in Singapore. Like everyone else on board, Sarah had fretted over her inability to send some kind of reassurance that they were still alive and well – and had to accept the fact that there was absolutely nothing she could do about it. There was no communication with Singapore now it had fallen into Japanese hands, and she could only pray that her father and Philip would recognise the announcement as a nasty piece of propaganda.

They had sailed on from Ceylon to Durban and around the Cape of Good Hope to Cape Town, where Sarah and the other women were faced with an unexpected dilemma. The South African authorities had put forward a tempting and very persuasive offer for the women with young children to remain in Cape Town for the duration. They pointed out that they hadn't yet been touched by the war, that the climate was closer to that in Malaya, and that food, housing and jobs would be plentiful. They had painted a very grim picture of England, with the cold, wet climate, the food rationing and air raids – and the fact that women with small children couldn't do their bit for the war effort, and therefore would become a burden on the country and be made to feel unwelcome.

Sarah had been sorely tempted, and Jane was quite excited by the prospect. But Sarah knew that their parents expected them to be in England, and to change their plans now would merely complicate things. It would be awful if their mother arrived in England only to find herself alone and still thousands of miles away from her daughters.

It seemed that the majority of the other women felt the same way, and once all this had been carefully explained to Jane, she accepted they wouldn't be staying in Cape Town, and began to look forward to arriving in England.

The temperature had dropped swiftly once they'd left the coast of Africa, and sitting on deck had soon become a thing of the past. The rough passage up the Atlantic with their escort of merchant ships was spent indoors, huddled on their mattresses cupping their hands round hot mugs of Marmite or Bovril – which were an acquired taste, but one they'd both come to rather like. Few of them had any warm clothing, and Sarah had raided their suitcases and emergency bundles so that when they arrived in the calmer waters of the Clyde that morning, they were wearing just about every stitch of clothing they possessed.

'We must look like refugee waifs and strays,' murmured Sarah as the ship dropped anchor late that afternoon at a place the Captain had told them was called Gurroch. She felt grubby and unkempt, for her hair needed a good wash and trim, and the jackets she'd used to make the bundles were horribly creased and stained.

'I think it's rather fun to be gypsies for a bit,' said Jane as they stood by the railings. 'But I do wish it wasn't so cold. Do you think it's always like this in England?'

'I hope not,' said Sarah, her teeth chattering. 'But this is Scotland, and we're still very far north, so Cliffehaven might be a bit warmer,' she said hopefully.

'Oh, do look,' said Jane, pointing to a tender coming towards them. 'Who do you think they are?'

Sarah watched as the sturdy little boat was lashed alongside and a group of women in dark green uniform began to climb aboard and disappear below deck, while the sailors unloaded huge cardboard packing boxes. 'I have no idea,' she replied, 'but they look very businesslike.' She grasped Jane's cold arm. 'Come on, let's get inside before we both turn into icebergs.'

It wasn't long before they discovered that the women who'd come on board were from the Women's Voluntary Service and were there to welcome them, and help smooth their way to their new and rather daunting futures.

They had set up at the trestle tables in the dining

room, the mysterious boxes now unpacked to reveal huge stacks of smaller boxes with long string handles. Sarah and Jane joined the long queue and awaited their turn to be seen. It seemed the smaller boxes held something that everyone had to put over their faces like a mask, and even the babies had to have a special sort of covered-in cradle. The noise was tremendous, for the children had become over-excited and the women were chattering nineteen to the dozen as they speculated over what these women in uniform might do for them – and whether they had any news of their menfolk back in Malaya and Singapore.

'Welcome to Scotland,' said a plump middle-aged woman on the other side of a table with a bright smile. 'Now, I will need your names first, and then we can get down to the real business in hand.'

Her accent was quite strong, and she had to repeat herself twice before Sarah fully understood what she was saying. 'Sarah and Jane Fuller,' she replied with an apologetic smile.

Their names and ages were duly noted down on an official-looking form. 'Now, my dears,' the woman said slowly and clearly, 'you must be fitted with a gas mask each.' She eyed them up and down and reached for two boxes from the stack behind her. 'Try these for size.'

They had seen the other women trying these things on and they both struggled to get the unwieldy, foul-smelling rubbery things over their faces. They were tight and hot and extremely unpleasant.

'I can't breathe,' shouted Jane, her voice muffled, eyes wide with terror as she tried ripping it off, only to get it entangled in her long hair.

Sarah rushed to help and then dragged her mask off too. 'Will we have to wear these all the time?' she asked in horror.

'No dear, only if there's a gas attack. But you have to keep them with you at all times. It's the law.' The Scottish woman eyed them both and gave a knowing smile. 'They're nae pretty, but they will save your life if Hitler decides to gas us.'

Jane looked at Sarah for reassurance, and Sarah squeezed her hand before helping her to pack the hated thing back into its box.

'Now we've sorted that,' said the woman, 'what else can I help you with?'

'Do you have any news of our family back in Singapore?' Sarah asked breathlessly. 'Only our mother was in the General Hospital when we left, and our father and my fiancé, Philip, were—'

'I'm so sorry, my dear,' the woman interrupted. 'We have no news concerning the situation in Singapore.' Her smile faltered as she saw the tears in Jane's eyes. 'There, there, wee lassie, no need for tears, not now you're safe. I'm sure they'll get a message to you as soon as they can.'

Sarah had clung to the hope that there would be news, just as every other woman had, and she swallowed her disappointment as she held tightly onto Jane's hand.

The woman folded her hands on top of the table. 'Now then, what sort of practical things can I get you to make you feel more at home here?'

'We need warm clothing,' said Sarah. 'We're both freezing.'

'We also need proper shoes,' said Jane as she woefully regarded her pretty sandals which were now falling apart.

'There is something else,' murmured Sarah as she leaned towards the woman, 'but it's a bit personal. You see, we both need—'

'Tha's nae problem, lassie,' she said quickly. 'They will be provided as a matter of course.' She smiled back at them. 'Now, I'll need to take some rough measurements,' she said, rising from her chair with a tape measure.

Once they'd been measured and their shoe sizes taken, they were handed emergency ration books and food stamps, and forms to fill in so they could apply for more when they reached their destination. Then they were dismissed with another cheery smile and the woman in the queue behind them took their place.

'I hope we never have to wear those horrid things again,' said Jane as they returned to their place below deck and she flung the gas-mask box onto her mattress.

'So do I,' replied Sarah as she sat down on her mattress. 'Because it will mean we're being gassed like those poor men in the trenches in the first war.' She realised Jane didn't know what she was talking about, and changed the subject. 'I wonder what sort of clothes we'll get,' she murmured. 'The things we've brought are worn to bits after wearing and washing them over and over.'

'I just hope we don't all end up in that horrid green uniform – we would look silly.'

'I don't care how silly we look,' Sarah said as she lay down and pulled the blanket up to her chin. 'I just want to feel warm again, and if that means wearing that uniform, then so be it.'

Jane was soon asleep, untroubled by the fears and doubts that assailed Sarah. She lay awake on the lumpy mattress for a long time, thinking about what tomorrow might bring. They were almost at the end of this journey, but there was still a long way to go before they would reach Cliffehaven, and she still didn't know if there was anyone there prepared to take them in. There had been no time for a reply to her father's telegram to get through before they'd had to leave Singapore. What if neither of the great aunts were alive, or if they were simply too old to cope? How on earth would she find somewhere else for them to stay when she had so little English money to pay for lodgings?

She turned restlessly and drew her knees up to try and garner as much warmth as she could beneath the thin blanket. She had no idea how big Cliffehaven was, or how badly it might have been affected by the war. Life was bound to be very different in England, especially during a war, and it would be hard enough to learn the way things were done, without the added worry over finding them both accommodation and some sort of job. Pops had said he'd made arrangements with the bank in Cliffehaven, but now Singapore had fallen, she rather feared that such arrangements were no longer valid. It was all very worrying, and it was a long time before she managed to fall asleep.

They awoke to discover the ship had steamed further up the River Clyde and was now docked at the quayside of a big harbour where everything seemed to be painted grey. It was a dull day, with an icy wind that whipped up the river from the sea and cut to the bone. Even the gulls sounded mournful, as if they too longed for a clear blue sky and a warm, tropical breeze instead of the colourless clouds and steely sea.

Just after lunch each woman was presented with a neat brown paper parcel which bore her name, and everyone raced back to their sleeping quarters to see what they'd been given.

'It's like Christmas,' said Jane as she wrestled with the string and tore back the paper. Her eyes widened as she pulled out a lovely blue woollen dress, two skirts, a hand-knitted cardigan and matching jumper, and a thick overcoat. There was a pair of sturdy lace-up shoes, two pairs of socks, warm vests and nightclothes, a pair of gloves, a beret and a scarf. 'What have you got, Sarah?' she asked excitedly.

Sarah found a tartan skirt, a navy dress and a pair of loose trousers. There were two thick woollen jumpers, a gabardine raincoat, shoes, thick stockings, warm underwear and a hand-knitted set of bright blue beret, gloves and scarf. The shoes were a bit worn and felt strange on her feet, but everything fitted very well considering how slapdash the WVS woman's measuring had been.

She bundled the spare clothes and sanitary pads into their cases and made sure Jane didn't leave her gas-mask box behind. Dressed in their new finery, they took one last look at their sleeping quarters with a touch of nostalgia, and headed back to the dining room where they'd been ordered to muster in preparation for landing.

Sarah glanced at Jane, who was looking so pretty in her red woollen beret and scarf and dark navy coat. She felt warm for the first time in days, but it wasn't just the clothes that heartened her – it was the generosity of those who'd given so much in a time of great austerity. The people of Glasgow had welcomed a ship full of strangers with such heartfelt kindness that it brought tears to her eyes.

It was late afternoon before they could disembark, and Sarah had to smile as she recalled the dire warnings the South Africans had given them about not being made welcome, for as they went slowly down the gangway to the wharf, they were greeted with loud cheers and cries of 'Well done!' and 'Welcome home!' from the waiting crowd. Flash bulbs went off as newspapermen took their pictures, and hands reached out to them with more gifts of woollen mittens and socks.

'Gosh,' breathed a wide-eyed Jane. 'It isn't as if we've done anything very special – but how lovely everyone is to give us such a friendly welcome.' She tucked her hand into the crook of Sarah's arm. 'I think I'm going to like it in England,' she said happily.

Sarah squeezed her arm. She checked that Jane hadn't mislaid her case or gas-mask box in the crush, then they followed the rest of the women and children on the short walk to the station. The doughty ladies of the WVS were waiting for them with warmed bottles and extra nappies for the babies, sticking plasters for scraped knees, and plates of sandwiches and biscuits and cups of hot tea.

'Eat while you can,' one of the women advised Sarah. 'There will only be drinking water on the train, and you won't arrive in London until tomorrow morning.'

Jane eagerly tucked into a sandwich and recoiled in disgust. 'Urgh! What on *earth* is this?'

'It's spam and margarine,' she was told rather firmly. 'You'll get used to the taste. Now eat up. Waste not, want not – there is a war on, you know.'

The woman strode away and Jane eyed the pink fatty meat and the smear of margarine, which tasted oily and most unpleasant. 'Do I have to eat this?' she whispered to Sarah. 'Isn't there anything else?'

Sarah had tasted her sandwich by now and agreed with Jane that it was quite disgusting. 'I don't think there is,' she murmured, 'but we'd better not throw these away in case we get into trouble.' She surreptitiously wrapped both sandwiches in her handkerchief, tucked them into her raincoat pocket and just hoped the grease didn't seep through and ruin her coat. 'Fill up on biscuits and tea,' she advised her sister before reaching for the plate of digestives.

The train was already in the station, puffing smoke almost contentedly from the stack as the sooty-faced driver and stoker leaned out to chat to the children until everyone had finished their tea and clambered aboard. The carriages were open ones, with hard, upright seats in serried ranks, and sturdy squares of black-painted wood were nailed over all the windows. The only light came from a couple of very dim bulbs in the ceiling.

Sarah and Jane put their cases in the rack above their seats and helped the other women with their babies and small children. It was going to be a long night, for the carriage was crowded, the seats were uncomfortable, the children were making a lot of noise – and they could barely see their way to get around.

But as the whistle blew and the great iron wheels began to turn, Sarah felt a surge of excitement that was tempered with sadness. They had spent two months getting here, and she still didn't know if her parents and Philip had managed to escape Singapore. She was miles from home, on her way to a place she'd never been, with a sister who needed caring for – but it was an adventure, and she had the feeling that she would remember this chapter in her life for the rest of her days.

Cordelia had spent another restless night worrying

about Sybil and her two daughters. She had hoped that Ron would have found out something by now – but almost a week had passed and he'd said nothing.

She got ready for the day, grabbed her walking stick and went downstairs to find Harvey snoring by the range and Peggy and the three girls at the breakfast table. Fran was babbling as usual, flashing her blue eyes and flicking back her fiery hair as she described the fun she'd had the previous night at a fund-raising dance.

'To be sure and you missed a treat, Suzy, so you did,' she said between spooning porridge into her mouth. 'There's a new swing band just started up, and they're very good. We danced until our feet were sore – and then went round to the side entrance of the Anchor, where Tommy let us all in for a drink.'

'So Tommy Findlay's breaking the licensing laws, is he?' said Peggy, her face stiff with disapproval. 'Rosie won't thank him if he gets her pub shut down.'

'Ach, Peggy, you worry too much,' said Fran lightly. 'Tommy's only doing what a lot of the landlords are doing – and you have to admit, the opening hours are far too short.' She turned back to Suzy. 'I'm on late shift today, but there's another dance at the weekend. We could go together, or make up a four.'

Suzy blushed and kept her gaze on her bowl of porridge. 'I'll see what Anthony's plans are, but yes, that sounds like fun.'

'So, how's it going with you two?' asked Rita as she finished her porridge. 'Had a run-in with Doris yet?'

Suzy chuckled. 'Not yet. Anthony was all for taking me home to tea so we could get to know one another a bit better, but I managed to dissuade him. Doris is daunting at the best of times, and I don't want to spoil things.'

'I don't blame you,' said Rita. She shot an apologetic glance at Peggy. 'Doris isn't the sort of mother-in-law I'd want, and that's a fact.'

'Oh, Rita, things haven't gone that far,' Suzy protested.

'From what I saw the other night, they seem to be going like a steam train,' retorted Rita. 'I saw you both huddled up in the shelter on the seafront so tight you couldn't have put a farthing between you.' She giggled. 'It was absolutely freezing, but neither of you seemed to notice. It must be love.'

Suzy's face went red. 'You could be right,' she murmured, 'but it's very early days yet.'

Cordelia watched this exchange with amusement. It was heartening to see how love had blossomed in Suzy – and it restored her faith in the human race. For despite the war and privations, the tragedies and the trials, love could still be found, and life still went on. She sipped her tea and tucked into her porridge. Perhaps today wouldn't be so bad after all.

'Where's Ron?' she asked as the girls bustled out to get on with their day.

'He must have gone out early,' said Peggy as she warmed a bottle for Daisy. 'Why, was there something you wanted him to do? Can I help?'

Cordelia hastily shook her head. 'I was merely curious,' she said. 'He doesn't usually miss his breakfast – and it's unlike him not to take Harvey.'

As if on cue, Harvey scrambled off the rug in front of the fire and dashed to the cellar door. Whining, he danced on his toes, his tail windmilling as the garden door slammed and Ron's heavy tread could be heard coming up the steps. As the door opened, Harvey leaped up, front feet on Ron's shoulders as he licked his face in delight.

'Will yer get down, you daft eejit,' he protested as he dodged the tongue and tried to get through the door. 'Lord love you, Harvey, anyone would think I've been away for days.'

'And where exactly *have* you been?' asked Peggy as she put Daisy on her lap and gave her the bottle of formula milk.

'We had an overnight exercise with the Home Guard,' he said as he took off his tin hat and dumped the hessian bag on a nearby chair.

'You seem to have those quite regularly,' she said dryly. 'Are you sure you haven't got some woman tucked away?'

He looked at her in amazement. 'Lord love you, Peggy girl – and what would I be doing with another woman when I have me Rosie?'

She regarded him levelly for a moment. 'Well, you've been up to something,' she said finally, 'and if it's not another woman, then it must be mischief. Just for goodness' sake don't get into trouble with the police. I have enough on my plate without having to get you out of a prison cell.'

Ron chuckled and filled a bowl with porridge. He sat down at the table, poured a cup of tea and began to eat. 'There'll be no prison and no police,' he said, 'and I'm old enough to stay out all night if I want to. Don't worry about me, Peggy girl. I'll not bring trouble to your door.'

Peggy finished feeding Daisy and deposited her in the playpen, then she went upstairs to check that the girls had stripped their beds properly so she could do the laundry.

'I have good news,' Ron said quietly as Peggy's footsteps could be heard on the upstairs landing.

Cordelia leaned closer so she could hear him properly, and when he'd finished, she grasped his hand thankfully. 'That's wonderful, Ron,' she said. 'How soon do you think we'll hear whether they're on their way here, or have stayed in South Africa?'

'My friend didn't say, but I would imagine they'd be in touch fairly quickly if they were wanting a place to stay here.'

Cordelia could feel her face going pink as he looked into her eyes and patted her hand. 'I must start organising their rooms just in case,' she twittered, all of a dither. 'Thank you, Ron.'

'Now, you're not to be upset if they've decided to stay in Cape Town,' he warned.

'Oh, I won't,' she said happily. 'Not now I know they're alive.'

Chapter Eighteen

The journey south seemed to take for ever. The seats were hard and uncomfortable, making it almost impossible to sleep, and there always seemed to be a baby crying somewhere or a toddler demanding attention. It was also frustrating not to be able to see out of the windows, and the stifling darkness soon became claustrophobic.

Jane eventually fell asleep, her head resting on Sarah's shoulder as the train chugged and chuffed and rattled along the rails with a gentle sway. But for Sarah, plagued by the worry of what lay ahead, it was a very long, sleepless night.

Eventually there was a change in the rhythm of the wheels and the swaying lessened. They were slowing down. With the aid of the pale glimmer of light above her head, Sarah glanced at her watch and realised they must be nearing London, for it was almost five in the morning.

The women around her began to stir as if they too sensed that their journey was almost over, and as they woke their children and prepared for their arrival in London, there was a tangible sense of excitement. Many of them had relatives living in London or the suburbs;

some had people in Kent and Surrey; others would have to take another train and head further west. But the knowledge that they were nearing journey's end seemed to give them added energy, and as they queued to use the lavatory and checked that everything was packed away, their voices rose in excitement.

Sarah nudged her sister awake and stood to stretch her tired, stiff limbs. The hours of sitting about had made her feel cold again, and she pulled on the coat, beret and gloves and wrapped the lovely soft scarf around her neck. The slightly unpleasant fug of too many people packed into a tight space was giving her a woozy head, and she was looking forward to fresh air and a bit of exercise to chase away the feeling of being stifled.

The train was going even more slowly now, the wheels clanking over the rails as the steam and smoke puffed more laboriously. Everyone was standing, reaching for cases and parcels, pulling on coats and hats, rounding up children and comforting babies.

Sarah pulled their cases from the overhead rack and handed Jane her gas-mask box. 'We're almost there,' she said, 'so when the train stops, let the others off first. I don't want to lose you in the crush.'

'Honestly, Sarah,' sighed Jane. 'I'm not a child, you know.'

Sarah smiled at her. 'Of course you're not,' she said, 'but humour me, Jane. We must stick together, otherwise *I* might get lost, and then where would we be?'

Jane grinned. 'I know we have to catch a train down

to Cliffehaven, and I'm sure a porter could point me in the right direction. If we do get separated, then I'll meet you by that train.'

Sarah digested this piece of wisdom and wondered if Jane's experiences over the past few months had somehow helped her to reason better now she didn't have her parents and Amah to fuss over her and make all her decisions. There had been fewer tantrums, certainly, and she'd knuckled down well into the routine of the ship, showing a much more adult and quieter side than ever before. Perhaps the doctors had been wrong – for Jane seemed to be slowly picking up the scattered pieces of her lost years and putting them together again in a coherent and mature order.

Sarah didn't have time to mull over this thought, for the train had come to a halt, and there was a flurry of activity as everyone tried to cram into the aisle and get to the door. She checked they both had their cases and gas-mask boxes and that they'd left nothing behind before she took her sister's hand and slowly joined the end of the shuffling crush. There were tearful goodbyes and promises to stay in touch, but the one thought that consumed them all was the feeling of having arrived at last.

They stepped down onto the platform and were instantly surrounded by the confusion of rushing people and deafening noise. Train whistles blew, steam billowed, and men and women scurried around piles of kitbags and suitcases, while children wailed and voices were raised to be heard above the unintelligible announcements that blared into the great, echoing building from several loudspeakers.

Soldiers, airmen and sailors in the uniforms of many Allied countries stood in huddles or marched purposefully past porters who pushed laden trolleys and shouted to one another. Women and children gathered in groups, greeting or saying goodbye to their loved ones as steam hissed and shrill whistles blew. Girls in uniform hurried importantly across the vast concourse, while others stood about gossiping by the refreshment room, sipping tea and smoking cigarettes as they pretended not to notice the admiring glances and wolf whistles from a group of passing Australian soldiers.

Sarah and Jane took all this in as they approached a young woman in the black uniform and peaked hat of the railway company who pointed out where they should go next.

'Thank goodness for the ladies of the WVS,' murmured Jane as they headed for the wonderfully familiar sight of green uniforms and a makeshift canteen. 'I never realised how big and confusing the station would be.'

Sarah was of the same opinion, and she was grateful for the clasp of her sister's hand as they crossed the concourse and joined their fellow travellers. They were fewer in number now, and even as they accepted a very welcome cup of tea and dry biscuit, they could see some of their friends being greeted by relieved relatives and bustled away. Those who were familiar with London had already left, and Sarah was beginning to fret that they might miss their connecting train.

Their names were called and they pushed their way to the front of the gathering. A middle-aged woman greeted them with a rather distracted smile as she ticked them off on her clipboard and handed them their rail passes. 'There is a bus waiting outside that door over there, which will take you to Victoria Station,' she explained. 'Your train is scheduled to leave at noon – although if there's an air raid, or the lines are up, it might be a bit delayed.' She shot them a smile. 'Don't worry. You'll get used to delays – there is a war on, you know.'

This seemed to be the stock explanation for most things, and Sarah smiled back at her. 'How long will it take to get to Cliffehaven?'

'About an hour and a half – unless there's a hold-up somewhere down the line. Do you have people waiting for you at the other end?'

'We're not sure,' Sarah admitted. 'But we do have two addresses to go to.'

The woman frowned. 'That area has suffered a fair bit of air-raid damage being so close to the Channel, and some people have had to move out of their homes and find billets elsewhere. If you have any problems, then go straight to the nearest WVS homing centre. They will help find you accommodation and so on.'

Sarah hadn't thought about the great-aunts having to move out, but she smiled her thanks, shifted the gas-mask box and handbag straps more firmly over her shoulder and picked up her case. 'Come on, Jane,' she said with studied cheerfulness, 'we can't afford to miss that bus.'

They walked through the milling crowd and eventually found their way out to where a double-decker bus stood by the kerb with its destination written on a large piece of card that had been propped inside the windscreen. Another WVS woman was waiting to check their travel passes, and she bossily ordered them on board as if they were schoolchildren.

Staring through the grimy window, Sarah got the impression that London had been bleached of any colour, for wherever she looked there was nothing to gladden the heart – nothing vibrant or exotic to catch the eye. Even the people looked dowdy in their black, brown and navy blue as they picked their way over the scattered remnants of shattered buildings beneath a leaden sky, their faces wan, their eyes downcast as if they couldn't bear to look at their surroundings.

The few surviving trees had a pale fuzz of new growth, but even that was coated in dust. Vast silver barrage balloons swayed above the colourless rooftops and piles of rubble that had once been buildings. Stacks of grubby sandbags guarded dark, gloomy doorways where men in black bowler hats with tightly furled umbrellas and briefcases dashed in and out. Skeletons of houses lay open to the elements revealing ash-coated furniture, ragged curtains and dun-coloured walls. There were grey pigeons pecking at the cracks in the broken pavements and dusty brown sparrows darted between hurrying feet in search of food.

Sarah blinked away her tears as a wave of home-sickness overwhelmed her. How she longed for the verdant jungles of Malaya where the birds were painted every colour of the rainbow and the flowers blossomed in gaudy, riotous brilliance, where the azure sky was matched only by the sea – and the beautiful saris of Amah and the other native women took on the vibrant hues of their tropical surroundings.

'It's all right,' murmured Jane. 'We'll soon be at the seaside, and it's bound to be nicer than this.'

Sarah squeezed her fingers, grateful for her comfort, but the woman in the station had said Cliffehaven had been hit by air raids – were they simply leaving one grey place for another? The thought was deeply depressing, and the longing for home, for family and for Philip weighed heavy on her heart.

The journey across a battered and fractured London was something of an eye-opener, for although Sarah and Jane had witnessed the effects of the heavy bombing raids in Singapore, they'd seen nothing like this. A shocked silence fell amongst the passengers as it slowly dawned on them that this once beautiful city had been ravaged by the years of war, and that although they had managed to escape the Japanese they now had to encounter another formidable enemy.

Delicate church spires tentatively poked their heads above the blackened ruins of houses, tenements and shops. Whole streets had been flattened, roads had been pitted and holed from bomb-blasts, and nearly every window had been boarded up. Tarpaulins were stretched across roofs; chimneys had toppled leaving remnants behind like broken teeth. Parks had been turned into vegetable plots; deep trenches offered dubious shelter during air-raids; and where there had once been ornate gates and railings there were only scarred pillars.

But Sarah realised that although there was no colour in London, there was a vibrant spirit which manifested itself in the defiant messages that had been plastered on walls and taped into shop windows. 'Open despite Hitler', said one. 'We're with you, Churchill', proclaimed another – and written on the wall below a boarded-up butcher's was 'Called up OHMS. Back as soon as we beat Hitler.'

Sarah returned Jane's rather wan smile, but there was nothing either of them could say that would relieve the awful sickness for home, so they sat hand in hand, lost in their own separate thoughts until they reached Victoria Station.

Yet another woman from the WVS was waiting for their group, and she led them into the large concourse where they were once more assailed by noise and an endless stream and eddy of hurrying people. Their travel passes were checked again and they were directed to the appropriate platforms for their destinations.

Jane said goodbye to the small children she'd helped to teach, while Sarah exchanged addresses and promises to write with the women. And then they were alone, waiting on the platform, their cases at their feet where the chill wind blew down the platform and stirred dust and bits of rubbish into tiny whirlwinds.

Sarah was just congratulating herself on how easy the journey had been so far when she heard the all-too-familiar shriek of the air-raid siren.

'Where do we go?' said Jane fearfully. 'What do we do?'

'We follow everybody else,' said Sarah. 'Grab your things and don't forget your gas-mask box.' She saw how everyone was making a beeline for one particular place and took Jane's hand. 'Stay close and don't let go of me,' she shouted above the terrible noise of the sirens.

They found themselves at the top of a flight of steep steps which disappeared into a dark tunnel. There was no turning back, for they were trapped in the crush of hundreds of people. Holding tightly to one another and their few possessions, they were almost carried down the steps and then deeper and deeper under the ground.

Sarah could hear the rumble and hiss of a train and felt the vibrations under her feet as it raced through the darkness nearby. She was terrified and knew Jane must be too, but they had no choice but to be swept along with the crowd.

As they reached the bottom of yet another long flight of stairs, the crowd thinned and the crush lessened as people began to disperse through the numerous tunnels that seemed to stretch in every direction. Disorientated and frightened, the sisters clung together. What were they meant to do? Where were they supposed to go now?

A portly man wearing a dark uniform and a determined expression came up to them. 'C'mon, girls, you can't stand about 'ere gettin' in the bleedin' way,' he shouted above the noise, his Cockney accent making it almost impossible for them to understand him. 'Shift yerselves and find a place on the bleedin' platform.'

'Where is the platform?' asked Jane nervously.

'Strike a light, you ain't gotta bleedin' clue, 'ave yer, darlin'?' he said as he scratched his balding head and adjusted his warden's cap. He took Jane's arm rather roughly and dragged her towards one of the tunnels. 'Over 'ere. Find a space and stay put until the bleedin' all-clear sounds.'

Jane glared at him as she wrenched her arm from his grip. 'I do *not* appreciate being manhandled,' she said imperiously.

He threw back his head and laughed. 'Bleedin' 'ell, love, you'll get more'n man'andling if Gerry drops 'is bombs on yer head.' He wandered off, still chuckling.

'What a horrid man,' muttered Jane as she brushed his dirty handprint from her coat sleeve. 'No porter in Malaya would *dare* touch me like that.'

'This isn't Malaya, and he's not a porter.' The cultured tones came from an elegantly dressed woman who was sitting on her suitcase by the tunnel entrance. She smiled up at them, her ageing face still bearing a faded reminder of her youthful beauty. 'Welcome to the London Underground,' she continued. 'If I squeeze up a bit, there's plenty of room to sit here.'

'Thank you,' said Sarah. She and Jane introduced themselves and perched on their cases, aware of the filthy floor which would damage their lovely new coats.

'Lucinda Sutton-Smythe,' said their companion. 'This might not be the most salubrious of surroundings, but it is considered one of the safest.' She smiled and patted Jane's hand. 'The ARP warden was only doing his job, dear. He meant no harm.'

She fitted a cigarette into an ivory holder, lit it and blew a stream of smoke towards the tunnel roof. 'My husband and I were in India for many years,' she continued, 'so I do understand why you objected to his mauling, but in times like these one has to forgive a certain lack of finesse.'

'He startled me, that's all,' said Jane as she gazed in wide-eyed wonder at the great crush of people sprawled from one end of the platform to the other.

Sarah could see chairs and beds set up at the far end, as though people were permanently camping down here, and everyone looked quite happy and settled as the siren continued to shriek above ground. She didn't like being buried so deeply – hated the sooty smell that was interlaced with the stink of sweat and much worse.

'How long will we have to stay down here?' she asked fearfully.

'For as long as it takes the Luftwaffe to shed their

bombs on poor old London,' said Lucinda. She regarded them with interest. 'You both seem far too tanned to have lived through an English winter,' she said dryly. 'I'm guessing you've just arrived on one of the convoys from the Far East. Why don't you tell me what it was like? It might take your mind off the raid.'

As Jane began to talk about their home in Malaya and their dash to Singapore, Sarah was astonished by how calm Lucinda and everyone else in the tunnel was, for she could now hear the rumbling of enemy planes overhead, and felt the vibrations of the exploding bombs tremble through the walls of the tunnel. Dust sifted down from the arched ceiling, and loosened tiles fell off the walls, but no one seemed to notice and simply carried on reading their newspapers or chatting as if this was just another ordinary day.

Realising how tense she was, Sarah eased her neck and loosened her grip on her handbag and gas-mask box. There was a certain sense of fatalism about sitting down here while the enemy dropped bombs – and she could hear it in the defiant song that had been started further down the track, and the happy laughter of several children who were playing hopscotch on the platform. If they were going to die, then they'd go out singing. It seemed one had to be stoic in England, to deal with the inconveniences and fears that haunted each day, and put on a brave face. But it was going to be an awfully hard lesson to learn.

The all-clear sounded over an hour later and they

slowly climbed back up the endless stairs to the station. The smell of burning was strong and there was a heavy layer of smoke blotting out the weak sun as fire engines and ambulances roared down the road, their bells ringing frantically to clear the way.

They said goodbye to Lucinda, who was on her way to Bournemouth to live with her sister, and headed back to their platform. Their train was delayed by at least another hour until repairs could be done to the lines.

'I'm hungry,' said Jane as they wandered back onto the concourse and she eyed the refreshment room longingly. 'Do you think we could have some breakfast?'

Sarah's stomach reminded her that they'd had nothing but biscuits since their last lunch on board the *Monarch*. She thought about the sandwiches which were still in her pocket, decided she couldn't face them no matter how hungry she was, and quickly dropped them into a nearby rubbish bin. Luckily, the grease hadn't ruined her coat.

'Pops managed to change some of our Malay dollars into British pounds, so as long as it isn't too expensive, we can find something to eat.' They smiled at each other, and feeling rather more cheerful, headed across the concourse in search of the traditional English breakfast of sausage, bacon and eggs that they'd heard so much about.

The refreshment room was painted an unappetising brown and cream; the floor had been covered in some sort of shiny, rubbery material that had worn right through in places; and the wooden tables and chairs bore the scars of years of wear. The overall smell was of old pipe and cigarette smoke laced with cheap perfume, stewed tea and burnt toast.

The woman who stood behind the high wooden counter had her hair covered with a knotted scarf, and her broad frame and large bosom were wrapped in some sort of flowery overall. She seemed to be deep in conversation with the lady at the end of the counter, and didn't look at all pleased to have her gossip interrupted.

'I can do you tea and toast, or a coupl'a sandwiches,' she replied to Sarah's query about breakfast. 'Eggs is orf, and of course bacon and sausage ain't been seen since Hitler mucked things up.'

'What's in the sandwiches?' asked Sarah warily.

'I can do you a round of spam with tomato sauce, or a round of corned beef with mustard.'

'I think we'll just have toast and tea.' She passed over a precious pound note.

The woman looked at it askance. 'Ain't you got nothing smaller?' At Sarah's apologetic shake of the head, she heaved a great sigh and scrabbled in her till, muttering about people having no idea how hard it was to get change – and didn't they realise there was a war on.

The tea was as weak as dishwater, and the toast had the merest hint of the infamous margarine smeared over it. There was no jam, and no sugar to put into the tea, and by the time they'd finished this meagre breakfast, they were still hungry.

They went back onto the concourse and Sarah bought a newspaper and a packet of Park Drive cigarettes. Then they settled down amid the ebb and flow of people while they waited for their train to be announced. Jane read the newspaper from cover to cover while Sarah lit a cigarette and tried not to think about how late it was getting. If the train didn't arrive soon they would get to Cliffehaven in the dark, and the great-aunts might already be in bed.

'Which aunt should we try first?' she asked Jane some time later.

'Cordelia,' said Jane. 'She's the younger of the two, and will probably be more likely to take us in.'

Once again, Sarah was surprised by Jane's mature good sense. She nodded and was about to reply when the announcement came over the loudspeaker. Their train had arrived. She stubbed out her cigarette, helped Jane gather her things and headed for the platform.

Their second-class carriage was very different to the one they'd had on the Glasgow train, and far more comfortable. There were two rows of four padded seats facing one another in the compartment, with luggage racks overhead and antimacassars on the headrests. The windows had blackout blinds but hadn't been boarded over, and could be opened by pulling on a leather strap, and there was a sliding door to shut out the draught that whistled along the corridor.

Settled on either side of the window, they

looked forward to actually seeing something of the countryside they would be passing through. And as other passengers joined them in the carriage they were relieved to see they weren't once again surrounded by squalling babies and fractious toddlers.

Then the guard blew his whistle and the train began to pull away from the station. They were on their way.

Soon the chugging train was crossing the Thames, and they both leaned forward eagerly to try and catch sight of the famous bridges and the Houses of Parliament. Then they were plunged into endless suburbs, where row upon row of terraced houses backed onto the railway embankments. Everything was unrelentingly gloomy, with soot-stained bricks, dreary backyards, untended gardens and abandoned bomb sites over which great palls of grey smoke swirled from the many chimneys.

They sat back in their seats, disappointed by the view, and while Jane dozed, Sarah smoked another cigarette and read the newspaper. That was all doom and gloom too, and she gave up on it with a sigh of frustration.

But as the train travelled further south the carriage emptied and the scenery changed. Now there were rolling fields, rivers and streams and tiny leafy hamlets. Little villages with ancient stone churches and thatched-roof cottages followed small, neat towns where the gardens had been turned to vegetable plots and bomb damage had been minor. Then there were great sweeps of forest and patchwork fields around isolated farms where huge, plodding Shires pulled ploughs and heavily laden wagons as flocks of birds trailed them.

'Oh, how lovely,' breathed Jane. 'I wish I could ride one of those. They look so gentle, so patient.' She turned to Sarah, her eyes glistening with tears. 'I do miss my poor Trixie. It wasn't her fault she fell over that fence and caught me with her hoof – I shouldn't have forced her to jump it when I knew she was so nervous.'

Sarah was startled by this declaration, for it was the first time Jane had ever mentioned the awful fall she'd taken when out riding four years before – and her parents had decreed that it must never be mentioned. 'I didn't realise you remembered what happened,' she said carefully.

'It's come back bit by bit – and of course I realise poor Trixie hadn't been sold like Pops told me. She must have broken her leg and been put down.' She was silent for a long moment as she continued to gaze out of the window, and the labourers stopped what they were doing and waved to the train. 'Those are girls,' she said breathlessly as she waved back. 'I wonder if they'd let me do that sort of work so I could be with the horses again?'

'I don't know,' Sarah replied hesitantly. 'Mother and Pops certainly wouldn't want you anywhere near horses. You'd have to be very strong and fit to take care of such big animals, and it looks like extremely hard work. Those girls are probably farmers' daughters and used to the life.'

'Maybe,' murmured Jane, 'but I saw a poster at the station, asking for women to join the Land Army. It didn't say anything about having to be a farmer's daughter – and Pops did look after trees, so that must count, surely?'

'We'll see,' Sarah replied non-committally. Her parents had laid down strict rules about Jane being kept away from horses, and although Sarah understood their well-meaning concern, she thought the ruling was harsh. Jane had always loved horses, was a competent rider and knew how to look after them – from what she'd just said it was clear she'd really missed not being around them.

An hour later and the scenery changed again, with huge stretches of marsh which were alive with birds, and fields where great flocks of sheep roamed. Farmhouses huddled close to where the hills were scarred with chalk and gulls hovered in the darkening sky above a glittering sea. They must be getting close to Cliffehaven.

The train chuffed into the station, where it was clear the enemy bombers had done their best to destroy every last bit of the station buildings. Clambering down to the platform, they hurried away from the clouds of steam and smoke and stood by the strange-looking hut that had 'Ticket Office' painted on the corrugated iron roof.

Breathing deeply of the refreshing salty air, they

looked to the bottom of the long hill and saw the sheen of the sea and felt revived. Cliffehaven might look very different to Singapore and Kuala Lumpur, but it wasn't dowdy at all despite the bomb damage, for there were trees bursting with blossom, white-painted houses and red roofs.

'Evening, girls,' said the elderly stationmaster. 'You look like you don't come from these parts. How can I help you?'

'We're looking for Havelock Road,' said Sarah, checking on the address.

'Nice for some,' he said enigmatically. He pointed down the hill. 'Go almost to the bottom of the High Street, and then take the last road on your right. You can't miss it. Havelock Gardens is on the corner, with a park on the other side, and if you go any further you'll be in the English Channel.'

Sarah thanked him and tucked the precious bit of paper back into her handbag before they began to walk down the steep hill. There were several bomb sites along the way, but there were also shops and a couple of places that looked like the pubs she'd heard about from her friends who'd visited England. A rather imposing Town Hall was protected by a wall of sandbags, as was a bank and a block of offices. It all felt very strange and rather daunting, for it was so different to anything she'd ever known, and she just hoped that they could find their feet quickly and be able to settle until it was time to go home again.

They continued down the hill, past another huge

bomb site, and the almost empty window of a large department store called Plummers. There was a shop called the Home and Colonial, which appeared to sell tinned food as well as other things, and a recruiting office for the RAF. The smell of the sea was very strong now, and they could hear the seagulls crying on the light wind which ruffled the waves, and see the barbed-wire barricades that had been erected all along the promenade.

'There's the park,' said Jane. 'Come on, we must nearly be there. I do hope Aunt Cordelia's in. I'm absolutely starving.'

It was certainly a very pleasant area, for there were trees and pretty gardens behind the high walls, and on the other side of the road was the park, which looked very green and tranquil in the swiftly fading light. Sarah looked at the numbers on the houses and came to an abrupt halt. Number thirty-nine and its neighbour had been obliterated.

'Perhaps the neighbours can tell us if the old lady got out alive,' said Jane hopefully. 'I'll go and ask, shall I?'

'We'll do it together,' said Sarah, trying her hardest not to show what an awful blow it had been. But there was no answer at number thirty-five, and it looked to Sarah as if it had been locked up for the duration, for every curtain was closed, and there was a padlock on the garage door.

The lady at number forty-one was very sympathetic, but didn't know anyone called Cordelia Fuller. She knew only that the family at number thirty-nine had lived there for some years and the mother had taken her children to the West Country while her husband was away with the Army.

Sarah swallowed her disappointment and thanked her before asking the way to Mafeking Terrace. It turned out to be some way to the north of the town, beyond the park and right beneath the towering hill that overlooked Cliffehaven. With heavy hearts they began to trudge back the way they had come.

Mafeking Terrace was a narrow cul-de-sac which was almost lost in a maze of similar streets that wound along the bottom of the hill and afforded the residents an excellent distant view of the seafront. Every red-brick bungalow looked the same, with a sloping roof over two heavily taped front windows and a short cinder path leading to a sturdy wooden door in which a circle of stained glass had been embedded. There was no real front garden, just a scrap of lawn and a small flower bed. 'Sea Vista' was halfway down.

Sarah took a deep breath, walked up the path and rapped the brass knocker. There was a flicker of movement behind the lace curtains at the nearest window, and Sarah grinned at Jane. 'At least someone's at home,' she murmured. 'Let's hope it's Aunt Amelia.'

But there was no sound of approaching footsteps – in fact there was utter silence. Puzzled, Sarah rapped the knocker again, and after another long moment of nothing happening, dared to push the letter box open just enough so she could see into the hall.

Her pulse began to race as she realised the occupant was standing in an open doorway at the end of the narrow hall. She could only conclude that the old lady must be frightened to open her door to strangers, and peering through her letter box was surely only making her even more nervous.

'Hello?' she called. 'Great Aunt Amelia Fuller? It's Sarah and Jane Fuller from Malaya. We didn't mean to frighten you, but do you think you could let us in?'

'Go away and leave me alone.' The voice came from the depths of the bungalow and was far from pleasant.

Sarah and Jane looked at one another in shock. 'She must have misheard,' muttered Jane. 'Try again.'

'Great Aunt Amelia, we're sorry to disturb you,' called Sarah. 'Didn't you get my father's telegram? His name's Jock Fuller, and his father was your brother, Charles.'

There was no response, so Sarah tentatively pushed the letter box open again. 'We've got nowhere else to go, Aunt Amelia. Please let us in,' she begged.

'If you don't leave my property I shall call the police. Now be off with you.'

Sarah stepped back in shock at her vehemence. 'Will you at least tell us how to find Aunt Cordelia?' she ventured. 'Is she still alive and living in Cliffehaven?'

There was the sound of a slamming door. If that old witch really was Great Aunt Amelia, then she clearly had nothing else to say.

'What shall we do?' asked Jane fearfully. 'It's getting late and it'll soon be dark.'

Sarah was close to tears, but she couldn't let Jane see how furious she was with that horrid old woman – and how frightened she was not having anywhere else to go. 'We'll go back to the High Street and see if there's someone at the Town Hall. I seem to remember seeing a WVS sign outside.'

'Hello, dear. Can I help you?' They both turned at the sound of the voice coming from the next bungalow's doorway. The speaker was a pleasant-faced elderly woman who came out to her garden gate to speak to them.

'We thought our Aunt Amelia Fuller lived next door to you,' explained Sarah, 'but we were obviously mistaken.'

The elderly woman shook her head. 'Oh, that was Amelia all right,' she muttered, 'but she's as mean as they come, and if she thinks you want something then she clams up.' She eyed their suitcases. 'I heard you say you've just arrived from Malaya.'

Time was of the essence, and Sarah didn't really want to get into a long explanation, even though this old lady seemed very pleasant. 'That's right,' she said, 'and we've been trying to get in touch with Amelia and her sister Cordelia. I don't suppose you know where we could find Cordelia? Only it appears that her house has been bombed.'

'I'm sorry, dears, but I don't get out much any more, so I've rather lost track of everyone. I remember Cordelia, though, nice little body.' She grimaced as she glanced to the bungalow next door. 'Not like her sister at all.' She thought for a moment and then shook her head. 'I seem to remember Cordelia moved into a boarding house with a local family after her husband died,' she murmured, 'but I can't for the life of me remember their name.'

Sarah felt a twinge of hope. 'What was her married name?'

The old lady frowned as she struggled to remember. 'Something like Sparrow or Thrush or Swallow.' She shook her head in frustration. 'I'm sorry, I've not been much help, have I?'

'You've been very kind, thank you,' said Jane.

'I'd offer you a bed for the night, but I already have two evacuees living in and simply don't have the room,' she said worriedly. 'I do hope you find Cordelia, and when you do, give her my regards. It's Olive Farmer.'

'Thank you, Mrs Farmer, we'll do that.' They hastily moved away before she could prolong the conversation and trudged their weary way back to the Town Hall. All the shops were closed now, and when they arrived, it was to discover there was no one from the WVS to welcome them and that every spare inch of space had been taken up with beds, baggage, prams and squalling children.

They stood with their suitcases at their feet in utter despair and bewilderment until a little woman in a wrap-round apron approached them with a screaming baby in her arms.

'It's all right, ducks,' she said after they'd told her their plight. 'No need to look so down in the mouth. I'll find you a couple of blankets and you can bed down in the Mayor's parlour for the night. He doesn't need it until tomorrow anyway.'

She gave them a cheerful wink and they followed her to the store cupboard, which she unlocked, and then she handed them two blankets and pillows. 'You're supposed to sign for them,' she confided in a stage whisper, 'but the office is locked, and I reckon you look honest enough.'

Sarah and Jane took the bedding and followed her into the Mayor's parlour, which was a sharp contrast to the crowded, echoing room they'd just come from. 'Thank you so much,' breathed Jane. 'You're a real lifesaver.'

The woman shrugged. 'In times like these we all need an 'and now and again,' she replied cheerfully. 'Just remember to be out of here by eight – the Mayor likes to make an early start.' She cocked her head and looked them up and down. 'This is a one-off,' she warned. 'You'll have to go to the authorities and get a proper billet in the morning.'

'Is there anywhere we can buy something to eat?' asked Jane.

'Yeah, there's a chippy just up the road. He'll do you a nice spam fritter if you ask him with a smile.'

After she'd closed the door behind her the sisters looked at one another and giggled. 'It looks as if we're going to have to get used to the awful spam if we're not to die of starvation,' said Jane.

'At least we've got somewhere to stay for tonight,'

said Sarah. 'Come on, help me push these heavy chairs together so we can make them like beds. And look, there's a gas fire. We can even have a bit of warmth as well.'

They pushed the chairs end to end and placed the blankets and pillows on them before trying to work out how to get the gas fire going. After a bit of experimentation they discovered it took sixpences, and were soon bathed in a satisfying warmth.

Sarah left Jane by the fire and ventured out again to find the mysterious chippy. She didn't really know what she was looking for, and then she smelled the mouth-watering aroma of frying fat and vinegar wafting towards her and saw the queue of people waiting. The taped window was steamed up but she could see the menu, and it appeared that chips and spam fritters were not the only thing on offer, and her spirits rose at the thought of some lovely fish.

Yet, as she stood patiently in the queue and listened in to the orders of those in front of her, she realised there wasn't any fish or sausages to be had. Like it or loathe it, spam was her only option.

Having overheard the way to ask for two fritters and something called mushy peas, with tuppenceworth of chips, she clutched the unfamiliar small change in her hand and managed to sound quite confident as she asked for an added splash of vinegar, a bit of salt and a pickled onion. Her mouth was watering so much she could barely speak, and once their supper had been carefully wrapped in newspaper, she put the right money on the counter and ran back to the Town Hall.

'It will probably taste better in batter,' she said to Jane as she unwrapped the newspaper and spread it on the floor.

'I don't care,' replied Jane, her mouth already full of golden potato chips. 'I'm so hungry I could eat shoe leather.'

The batter was crisp and golden around the thick slice of spam, and they dunked this greasy offering in the little paper twist of lurid green mashed peas, and shared the pickled onion. It was as good as a feast, even though they were eating with their fingers out of newspaper. Their mother would have had a fit if she could have seen them now.

But, in a way, it was all a part of this strange and rather wonderful adventure they were having. Although they were homeless and Aunt Amelia had proved to be a beastly old curmudgeon, they had temporary shelter and warmth and food in their stomachs – and were actually quite enjoying themselves.

Chapter Nineteen

'Oh, do look,' said Cordelia excitedly, 'there are pictures in the newspaper of the women and children arriving on the ships in Scotland.'

Peggy spooned a bit of porridge into Daisy's mouth and scanned the rather blurred photographs. 'There are certainly a lot of them,' she replied, 'and that's just one ship. But at least it looks as if they've been given a warm welcome.'

'The article says the *Monarch* docked two days ago, but there's no list of the passengers.' She put on her glasses and took a closer look at the hundreds of people who were lining the decks and gave a deep sigh. 'I don't know why I'm trying to find them,' she said as she closed the paper. 'It's impossible to see any faces, and I have no idea what they look like anyway.'

'We'll no doubt get a telegram at some point,' said Peggy as she finished feeding Daisy and went to warm her bottle of milk. 'Perhaps we should make a start on their rooms when I get back from the Town Hall?'

'You do enough,' replied Cordelia. 'I'll make the beds and dust around this morning. If there's anything heavy to lift, I'll ask Ron to help me.' She set the newspaper aside and sipped her tea, her expression thoughtful. 'They're going to find things very different here,' she mused, 'what with the weather, the different money and all the restrictions on travel and food and everything. I do hope they don't get lost.'

Peggy tested the heat of the milk on the back of her hand before giving it to Daisy, but her mind was elsewhere. She'd had a sudden dreadful thought and wondered how on earth neither of them had had it before. The telegrams had gone to Cordelia's old house and to her sister's – but Amelia had made it clear she would have nothing to do with her brother's family, and Cordelia's house was a bomb site. Sybil and her daughters would have no way of discovering where Cordelia was – for the telegram had been sent to Miss Cordelia Fuller.

'What's the matter, Peggy? Why are you frowning?'

Peggy shook off the worrying thoughts and gave her a bright smile. 'Nothing,' she said, 'just thinking about all the things I need to do today.' She couldn't discuss this problem with Cordelia, who didn't know that her old place had been bombed, or that her sister had already nastily refused to have anything to do with Sybil or her daughters. This was something she had to deal with alone, but where on earth did she start?

'I'll clear up everything in here,' said Cordelia, 'and then make a start on the bedrooms. If they haven't decided to stay in South Africa, then they could be here within hours. It said in the paper that they left Glasgow the day they docked and took the night train to London. I wonder if we telephoned the station, Stan might be able to tell us if they've arrived.'

'That's a very good idea,' said Peggy. 'I'll ring as soon as Daisy's finished her breakfast. Stan knows all the locals, so he's bound to notice strangers.'

While Cordelia began to clear the table and start on the washing-up, Peggy finished feeding Daisy. Putting a clean bib over her clothes, she tucked her into the pram and wheeled it into the hall. Picking up the receiver, she waited for the operator to answer.

'Hello, Phyllis,' she said. 'It's Peggy. Could you please ring the station for me?'

The ringing tone went on and on, then Phyllis came back on the line. 'Stan must be working on his allotment,' she said. 'D'you want me to try him again in half an hour?'

'No, it's all right, Phyllis. I'll pop up there later.'

She went back into the kitchen. 'He's not answering,' she said, 'so I'll go up there before I start at the Town Hall.' Finishing the lukewarm cup of tea, she was about to help dry the dishes when the telephone rang. 'Maybe Phyllis managed to get hold of him after all,' she murmured.

'Hello there, me darlin' girl. How's things in Cliffehaven?'

'Jim,' she breathed, 'oh, Jim, what a lovely surprise. Are you coming home on leave?'

'No, me darlin',' he said sorrowfully. 'We're stuck up here for a while yet, and there'll be no embarkation leave for either of us. I'm sorry, Peg.'

'But that's not fair,' she protested. 'Everyone gets—'

'Peg, I don't have much time, so please listen. We've got our orders and I'll be going further north for a while – can't tell you where, but it is a Blighty posting, so you don't need to worry.'

The relief was tremendous and she slumped against the wall. 'Thank God,' she sighed. 'But what about Frank? Are you still together?'

'He's going to the Midlands, and will probably stay there for the duration. All I can tell you is we'll both be involved in repairing bridges and tracks. I'll write and tell you more soon.' The pips went. 'I love you, Peg,' he shouted down the line. 'Give Daisy a kiss for me and tell Da we're both fine and—'

Peggy clutched the receiver, hoping he might be able to get back on the line, but there was only the disconnected burr. She replaced the receiver and closed her eyes. At least he was safe, and wouldn't be sent off to some hellhole in Africa or the Far East. He would write soon and she'd know more. But, Lord, how she missed him. How hard it was to hear his voice from so far away and not be able to see him or touch him.

'I know it's difficult,' said Cordelia as she came into the hall and took her hand. 'But at least you've had the chance to talk to him – and I'm sure he'll try again when he can.'

Peggy blinked away the tears and did her best to be positive. 'Of course he will,' she replied, 'and he's promised to write, so I'll have an address of sorts for my own letters.' She took a deep breath and gently squeezed Cordelia's fingers. 'I'd better get on,' she said firmly. 'The day's going to be busy enough, without me standing about here feeling sorry for myself.'

An hour later Peggy was pushing the pram down the High Street to the Town Hall. Stan had been most helpful, describing in minute detail the two pretty young women who'd obviously come from abroad, and how they'd asked the way to Havelock Gardens. They'd sounded very posh, apparently, and he hadn't been at all surprised when they wanted that side of town. But he'd been adamant that there was no older woman with them. Peggy could only conclude that if it was Sarah and Jane, then their mother wasn't travelling with them – which meant they would be feeling very lost and alone. She just hoped to God they hadn't found the bombed-out house and gone in search of Amelia Fuller.

She parked the pram in the lee of the wall of sandbags outside the Town Hall and ran up the steps to find the WVS supervisor. 'I'll be a bit late starting today,' she said to the motherly Mavis Watkins, who seemed to have her hands full with a particularly belligerent mother who was demanding instant housing for her and her eight small children.

'I could do with you being here this morning,' Mavis said after she'd quelled the woman's demands and sent her off to the Billeting Office. 'We're short-staffed, and everyone seems to be in a foul mood today.'

'I'll only be about another hour,' said Peggy, and went on to explain her mission.

'Goodness, well of course you must find them,' said Mavis. 'Though they might have been here already, because I got some garbled message from Mrs Frost about two young women staying here overnight. I wasn't too happy about it, actually,' she confided. 'It seems they spent the night in the Mayor's parlour and didn't even sign for their blankets and pillows.'

'So you don't have a name for them?'

Mavis shook her head. 'Mrs Frost didn't think to ask, and there was no sign of them by the time I got here. Sorry, Peggy, but I have no idea where they could have gone. You could try the Labour Exchange, I suppose. They might be registering for ration books and things. And then of course they could be at the Billeting Office.'

'I'm not absolutely sure it is them,' Peggy confessed. 'But if a Sarah and Jane Fuller come in looking for help, will you please keep them here until I get back?'

'Don't worry, Peggy. I'll make sure they won't stray again if they do come back.'

Peggy hurried back out of the Town Hall and headed for the Labour Exchange. She didn't really think they would have gone there, but she had to make sure. She parked Daisy outside and went into the warm fug of a crowded room where endless lines of people waited to be seen. She scanned the many faces, hoping to spot two young women with tanned skin and brightly coloured berets and scarves – but all she could see were the wan Monday morning faces of harassed mothers, woebegone children and bewildered elderly men and women.

Having had no luck at the Billeting Office either, she decided to go to Havelock Road and ask if anyone had been approached by the girls. If they had gone there the previous evening and seen the destroyed house, then it was logical they would ask about the occupants.

Havelock Road was deserted as she pushed the pram along the pavement. She knew that several of the residents had moved out for the duration, but there were still some around, so she went from door to door in the hope someone might have spoken to them.

When she heard that two young women had been asking for Cordelia Fuller and that they had then asked the way to Mafeking Terrace, Peggy knew it had to be Sarah and Jane. Fearing that they would have been met with a less than friendly reception from Amelia, she hurried back up the hill and made her way along the cul-de-sac to the spinster's bungalow.

There was no reply to her knock, but she saw a twitching curtain in the next-door front window and guessed this was a nosy neighbour who probably knew everything that went on in Mafeking Terrace.

She was proved right, and within minutes Peggy was heading back down the hill towards the Town Hall. It was a good thing Amelia had not been at home, for if she had, Peggy would have given the mean-minded, nasty old cat more than just a piece of her mind.

She was exhausted by the time she got back to the

Town Hall, but there was no one around to help her with the pram. She dragged it step by step up to the door and pushed her way into the reception area. Once she'd parked Daisy alongside the other prams, she went in search of Mavis again.

'They haven't come back yet,' Mavis said, 'but I've asked everyone to keep an eye out for them. Mrs Frost has given us a good description, so at least we'll know them when we see them.'

'Thanks, Mavis. Now, if you don't mind, I'd like a cup of tea before I get started on those parcels.' She went into the canteen and sank onto a hard wooden chair, lit a cigarette and tried to relax. But her gaze remained on the door, her ears tuned to the many voices of the women around her as she sipped the welcome tea and wondered where on earth the girls could have gone.

Sarah and Jane had woken early, feeling stiff and cold after their night on the chairs. Their sixpences for the gas fire had run out shortly after they'd eaten their supper, and, not wanting to disturb anyone, they'd slept in their clothes beneath the thin blankets.

The Mayor's parlour looked rather shabby in the early light, and there was a strong smell of fried food and vinegar emanating from the newspaper, which they hoped he wouldn't notice. Having tidied away the chairs and disposed of their supper wrappings, they'd gone in search of the bathroom. But the Town Hall didn't provide such luxuries – only a couple of lavatories – and they were directed by one of the other women to the town baths which were situated down near the seafront.

They had never used a public bath before and had no idea what to expect. The building turned out to be long and narrow, with peeling paint and small windows heavily protected by metal slats. They paid their money to the elderly woman at the turnstile, collected a towel each and a sliver of rather dubious-looking soap, and found their appointed cubicles.

There were notices everywhere that water was restricted, and that only two inches were allowed. This rule appeared to be overseen by another woman, who stood by a large array of switches and wheels which seemed to regulate the water flow. No sooner had the bottom of the bath been covered than the wheels creaked into action and the water was stopped.

The cubicles left little room to manoeuvre. Wooden dividers gave some privacy, but the door didn't reach either the top of the divider, or the floor. A bitter draught whistled in from the entranceway which made the door rattle against the flimsy latch, and the rough concrete floor would be cold under their bare feet. The bath itself was a great white tub with clawed feet, and several large chips in the enamel – but it looked clean enough, despite the rust marks beneath the taps.

Sarah hurried to get undressed, putting her clothes on the wooden chair standing next to the bath. Once the water stopped flowing, she stepped in and washed as quickly as possible, her teeth chattering and her skin prickling with the cold.

'How are you getting on in there?' she called through the divider.

'I'm freezing to death,' replied Jane. 'I don't think this was such a good idea.'

'Me neither,' Sarah murmured. She used the thin scrap of towel to dry herself and fumbled to dress before she lost all feeling in her fingers and toes. 'We'll go and find some breakfast after this. A hot cup of tea or coffee will soon make us feel a bit better.'

'But we still have to find Aunt Cordelia,' said Jane, her voice muffled as she pulled on a sweater. 'We can't just wander about all day.'

Sarah had realised that, but she didn't really know how they'd ever find the old lady when they didn't even know her surname. 'We'll go back to the Town Hall,' she said decisively. 'The WVS people should be there by now, and they'll tell us what to do for the best.'

She sounded very sure of herself, but in fact she was extremely worried. If they didn't find Cordelia soon, they would have to bed down at the Town Hall again, for it was clear from the sheer numbers of people they'd seen last night that there were very few places to stay in Cliffehaven.

Wrapped warmly in their second-hand clothes, they gathered up their cases, gas-mask boxes and handbags, returned the damp towels and soap and went out into the bright spring day. But the sun was deceptive, for a brisk wind blew off the sea and seemed to find every inch of exposed skin. Ducking their heads and pulling up their collars, they hurried back up the High Street.

The Town Hall was seething with life, and Sarah wondered where on earth she should go to ask for help. There were long trestle tables groaning under the weight of clothes and shoes and household appliances; more tables where women were packing boxes with socks and tins and packets of cigarettes; and long lines of patient people waiting outside a door marked 'Almoner's Office'. Small children ran about, getting under everyone's feet and making enough noise to beat a band, and there were prams lined up against one wall, the occupants either asleep or wailing. Several harassed-looking women darted back and forth with clipboards clasped to dark green uniformed bosoms.

'There's a sort of canteen in that room over there,' said Jane as she pointed. 'Let's get a cup of tea and something to eat, and perhaps the lady behind the counter will tell us what to do.'

Sarah nodded, grasped her case and followed Jane into the slightly less noisy room at the back of the hall. Her stomach growled at the thought of food, and she realised that if spam was the only thing on offer, she would be glad to eat it.

The woman behind the counter was flushed in the face as she did battle with a vast tea urn, and she didn't look up as they approached her. 'I'll be with you in a minute,' she muttered. 'Only I've got a blockage in the tap, and can't seem to shift it.'

'Would you like me to help?' asked Jane.

'Bless you, dear, but no, I think that's got it.' The

woman looked up with a broad smile of achievement, and then gaped at them in surprise. 'Goodness me. Are you Sarah and Jane Fuller?'

'Yes,' said Jane with a frown. 'But how on earth do you know that?'

'Someone's been looking for you,' she replied delightedly, as she came round the counter. 'Come on, I'll take you to her.'

They were herded back towards the room where women were swiftly packing cardboard boxes with the piles of things laid out next to them. 'Those are comfort parcels for our boys who're fighting abroad,' the woman explained. 'Now where is . . .? Ah, there. Peggy!' she shouted above the cacophony. 'Peggy, look who I've found!'

Sarah saw a short, slender, dark-haired woman look up from the box she was packing, and watched in some confusion as the woman broke into a beaming smile and hurried towards them. She had no idea who she was, or why she'd been looking for them, but her smile was warm and she looked very friendly.

'Hello, dears,' she said breathlessly. 'I'm Peggy Reilly, and I've been so worried about you. I've spent half the morning going back and forth trying to find you, but you'd disappeared completely. Now, which one is which?'

'I'm Sarah, and this is Jane,' she replied, still puzzled by who this pleasant little woman could be. 'Are you a relative of our Great Aunt Cordelia?'

'Goodness,' said Peggy, 'here's me rattling on and

you've absolutely no idea who on earth I am.' She grinned delightedly at them. 'Cordelia Finch has been living at my boarding house for several years, and she'll be absolutely thrilled that you've made it here safely.'

Sarah was almost overwhelmed with relief. 'We thought we'd never find her. We've been all over the town asking about her, but without her married name, we realised fairly quickly we didn't stand much chance of tracking her down.'

'Well, we've found each other now, so you can relax.' Peggy reached for her coat and handbag. 'Let's get going before I'm given something else to do. It's not far to walk, and then we can all sit down and have a nice cup of tea while you tell us about yourselves and your journey.'

Sarah and Jane grinned at one another before they hurried after the bustling little figure who weaved her way through the melee to the other side of the room. 'I think she's lovely,' murmured Jane. 'We're very lucky to have found her.'

'Let's just hope Aunt Cordelia is as nice,' muttered Sarah, 'and not like that old dragon Amelia.'

Peggy turned and smiled at them. 'Amelia will get the sharp edge of my tongue, never you mind,' she said firmly, 'and you've nothing at all to worry about with Cordelia, she's an absolute treasure.'

'That's a relief,' said Jane. 'Amelia was simply horrid when we knocked on her door.'

'I know,' said Peggy. 'The neighbour told me.'

She stopped by one of the prams. 'This is Daisy,' she said as she proudly drew back the blanket. 'She's my youngest, and is just over three months old.'

Jane was delighted with Daisy, who was beginning to stir from her sleep. 'How lovely,' she cooed. 'Are your other children back at your house?'

Peggy laughed and shook her head. 'The two youngest boys are down in Somerset with their sister and my granddaughter, and my other daughter is in the WAAF, so rarely comes home any more. It's just me, my father-in-law Ron, Cordelia and my evacuee, Rita, and the two nurses Fran and Suzy now. My husband Jim was called up two weeks ago.'

Sarah noted how the smile faded somewhat, but the tilt of her chin remained determined. Peggy was obviously trying her best to be stoic. 'Let me help you get the pram down the steps,' she said.

'Thank you, dear.' Peggy's dark eyes regarded her as they reached the pavement. 'We were expecting your mother to come with you,' she said quietly. 'I do hope everything is all right with her?'

'We don't really know,' said Jane, her voice a little unsteady. 'She was in hospital with dengue fever when we had to leave Singapore. We were very worried about her because she was expecting a baby and the fever can be quite dangerous.' She took a deep breath. 'But Daddy promised he would get her on the next available ship – so she might turn up any time now with her new baby.'

'Goodness me,' breathed Peggy as her soft heart

went out to them. 'How awful for you all. Your poor father must have been worried sick.'

'I don't suppose there have been any letters or telegrams, have there?' asked Sarah. 'Only we have no idea if our parents or my fiancé managed to escape before Singapore fell.'

'I'm so sorry, my dears,' said Peggy, 'but there has been nothing – and of course the news bulletins don't tell us anything, really – only what Mr Churchill's government wants us to know.' She made a visible effort to remain cheerful. 'I'll inform the Post Office of your address so that if anything goes to either Mafeking Terrace or Havelock Road it will be redirected to Beach View. I'm sure you'll receive news any day now – and in the meantime we must get you settled.'

They walked on either side of her as she steered the pram down the High Street and eventually turned left into a road that seemed to wind its way east, parallel to the seafront.

'This is Camden Road,' explained Peggy. 'The council took all the road signs down at the beginning of the war to confuse the Germans if they invaded. It's the same at railway stations and all along the main roads.' She smiled back at them. 'I realise it must all seem very strange after living in the tropics, but you'll soon get used to things,' she reassured them.

'Does it ever get any warmer than this, Mrs Reilly?' asked Jane.

'You must both call me Peggy,' she said with a smile, 'and yes, in the summer it can get quite hot. Cliffehaven used to be a favourite spot for summer holidays, and we would have hundreds of visitors coming down to enjoy paddling in the sea and going on the pier. There was always a brass band playing, and candyfloss and toffee apple stalls all along the promenade, with deckchairs to sit in while you ate your fish and chips out of newspaper.'

'We had spam fritters and chips in newspaper last night,' said Jane. 'It tasted much better than the sandwiches they gave us in Scotland.'

'Have you eaten since then?' asked Peggy. As they shook their heads, she quickened her pace. 'In that case let's get home quickly and I can make you some lunch. I don't know what's in the larder, but there's bound to be something I can rustle up.'

'We heard about the rationing,' said Sarah. 'Is it very strict?'

'It has to be,' replied Peggy. 'Our little island depends upon the convoys to bring in our food as well as other essentials, and with Hitler's U-boats causing so much trouble, things are in very short supply. But not to worry, Ron usually has a rabbit or something for the pot, and his vegetable garden provides us with fresh spuds and cabbage and suchlike.'

Sarah and Jane exchanged glances. Neither of them had seen a rabbit outside a children's picture book, let alone eaten one, and the thought was unappealing. There were so many questions they wanted to ask, so many things they didn't understand. But as they hadn't expected to be accommodated in a boarding house, there was one question that Sarah knew must be answered before they moved in.

'We don't have a lot of money, Peggy,' she began. 'Our father made arrangements with the bank here, but there's no guarantee that the funds will have come through. We will of course both find jobs, but we might not be able to pay you rent until we do.'

'Please don't worry about things like that,' said Peggy quickly. 'The Government pays me for your billet, and I will take charge of your food stamps. All I expect from my lodgers is help around the house, like cooking, cleaning and a bit of washing. As long as you keep your rooms clean and don't bring men into the house, we'll all get along just fine.'

'I'm engaged and Jane's too young to be bringing men home,' retorted Sarah, rather more sharply than she'd intended.

'I'm not being personal,' said Peggy hastily, 'it's just a rule of the house. When you've been in the business as long as I have one learns to put people straight right at the start so there can be no argument.' She eyed them rather bashfully. 'I do hope you didn't think I was being rude.'

Sarah flushed a deep red and shook her head, realising she was being a bit over-sensitive. It was probably the lack of food and drink, and the exhaustion brought on by the endless journey down here and the worry it had entailed. 'We won't do anything to upset you, Peggy,' she said softly. 'You've been so kind to take us in when it's clear you already have a houseful.'

Peggy waved away her apology with a smile. 'I enjoy having young people around me, and of course they all help with Daisy, which is a bonus. Cordelia does her bit too, even though she's getting on and is rather frail.' She chuckled. 'I should warn you that Cordelia often forgets to turn on her hearing aid, so you might find yourself in the maze of a very strange conversation. Don't let it worry you; she's got all her marbles and can be great fun.'

'She sounds lovely,' said Jane.

'She is,' agreed Peggy. 'So much so that she's an intrinsic part of my family, and even the girls have taken to calling her Grandma Finch.' She fell silent for a moment. 'I wouldn't mention the fact that her house has been bombed – or tell her about your run-in with Amelia. Cordelia and she have never got on, and it would only upset Cordelia to know that her family home has been destroyed and her sister had been so mean.'

'Don't worry, Peggy,' said Sarah. 'We won't say anything.'

As they continued to walk down Camden Road, Peggy pointed out the fire station where her evacuee Rita worked as a driver, and the hospital where Suzy and Fran nursed. 'These are my local shops,' she explained. 'My ration books are registered here. And that's the Lilac tea rooms, which often has some lovely fresh scones and jam to go with their good strong tea. That ugly great building is the old dress factory. They make uniforms now.'

There was bomb damage here too, Sarah noticed, but with bright yellow flowers bobbing their heads in the wind through the rubble, it didn't seem too awful. They continued along past the Anchor pub and the general store, and came to a junction.

'The sea's down that way, and we're across over there,' said Peggy as they waited for a convoy of Army lorries to trundle up the hill. 'Beach View has been in my family for years, but of course the war brought an end to the tourist trade, and now it's home not only for my family, but for the waifs and strays who find their way to our door.'

They crossed the road and Peggy drew to a halt at the entrance to Beach View Terrace. 'As you can see, we've had a bit of damage – a gas explosion took out the last two houses at the end – but so far we've managed to escape anything too serious.'

The house was one in a line of tall terraced buildings, with steps leading from the pavement over a basement window to the front door. Each house carried the scars of bombing raids, and most of the windows had been boarded over where the glass had been shattered. The front door to Beach View Boarding House appeared to be a replacement, for it bore no resemblance to the others in the short cul-de-sac, and the smart brass knocker and letter box looked rather incongruous against the cheap wood. A pile of rubble at the end was all that remained of the two houses which had once stood there, but again, the spring flowers that had struggled through the debris brought a dash of colour.

Jane helped Peggy with the pram while Sarah took the cases and gas-mask boxes. They stepped through the front door into a square hall which had dark red and blue tiles on the floor, and cheerful yellow paint on the wall above the dado rail. The house smelled of furniture polish and cooking, and was warm and quiet after the chaos of the Town Hall and the loneliness of wandering the streets.

Peggy put her finger to her lips, her eyes sparkling with fun. 'Let's give Cordelia a lovely surprise,' she whispered. 'Stay here until I call you.'

Sarah put their cases and gas-mask boxes on the floor beside the front door and unwound her scarf as Jane slipped off her coat and stuffed her beret in the pocket. The hall was quite large and the stairs were of some old dark wood that had been polished to a gleam. A runner of brown carpet was held in place on each step by a shining brass rod, and although the paint was a bit faded on the walls and some of the wallpaper was peeling off below the dado rail, it felt homely.

Peggy came back out of the kitchen with a worried frown. 'She doesn't seem to be there, or in the garden,' she said. 'I wonder if—'

'There! Over there, woman! Will you be after shutting the door quickly before she gets out?'

Startled, they all looked up as the strongly accented male voice roared from the upper floor accompanied by the excited barking of a dog.

'Quick, quick – under there, Harvey!'

'What on earth?' Peggy's face tightened and her

eyes narrowed, but before she could move towards the stairs she was confronted by a dark brown ferret streaking towards her, Harvey in hot pursuit.

Sarah and Jane screamed and leaped back as the long furry creature flashed past and the dog almost bowled into them. 'It's a rat!' shouted Jane in terror.

'It's a flaming nuisance,' snapped Peggy, 'and what it's doing upstairs I have no idea.' She ran up the stairs to the first landing. 'Ronan Reilly!' she yelled. 'You get down here this instant.'

'To be sure I would, Peggy, but Dora's gone missing and I have to find her.' His reply was muffled by distance, but nothing could disguise the high note of panic in his voice.

'Dear God,' breathed Peggy. 'I knew those damned things would be trouble.'

Harvey came trotting into the hall holding a dangling ferret in his soft mouth as if it was a fine trophy. He went to each of them in turn to show off his prize, and having received less than rapturous praise, galloped up the stairs to give it to Ron.

Peggy took a deep breath and turned back to the girls who were cowering against the front door. 'Welcome to Beach View Boarding House,' she said with a wry smile. 'We do things rather differently here, but you can be assured that this particular event will not be repeated.'

'What was that creature?' asked Sarah.

'It's a ferret, dear. She won't hurt you unless you get too close to her sharp teeth, and although she's related to rodents, she's actually quite sweet when she isn't running amuck in my house.' She took a deep breath. 'Ron uses them to help hunt down rabbits. He's *supposed* to keep them in their cages in the cellar.'

She glared back up the stairs where a great deal of shouting and barking was going on. 'I'll have to sort this out,' she said apologetically. 'Go into the kitchen and make yourselves a cup of tea while I deal with Ron. I won't be long.'

Sarah and Jane watched her run up the stairs but didn't move from the hallway. They didn't know how many ferrets there might be, and certainly didn't want to bump into any that might be lurking in the kitchen – no matter how sweet they might be.

'Do you think it's always like this?' asked Jane.

'I don't know, but it's all rather fun, isn't it? Should we join in the chase, do you think?'

'Why not?' said Jane and grinned. 'It's not every day we get a chance to do something as mad as this – and I'm game if you are.'

They crept up the stairs, wary of flying ferrets and dashing dogs as they followed the sound of trampling feet and loud voices.

'It's there,' shouted Peggy. 'I can see it under the bed. Get it out, Ron.'

'Ach, to be sure, Peg, you're frightening her. Stop yelling and give the poor wee creature time to catch her breath.'

'She'll be lucky to have any breath to catch if I get hold of her,' Peggy snapped.

'It was all my fault,' quavered an elderly voice. 'I didn't know Ron had got them out of the cage when I opened the cellar door.'

'It's all right, Cordelia,' said Peggy. 'I'm not blaming you. Ron shouldn't have let them out in the first place.'

Sarah and Jane reached the bedroom door at the top of the house and peeked round it. Cordelia Finch was a little elderly lady with a shock of white hair and a round, sweet face which was quite flushed with all the excitement. Ronan Reilly proved to be a broad-set man in his sixties, with a mane of shaggy hair, wild eyebrows, and a dubious sense of dress, for he was wearing a much-darned shirt, baggy corduroy trousers and muddy wellingtons which had left great clods of muck all over the polished floor.

The ferret eyed them all from beneath the bed, whiskers twitching, bright eyes glinting in the shadows as the large brindle dog danced about and barked furiously.

And then suddenly the ferret made a dash for freedom. She shot between the girls' feet, along the landing, and down the stairs. Sarah was almost knocked flying as the dog gave chase, swiftly followed by Ronan and Peggy.

Cordelia Finch caught sight of them standing in bewildered amusement on the landing and her little face split into a broad welcoming smile. 'You must be Sarah and Jane,' she said rather unsteadily. 'Oh, how wonderful. How simply wonderful.'

The tears sparked in her eyes as she held her arms

open in welcome. 'Come and give me a hug. I've been waiting so long to meet you, and I'm so glad you decided not to stay in South Africa.'

They tentatively hugged her, aware of brittle bones and unsteady feet. She was very tiny and aptly named, for she was as delicate as a little bird. 'It's lovely to be here,' murmured Sarah, 'and to meet you at last. I hope our father's telegram didn't put you to too much trouble, only he didn't have anyone else to turn to.'

Cordelia dabbed her eyes with a handkerchief. 'Silly old woman, aren't I?' she managed, 'but it's so lovely to see you – and of course you had to come to me. You're family, and family has to stick together in these troubled times.'

'Everyone has been so kind,' said Jane.

Cordelia twittered as she dabbed her eyes and tried to pull herself together. 'I don't know what you must think of us,' she giggled. 'Ron's ferrets were bound to cause trouble sooner or later – but goodness me, we've had some fun trying to catch them.'

'How many are there?' asked Jane, looking warily about the room.

'Two,' said Cordelia. 'We've yet to find Dora,' said Cordelia, 'but I suspect she's found a nice warm dark corner to hide in. Harvey will sniff her out, never you mind.' She looked up at them, her little face radiant with happiness. 'Let me show you your room, and then we can go down and see what's happening. Poor Ron is no doubt getting a terrible lecture from Peggy, and I really should share the blame.'

She led the way down to the first landing and headed for a door which stood ajar at the far end. 'It's the best room in the house,' she said, 'and I've made it all nice and fresh for you.'

The three of them came to a halt as Cordelia pushed the door open to reveal two single beds and a long furry body stretched out contentedly in the shaft of sunlight that fell across one of the bedspreads. They had found Dora.

'We'll just shut the door on her and leave her to it,' murmured Cordelia. 'Ferrets have sharp teeth, and Ron will know how to handle her properly.' She grinned up at them. 'Don't worry, I'll make sure everything's clean again before you go to bed.'

Jane giggled. 'What fun,' she said as she took the old woman's arm and steadied her down the stairs. 'I had a pet lizard in Malaya, and she used to sit on my dressing table and chirrup at me, but I've never seen a ferret before.'

'It's never dull around here,' said Cordelia as they reached the hall. 'I just hope you'll forgive our rather rude welcome.'

'It was certainly different,' laughed Sarah, 'and Peggy seems very nice when she's not being confronted by runaway ferrets and hurtling dogs.'

'She's an absolute treasure, and I'd be lost without her,' Cordelia replied.

'That's exactly what she said about you,' said Jane happily. She giggled as she heard Peggy telling Ron exactly what she would do to him if the ferrets got out again. 'But I don't think Peggy regards Ronan as a treasure at this very moment,' she added with a twinkle in her eye.

'They adore one another really,' said Cordelia as she led the way across the hall to the dark and rather cluttered kitchen. 'Ron and Peggy are the glue to this household now Jim's been called up, and although there will be a lot of shouting and name-calling, it's always followed with laughter.'

She paused in the doorway and looked up at them. 'This is a house full of love, girls, and everyone who has made their home here would defend it to their last breath. I do so hope that in some small way it will compensate for the loss of your own home.'

Sarah simply nodded, for she could feel the tears gathering. Nothing could compensate for home and family and the assurance that her parents and Philip had survived the fall of Singapore. But this large house and the friendly people who lived here were doing their level best to make them welcome, and she would see to it that she and Jane fitted into this new and strange way of living.

Peggy was stomping up the cellar steps as they came into the kitchen. 'Honestly, I don't know what you must think of us,' she said crossly as she placed the kettle firmly on the hob. 'What with ferrets and dogs and daft old men traipsing their muddy boots about my house, I'm amazed I've managed to stay sane.'

'Flora's in her cage,' said Ron as he tramped into the kitchen still wearing his wellingtons. 'I'd better go and find Dora before there are more ructions.' He grinned at Sarah and Jane. 'To be sure, 'tis a house of chaos – but we're pleased you managed to get here all in one piece.'

'Dora's in the girls' bedroom,' said Cordelia. 'When you've caught her and put her away safely, you can put clean pillowcases on and find another bedspread.' She waggled a finger at him and tried to look fierce. 'And if I find one dropping or puddle anywhere, you'll get a poke from my walking stick.'

'Ach, to be sure,' he sighed, his eyes downcast, 'the divil must be laughing, for it seems I'm to be a martyr not only to me moving shrapnel, but to a house full of bossy women.'

'Take those boots off before you go a step further, Ronan Reilly,' warned Peggy, her mouth twitching with laughter at his woebegone face. 'And you'll clean every bit of mud from my floors before you get a drop of tea.'

Sarah slipped off her coat, hat and gloves and settled beside Jane on one of the hard chairs that surrounded the table. There was a strange sort of slippery cloth over it that felt rather rubbery under her fingers, and there seemed to be more of it in a different pattern on the floor. The kitchen was like nothing she'd ever seen before, with its dark, heavy dresser, the black range, stone sink and mismatched armchairs. But despite the clutter and the lack of any real light coming through the heavily taped window, there was a glow eminating from the range fire and a warmth of homeliness about it.

Sarah smiled at her sister. They would be all right here with Peggy and Great Aunt Cordelia until it was time to return home to Malaya.

Chapter Twenty

Peggy couldn't face another night alone in that big bed even though she was bone weary, so she'd settled in front of the range and let Daisy sleep on in her pram in the corner of the kitchen.

Hearing Jim's voice on the telephone had been wonderful but it had also depressed her, for it meant he was too far from home to be able to come back on any leave he might get, and that their enforced separation would continue. And yet she had to be thankful he and his brother wouldn't be sent overseas, and could only pray that the Army didn't change its mind for once. She'd heard of other husbands being sent off at a minute's notice to the heart of some fly-infested battlefield, and didn't want the same happening to Jim or Frank.

She gave a deep sigh, then took another sip of her tea. Lord only knew how Jim was getting on if he was being made to repair bridges and railway lines. He hadn't done a stroke of labouring since the previous war and had grown soft after sitting in that projection room for years. At least Frank was hardier, but they would both find it tough having to obey orders again.

She leaned back against the cushions and stared into

the glowing fire. Cordelia had gone to bed happier than she'd seen her in a long while, and the two girls had seemed to get along just fine with the others – especially with Suzy, who talked just as posh and appeared to be surprisingly knowledgeable about the Far East. During the course of the evening, Suzy had revealed that her grandfather had made his money out of the tea plantations he'd once owned in Ceylon, and that she'd actually been born there. Her mother's delicate constitution had brought them back to England, but she could still remember the vividness of the green tea bushes, the colourful saris of the women pickers, and the way the clouds would hang over the nearby mountains of Kandy.

Peggy had noted she wasn't the only one to be amazed at how little they knew about Suzy and her family. She'd always just been Suzy: a hard-working, cheerful young nurse who had become a stabilising influence for the more rambunctious Fran, and had never caused her a moment of worry. Peggy smiled. It just went to show how easy it was to take things at face value and not see beyond to the hidden depths of the people she'd thought she knew so well – and it made her wonder whether there was more to Fran.

She stared into the fire, enjoying these few moments to herself. Ron had taken Harvey out for a last run and everyone else was in their bedrooms, so the house was still but for the usual creaks and groans of old timbers and pipes. There had been a couple of warning pips earlier, but they'd come to nothing, so there had been no mad dash for the Anderson shelter and they'd had a peaceful evening.

Half an hour later the cellar door creaked open and Harvey came in panting. After slopping water all over the floor from his bowl, he flopped down at her feet in front of the fire. Ron kicked off his boots and padded over to pour himself a cup of tea before he checked Daisy, who was still asleep in her pram.

He sank into the second armchair and eyed her from beneath his shaggy brows. 'You should be in bed, Peggy,' he said gruffly as he blew on his tea. 'You look worn out.'

'It doesn't help matters when ferrets are let loose and someone traipses mud all over the house,' she said without rancour.

'Aye, well, I've said I'm sorry,' he muttered before slurping his tea. 'It will not be happening again.' He set the cup aside and reached into his pocket for his pipe. 'Our new lodgers seem pleasant enough,' he said as he packed the pipe with tobacco. 'And Cordelia's certainly perked up since their arrival. But they're going to find it hard to settle in after coming from the other side of the world.'

Peggy smiled. 'They certainly will,' she agreed. 'D'you know, Ron, they've never cooked a meal, or done laundry – or even had to buy groceries? They had servants to do everything – even drive them about. It's not going to be easy for them with so much to learn.'

'Sarah seems capable enough,' he replied. 'She told me she worked in her father's plantation office, so she has some skills. But Jane . . . I get the feeling she's a wee bit too young for her age.'

Peggy nodded. 'I got the same impression, and Sarah certainly keeps a careful eye on her. I suppose it's their posh upbringing and the life they led out there – but Sarah's very sophisticated for nineteen and is already engaged. It's all very strange.'

'Things are different in the tropics,' said Ron, who'd never travelled further than the trenches in France and Belgium. 'I expect it's got something to do with all that heat.'

She smiled as she hunted out her packet of cigarettes. Heat probably had very little to do with it, and she suspected it was more to do with money and class and the fact they were white. There was an old lady she'd once known who'd lived in India for years, and she spoke as if she had a plum in her mouth too. Her tales of Colonial rule had painted a rather dubious picture of life in the tropics, and her snobbish attitude to the natives and those white settlers she deemed beneath her, had really turned Peggy against her.

At least Sarah and Jane didn't seem to hold the same biased views, for they'd appeared to be genuinely upset when they'd talked about the death of their Burmese driver and having to leave their Amah behind. She couldn't begin to imagine what they'd gone through to get here, or how they were coping with the worry over their parents.

She lit a cigarette. 'I'll have to take them into town tomorrow to register them officially as lodgers, and then go with them to the bank and the Labour Exchange, and introduce them to the local tradesmen. Sarah's old enough to be called up, and Jane seemed keen to do something towards the war effort – though goodness knows what practical use she might be considering she's never had to lift a finger before now.'

'They'll find their way,' said Ron around the stem of his pipe. 'But don't try to rush things, Peg. They've got a lot to get used to, and not knowing what's happened to their parents must be a terrible worry.'

'Yes, it must be absolutely bewildering for the pair of them,' she agreed. 'We'll just have to do our best to make sure they fit in. I want them to be happy here, Ron, for their own sake as well as Cordelia's.'

The room was in total darkness due to the heavy blackout curtains which Peggy had insisted must be drawn before any light went on. But despite the exhaustion she felt after the long and confusing day, and the comforting warmth of the stone hot water bottle at her feet, Sarah lay awake long after Jane had fallen asleep.

The worry about getting here and finding Cordelia had drained her almost completely, and she'd thought she would be able to relax a while – but now she had other things to fret about. Jane might be slowly recovering, but would she be able to find her feet here, and how would she cope if she was called up? What sort of work could she possibly do? She was barely out of the schoolroom, had been pampered and spoiled by their parents and Amah, and protected from everything that might upset or harm her. She was ill-prepared for life in general, let alone some job in a factory or on a farm.

Sarah turned onto her side, her mind in a whirl with all the new sights, sounds and experiences she'd been bombarded with over the past months. Their arrival in Cliffehaven was only just the beginning of a whole new life, and she was daunted by the thought of how much there was to learn – and how Jane was going to cope with it all. Peggy would help, she was sure, for she'd proved to be a lovely little woman with a firm hand on the reins of the household, and a no-nonsense, practical approach to everything which was very reassuring. And then there was Ron, who she suspected had a sharp mind behind those twinkling, mischievous eyes, and would no doubt do what he could to help ease them into the way of life here.

Sarah rolled over onto her other side and snuggled beneath the lovely soft blanket. She'd forgotten how comfortable a real bed was after so many weeks of sleeping on a lumpy mattress in the bowels of a ship, and she revelled in the downy pillow and the reassuring weight of the eiderdown. Beach View Boarding House might be a bit run-down and shabby, and not at all what she was used to – but no one could deny that the atmosphere was homely.

Great Aunt Cordelia had been a revelation after encountering her sister Amelia, and it was obvious that she'd been overjoyed to see them. She was a sweet old dear, and Sarah could see that Jane had taken to her just as much as she had. It would be fun to have a grandmother-figure at last, for she'd never met Sybil's parents, who lived in Western Australia, and had been born long after Jock's mother had died. She closed her eyes and thought about their first day at Beach View.

Lunch had consisted of boiled egg sandwiches and plenty of tea, and once their hunger was sated, they'd been properly introduced to Flora and Dora. Jane had taken an instant liking to them, but Sarah wasn't at all sure she trusted them not to bite. Having never had a dog before, they were both a bit wary of the over-excitable, bouncing Harvey. However, he seemed to like his tummy being rubbed and as long as he didn't try to lick her face, Sarah rather took a shine to him, and to scruffy old Ron, who clearly adored his animals despite calling them 'eejit, heathen beasts'. She smiled at the memory and let her thoughts wander to the rest of the day.

They had returned to the kitchen after meeting the ferrets, and had settled down with Cordelia to look through her box of treasures. It had been interesting to see the old photographs and hear about their grand-father's family, even though Cordelia couldn't really remember much about Charles – and she and Jane had been happy to fill in the blanks for her and talk about their life in Malaya. But the memories of home were still so raw that it had proved quite hard not to break down and cry – and Cordelia had seemed to understand this, for she'd swiftly changed the subject and asked them about their journey on the *Monarch*.

And then the other girls had come home and the mood had lightened considerably as Fran regaled them with stories of dances and parties, and Rita told them about her motorbike and what fun it was to drive a fire engine when she wasn't involved in the dirt-track races she organised. Then Suzy had told them of the time they'd painted their legs with cold tea and drawn a pencil line down them so it looked as if they were wearing nylons.

There had been some teasing chatter over a delicious supper of stew and potatoes – mainly aimed at Suzy and her boyfriend Anthony, who was Peggy's nephew. Fran had then treated them all to a hilarious parody of Anthony's mother, with only a nod of apology to Peggy, who didn't seem to mind at all that her sister was being made fun of.

Sarah smiled into the pillow. The three girls were all very different, but had certainly made Sarah and Jane welcome. If it had been Malaya there would have been whispers behind hands, watchful eyes and probing questions into their father's profession and their mother's pedigree before they were accepted – or rejected as 'not quite the thing'. It was the one aspect of Malaya and Singapore that Sarah had found abhorrent. Not being the daughter of an Army bigwig or a wealthy, well-connected businessman or government official meant she'd never been accepted as one of the social elite. Not that she'd wanted to be. She couldn't stand the cattiness and the snobbery of it all, and preferred to be amongst people who didn't put on airs and graces.

These girls were friendly and jolly and seemed to accept them without reservation – and it was marvellous that Suzy had a similar background and could relate to so much of their lives in Malaya. She and Suzy had taken an instant liking to one another, and as they chatted and laughed together, Sarah had begun to feel a little easier about fitting in.

Her thoughts turned to home and Philip as she pressed her engagement ring to her lips and silently sent up a prayer for his and her parents' safety. She was about to embark on a new life in a different sort of world, and she could only keep faith that they too had found some sort of sanctuary.

Breakfast was a noisy, bustling affair with Harvey trying to beg scraps as Ron slurped his tea, Daisy yelled for her breakfast, and the other girls raced about getting ready to go on duty. Sarah eyed them enviously, for they had a routine – somewhere to go and something important to do in the battle to win this awful war.

Peggy seemed to notice this and patted her hand. 'We have a lot to do today,' she said, 'and you'll be rushing about soon enough, so I'd take it easy while you can.'

'But what sort of jobs can we do, Peggy?' asked Jane as she scraped the merest hint of the horrid margarine on her brown toast. 'Sarah will be all right – she can type and run an office – but Mummy and Daddy said I was too young to give up my schooling just yet.'

Sarah looked at her sister in surprise, for it was clear she'd also been worrying about the part she would have to play in this new chapter of their lives.

'I'm sure there are lots of things you can do,' said Peggy. 'What do you like best?'

'Sums, figures, puzzles, that sort of thing,' Jane said vaguely. 'I used to be very good at riding and looking after horses, but Mummy and Daddy wouldn't let me ride again after my accident. But my writing's getting better, so perhaps I could learn to type or something.'

'And what accident was that, Jane?' asked Cordelia quietly from the other side of the table.

'I fell off my horse and she kicked me in the head by mistake,' said Jane matter-of-factly. 'But I don't have headaches any more and things are a lot clearer in my mind than before, so I think the doctors were wrong, and I'm getting better.'

'You've certainly proved that over the past couple of months,' said Sarah into the awkward silence. 'I think it's done you good to get out of the schoolroom and have a taste of real life for a change.' She smiled at her sister. 'I'm sure there are lots of things you could do, Jane. Don't worry about it.'

Peggy had finished feeding Daisy and was now bathing her in the kitchen sink, where every kick and splash sent water flying as she gurgled in delight. 'If you like doing sums and things, I'm sure someone will be only too delighted to take you on,' she said as she wrestled Daisy out of the sink and wrapped her in a soft warm towel. 'What with so many men being called up, banks, post offices, small business and accountancy firms must be crying out for help.'

Jane's eyes widened in delight. 'Do you really think so?'

'I don't see why not. I'm not much good at that sort of thing myself,' Peggy admitted, 'but my nephew Anthony could certainly give you a few tests to see what you can do. He taught maths and physics at the local private school for boys. He got a double first at Oxford, so we're all very proud of him. If he agrees, he might write you a reference, which would help no end.'

'Would he?' Jane's eyes sparkled. 'That would be fun. When can I see him to do the tests?'

'Anthony is a busy man, but he's coming to pick Suzy up tonight, so we'll ask him then. I'm sure he won't mind taking half an hour out of his evening – they're only going for a drink.'

Sarah saw the excitement in her sister's face and silently blessed Peggy for her kindness. There was little doubt that Jane would shine in the tests, and with a good reference, she would find it much easier to get the sort of work she'd feel comfortable with.

Peggy was unaware of the goodwill radiating from both girls as she swiftly put a clean nappy on Daisy and then dumped her in Jane's lap. 'Finish drying her off and then get her dressed for me, while I clean up this mess and have a cup of tea. Her fresh clothes are on the sideboard.'

Sarah watched in trepidation as Jane cuddled the

baby and carefully dried all the little creases around her arms and legs, talking all the while and smiling down at her as she slowly pulled on the tiny cotton vest and grappled with the knitted leggings and cardigan. Jane was proving to be quite expert at handling babies, and Sarah breathed a sigh of relief.

'You seem to know what you're doing,' said Cordelia with a smile of approval.

'I had lots of dolls to play with,' said Jane, 'and I've always loved babies.' Her bright smile faded. 'I was so looking forward to Mummy's baby, but I suppose it could be a long, long time before I get to see it now.'

'Oh,' said Cordelia, her little face clouded with concern. 'I didn't realise your mother was expecting. How very worrying for you all.'

'Well, you can look after Daisy for me until we can find you something more interesting to do,' said Peggy firmly. At Jane's wide-eyed pleasure, she grinned. 'She's not always that easy to deal with,' she warned. 'She has a bit of a wilful way about her, and can cry loud enough to drown out the air-raid sirens when she's unhappy about things.'

Jane cuddled Daisy and kissed the dark curls. 'I'm sure she's absolutely perfect all the time,' she murmured.

'Shows how much you know about babies,' said Peggy and laughed. 'Come on, we have a lot to do today and time is wasting.' She finished clearing the table and put everything on the draining board. 'We'll do that when we get back.'

'Ron and I will do it,' said Cordelia. 'You see to my girls – that's the important thing.'

Sarah gathered their coats, handbags and gas-mask boxes together while Jane carefully tucked Daisy into the pram. Once everyone was ready and they'd kissed Cordelia goodbye, she helped Jane get the pram down the front steps.

'Can I push the pram?' asked Jane.

'Be my guest,' said Peggy as she pulled on her gloves.

Sarah walked beside Peggy as Jane proudly pushed the pram along the pavement, and when she caught the older woman's eye, she smiled her silent gratitude. Jane was feeling useful – probably for the first time in her young life – and the happiness that brought was worth a fortune.

They were introduced to Fred the Fishmonger and Alf the butcher, and then to Ray the ironmonger, whose shop was a treasure trove of all sorts of weird and wonderful things they would have loved to rifle through and explore. But they weren't allowed to linger, for Peggy had warned that the Labour Exchange and Billeting Office got very busy early on, and if they didn't want to spend most of the day sitting about, they needed to get there as it opened.

Sarah was amazed by the length of the queue already waiting outside the Labour Exchange, and it was at least an hour before it was their turn to be seen and Peggy could register them for their ration books and clothing coupons. There were lots of forms to fill in, and this took another half an hour.

The Billeting Office was even worse, and they spent two hours sitting about waiting until they had more forms to fill in. Finally Peggy was given the official document so she could claim her allowance from the Government, and they left the musty-smelling office with a sigh of relief, and headed further down the High Street to the bank.

Sarah explained to the woman behind the counter why she was there, and within minutes the manager, Mr Duffy, came out to greet them. Peggy stayed with the pram while they went into his office and sat down in leather chairs.

Mr Duffy was a rather pompous, portly man of late middle-age who peered at them through such thick-lensed spectacles that his pale blue eyes were magnified to an almost alarming degree. 'I did receive your father's telegram, and the notification from his bank in Singapore,' he said as he steepled his fingers beneath his double chin. 'Unfortunately no funds were able to be transferred before the fall of Singapore, and until the situation has been resolved with the Japanese, there can be no further transactions.'

'So there's no money,' said Jane flatly.

'I didn't say that,' he replied. He pulled a folder towards him and opened it. 'Your grandfather opened this account many years ago for your father, and there are some funds in the account, which have gathered interest over the years. But it is hardly a fortune.'

'How much is there?' asked Sarah.

'A little over five hundred pounds,' he replied, pushing the statement towards them.

'But that's a lot of money,' breathed Jane.

'Not if we're stuck here for several years,' replied Sarah, trying hard to swallow her disappointment. She pushed the statement back across the desk and opened her handbag to fish out the precious envelope her father had given her the night before they'd left Singapore. 'I have over five thousand Malay dollars here,' she said. 'Is it possible to exchange them for English pounds?'

'I'm afraid not,' he replied, his expression rather mournful. 'You see, the Japanese have brought in a new currency, and the Malay dollar is no longer viable.'

'But apart from two five pound notes, it's all the money we have,' gasped Sarah. 'Father gave it to me only two months ago. Surely you could exchange it for sterling after all the years our family has had an account with you?'

His expression was implacable. 'I'm very sorry, Miss Fuller, but I am not authorised to deal in untradeable currency.'

Sarah battled to keep the tears from falling as she shoved the envelope of useless money back into her handbag and closed it with a snap. He didn't look a bit sorry, and she was damned if she was going to let him see how upset she was.

'I could arrange for you to have a small loan,' he said. 'The bank is always willing to lend to our loyal customers, and the interest rate is quite good at the moment.'

'I don't think that would be a sensible idea at all,' she muttered as she got to her feet. 'Good morning, Mr Duffy,' she said stiffly as she was forced to shake the rather unpleasantly damp, limp hand.

Without waiting to see if Jane was following, she wiped her hand down her coat and marched out of the horrible little man's office, straight past a startled Peggy and out onto the pavement. She was so angry and upset that she lit up a cigarette and puffed furiously on it, not caring that her mother would have been appalled at her doing such a thing in the street.

'Jane told me what happened,' said Peggy as she came to console her. 'Never mind, you'll have enough to keep you going until you can get a job.'

'But it's so unfair, Peggy. Pops worked hard for that money, and now it's worthless.' She could feel the tears pricking again and angrily blinked them away. 'Duffy was a pompous ass, and I had to get out of there before I was very rude to him,' she added, crushing the half-smoked cigarette under her shoe. 'He even had the gall to offer me a loan when he knew I'd have a struggle to pay it back,' she muttered crossly.

'We should close the account and find another bank,' said Jane. 'That would teach him.'

Sarah's fit of pique dissolved swiftly and she hugged her sister. 'Maybe it would, but I really can't be bothered to fill in any more forms today.'

Peggy pulled on her gloves. 'I propose we go and have a cup of coffee – my treat – at the Lilac tea rooms.

That will cheer us all up and then we can see about finding you both a decent job.'

'But I thought Anthony was going to test me for a job,' said Jane as she wheeled the pram into Camden Road.

'No, Jane,' said Sarah patiently, 'he's going to test how good you are at mathematics, and maybe give you a reference. He can't give you a job as well.'

Peggy led the way into the tea rooms and they sat at the window table so they could keep an eye on Daisy. The warm, friendly atmosphere and the smell of proper coffee and baking cheered them all up, and once they'd eaten their scones and drunk all the coffee, they were back out into the spring sunshine again, feeling restored.

'Thanks for that little treat, Peggy,' murmured Sarah as she tucked her hand into the crook of her arm. 'I don't usually behave like a spoilt brat, but it was all such a shock to discover that everything we'd been counting on proved to be worthless.'

'You'll be surprised how quickly you'll adapt,' said Peggy with a smile. 'My life has been one long adventure of feast and famine, but Jim and I got through all right.' She became businesslike. 'There are several recruiting places, but I think the best one is in the Town Hall. They have no allegiance to any of the services, and there's a far wider choice.'

'Well, I won't be trying for a job *there*,' said Jane as they passed the bank. 'And if all bank managers are like that, I'll find something else to do.'

'That's good fighting talk, Jane,' said Peggy. 'Come on, let's see what's on offer in the way of jobs, and then we'll read all the bumph they're bound to give us, and discuss all the options.'

The recruiting office was very busy, so they helped themselves to the endless number of pamphlets and slips of paper, and then sat in the WVS canteen and trawled through them.

There was every job imaginable on offer, for it seemed there was an urgent need for women to play their part in the war effort now that so many of the men had been called up – from factory production lines to boiler-making, welding, painting, engineering, fire-fighting, plumbing, secretarial, hospital assistants, milk delivery, and on to farm work, forestry and animal husbandry.

'I like the look of that,' said Jane, pointing to the leaflet about the Women's Land Army. 'I saw a poster in London, and there were girls out with those big horses in some of the fields we passed in the train.'

'It's a tough job,' warned Peggy, 'and you'd have to start very early and work until it gets dark again. I think it might be better if you went for something a little less labour-intensive to begin with, and if you really do have a skill at mathematics, then it would be a shame to waste it.'

'But I don't want to work in an office, or learn to be a plumber. I want to be out in the open with trees and fields, and horses.' She turned to Sarah. 'What about you?' she asked. 'Have you decided what you want to do yet?'

Sarah really wasn't at all sure about anything, but knew they both had to do something, and if Jane was determined to work on the land, then it would be better if she went along with her – although she didn't fancy the sound of it one bit.

'I think we should go and ask about the sort of things we'd be expected to do,' she said quietly. 'Then we can have a clearer idea of whether we're suited to it or not. But Peggy's right, Jane, we'd both be wasting our skills if we ended up digging potatoes all day.'

'Why don't you go and talk to Vera Watkins?' said Peggy as she stubbed out her cigarette and got to her feet. 'I've known her since we were at school together, and now her children are off her hands and her husband is away in the Navy, she's doing sterling work for the recruitment people. She's very nice, and might be able to point you in the direction of something where your skills could be put to their best advantage.' She shoved her gloves in her pocket and picked up her handbag and gas-mask box. 'While you do that, I'll fill in the time by helping out with the comfort boxes. I'll be in the big hall when you've finished.'

Sarah stubbed out her own cigarette as Peggy bustled off. 'Let's see what Vera has to say and then we'll have a clearer idea of what being in the Land Army entails.' She stilled Jane as she hurried to gather up all the leaflets. 'It sounds a tough sort of life, and it won't all be riding horses and drifting about stables, you know.'

'I realise that,' Jane said flatly. 'But anything's got to be better than waiting about until the Government calls us up and we're made to work in some horrid factory. Besides, we're only asking today, and if Anthony gives me a reference, then I can look at other options.'

Jane was being quite mature about things, so Sarah said no more and headed back to the office to see Peggy's friend Vera. There were more long forms to fill in while they waited their turn, but it helped to pass the time until Vera was free to see them.

'We'd like to know more about working for the Women's Land Army,' said Jane as they sat in front of the cluttered desk.

Vera smiled at her enthusiasm and took their forms. 'Let me have a quick look through these first, then I'll have more idea of who you are and what you can do,' she said.

She read each form carefully and then placed them neatly on the blotter in front of her. 'I see you've just arrived from Malaya, and that you lived on a rubber plantation there,' she said, looking eagerly at Sarah. 'You worked in the plantation office?' At Sarah's nod, she hurried on. 'Do you have any experience of assessing the amount of timber in a tree, of measuring the amount of timber felled, or surveying new woodlands and identifying trees for felling?'

Sarah frowned, for this didn't sound like farming at all, more like forestry. 'Our father was a plantation manager, and over the years he taught me how to measure and survey, as well as how to tap for rubber and plan new plantings. I worked in his office after I left school, and prepared lading dockets, shipment schedules and the transport and customs documents. I have shorthand and typing qualifications, and a basic knowledge of book-keeping.'

Vera smiled. 'I can see you're a bit confused,' she said, 'but you see there are different parts of the Women's Land Army that you could join.' She leaned back in her chair. 'There's a great need for women to work on farms and see to it that our crop yields continue to meet the heavy demand now the convoys are finding it so hard to get through. But there's also a huge demand for timber, and the country needs women to take over the sawmills and work as foresters – which is why a new Women's Timber Corps is starting up. With your background and skill, you'd be a perfect candidate.'

Sarah felt uneasy beneath her enthusiastic gaze, for she'd never done any of the labouring on the plantation, and didn't have a clue about running a sawmill. 'I don't really think either of us are cut out to chop down trees,' she said. 'What would this work entail, exactly?'

'Goodness me,' said Vera, 'I wasn't suggesting you should work as lumberjills; you're both far too small and slender.' She smiled brightly at Sarah. 'With your qualifications, you'd be in the administration office most of the time, dealing with the wages, preparing dockets and organising transport of the timber, and of course filling in the documentation for the Ministry of Supply. You would be expected to measure and grade the timber, and from time to time, you might be asked to help fire the brushwood and prepare for replanting. You might even have to do a bit of heavy lifting on the odd occasion – but all in all, you would be in an administrative position and not expected to do manual labour.'

Sarah was warming to the idea. 'It certainly sounds interesting, and I feel quite confident that I could do it, but this is all a bit sudden and I need time to think about it.'

'Of course, dear, I quite understand you don't want to be steamrollered into something so soon after arriving here.' She turned her bright blue gaze on Jane. 'And what about you, dear?'

'I haven't worked at anything yet,' said Jane with innocent honesty, 'but I'd love to be with those lovely big horses out in the forest, and if Sarah and I can work in the same place, it would be even better.'

Vera glanced appraisingly at Jane's slight figure and soft, elegant hands. 'As I said before, I don't think the Timber Corps would suit you, dear. The work is very hard, and you would need to be quite robustly built to be sawing down trees, and lifting heavy telegraph posts and loading them onto trucks.'

'I know I'm short and thin, but I'm stronger than I look,' said Jane firmly. 'Do they have horses in the Timber Corps too?'

Vera clasped her hands on the desk. 'Yes, they do,

but because they take so much heavy handling, they are always looked after by an experienced male forestry manager or the foreman.' She must have noted Jane's disappointment, for she hurried on, 'Let me tell you what is involved in the WTC, and then you'll have a clearer picture of how unsuitable I think you would find it.'

Jane glared at her and folded her arms, determined not to be put off by anything.

'The WTC includes all the jobs involved in forestry, like felling, stripping bark, loading, crosscutting, driving tractors and trucks and running the sawmills as well as working with the men who are either too young or too old to be called up. There would be an initial training course of four to six weeks for the unskilled, after which you would be posted to your work area.'

'You mean I would have to leave Cliffehaven? Would Sarah come with me?'

'The training camp in this south-eastern sector is in the Weald, about forty miles away. Sarah would stay here and begin work on the Cliffe estate almost immediately if she got the job, and there is no guarantee that you would be posted back to Cliffehaven. The WTC have nine geographical areas, and you could be sent to Scotland, the Midlands, the West Country or Wales. You would have no say in where you were to be posted, I'm afraid.'

'I see,' murmured Jane.

Vera turned to Sarah. 'The WTC have taken over

Lord Cliffe's estate, and as you already have a billet with Peggy, you'd be able to get there each day without too much effort.'

'But once the forest has been cleared and replanted, I would be posted somewhere else?'

Vera nodded. 'But that is many months, perhaps years ahead. It's a huge forest and the work is slow.'

'What about the Land Army?' asked Jane. 'Are there local farms I could work on?'

'There are, but again the labour is intensive and you'd need to be tough both physically and mentally to be able to cope with the conditions. The hours are from dawn to dusk, regardless of the weather, and you would be expected to plough and harrow, dig and harvest, look after the animals and help make repairs to outbuildings. You would find some of the old farmers wouldn't treat you kindly, for they still hold the opinion that women shouldn't be let loose with farm implements or their livestock. Thankfully, that attitude is slowly changing.'

'But couldn't I just work with the big horses and look after them?'

Sarah was becoming quite alarmed at how determined Jane seemed to be about working with horses, and could only hope that Vera would continue to dissuade her.

Vera shot a glance at Sarah before replying to Jane. 'They are only a tiny part of the work involved, Jane, and not all farms have them now there are more tractors about. Farming is a tough way of life, and only a very few girls settle down to it successfully. They seem to have this dewy-eyed image of floating about in cornfields in a cotton frock, or sitting on hay bales in a sun hat, but that's the poster image – the reality is far harsher.'

Sarah had hoped that Vera's bleak description would make her see sense, but Jane still didn't look convinced.

Vera seemed to realise this too, for she regarded Jane, took a deep breath and plunged on. 'Imagine that it's four in the morning, Jane,' she said quietly, 'and the freezing wind and rain are lashing the muddy yard. The cows have to be fetched from the field to be milked, and once that's done, they have to be herded back out again so you can scrub the milking parlour clean of all their filth. And this is even before you've had time for a cup of tea, let alone breakfast. And then the rest of the day would be spent out in the windswept fields, battling with tractors that won't start, or trying to plough a straight furrow in mud that reaches to your knees.'

Jane grinned at Vera. 'You don't have to say any more,' she said. 'You've been very convincing, and the picture you've painted is nothing like the poster I saw at Victoria Station.'

'The reality rarely is, but the recruitment is vital if we're to win this war,' she replied, and gave her a warm smile. 'You must think I'm an odd sort of recruiting officer for putting you off, but I think it's best to try and steer people to the jobs where they'll get the most satisfaction. My daughter worked in the Land Army, and she lasted four weeks and was utterly miserable. Now she's a WREN and driving an Admiral about, and is as happy as a lark. So you see there is a job for everyone – it just might take a bit of time to find out what suits and what doesn't.'

'The trouble is,' sighed Jane, 'I'm not much good at anything really – only mathematics and puzzles and stuff – and I can't see how they would help at all.'

'Don't get downhearted, Jane,' soothed Sarah. 'We'll see Anthony tonight, and then you'll have a much clearer idea of what to do next.'

'There are lots of administration and book-keeping jobs going,' said Vera cheerfully. 'I'm sure we could find you something.'

'You've been very kind,' said Sarah as she got to her feet. 'I'll think about the WTC and let you know one way or the other tomorrow.'

They were almost out of the door when Vera called out, 'Hold on a minute. I've had a marvellous idea that might just be perfect for Jane.'

They looked at one another, shrugged and returned to the desk with apologetic smiles at the woman who was next in line.

Vera's face was alight with eagerness as she rummaged through the great pile of paperwork on her desk and pulled out a leaflet. 'The local dairy needs someone to load up and deliver the milk each day. The lad they had working for them has been called up and Alan Jenkins is finding it difficult to run his usual number of rounds. It will involve getting up very early, for the round starts at five in the morning, but you'd be finished by lunchtime.'

Jane's expression wasn't at all enthusiastic. 'I don't know,' she murmured. 'Delivering milk isn't exactly going to win this war, is it?'

Vera laughed. 'You'd be surprised how important our daily delivery is, Jane. It's a tradition that not even Hitler has been able to break, and we need milk to keep our teeth and bones healthy now rationing is getting so tight.' She leaned across her desk, her face beaming and her eyes twinkling. 'And do you know how that milk is delivered, Jane?'

Jane shook her head and gave a tiny shrug, clearly not at all excited by the idea.

'Alan Jenkins has four Shires which pull the delivery drays, and the person delivering the milk is responsible for the care of their horse.'

Sarah's spirits plummeted as Jane sat bolt upright, her eyes sparkling with excitement. 'You mean I'd have to muck out and groom and feed it – and check its hooves for stones and make sure it has enough water and feed?'

Vera laughed. 'I suppose you would, though I know nothing about keeping horses.' She passed the piece of paper over to Jane. 'This is the address. Why don't you go and talk to Mr Jenkins and find out what the job entails? The money isn't much, but it is only part-time, and you could always find something else to do in the afternoons.'

'Oh, I will,' Jane said, clutching the paper to her

heart, her face glowing with hope. 'I'll go this very minute.' She headed straight for the door, forgetting her handbag, coat and gas-mask box in her eagerness to find the dairy.

Sarah smiled at Vera as she gathered up their belongings. 'She gets a bit over-enthusiastic about things at times,' she said softly.

Vera nodded. 'I had a feeling she might,' she replied with a knowing look. 'Good luck, Sarah, and I hope that tomorrow you'll have decided about your work. I have a feeling that the WTC would suit you down to the ground.'

Sarah smiled her thanks and hurried after Jane, who'd already found Peggy and was excitedly telling her all about the job at the dairy.

'Well, we'd better go and see Alan then and make sure he gives you the job,' said Peggy with a sideways glance at Sarah. 'But you will need to put your coat on – it's still very cold outside.'

Jane blushed as she pulled on her coat and took her handbag and gas-mask box from Sarah. 'I got a bit carried away, didn't I?' she said ruefully.

'I'd call it youthful enthusiasm,' said Peggy, 'and there's nothing wrong with that.'

Sarah wished Peggy wouldn't encourage her. Jane had been very carefully brought up, and delivering milk was not the sort of occupation her parents had envisioned for her.

'I really don't think you should apply for this, Jane,' she said firmly. 'Mother and Pops have been quite specific about you staying away from any kind of horse, let alone those huge Shires. They will take a great deal of strength to handle – and you haven't been near a horse in years, so it would be very dangerous.'

Jane blushed a deeper red. 'I have, actually,' she confessed. 'Sally Bristow used to let me exercise her horses and help around the stables.'

'What?' Sarah stared at her in shock and horror.

'Mrs Bristow knew,' Jane ploughed on, 'but Sally swore her to secrecy, and once she'd seen I wasn't going to fall off or do anything stupid, she even began to teach me how to drive a carriage and pair.'

'Good grief,' breathed Sarah. 'I can't believe Elsa Bristow would do such an underhand thing when she knew how much Mother and Pops dreaded you having another accident. It's a good thing they never discovered what you were up to, because you'd have been put under virtual house arrest and they would have fallen out very badly with the Bristows over it.'

'Well, they didn't find out,' Jane said defiantly, 'and they're not here to stop me now. I want this job, Sarah, and I'm determined to have it.'

Sarah could see that determination in her eyes and knew there was little point in arguing. But she felt quite sick at the thought of her excitable, naïve sister in sole charge of a huge Shire – and if her parents ever found out, they would be furious with both of them – especially with Sarah, for she'd promised to keep her sister safe.

She kept these thoughts to herself as she helped

Peggy down the Town Hall steps with the pram. All she could do now was hope that the job was already taken, for it would be easier to deal with one of Jane's tantrums than have to face her parents' wrath.

They set off up the High Street, taking the narrow road past the station which led to a maze of streets that radiated from what remained of the high brick wall that ran beside the railway lines. There was a lot of clearing and building work going on amid the shattered remains of street after street of houses.

'Our little Rita used to live in this area,' said Peggy. 'The whole lot was flattened when the Luftwaffe dropped their blast-bombs. A lot of people were killed, but luckily she wasn't at home at the time and her widowed father was away with the Army.'

Peggy eyed the miserable remains of the terraced hovels as they walked past. 'It was a blessing in a way,' she added, 'because the houses were no better than slum tenements, and these nice new asbestos ones will certainly do until after the war.'

Sarah thought they looked no better than boxes, and, with their flat roofs, pipe chimneys and plain grey walls, they reminded her of the native shanties back in Singapore.

Peggy pointed out the allotments and the new factories and warehouses that had sprung up over the past three years, and explained that the barrage balloons which swayed high above the industrial area were there to deter the enemy planes from getting too close.

She came to a halt finally outside a high brick wall which had 'Jenkins' Dairy' written on a large board above a double gate. 'Here we are,' she said, puffing rather from the uphill walk. 'Open the gate, Jane. Alan's been our milkman for years, and he won't mind if we take the pram in.'

Jane pushed open the right-hand gate and came to a halt as she was confronted by a cobbled yard and a wooden stable-block. Most of the stables were empty, but there were four handsome, inquisitive heads poking over the doors, and they snorted and stamped their great iron-shod hooves as they greeted their visitors.

Jane left the pram to Peggy and, before Sarah could stop her, quietly walked towards them.

'Hello, beauties,' she murmured to each of them in turn as she stroked their broad noses and let them snuffle the palms of her hands. 'I'm sorry, but I don't have any carrots or sugar for you today.'

Alan came out of his office to see what all the noise was about, and once Peggy had told him why they were there, he eyed Jane up and down and scratched the grey stubble on his chin. 'I was hoping for another lad to help me,' he said in his thick Welsh accent. 'Would she be strong enough to keep one of my girls under control, and has she ever driven a dray before?'

'She's never driven a dray,' said Sarah, 'and hasn't worked with such big horses before.' She felt mean at trying to spoil things for Jane, and quickly added,

'But she's good with horses and knows how to handle them.'

'I've heard that before,' he said darkly. 'But I do need help, so I'll give her a fair chance to show me what she can do.' He stumped across the yard and shook Jane's hand, and after a few words they couldn't catch, he got her to open one of the stable doors.

Sarah's pulse raced as she saw how enormous the Shire was. It towered over little Jane and snuffled at her hair as she nimbly squeezed past, avoided the great restless hooves and quickly got it tacked up. Within minutes she emerged with a beaming smile, leading the great beast into the yard and tying it to a ring that had been set in the wall.

Alan Jenkins pointed to a large wooden dray that had been propped against a nearby wall, and Sarah gasped. 'Surely he doesn't expect her to manoeuvre that? It looks like it must weigh a ton.'

'It appears so,' muttered Peggy. 'Who would have thought there was so much strength in that little body?' she added in amazement as Jane got the dray into position and set about coaxing the Shire back between the long wooden shafts.

Sarah's initial fear was replaced by a swell of pride as Jane expertly secured the harness to the dray, petted the horse, and then clambered up onto the seat. Her little sister had clearly lost none of her talent for dealing with horses, and her face was simply glowing with pleasure. They watched in awed silence as she quietly spoke to the animal before slapping the reins against the broad back and getting it to plod across the yard and down towards the sprawling building at the far end.

Alan laughed and ran his fingers through his mop of snow-white hair. 'She'll do all right,' he said, 'though goodness knows where she learned to do that. She looks as if a puff of wind would blow her away.'

Jane brought the horse and dray back into the yard, clambered down and patted the animal's muscular neck before looking up at Alan. 'Did I do it well enough, Mr Jenkins? Have I got the job?'

He stroked the animal's broad nose and ran his fingers through the pale mane that drifted over the animal's gentle eyes. 'What do you think, Mabel? Can you and her get on?'

Mabel snorted and slobbered on his shoulder, and he laughed. 'It looks like you've got Mabel's approval, so I suppose you'd better start tomorrow.'

Sarah could see that Jane was struggling to keep her joy restrained, for she was almost dancing on the spot as she grinned up at him. 'What time tomorrow?' she breathed.

'I expect you here at four-thirty every morning except Sundays. You'll muck her out and groom her so she's all clean and ready for the round, and when you get back you must groom her again and see that she has plenty of feed in her nosebag, fresh straw in her stable and clean water in her bucket. I pay two pound ten shillings a week and provide a uniform of sorts – but I warn you, it's very basic.'

Jane's face was glowing. 'Thank you, Mr Jenkins,' she managed. 'Thank you so much, and I promise to never be late, and to look after Mabel as if she was royalty.'

He grinned back at her and stuck out his hand. 'Have we got a deal then, Jane?'

'We've got a deal,' she said as she clasped his hand and beamed up at him.

Chapter Twenty-One

Ron had let Cordelia boss him about for half the morning, and after fetching and carrying and sweeping, he felt he'd earned a couple of hours up in the hills with Harvey and his young ferrets. With Dora and Flora neatly tucked into the inside pockets of his poacher's coat, and carrying a sharpened spade over his shoulder, he'd followed the galloping dog up the steep hill and down into the valley copse where he knew there was a small rabbit warren. He didn't want to risk his babies getting lost in one of the larger warrens that burrowed for miles beneath the windswept hills, but he needed to see what they could do.

'This is always the tricky moment,' he murmured to Harvey, who was eagerly watching him place the pocket nets over the rabbit holes and secure them with pegs. He gently lifted the two ferrets from his pockets and stroked their bellies. 'Now,' he muttered, 'you've to find me a rabbit or two and then come back. I don't want you getting lost down there.'

Flora and Dora's whiskers twitched as he lowered them one after the other beneath the pocket net. They didn't look back, but disappeared down the rabbit hole eagerly.

Ron sat on a hummock of grass and lit his pipe. 'Now we wait, Harvey, and hope we see them both again.'

Harvey flopped down with his nose on his paws, his eyebrows wriggling as he followed the sounds beneath the earth that Ron couldn't hear. He was used to waiting for ferrets and looked relaxed, but he was coiled like a spring, alert for the first sight of a rabbit running into a net.

Several minutes later a small rabbit shot into one of the nets, Dora at its heels. Ron left Harvey to grab the rabbit while he snatched up Dora before she could run away. 'Good girl,' he praised, as he fed her some of the milk-soaked bread he'd brought in an old biscuit tin, and made a fuss of her before sending her back down another hole.

Fifteen minutes passed and three more rabbits shot into the nets as they fled the ferrets, but there was still no sign of Flora. After another half-hour had gone by, Ron was beginning to worry that she'd got lost, or had simply caught a rabbit and was down there eating it. Ferrets could stay underground for days, making a feast of an entire warren of rabbits, and he didn't want her to get into that habit.

Dora chased another rabbit into the net and Ron decided she'd done enough on her first outing. He gave her some more food and placed her back in his coat pocket, where she wriggled about and finally curled up and went to sleep.

Harvey began to sniff one of the rabbit holes and

whined as he heard something. Ron lay on his stomach and listened. He could hear Flora now, and she sounded as if she was in some distress. He knew it was a stupid thing to do, and experience had taught him it was foolhardy to offer a trapped ferret anything she could bite. But he had no other option if he was to get Flora out of there.

He gingerly put his hand down the hole, reaching as far as he could, his fingers scrabbling through roots in search of his trapped ferret.

'Ow, bejesus, that hurts!' he yelled as Flora's teeth fastened on his finger. 'Let go, ye heathen creature.'

But Flora had no intention of letting go, and now they were both stuck – Ron with his arm firmly jammed into the rabbit hole up to his shoulder, and Flora more than likely trapped among the roots in a narrow tunnel.

Ron closed his eyes and tried to ignore the agony in his finger and relax. He knew that if he tried to pull his finger from her teeth he would probably lose it. Ferrets' teeth were lethal and their jaws locked like a steel trap. He lay there with Harvey panting alongside him for what felt like hours until Flora's jaw relaxed and she got bored with the game.

Pulling his arm out of the hole, he eyed his finger, which was bleeding profusely, and cursed as he wrapped a rather grubby handkerchief around it and then picked up the spade. 'There's nothing for it, Harvey,' he muttered crossly. 'I'm going to have to dig her out. A bit of help from you wouldn't hurt, if you could bear to stop lying about being useless.'

Harvey barked and began scrabbling at the entrance of the hole as Ron assessed where Flora must be and began digging a couple of feet behind her. It was hard work, for the earth beneath the wiry grass was rock hard, and interlaced with thick roots. 'Be ready to catch her,' he warned Harvey. 'She'll shoot out of there like a cork out of a bottle.'

Ron was sweating and his injured finger was throbbing as he dug into the unforgiving earth and severed through the roots that he could now see were trapping Flora.

Flora suddenly wriggled free and streaked out straight into Harvey's jaws and dangled there, limbs waving furiously as she squeaked and squirmed. Harvey stood patiently waiting for Ron to take her from him, his teeth holding her just enough to keep her prisoner, but not hard enough to hurt her. He was a good hunting dog with a soft mouth, and could carry an egg without breaking it.

'Good lad,' said Ron as he took the squirming ferret, checked that she hadn't been harmed, and tried to soothe her. 'To be sure, I think we've all had enough adventure for one day,' he said as he gave her some of the bread and milk and then popped her into his pocket alongside Dora.

Once he'd picked up all his little nets and stowed them in yet another pocket, he tied the dead rabbits together, got his pipe going again and picked up the spade. 'Let's go and find that wee hole we made in the fencing round the estate,' he murmured. 'To be sure, a couple of rabbits will not be enough for the pot.'

They set off across the hills, man and dog in harmony with their surroundings as Flora and Dora curled up and went to sleep, snug in his deep pockets. The sun was shining, and although the wind was still keen, there was definitely a touch of spring in the air, and a promise that the warmer weather was just around the corner.

The high fence stretched as far as the eye could see, and Ron tramped along the perimeter heading for the spot where he'd managed to cut through it. He found the forked stick in amongst the scrub which he'd left as a marker, but the hole had been repaired, and he hadn't brought the wire-cutters with him today.

'You looking for something, old man?'

He looked up to find a burly stranger with a rifle watching him from the other side of the fence, a thick-set mastiff snarling at the end of a short leash. 'I was just wondering what was going on in there,' he said blithely as Harvey growled deep in his throat at the other dog.

'Nothing that concerns you,' replied the man gruffly, his gaze suspicious beneath the low brim of his hat. 'This is off limits to civilians,' he said darkly, 'and damage to Government property is a serious matter.'

'Aye,' said Ron innocently, 'I would imagine it would be.' He regarded the man, who was dressed in thick trousers, boots and tweed jacket, and decided he didn't like the look of him or his dog. 'Are you His Lordship's new gamekeeper?'

'Something like that,' he said flatly. 'Now be off with you.'

'I'll go when I'm ready,' said Ron, taking offence at his rudeness. 'You might be in charge of everything behind that fence, but I'm free to come and go as I please on this side.'

Harvey was stiff-legged, hackles bristling as he continued to snarl at the other dog, and Ron left him to it while he settled down on a flat ledge of chalk that jutted out from the tangle of briar and gorse and relit his pipe. But his gaze never left the other man's face. He didn't like his manner or his looks, and suspected nothing much got past him either – unlike the old gamekeeper, who could be persuaded to be deaf and half-blind when it came to sharing out the spoils of a night's poaching.

Harvey continued to snarl and growl as he cocked his leg and urinated against the fence to mark his territory. The other dog danced on his back legs and began to bark furiously. But he was restrained by the leash attached to his thick collar, and his barks turned to frustrated howls as he realised he couldn't get to either Ron or Harvey.

The man grunted and yanked on the leash. 'If I catch you tampering with this fence again I'll come looking for you, old man,' he muttered. 'And that mangy mutt of yours.' He yanked again on the leash and had to almost drag the slavering mastiff along as he stomped off back into the woods.

Harvey barked at the retreating figures, his hackles still up, ears flat in dislike.

Ron gave him a hefty pat as he returned to his side and flopped down in the grass. 'That showed them, eh?' he murmured. 'It comes to something when strangers can tell a man what to do on his home territory.'

He smoked his pipe as Harvey groomed himself and calmed down. When the tobacco was burnt to nothing, he knocked the dottle from the pipe, gathered up the string of rabbits and his spade, and stood up. 'We'd better go,' he said. 'But I'm damned if I'll let that eejit get the better of me, Harvey. We'll find a way to outwit him, if it's the last thing we do.'

Cordelia didn't need to turn her hearing aid up to listen to *Workers' Playtime*, for she could put the dial right to the top on the wireless when she was alone in the house, and sing along to Glenn Miller's 'Kalamazoo' as she dusted. She loved listening to the jolly music they always played – and although she had no idea where Kalamazoo was, she enjoyed the catchy tune and knew most of the words now.

'I gotta gaaaaal in Kalama-zoo, zoo, zoo,' she trilled.

'You sound as if you're having fun,' said Jane as she came into the kitchen with Peggy and Sarah. She gave Cordelia a hug. 'I've been having fun too,' she said, her eyes sparkling.

'Goodness me,' gasped Cordelia as she took in the

bright eyes and rosy face. 'What on earth have you been up to? You look as if you've been having fun.'

'Well, I've got a job,' Jane replied as she hastily turned the knob on the wireless and shut off the lovely music. 'I'm going to deliver the milk every morning and look after Mabel. She's lovely – a great big Shire, with the kindest eyes – and Mr Jenkins says he thinks I should get on very well with her and—'

Cordelia frowned and grabbed her hand. 'Why have you got a hob and a table for hire? And why shouldn't I tell Mr Jenkins about the liver and milk? It doesn't sound at all the sort of thing you should be doing, and I'm sure your parents wouldn't approve of such shenanigans.'

She saw Jane tap her ear and make winding signs with her hand, and when she looked at the others, she realised they were giggling, and couldn't for the life of her think what they were finding so funny. She fiddled with her hearing aid, most concerned that Jane seemed to be setting up some sort of black-market stall behind Mr Jenkins' back. 'Now dear,' she said as she sat at the table. 'I think you'd better tell me what this is all about.'

She listened as Jane carefully told her about the job at the dairy, but she lost half of what she was saying because each word seemed to run into the next as Jane's excitement grew. But she got the gist of it. 'I don't know that your parents would like you doing a job like that,' she said fretfully. 'It's not really suitable for young ladies, and those big horses are dangerous.'

'Mabel is the sweetest, dearest old thing,' said Jane, 'and it doesn't matter if I'm only delivering milk – Mr Jenkins said it was a very important job, and I think it's perfect.'

'It's a fair way from here to the dairy,' said Peggy as she mashed some of the leftover vegetables for Daisy's lunch. 'I won't be using my bicycle for a long while yet, so you'd better have it. Ron can make sure everything's oiled and the tyres are pumped up.' She looked up from her task. 'I'm assuming you can ride a bicycle?'

As Jane nodded and clapped her hands in delight, Cordelia realised that the girl had found something to excite and satisfy her. Yet she had a feeling that Sybil and Jock wouldn't approve of such a lowly job for their youngest, rather pampered daughter – but Sarah seemed to accept it, and she didn't suppose it mattered much if their parents approved or not seeing as they weren't here.

'I'm delighted you're so happy,' she said as she patted her slender hand and noted how soft it was. 'I'd better find a pair of my leather gloves for you,' she added. 'Your hands will be ruined.'

Jane hugged her again and kissed her cheek. 'Mr Jenkins has gloves for me, though they're a bit big, and I'll be wearing a white overall over trousers and a jacket, and there's a big striped apron to go over it and a peaked hat with a badge on the front. I'm going to look very smart.'

Cordelia laughed. 'I'm sure you will, dear. Now, let's

have a cup of tea to celebrate and then Sarah can tell me what she's planning to do while you're delivering milk.'

She placed the kettle on the hob and hunted out cups and saucers as Peggy fed Daisy the mashed vegetables. Everyone else would have to have cod roe on toast for lunch, with lots of tomato sauce to take away the horrid taste.

Cordelia made the tea and was just sitting down to talk to Sarah when Ron came tramping in with Harvey. 'You must have smelled the tea,' she said wryly. 'It never fails to amaze me how you turn up the moment I've brewed a fresh pot.'

'Well now, I've a terrible thirst, and me nose tells me that's a proper pot of tea and not the usual dishwater we have around here.'

'The weather was nice, so I went out and bought some this morning,' she said proudly. 'It's incredible how a bit of hobbling and sighing can get you to the front of the queue.' She giggled as he waggled his eyebrows at her. 'But then I've learned to be crafty after living with you all these years,' she added.

'Aye, well, there's no shame in that,' he said as he shooed Harvey away from Daisy, who had most of her lunch down her front. He carefully adjusted his coat and patted his pockets before he sat at the table.

'What have you got in there?' asked Peggy sharply.

'To be sure Flora and Dora are asleep, and I'm not wanting to disturb them.' He reached into another pocket and pulled out the dead rabbits. 'They got these this morning,' he said as he dumped them on the table, all glassy-eyed and stiff. 'I'll skin them after I've had me cup of tea.'

Cordelia noticed how distressed Jane was at seeing those poor dead creatures and slapped Ron's arm. 'You'll put them on the draining board, and cover them up. The kitchen table's no place for dead things.'

He heaved a great sigh and carried them over to the sink, where he covered them with a tea towel. 'They don't offend you when they're in a stew,' he grumbled.

'We can't see what they are by then,' she retorted. She saw the grubby, bloodstained handkerchief around his finger as he hung his coat on the back of the kitchen door and checked that his ferrets were all right. 'That doesn't look very hygienic,' she said. 'What have you done?'

'Ach, 'tis nothing. I'll clean it up later.' He glared at them all, daring them to cause him further delay in getting to his cup of tea. 'So what have you four been up to?' he asked after that first satisfying gulp of hot, sweet nectar. 'You're all looking very pleased with yourselves.'

Cordelia told him about Jane's job. 'We were about to hear how Sarah got on when you came in and interrupted,' she said with a sniff of disapproval. 'And I do wish you wouldn't bring that horrible old coat in here – it smells to high heaven.'

He winked at her. 'Well now, it seems I can't be pleasing you at all today, Cordelia. 'Tis a good thing I'm not one to take easy offence.'

'When you two have quite finished arguing,' said Peggy, trying not to laugh, 'I think we should hear about Sarah's morning.'

Sarah blushed as they all turned to look at her. 'I haven't got very much to tell you,' she said shyly, 'but there is a job I quite like the sound of, and now Jane's suited – well, I think I might go for it.'

'What is it, dear?' Cordelia asked. 'Not thinking of joining the WAAF like Cissy, are you?'

'It's with the Women's Timber Corps,' said Sarah. 'I'd be working in the office at the Cliffe estate if I got the post – and it sounds very similar to the sort of thing I used to do for my father back home in Malaya.'

As Cordelia struggled to hear what Sarah was saying about the work involved, she suddenly noticed how Ron had perked up. He was listening avidly, and there was a gleam of mischief in his eyes that she was all too familiar with. 'That sounds perfect,' she said rather distractedly once Sarah had finished talking.

'To be sure, you'll fit in there like a hand in a glove,' said Ron as he filled his pipe. 'You'll be after going down to the recruiting centre first thing tomorrow before someone else snaps it up. A job like that doesn't come along every day.'

'Yes, I rather think I will,' said Sarah. 'It's work I'm familiar with, and although it sounds as if the estate is quite a long walk away, and I'll have to get up very early to be there on time, I think I might find it all very interesting.'

'I could take you up there this afternoon and show you where it is,' said Ron casually.

'That's very kind of you,' said Sarah, 'but I think I should wait and see if I actually get an interview first.'

'You'll get through all that with flying colours,' he said airily. 'And I'll be glad to show you the way. It's easy to get lost up in the hills if you don't know them well, and so I'm thinking it might be an idea if Harvey and I came with you for the first few days until you've got your bearings. Harvey will appreciate the walk.'

Cordelia realised suddenly what Ron was up to. 'I'm sure you'll both benefit from the exercise,' she said dryly.

He widened his blue eyes with a commendable show of innocence. 'Now, Cordelia, what *could* you be meaning by that?'

'You know very well what she means,' said Peggy. She turned to Sarah. 'Don't trust him an inch, love. His heart's in the right place and his offer is genuine – but he's been trying to find a way into the estate ever since they put up that fence.'

'But why can't he just go through the front gate?' asked Sarah with a frown.

Peggy laughed. 'Poachers never use the front entrance, not if there's a convenient hole to crawl through.'

Sarah giggled. 'Ron,' she teased, 'I never realised. You are naughty.'

'Aye, well,' he said as he shifted about in his chair, 'you don't want to be listening to these two. They have a poor opinion of me, so they do – but they never refuse a nice bit of fish or a few birds for the pot.'

'But wouldn't you get into fearful trouble if you were caught?'

'Yes, he would,' said Peggy grimly, 'and I've heard about the new gamekeeper up there. He's sharp and unpleasant, and the sort who shoots first then asks questions.' She turned to look at Ron. 'You're to promise me you won't go spoiling things for Sarah,' she said sternly.

'Ach, Peggy,' he protested, his hand over his heart. 'You cut me to the quick, so you do, with your suspicions. To be sure I'm a reformed man.' He winked broadly at all of them and returned to slurping his tea.

Sarah and Jane giggled as Peggy and Cordelia tried to keep straight faces. Ronan Reilly was a mischievous old rogue of long-standing. He simply didn't know how to change the habits of a lifetime – and in truth, none of them wanted him to.

While Ron skinned the rabbits and prepared them for the stew, Peggy put Daisy in her playpen surrounded by her toys while she did some housework. The girls had all been very good about tidying their own bedrooms and keeping the bath clean, but the carpet on the landing needed hoovering, and it was about time the hall floor was scrubbed. The tiles were looking decidedly grubby with so many feet trampling over them every day.

She was humming quietly to herself as she ran

the vacuum cleaner over the carpet, and tried not to notice the cobwebs that were hanging from the ceiling and drifting along the picture rails and over the lampshade. The whole place needed spring-cleaning, but she just didn't have the time – and with all the girls so busy, it seemed unfair to ask them to get up stepladders with brooms. At least there weren't that many windows to wash any more, so that was a blessing, but she did wish everything didn't look quite so shabby.

Having finished upstairs, she went into the kitchen, fetched the mop, and filled a bucket with hot water. Ron was outside in the back garden with Jane, showing her how to repair the flat tyre on the bicycle as Harvey dozed in the spring sunshine beside Cordelia's deck-chair. Sarah was examining the Anderson shelter and, by the look on her face, didn't rate it very highly.

Daisy gurgled and rolled over onto her stomach, and as Peggy watched, managed to push herself up on her hands and kick her feet. She looked a bit like a floundering fish, but it was her first attempt at crawling, and Peggy swept her up and covered her face in kisses.

Daisy squirmed and wriggled and Peggy put her back in the playpen, where she immediately rolled onto her stomach and chuckled at her cleverness. Peggy blinked as tears pricked. They grew up so fast, and Jim was missing his daughter's first attempt at crawling. He would also miss her first tooth, for it had come through only the other day, and she could feel two more under her bottom gum. 'Damn you, Hitler,' she muttered. 'Damn you and this bloody, bloody war for tearing my family apart.'

'Oh, Peggy, what's got you so upset?'

She hadn't heard Suzy come in, and she turned to face her, feeling rather embarrassed at being caught feeling sorry for herself. 'I'm just letting off a bit of steam,' she said. 'It's been quite a day and we're only halfway through it.'

Suzy took off the lovely blue woollen cape with its red lining, and hung it over the back of a chair before she sat down and eased off her sturdy rubber-soled shoes. 'I know how you feel,' she said as she rubbed her toes. 'Matron's been in a foul mood all night and I couldn't wait to come home.'

Peggy quickly poured boiling water over the cooling tea leaves and placed the cup in front of her. 'Are you still seeing Anthony this evening?'

'Yes, though how long I'll manage to stay awake, I don't know. But at least I'll get a lie-in tomorrow.' She sipped her tea and closed her eyes as she gave a deep sigh of pleasure. 'Heaven,' she murmured. 'Hot tea, a quiet kitchen and no one wanting anything from me.'

'Actually,' said Peggy awkwardly, 'I was wondering if you could do me a bit of a favour?'

Suzy opened her eyes and sat up, her expression immediately concerned. 'Of course, Peggy. How can I help?'

'I understand that Anthony gave you the number for his direct line at work?'

'Well, yes,' she said with a frown. 'But he's told me not to telephone unless it's important. His bosses don't like personal calls during working hours.'

'This is a bit important,' said Peggy and went on to explain about Jane and her new job, and the possibility that she had skills which could open far more promising doors. 'I know it's an awful cheek,' she finished in a rush, 'but if he could rustle up a few tests for her to do, I'd feel I'd kept my promise to her.'

'I'll ring him now, and see what he says.' Suzy smiled. 'Then I'm going to bed to snatch a few hours' sleep before supper.' She finished her tea, grabbed her cape and headed for the hall.

Peggy tried not to listen in as she found the scrubbing brush and cloth from under the sink, but there was a lot of murmuring and cooing going on, and it reminded her too sharply of her own courting days. She blinked and sniffed and determinedly tugged the curtain back over the shelves of household cleaning materials.

Suzy stuck her head around the door. 'He said that's fine, and he'll come over about seven. Now I'm off to get some beauty sleep.'

Peggy couldn't help but smile as she gathered everything up and headed into the hall. There was nothing like a bit of romance to liven things up, even if it did bring back painful memories of her youth – and if Jane did prove to be as adept as she said, then who knew where it might lead? Anthony had lots of contacts, and although she had no idea what he actually did for the MOD, she was sure it was terribly important. How marvellous if he could find Jane something really interesting to do.

Sarah had watched carefully as Peggy and Cordelia made the stew, for there would come a time when she would have to take her turn at cooking, and if she wasn't going to poison everyone, she had to learn quickly.

She and Jane had prepared the vegetables and cored the cooking apples Ron had stored in the cellar since the previous summer, so they could be baked in the oven and then served with the cream from the top of the milk. It seemed that English food was plain and heavy, but then it was still very cold, and she supposed they needed all that weight to keep them warm. She missed the lightly baked fish and aromatic chicken that Wa Ling used to prepare – and the noodles and fragrant rice, and the exotic fruit that was always in abundance. This morning's trip into town had been an eye-opener, for the shops were almost empty and there was no fruit on display at all.

Fran came back from the hospital just as everyone was sitting down for their evening meal at six o'clock. 'Matron has been on my case all day,' she said dramatically as she swept off her cape and flung her cap onto the sideboard. 'I don't know what's eating her, but I wish it would gobble her up and get rid of her once and for all.'

'She's probably as tired and fed up with things as

everyone else,' said Suzy, who was looking very pretty in a twinset of blue wool that matched her eyes and a short cream skirt she'd made out of an old dress. 'I'm sure she'll be on better form tomorrow.'

'She needs a bit of romance to soften her up,' said Fran with a glower. 'Though no man in his right mind would go anywhere near the old dragon.'

'Men aren't the answer to everything, Fran,' said Rita with her usual bluntness. 'Honestly, if you had to work with them day in and day out, you'd soon wish you were back on the wards with Matron.'

'Well, I'm going to be working with horses,' said Jane, unable to keep her news to herself any longer, 'and horses are nicer than people any day.'

Sarah smiled as Jane chattered on about her job. It was lovely to see how well all these girls got on, and it was clear that Jane was relishing these new friendships. She turned to Peggy. 'Are they always this happy together?' she asked quietly.

'There have been a few minor spats over the years – one can't expect a bunch of girls to live together without there being fits of pique or temper tantrums over make-up or belongings. But on the whole they rub along nicely, and I'm glad you and Jane are fitting in so well.'

Fran's voice made them return to the conversation around the table. 'Well, you can't go working with horses with your hair hanging down your back like that,' she said. 'I'll show you how to fix it in victory rolls if you like. It'll be much neater, and you've got such a pretty face, you shouldn't hide it behind all that hair.'

Jane blushed. 'Won't it be a bit too grown-up? Mummy said I shouldn't put my hair up until I'm eighteen.'

'When's your birthday?' asked Rita.

'July the ninth.'

'That's only four months away,' said Rita, 'and close enough not to make much difference. I'd give it a go, if I were you.'

'I'll show you after tea,' said Fran, 'and while I'm at it, I'll do something about Rita's mop. She's looking more like a shaggy sheepdog every day.'

'You should see to your own,' muttered Rita as she eyed the amber and gold tangle of riotous curls which had escaped the pins. 'It's like a brush fire.'

Jane explained she might not be able to get her hair done immediately after supper because of Anthony and the tests.

Fran laughed. 'To be sure, it seems we all want something from the poor wee man. It's a good thing he's so smitten with our Suzy – I swear to all the saints, we wouldn't see him for dust otherwise.'

'And I know how he must feel,' grumbled Ron. 'To be sure, 'tis the divil's curse to be surrounded by demanding, chattering women every day. A man is never left in peace.'

'We all know you love it really,' teased Fran, 'so don't come the old soldier, Ron. It doesn't wash.'

'A martyr I am,' he said woefully to Sarah. 'With me

shrapnel on the move, and no one to care. You see how they treat me?'

Sarah smiled uncertainly. 'I didn't know you were injured,' she murmured.

Ron brightened immediately. 'I was wounded in the first war,' he said. 'Came home with a medal and a lump of metal in me back, and do you know—'

'I don't think this is a suitable topic of conversation for the tea table,' interrupted Peggy quickly. She turned to Sarah and smiled. 'Ron enjoys talking about his war wound, and we've heard about it too frequently to mention. But the tale gets longer and more heroic with every telling, so be warned.'

Ron grinned. 'Now, Peggy, you wouldn't be doubting me, would you?'

'Not at all,' she retorted, 'but you have to admit, Ron, there's more blarney in your tale than there is in the whole of Ireland.'

This was greeted with a chorus of giggles, and Sarah happily continued eating the baked apple. It was very sour, but clearly it was the only fruit available. She liked Ron, who was as entertaining as he was scruffy, and she wondered what her father would make of him. They'd probably get on like a house on fire, she realised, for they could both tell a fine tale.

Once supper was over, Peggy and Cordelia were ordered to sit down by the fire and relax while Sarah and the others cleared the table and did the washing-up. With that done, they made a pot of tea, and Fran ignored Rita's protests and started trying to bring some order to her dark mop of hair.

Sarah sat beside Jane and watched in amusement as the two girls battled to get their own way.

'Will you be sitting still?' hissed Fran as she wrestled hairpins through the thick roll of hair.

'I would if you didn't keep stabbing me.' Rita winced. 'That's the third time.'

'You have to suffer if you want to be beautiful,' said Fran.

'But I'm quite happy with the way I am,' protested Rita. 'How on earth am I supposed to get my fireman's helmet over the top of all this?'

'Don't wear one,' said Fran as she continued to stab and roll and stab again. 'Bejesus, Rita, you've a head of hair, that's to be sure.'

'Have you seen yourself lately?' Rita asked crossly. 'Talk about the pot calling the kettle black.'

'I think you've both got lovely hair,' sighed Jane as she fingered the thick plait that hung over her shoulder. 'Mine's always been just straight, and hanging. I tried putting curlers in once, but they did no good at all.'

'Count yourself lucky,' said Fran. 'It's the very divil to get a comb through it in the mornings, and when it rains it frizzes up and looks a fright.'

'Then you should understand how painful it is with you jabbing and pulling at me,' said Rita, who was still in a bit of a huff.

The argument was interrupted by a knock on the front door, and Harvey barked as Suzy raced to answer it. There was murmuring in the hall followed by a long silence, and Fran and Rita exchanged knowing looks. 'It would seem Romeo has arrived,' said Fran in a hoarse whisper.

'Shhhh,' admonished Peggy. 'It'll be your turn one day, and you wouldn't like it if we all listened in and made comments.'

Sarah thought of Philip and the few moments they'd managed to snatch before they were torn apart. The ache for him was always there, just beneath the surface, waiting to emerge at moments like this. She looked at Peggy and wondered if she too felt that ache, and suspected that she did, for although she'd never met Jim, she'd learned enough about him from Peggy to suspect that he was the love of her life.

Anthony was quite a surprise, for Sarah had expected Suzy's young man to be rather dashing after all she'd said about him. But he was very ordinary-looking, with dark hair and glasses, his tall, slender figure dressed conservatively in slacks and a tweed jacket which had leather patches on the elbows. But when he smiled she could see why Suzy was attracted to him, for it was a shy, gentle smile that lit up his face and made him handsome.

Suzy introduced him to Sarah and Jane while Peggy hurried to pour him a cup of tea.

Anthony unwound his college scarf and stuffed it into the sagging pocket of his jacket as he smiled shyly at Jane. 'Suzy said you enjoyed mathematics and puzzles, so I've brought some of my old examination papers and a couple of out-of-date code books,' he said as he reached into his rather battered briefcase. 'Why don't you make a start, and see how far you can get?'

'Go into the dining room, Jane,' said Peggy. 'I've cleared a table in there and it'll be quiet.'

'How long do I have?' she asked.

He pushed his glasses up his nose and glanced at the mantel clock. 'Shall we say half an hour?'

Jane nodded and rushed off.

Sarah tried to concentrate on the chatter around her, but her mind was on Jane in the other room. She just hoped she wasn't rushing things and therefore being careless, for it was important she showed Anthony how good she was so that she could find something more sensible to do than deliver the daily milk.

The half-hour seemed to drag as the others talked about their plans for the weekend, and tried to get her to join in the conversation and agree to go out with them. 'I don't know if I'll be able to,' she said. 'I might have a job by then, and as I'm not sure of the hours, it's difficult to make plans.'

'Well, all work and no play makes a girl very dull,' said Fran as she finished doing Rita's hair. 'The offer's there if you want it.'

'What do you think?' asked Rita, turning her head this way and that.

'I think it's lovely,' said Sarah truthfully. 'It makes you look very feminine and grown-up.'

'It makes me feel as if my head's been clamped in

a steel helmet,' muttered Rita as she tried to see her reflection in the glass covering the picture of the King and Queen which hung above the mantelpiece.

'You look very pretty,' said Cordelia as she regarded her over her half-moon glasses. 'It's nice to see you as a girl again and not a tomboy. All you need now is a pretty frock and proper shoes, and you would be the belle of the ball.'

Rita pulled a face and tried to appear nonchalant, but Sarah suspected she liked her new appearance.

Jane came back into the room and handed Anthony a wad of examination papers and one of the code books. 'I couldn't do some of it, but I'd like to keep the books if I may. I love puzzles, and these are really good ones – they made me think very hard.'

Sarah watched closely as he took the papers and sifted through them quickly. She saw how his eyes widened and his carefully guarded expression sharpened as he examined page after page of neat figures. He was impressed, she could tell, and she felt a great swell of pride for her little sister's amazing ability.

She continued to watch as he took the code book and read the pieces of paper on which she'd written the answers. When he'd finished he looked up at Jane, his expression unreadable. 'That's very good, Jane,' he said, his voice sounding rather stiff. 'I can see you have a real talent for both maths and puzzles, but I'll be interested to see how you cope with something a little more advanced.'

'Really? So I did all right then?' she asked eagerly.

'You did very well,' he said, his tone non-committal as he reached into his briefcase and pulled out a sheaf of papers. 'Take these into the other room. You have ten minutes to solve one of these.'

'I thought we were going out?' murmured Suzy as Jane dashed off.

He smiled at her. 'We are, I promise. Just give me another ten minutes, and then I'm all yours.'

Suzy giggled and went off to powder her nose and fetch her coat, while Sarah wondered what sort of thing Anthony was testing her sister with now. But Anthony was deep in conversation with Cordelia, so there was no chance to ask him.

Jane returned exactly ten minutes later. 'I did two,' she said as she handed over the sheets of paper. 'I hope you don't mind.'

'Well done,' Anthony murmured as he quickly read through the pages. When he'd finished, he stuffed them back in his briefcase and fastened the lock, his expression inscrutable. 'I'll write you a reference with pleasure,' he said, 'and bring it round in a couple of days when I next have time off.'

'Thank you,' breathed Jane. 'You've been very kind.'

'Not at all.' He turned to Peggy. 'May I leave this here, Aunt Peg? I'll fetch it before I go home.'

Peggy took the briefcase. 'I'll put it in my room,' she said as she eyed him questioningly.

'Oh, there's nothing of any importance in there,' he said lightly, 'but I don't want to be carrying it about all evening.'

Suzy fastened the buttons on her coat and tied the belt around her waist before slipping her hand into the crook of his arm. 'I need that drink now,' she said. 'It's been a long day.'

Anthony smiled down at her, his face radiant with love. 'Your carriage awaits,' he said. 'I managed to borrow an Austin from the castle car-pool. We have it until eleven.' They waved goodbye and were gone.

There were a lot of questions Sarah wanted to ask Jane, but she was chattering away to Fran, who'd started to brush her hair and roll it into shining coils away from her face.

'So what sort of tests were they?' she asked as soon as Jane stopped for breath.

Her sister shrugged. 'Just mathematical problems and a few codes. Some of the codes were a bit tricky and I would have needed much longer than ten minutes to work them out, but I think he was pleased, don't you?'

'He wouldn't have offered to write the reference if he hadn't been,' said Peggy.

'Do you think he might find me a job as well?' asked Jane breathlessly. 'Only I really enjoyed doing those tests.'

'I really don't know,' admitted Sarah, 'but if you do get an office job, you'll have to tell Mr Jenkins you won't be able to deliver his milk.'

'Oh, no,' Jane retorted fiercely. 'I'll stay at the dairy and do something in an office as well if I get the chance.'

'But I don't like the thought of you—'

'Don't fuss, Sarah,' she retorted. 'I'm perfectly capable of looking after myself.'

Sarah suddenly realised that Jane had a new confidence about her, and that she was indeed quite capable of making her own decisions about things. The Japanese invasion of Malaya and their flight from Singapore had wrought a huge difference in her little sister. Without the smothering love of her parents and Amah, who'd protected her too well, she was blossoming into the young woman she was meant to be.

Chapter Twenty-Two

Sarah was woken at four in the morning by the deafening clamour of Peggy's alarm clock. She quickly reached out and silenced it before it woke the whole house, and then stayed beneath the blankets as Jane raced around the room and got ready for her first day at work. 'How are you feeling?' she asked as her sister pulled on a sweater.

'Nervous,' she admitted, 'but excited too. I hardly slept a wink last night.'

Sarah smiled as Jane tied the laces on her shoes and adjusted the waistband of the trousers Sarah had been given in Glasgow. They were a bit large for her, but she held them up with a belt Rita had lent her, and then reached for her hairbrush and tried to emulate the style Fran had created the previous evening. What a very different girl she was to the pampered and childish Jane who had left the plantation, for now she had a purpose, and she was beginning to make her own way.

'I can't get this right,' Jane said in exasperation, 'and if I spend any longer on it, I'll be late.' She put down the brush, twisted her hair into a knot on the top of her head and tethered it with pins. 'That will have to do, and no one will see it anyway once I've got my cap on.'

Sarah noticed the doubt suddenly cloud Jane's excitement and hurried out of bed to give her a reassuring cuddle. 'It will all feel very strange to begin with, but you'll soon get the hang of things.'

Jane nodded. 'I'll have Mabel to help me,' she said, 'and she's been doing that round for years. Mr Jenkins said she could probably do it on her own by now, but of course she can't pick up the empties and put the new ones on the doorsteps.' She giggled. 'I'm babbling, aren't I?'

Sarah smiled. 'Just a bit. Do you want me to come down with you and see you off?'

Jane shook her head, her expression earnest. 'I have to do this on my own, Sarah. You do understand, don't you?'

'Yes,' she said softly, 'and I'm very proud of you.' She kissed her cheek and gave her a gentle nudge towards the door. 'Don't get lost on the way or fall off that bike – and don't forget to take the wellington boots Ron dug out for you, and to make a flask of tea to take with you.'

Jane rolled her eyes. 'Go back to bed, Sarah,' she said firmly. 'And good luck with your interview. I'll see you later.'

Sarah climbed back into bed after she'd shut the door, and tried to imagine her sister in the kitchen making a thermos of tea the way Peggy had shown them, and then getting the bike out of the cellar without disturbing Ron and his animals, before cycling through the silent twilight to the very northern border of Cliffehaven.

She snuggled down beneath the blankets and tried to relax, but there was a knot of anxiety in her stomach. Jane would be all right, and so would she – but if the job with the WTC had been taken, then she would have to find something else, and quickly before their money ran out. She was loath to dip into the bank account, for it might be needed in an emergency, and she had absolutely no intention of selling her mother's earrings and bracelet, which she'd unpicked from the hems of her dresses and hidden, with her pearls, on top of the very tall wardrobe. With only five pounds in her purse to see them through until they were paid, it was imperative she got a job – and soon.

'You're up early,' said Peggy, who was already bathing Daisy in the sink as the kettle sang on the hob. 'Take that off and make us a pot of tea, dear. All that whistling is giving me earache.'

Sarah made the tea and, as Peggy told her where everything was kept, began to lay the table for breakfast. 'What time does the recruitment place open?' she asked as she stirred the porridge carefully.

'Nine o'clock sharp, but you'll need to get there at least half an hour earlier if you don't want to stand about for ages in a queue.' Peggy looked Sarah up and down, taking in the tartan kilt and dark green sweater, the neat hair pinned back in a shining blonde pleat, and the hint of lipstick, powder and mascara to enliven her face. 'You look very smart,' she said. 'I'm sure the WTC will snap you up.'

Sarah silently hoped so, for a lot was riding on today, and she had no intention of letting little Jane become the breadwinner.

Sarah didn't have much appetite for breakfast; she was too nervous. She left Beach View almost an hour and a half too early, with everyone's best wishes ringing in her ears, and started to walk down Camden Road.

Her mouth was dry and her pulse was racing, but she was determined not to show how much this interview meant to her. And yet it was a strange feeling to be so nervous. After all, it was just a job and, by the sound of it, one she could do very well – but then she'd never expected to be in this situation, and hadn't realised how easy and privileged her life had been until now. It wasn't only Jane who had to learn to adapt to this strange and rather frightening new way of things, and Sarah's usual confidence wavered as she reached the High Street.

It was already busy, with Army lorries roaring back and forth and delivery boys on bicycles dodging the office workers, and the tram rattling past. A few hardy souls had already started queuing outside the Home and Colonial. There was a blue sky overhead, which boded well, but despite the early sunshine, it was still chilly, and Sarah pulled up the collar of her coat as she headed for the Town Hall.

The office wasn't open, so she decided to find a table close to the door in the WVS canteen and have a cigarette while she kept an eye on any queue that might form outside the office.

'Hello, dear, you're an early bird.' Vera Watkins was having a cup of tea and a cigarette, and she waved to Sarah. 'Come and join me,' she said pleasantly.

Sarah sat down and gave her a nervous smile. 'I've come to tell you I'd like to apply for the WTC post,' she said.

Vera's welcoming smile faded. 'Oh,' she said. 'I see.'

Sarah's spirits tumbled. 'Someone else has got it, haven't they?' she said unsteadily. 'I knew I should have come back yesterday afternoon.'

'It probably would have been wise,' murmured Vera, 'and I was going to telephone Peggy to get you back here, but you know how it is – the day just flew past, and what with one thing and another, I forgot.' Her gaze was sympathetic. 'I'm sorry, dear.'

'It's not your fault,' said Sarah, trying hard not to show how bitterly disappointed she was. 'I'm sure there must be something else I can do.'

Vera smiled as she stubbed out her cigarette. 'All is not lost,' she said cheerfully, 'and as you're here so early I'm sure I can persuade Mr Cruikshank to fit you in.'

Sarah frowned. 'Mr Cruikshank?'

Vera checked her lipstick in her compact mirror and then smiled. 'He's the forester who's been in charge up there for as long as I can remember. He's holding the interviews in the estate office today, so you see, you still have a chance.'

Sarah's hope rose again. 'How many girls are going for it?'

'Six,' said Vera, 'all with secretarial and book-keeping experience, but none with your knowledge of measuring and essaying.' She cocked her head. 'Still interested?'

'Oh, yes please,' breathed Sarah.

'Then we'd better get on.' Vera gathered up her gas-mask box, handbag and briefcase. 'I'll telephone Mr Cruikshank to warn him he has another candidate, then we can deal with all the paperwork and answer your questions before I have to open the office. That way you'll get up to the estate in time for your interview – but it is quite a walk, and time is of the essence.'

'This is very good of you, Vera.' Sarah followed Vera into her office.

'It's my pleasure,' said Vera simply as she settled behind the desk and reached for the telephone. 'How did your sister get on at the dairy, by the way?'

Sarah grinned. 'She started this morning and has fallen in love with Mabel the Shire.'

'That's excellent news. Mr Jenkins is a fair employer and she should be happy there.' Vera fell silent as she waited for her telephone call to be put through, and then smiled. 'Good morning, Mr Cruikshank, so sorry to bother you this early, but I have another candidate for you.'

Sarah listened anxiously as Vera expounded on her

skills and coaxed a clearly reluctant Mr Cruikshank into giving her an interview.

'Twelve-fifteen, then,' said Vera. 'No, she won't be late, I promise.' She shot Sarah a warning glance, said goodbye to the man at the other end of the line and put down the receiver. 'We haven't much time at all,' she said, 'and as you probably heard, he wasn't that happy about extending the interview time to accommodate you. But I think I managed to persuade him you were a worthy candidate.'

Waving Sarah's thanks away, she became very businesslike. 'You already know what the job entails, and Mr Cruikshank and the administrators from the Women's Land Army and MOS will fill in any of the smaller details.'

A shaft of dread made Sarah go cold. 'So it won't just be Mr Cruikshank doing the interview?'

'The WTC is part of the Land Army, and they answer directly to the Ministry of Supply, so they need to oversee everything and make sure they have the right candidate before everything is set up and finalised,' said Vera distractedly as she hunted through the pile of paperwork on her desk.

Sarah digested this information and tried not to let her nerves get the better of her. She'd never been to a job interview and had absolutely no idea what it might entail, but the thought that she would have to impress not only the forester, but the officials from the Women's Land Army as well as the Ministry of Supply, was daunting.

Vera seemed oblivious to Sarah's rising panic as she retrieved a wad of papers and removed the bulldog clip that held them together. 'As you have so many of the necessary measuring and assessing skills, you'd be on the top wage of four pounds a week if you get the post. Lunch would be provided, so that's good.'

Sarah's answering smile was a little stiff. 'Would I have to wear some sort of uniform, or could I just go in my everyday clothes?'

'As a member of the WTC you would have to wear a uniform, even though you'd be in an office for most of the time.' Vera gave a rueful smile. 'It's not terribly flattering, I'm afraid. You'd have to wear a green jersey, gabardine trousers that bear a faint resemblance to riding breeches, woollen knee socks, a beige shirt, boots, and a green beret with a WTC badge.' She smiled and shrugged. 'It doesn't sound frightfully appealing, does it, but as you're not preparing for a fashion parade and all the girls look the same, it wouldn't really matter.'

'You said before that I'd be in charge of the payroll. What sort of wages are the others earning?'

'Anything from thirty-five to forty-six bob a week. That's between one pound fifteen shillings and two pounds six shillings,' she explained as Sarah was trying to work it out. 'You'd better brush up on your pounds, shillings and pence before you get started,' she added wryly. 'If those pay packets are wrong at the end of the week there'll be a riot.'

Sarah nodded. She'd already wrestled with the

strange sterling currency in which there were twenty shillings to the pound, and twelve pence to the shilling. The Malay dollar was easy, for everything was in tens. She'd have to keep her wits about her if she got the job – or horror of horrors, the interviewers decided to test her.

Vera passed a piece of paper across the desk. 'This is a map of the estate which shows how to get there.' She ran her finger over the map, following a northward trail that seemed to go on and on. 'It's a bit of a trek up that hill from Peggy's, but once you're on the top it's downhill all the way.'

'Thank you, Vera, but Ron said he'd go with me for the first few times.'

Vera raised an eyebrow. 'And how is Ron? Still as disreputable as ever?'

Sarah giggled. 'He's an old rascal,' she said, 'and he has us all in stitches when he starts telling his war stories.'

Vera grinned and pushed a form towards her. 'Fill that in,' she said. 'I know it's a nuisance, but this war can only be won if we fill in endless forms – and you'll need to take it with you today.'

Once Sarah had filled in everything she handed it back for Vera to check. 'That all seems to be in order,' she said and clipped it with the other papers. She smiled back at her. 'Good luck, Sarah. I hope you get it, but if you don't, well, you know where I am.'

Sarah gathered her things together, tucked the paperwork and map in her handbag and shook Vera's hand. 'Thank you for everything,' she said gratefully. 'You've been very kind.'

'Just let me know how you get on,' she replied. 'Now hurry up, it's a long walk and you can't afford to be late.'

Peggy had a row of pristine white nappies flapping on the line, and because it was such a lovely day, she'd decided to put Daisy's pram out in the back garden so she could get some fresh air. It got awfully stuffy in the kitchen, what with the fire in the range, the cooking and washing and Ron's pipe-smoke, and she was sure it didn't do Daisy any good at all. Yet she looked healthy enough, kicking her legs and waving her arms as she gurgled at the dappled shadows of the neighbour's tree that danced across her pram.

Peggy sighed. It would have been lovely to sit in a deckchair for a while and just let the world go by, but there was too much to do, and if she sat still for any amount of time she thought about Jim and how far away he was – and that just made her sad. She wiped her hands down her wrap-round pinafore, picked up the laundry basket and headed back into the kitchen where Cordelia was doing the ironing as she listened to the wireless.

Peggy winced and turned the volume down to a bearable level, then signed to Cordelia to turn up her hearing aid. The neighbours would start complaining soon, and they'd all be deaf before too long if they had to stand that every day.

Cordelia ran the hot iron over a pillowcase, then folded it neatly and placed it on the pile of freshly laundered linen that sat on the kitchen table. 'I enjoy ironing,' she said as she put the flat-iron on the hob to heat up and picked up the other one. 'There's something very satisfactory about a pile of sweet-smelling, freshly ironed washing.'

Peggy agreed with her, but looking at the state of Ron's shirt, she wondered if it was worth washing it any more – she had better-looking cleaning rags under the sink. She plucked it out of the pile of washing yet to be ironed, found two more that were hanging together by threads, and stuffed them into her ragbag. 'I'll have to winkle some of his clothing coupons out of him and get new ones,' she said with a sigh. 'He's beginning to look like an old tramp.'

Cordelia smoothed the hot iron over a blouse. 'It'll be a good thing when Rosie comes back,' she said. 'Ron takes care of his appearance when she's around.' She looked over at Peggy, who had begun to scrub the larder shelves. 'Has there been any news of her?'

'None that I know of, and I'm sure Ron would have told us if she'd written to him.' Peggy sat back on her heels and grimaced. 'Findlay's still in charge at the Anchor. I saw him leaning in the doorway as if he owned the place the other morning. There's been talk about women staying there overnight and all sorts of shenanigans going on in the bar. If Rosie doesn't get back soon, she'll have no pub to run.'

The clatter of the letter box got Peggy to her feet

and she hurried expectantly into the hall. There were several letters for the others, but there was only one that lightened her heart, for she'd have recognised that writing anywhere.

'I've got a letter from Jim at last,' she said excitedly as she sat at the kitchen table and tore open the envelope.

Her spirits plummeted as she pulled out the three pages which almost fell to pieces in her hand. 'The censor has cut it to ribbons,' she said crossly as she showed Cordelia the gaping holes and the thick black lines that had been scored through some of the words. 'It's almost unintelligible.'

'I suppose it's to do with security,' sympathised Cordelia, 'but I hardly think Jim's in possession of state secrets.'

Peggy read what was left of the letter and felt the prick of tears as she folded it back into the envelope. 'He's well, and the food is plentiful but not up to my standards, evidently,' she said as she sniffed back her tears. 'He's enjoying the company of the other men, but the work is hard and the Sergeant Major is a little man with a big ego and a voice that can probably be heard in the next county. Jim's back is playing up, the boots have given him blisters, his hands are covered in calluses and he's moaning about being out in all weathers. Apart from that, the beer is good, and he's made a couple of good mates, but he misses everyone, and sends his love to us all. He's hoping to get a week's leave in a couple of months' time but can't promise anything, because he's so far away.'

'I suppose we're not allowed to know where?'

Peggy shook her head. 'He started out in Yorkshire and has been sent north, so he could be anywhere – but the censor cut that bit out.' She heard Daisy gurgling happily outside. 'I'll look out the box brownie and take some snaps of Daisy when we get back from the clinic,' she said. 'He's going to miss so much of her growing up, and it's the only way to keep him up to date with how she's doing.'

'He'll enjoy getting some photographs,' agreed Cordelia as she finished ironing the last skirt. 'And while you're at it, you should send some of you as well. I'm not much good with such things, but I'm sure one of the girls would be happy to use the camera.'

Peggy put the letter behind the clock on the mantel and returned to scrubbing the larder. Life without Jim would be unbearable if she gave herself time to think about it – but as long as she kept battling through each day, and continued to be positive about things, she would get through this. And then, when the war was over and Jim had come home along with the rest of her family, they could return to how it had once been.

Sarah was out of breath, and her second-hand shoes had given her a painful blister on her left heel. She hurried across the street and made her way along the narrow lane between the houses and into the back garden of Beach View, wondering how she would manage to walk all the way to the Cliffe estate with her heel hurting the way it did.

There was no sign of Ron or Harvey as she hurried into the basement, and her spirits flagged as she realised the ferrets were not in their cages. She hobbled up the steps to the kitchen. 'Where's Ron?' she asked as she sank gratefully into a chair.

'He went out just after breakfast,' said Peggy. 'Why? Did you need him for something?'

Sarah nodded and gingerly eased off her shoe and ankle sock. 'I've got an interview on the estate at a quarter-past twelve, and I need him to show me the way.' The blister was large and threatening to pop at any minute. 'Will he be back soon, do you think? Only I don't have much time and this is going to slow me down.'

Peggy chewed her lip. 'He's a law unto himself,' she murmured, 'and could be out for hours yet.' She examined the blister. 'I'll pop that and put some surgical spirit and a plaster on it. But you'll have to change those shoes.'

'They're the only ones I have except for my sandals,' said Sarah, close to tears with frustration and anxiety, 'and I can't go for an interview in them. No one would take me seriously.' She glanced fretfully at the clock on the mantel. It was already past nine-thirty.

'You could wear the sandals and carry your shoes,' said Cordelia as she fetched the first-aid box from the dresser.

'That's a very good idea,' Sarah replied thankfully, 'but I'm not really sure how to get to the estate. Vera gave me a map, but I've never been very good at things like that, and I can't afford to get lost up there and be late.' Her voice wavered as she blinked back the tears. 'Could you come with me, Peggy?'

'I'm so sorry, but I can't – not this morning. I have to take Daisy to the clinic for her immunisation, and after that I'm due to see the doctor for a check-up.' Peggy carefully popped the blister and dabbed it with surgical spirit before expertly applying a sticking plaster. She patted Sarah's knee. 'Let's have a look at that map, and I'll mark out things you should look for on the way.'

Sarah could feel the blister stinging, but it was a small discomfort compared to the rising panic, which was making her feel a bit sick. She pulled the map out of her bag and spread it on the table.

Peggy got a stub of pencil from a jar on the mantelpiece and began to mark the gun emplacements and the fire-watch stations. 'When you get here, you will see the ruins of an old farmhouse. Go down the hill keeping the ruins on your right, and you'll see the valley spread out below you. The estate will be on your left – follow the line of trees right round until you come to the lane which leads to the little village where my daughter and her husband have a cottage. But don't go towards the village, go to the left. The estate entrance will be on your left, about four hundred yards down the lane, and Cruikshank's office is down the right-hand fork in the long drive. That will lead you to the forest, and his office is about a hundred yards into the trees on your left.'

Sarah tried to absorb all this information as Peggy

drew the line on the map and marked each landmark with an x. 'How long will it take me?' she asked.

'A good hour or more, so you'll have to leave soon.' Peggy smiled at her. 'Fetch your sandals while I stick some cotton wool into the back of your shoes. Then you can sit and have a cup of tea and a cigarette while you settle those nerves.'

Sarah ran barefooted up the stairs to fetch her sandals. A glance in the mirror showed that her hair was escaping the pins, there was a smudge of mascara under her eyes and she'd chewed off most of her lipstick. 'You look a mess,' she muttered as she cleaned away the smudge and swiftly pinned her hair up again. 'Calm down, Sarah, or you'll look a complete fright by the time you get there.'

Returning to the kitchen with the flat thonged sandals, she drank the welcome cup of tea and smoked a cigarette. Feeling only slightly calmer, she repaired her lipstick, dumped her socks in her handbag alongside the papers Vera had given her and snapped it shut. It was now almost a quarter-past ten, and although there were two hours to go before the interview, she had to make allowances for her lack of fitness and the very real possibility of getting lost.

'Good luck, dear,' said Cordelia as she squeezed her hand. 'Peggy and I will keep our fingers crossed for you.'

Sarah stuffed her shoes into her raincoat pocket and picked up the map and gas-mask box. She tried to return their encouraging smiles, but the muscles in her face were too tight with anxiety. She headed back down to the cellar and hurried along the garden path, her sandals slapping against the flagstones.

She turned in the gateway and saw Cordelia and Peggy standing at the kitchen window. She waved back to them, hitched the straps of her handbag and gas-mask box over her shoulder, and with the map firmly clenched in her fist, began the long, unfamiliar walk up into the hills.

Sarah was out of breath from the steep climb to the brow and the sandals kept slipping on the grass, which slowed her down. They hadn't been made for treks like this, and the delicate leather thongs between her toes were beginning to rub. But she knew she had to ignore the discomfort and keep going, and, as she caught her breath and checked the landmarks on the map, she began to feel a bit more confident. Peggy had marked everything well, and she could see clearly which way she had to go.

She set off again, hardly aware of the blue sky and the sharp, salty wind that blew in from the sea as she followed the pencil line on the map and mentally ticked off each landmark. The ruined farmhouse came into view and she drew to a halt. There was the broad valley and the forest of trees which had now been fenced in. She hitched the straps over her shoulder and tentatively made her way down the steep slope into the valley.

The soles of her sandals were smooth and slippery

and several times she almost ended up on her bottom, but she made it finally and stopped for a moment to catch her breath and check the time. It was half-past eleven, and although it didn't look as if she had much further to go, the distances on the map had proved deceiving, so she couldn't afford to be complacent.

The grass was greener in the valley and there were vibrant yellow flowers on the dark spiny bushes that seemed to grow everywhere. She followed the tall wire fence that Ron had moaned about and was beginning to wonder how much further she had to go when she saw the country lane. It wound along the valley between fields and hedgerows and disappeared into the distance, where she could just see the top of a church spire. That must be the village where Peggy's daughter Anne had a cottage, so she had to turn left.

Feeling rather pleased with herself, and relieved that her journey was almost at an end, she hurried down the rough country lane, her sandals scuffing up the dust. But now she seemed to have gone further than four hundred yards and there was still no sign of the two big pillars that guarded the entrance to the estate. She was beginning to panic that she'd gone the wrong way. But as she followed yet another long bend in the lane she saw them, and the relief was so great she found she had to stop because she was shaking so much.

With the entrance in her sights, she sat on the grassy bank at the side of the lane and took off her sandals. Her feet were filthy and there were small red marks between her toes where the thongs had begun to rub yet more blisters, but she wasn't going to let a bit of pain defeat her – not now that she'd made it this far.

She cleaned her feet as best she could with her handkerchief and pulled on the ankle socks. The second-hand shoes felt tighter than ever with Peggy's bits of cotton wool in them, so she discarded them and gingerly stood up. The blister on her heel didn't feel too bad now it was cushioned by the plaster, and as long as she didn't have to walk very far, she was sure she could manage.

Checking her appearance in her compact mirror, she tidied away the few wisps of hair that had escaped the pins, refreshed her lipstick and tucked the map in her coat pocket alongside her sandals. Then, beneath the watchful gaze of the two stone stags that stood imperiously on top of the imposing pillars, Sarah took a deep breath and stepped onto the driveway.

The gravel crunched under her shoes and the blister throbbed on her heel as she walked past sweeping lawns and great banks of brightly coloured azaleas and rhododendrons. Ornamental trees rustled in the breeze, their lime greens and russet reds contrasting wonderfully against the blue of the sky and the green of the lush lawns. There was beautiful birdsong, and in the distance she could see a flock of sheep grazing in a field. This really was so quintessentially English and picture-perfect that it almost seemed unreal.

At the end of the driveway she could see the mansion, which looked as if it had been standing there for centuries, its honey-coloured stone gleaming in the sun. Tall, elegant windows looked over the grounds from beneath veils of jewel-bright droplets of purple wisteria. A bronze statue of a boy riding on the back of a dolphin rose up from the silent fountain which stood in the centre of the driveway turning circle, and imposing white pillars and a portico shaded the sturdy oak front door.

Sarah was enchanted, and she tried to imagine what it was like behind that front door and who the people were who had the privilege of living in such a beautiful, peaceful place.

'Who are you? And what are you doing here?'

Sarah spun round to face the speaker and immediately took a step back. He was a big, ugly man with a sour expression and a gun hanging over his arm. The dog growling at the end of the leash looked just as unfriendly. 'I've come for the interview with Mr Cruikshank,' she said, her gaze flitting anxiously to the dog, which had bared its teeth and was snarling at her.

He eyed her suspiciously from head to toe. 'You're not allowed up here,' he snapped. 'The forester's office is down there and off to the left.'

Sarah edged past him. 'Sorry,' she muttered, her gaze locked on the vicious dog which was straining against the leash to get at her. 'I didn't realise . . .' She scuttled back down the driveway, feeling the eyes of both man and dog boring into her back as she desperately sought the pathway she'd missed.

It was almost hidden between two dense banks

of rhododendron, and she hurried down it, praying fervently that this really was the right path. It seemed to wind on for ever, but she could see the dark trees of the forest ahead of her now, and there, finally, was the wooden cabin she'd been looking for.

She paused to catch her breath and could only hope she didn't look too flustered. Ignoring the pain in her heel, she climbed the steps to the door. There was a notice pinned to it informing the candidates to use the door at the side, so she followed the arrow, took a deep breath for courage and walked inside. She had five minutes to spare.

The inside of the cabin was sparsely furnished with a desk, two chairs and a line of filing cabinets – and it reminded her so much of her office back in Malaya that she immediately felt at home. She smiled at the middle-aged, rather motherly-looking woman who sat behind the desk. 'Good morning. I'm Sarah Fuller and I'm here for the interview.'

'Hello, dear. I was beginning to wonder where you were.' She gave Sarah a broad smile and shook her hand. 'I'm Mrs Cruikshank, and if you get the post I'll be the one to help settle you in. You'll be taking over my job when I leave.' She cocked her head. 'You look a bit flustered,' she said, 'but it's all right. The interviews are running a bit behind schedule, so you've got time to get your bearings.'

Sarah handed her the paperwork and sat down on the other side of the desk. She could have done with a cigarette to help calm her nerves, but there were no ashtrays about, and she didn't like to ask in case it wasn't the done thing to smoke in here.

'That all seems in order,' said the older woman. 'Now I'd like to give you some dictation which you will type up.' She turned the heavy black Imperial typewriter round to face Sarah, pushed a pencil and pad across the desk and immediately began to dictate a letter to the Ministry of Supply.

Sarah's hand was shaking, but she managed to catch up and soon the page was full of Pitman's shorthand, which amazingly enough was actually legible. 'How many copies do you need?' she asked as she looked at the pile of headed paper stacked beside the flimsy black carbon paper.

'Three, and I want the type justified, with indentations at the start of every paragraph.'

Sarah quickly adjusted the tabs, settled the carbons the right way round between the sheets of headed paper and neatly rolled them over the cylinder and held them in place with the bail. It was always a tricky enterprise, for the ink invariably got onto her fingers, and if she wasn't careful, she'd leave a smudged mark on the top copies. She adjusted the chair so she was closer to the desk and rested her fingers nervously on the keys. She was all too aware of the other woman watching her, and knew she had to overcome her nerves and not make any mistakes.

Concentrating hard on her shorthand, she let three years of practical experience take over and her fingers flew over the keys. Drawing the pages out of the machine, she took out the carbons, checked everything was perfect, and confidently handed the finished letters to Mrs Cruikshank.

'Thank you.' She swiftly read through one copy and then set it aside. 'Now I'd like you to convert all these lengths and girths into cubic feet of timber, and prepare a docket for the stationmaster at Cliffehaven, and another for the colliery in North Wales.'

Sarah swiftly did the conversions, and then read the dockets carefully before she filled them in and signed them.

Mrs Cruikshank smiled and took the dockets, checked them and pushed back from her desk. 'I'll be back in a minute,' she said as she gathered up the letters and the paperwork Vera had provided and opened the door behind her desk.

Sarah sat and fidgeted nervously as she stared out of the window to the deep shadows of the surrounding trees. She knew she'd passed the first test, but what was to come?

'They're ready for you now.' Mrs Cruikshank held the door open. 'And don't worry, dear,' she said quietly. 'They might look daunting, but they won't bite.'

The two men stood as she entered the room, but the hatchet-faced woman beside them simply glared at her as she sat down to face them and tried not to look too nervous.

Mr Cruikshank was a tall, vigorous-looking man with a weathered face and labour-roughened hands. The man from the MOS had a bald head and drooping, tobacco-stained moustache, and wore a dark rather shiny suit, which made him look like a well-fed walrus. The woman from the WLA was as thin as a rake, the green uniform sweater and felt hat doing her sallow complexion no favours. She continued to watch with eagle-like intent as the two men asked Jane about her background and experience.

Sarah felt she was doing well, and she'd caught the look of approval that had passed between the two men. As silence fell and it looked as if the interview was over, the woman leaned forward and spoke for the first time. 'I see you're engaged,' she said abruptly 'When are you planning to get married?'

Sarah fiddled with her precious ring. 'My fiancé is still in Singapore,' she replied. 'We haven't set a date yet.'

The woman sniffed disdainfully. 'You may go, Fuller,' she said. 'The successful candidate will be informed within ten days. Use that door.'

Rather taken aback by her rudeness, Sarah nodded and tried not to let any of them see how disappointed she was that a decision wouldn't be reached today. She walked into the dappled sunlight, closed the door softly behind her and let out a long breath, glad it was over.

'Ghastly, isn't it?' said Mrs Cruikshank as she suddenly appeared around the corner. 'I remember my first job interview, and I thought I would faint at one point.' She grinned as she pulled her thick cardigan over her large bosom. 'I'm off in a fortnight to be with my daughter, who's expecting her first baby, so they'll make their minds up quickly.' She leaned forward with a conspiratorial whisper, 'I put in a good word for you, dear, so I hope you get it.'

She bustled off down the track and was soon camouflaged by the dark shadows beneath the surrounding trees.

Sarah watched her go and then heard movement in the office behind her. She didn't want to get caught standing here – they might think she was trying to eavesdrop – so she hurried back down the winding path. Emerging onto the driveway, she glanced nervously about in case the horrid man and his dog were still lurking, and then rushed towards the gates and out into the lane.

Her heel was hurting so badly now that every step was agony, but she hobbled on until she was out of sight of the manor house, and well hidden by the curve of the treeline. Sinking down onto the grass, she cautiously eased off her shoes and socks, stuffed the hated shoes in her gas-mask box and wriggled her toes. The plaster had shifted and the blister was red-raw and weeping. No wonder it hurt so much.

She fixed the plaster back into place, fished her sandals from her coat pocket, and got to her feet. The hill challenged her and she determinedly plodded up it, knowing that once she'd reached the top it would be relatively flat and then downhill all the way to Beach View. But when she reached the top she paused in awe as she became aware of the wonderful view.

She could see the Channel glittering in the afternoon sun, and the gleam of the white cliffs that towered over the inlets and beaches that were studded all the way along the coast. Cliffehaven sprawled between the sheltering arms of the hills, and the size and spread of it surprised her, for she hadn't realised how big it was until today. She looked for recognisable landmarks and tried to trace a path between the station and Beach View, but soon became confused by the maze of buildings, so turned her attention back to the ruined pier and the wide sweep of blue that rippled like silk beneath the azure sky.

Sarah heard the twittering of small birds congregating in the nearby trees and watched the shrieking gulls dip and soar over the cliffs and the rooftops. She sat down on a grassy mound to absorb it all, for there was no rush now and she could relax and enjoy this lovely afternoon.

Lighting a well-earned cigarette, she lifted her face to the sun and revelled in its gentle warmth. It was so peaceful here with only birdsong to keep her company, and she could understand why Ron spent so much of his time up here – but it was so very different to the steamy, vibrant jungles of Malaya with their screeching parrots and hooting monkeys, and she was surprised at how deeply it was affecting her.

She looked around, not at all inhibited by this unusual solitude – in fact she embraced it, for this was the first time she'd been alone for months, and this small corner of England seemed to touch her heart with its soft hues and the calm assurance of centuries-old history. This was the essence of England and she could understand the almost ferocious tenacity of her people to keep it safe and free from Hitler's tyranny.

And yet, as she sat there in the spring sunlight with the salty breeze ruffling her hair, she was overwhelmed by a yearning for home and Philip and her parents. She'd kept a brave face for Jane, had borne the terrors of their flight to Singapore, the anxiety for her loved ones and the uncertainties of their arrival here with a fierce determination that had taken every ounce of her strength. Alone now, she could at last be free to let those emotions through, and as the great wave of loneliness and pain engulfed her, she curled into it and wept bitter tears for all that she'd left behind.

Chapter Twenty-Three

Cordelia had been anxiously watching the clock ever since Sarah had left the house. She had only a vague idea of how far the girl would have to walk – she'd never been one to go tramping hills – and Peggy had told her it would be highly unlikely for her to get back much before three. But it was now past four and there was still no sign of her.

'I do hope she hasn't got lost up there,' she fretted as Peggy walked into the kitchen.

'I expect the interview took longer than expected,' she replied. 'And it's a lovely day, so she might simply be enjoying a leisurely walk home.' She took off her headscarf and overcoat, and fluffed up her curly dark hair. 'Where's Jane?'

'She's gone down to the seafront to have a look around.' Cordelia took up her knitting again, and tried to figure out where she'd dropped that stitch. 'How did you get on at the clinic?'

'Daisy didn't like the injection. She cried and cried, but I don't blame her. I hate needles too.'

Cordelia eyed her over her half-moon glasses. 'And what about you? Did the doctor give you a clean bill of health?'

Peggy smiled. 'All tickety-boo, Cordelia. But the clinic was packed as usual, and I seem to have been talking all afternoon. Now I'm desperate for a cuppa.'

Cordelia watched as she put hot water over the used tea leaves and gave them a stir before pouring the pale brown liquid into their cups. There was the fresh packet of tea in the larder, but it wouldn't be dipped into until the old leaves had been wrung completely free of taste. They'd run out of sugar yesterday and now the tea was so weak it seemed pointless to add milk.

Cordelia set the knitting aside, for she couldn't concentrate on anything much until she knew that Sarah was back safely. 'Perhaps she bumped into Ron up there,' she said hopefully. 'That could explain why it's taking so long.'

Peggy shook her head. 'I saw Ron lurking about outside the Anchor. The police had been called in again following some fight that had broken out at lunchtime, and Ron was all for confronting Findlay.' She gave a deep sigh. 'I think I managed to dissuade him, but you know Ron, he'd defend Rosie and her pub to his last breath.' She lit a cigarette. 'If she doesn't get back soon, then Ron could get himself into real trouble. I just wish she'd at least write to him and explain what's going on.'

'It's certainly out of character,' agreed Cordelia. 'One does wonder if she left a letter for Ron, and Findlay hasn't passed it on.'

'I wouldn't put it past him,' muttered Peggy, 'but

Rosie knows what her brother's like, and she wouldn't have trusted him to deliver anything.' She shook her head. 'It's a mystery, Cordelia, and one that won't be solved until she comes back.'

Cordelia drank the weak, almost tasteless tea, glancing up at the clock repeatedly as the time ticked away. Her spirits rose when she heard someone coming through the front door, but it was Jane, all rosy from her walk along the seafront.

'It's lovely down there,' she said as she took off her beret and scarf and shrugged off her coat. 'But it's such a shame they had to put all that horrid barbed wire along the esplanade.' She looked around the kitchen. 'Where's Sarah? I thought she'd be back by now.'

'I'm here.' Sarah came up the cellar steps, dropped her handbag and gas-mask box on the floor, and sank gratefully into a chair. 'I can see that I'll have to toughen up if I have to do that every day,' she said. 'I don't think I've walked that far in years.'

Cordelia looked at her sharply. The girl's eyelids were puffy, and despite the powder and lipstick, she looked rather pale and forlorn. Something – or someone – had made her cry, but it was clear she wasn't prepared to let it show, so Cordelia resisted the temptation to probe too deeply. 'We were worried that you'd got lost,' she said.

'I'm sorry, but it was such a lovely day and the view from the top is quite magnificent.' She smiled ruefully. 'I didn't mean to worry you, Cordelia. I simply lost track of the time.'

'I'm just relieved you made it back in one piece,' she replied, mollified. 'How did the interview go?'

Sarah told them all about it, making light of her run-in with the gamekeeper, and the small terrors she'd had about getting lost, and giving sharply observant descriptions of the interviewing panel which made the others smile.

'I have no idea how well I did,' she finished, 'but I just hope the casting vote isn't made by that awful woman. Honestly, if looks could kill, I'd be stone dead by now.'

'What was her name?' asked Peggy, who'd taken up her own knitting.

'Mrs Cornish. And she had an expression that would sour milk.'

'Ah,' said Peggy. 'I know Gladys Cornish – or at least I know of her. She was married to a particularly nasty little man who'd been a sergeant major in the Army before he retired. He was a bully, by all accounts, and rumour has it that it was a bit of a relief to Gladys when he had a massive heart attack and dropped down dead in the middle of one of his rants.'

'One can't really blame her for being sour, then, I suppose,' murmured Cordelia. 'But it's unfair to take it out on young girls like Sarah.'

'I agree,' said Peggy, 'but I suspect she gave as good as she got with that husband of hers, for she's aggressive and rude on all the committees she runs, and everyone is so terrified of her they daren't tell her to sling her hook.'

'It's a great pity she hasn't crossed paths with your sister Doris,' said Cordelia dryly. 'She wouldn't be able to bully *her*.'

Peggy giggled. 'They've had their spats, believe me, and Gladys is now very careful not to be on the same committees as Doris. But I'm surprised she's joined the WLA. Perhaps she thinks the uniform will give her added clout.'

'The green doesn't suit her,' said Sarah, 'and that hat looks like a pudding basin.'

Jane's eyes widened in surprise. 'You're not usually so sharp about people,' she spluttered. 'She must have really got to you.'

Sarah shrugged. 'I didn't like the way she tried to intimidate me by glaring all the way through the interview. But she didn't put me off,' she added and grinned. 'I've run the gauntlet of Brigadiers' and Commodores' wives back in Malaya, and they could certainly give Gladys Cornish a run for her money in the glaring stakes.'

'Good for you,' murmured Peggy. 'Did you see any of the other candidates so you could gauge who you were up against?'

Sarah shook her head. 'I was the last one, and at the end of the interviews we had to leave by another door which led straight back outside.' She eased off her sandals and regarded her filthy feet and the angry blister. 'I'll just have to keep my fingers crossed and wait to hear if I've got it,' she said, 'but whatever the outcome, I will have to get new shoes.'

Cordelia knew how little money Sarah had, and although the clothing coupons would go some way towards buying new shoes, the girl was still going to struggle to pay for them. She bundled her knitting into the large carpet bag that always sat by her chair, and tried to remember how much she had in her purse after her shopping expedition the previous day. Sarah would probably refuse to take it, but there were ways and means of getting a pound note into a purse without being seen.

Feeling rather pleased at how devious she could be, Cordelia went to fetch the first-aid box so Sarah could attend to that very painful-looking heel.

Sarah thanked her, and glanced up at her sister as she bent to clean and bandage the blister. 'So, come on then. Tell me all about your first day.'

'It was jolly hard work,' Jane said cheerfully, 'but I loved every minute of it. Mabel was perfectly well behaved and we delivered all the milk on time.' She shrugged happily. 'We had to stand about a bit while people gave her a carrot or a cooking apple, but she seemed to expect it, so I didn't mind. Everyone was pleased to see me and asked me lots of questions, and I could have been kept talking all morning – but I knew Mr Jenkins was waiting for me back at the dairy, so I didn't dare stay out too long.'

'What's he like as a boss?'

'He's very kind, but he has strict rules about things and likes them done in a certain way.' Jane grinned. 'The three boys who drive the other drays were a bit put out to have a girl working with them, and they moaned a bit. But Mr Jenkins stood up for me and I proved I could do all the same jobs, so they were quiet after that, and even offered to share their sandwiches with me.'

Sarah smiled. 'Well done, Jane,' she said softly.

Jane grinned back. 'Well, I couldn't let a bunch of spotty boys get the better of me, could I?' she said.

'So, what did you do when you got back from your round?' asked Cordelia. 'It was almost lunchtime before you came home.'

'I had to help unload the crates and carry them into the shed where Mrs Jenkins was in charge of washing and sterilising them in the big baking oven. She has her niece to help her, and her name's Stella.'

'That's good – there's another girl for you to pal up with,' said Cordelia.

'She's very shy,' said Jane, 'and Mrs Jenkins told me on the quiet that she's a bit slow, and not to worry if she doesn't take to me straight away. But I think she just needs a bit of time to get used to me – like Lucy did back in Malaya.' She quickly explained about Lucy, who'd been slow of mind and inclined to sit in corners away from everyone.

Jane rushed on enthusiastically. 'After unloading the crates, I had to see to Mabel. I groomed her and then let her into the paddock with the others while I mucked out her stable and put down fresh straw and topped up her feed manger.' She gave a happy sigh. 'Mabel and her friends loved galloping about the field; it's surprising how fast such big horses can go.'

She paused to take a breath. 'I was given hot cocoa when I'd finished mucking out, and Mrs Jenkins gave me a huge cheese sandwich for my breakfast. They make their own cheese and cream and butter there, you know, and Mr Jenkins said he'd show me how he does it when he's got time to spare.'

'It all sounds great fun,' said Cordelia. 'I love to see those beautiful animals coming down the street during the summer parade. I do so hope they still have it this year. Mr Jenkins grooms them to a gleam and ties bright ribbons in their manes and tails, and fluffs up their snow-white feathered feet. He dresses their harnesses with brasses and has the four of them pull his really big wagon which he's painted red and gold, and he sits up at the reins, all dressed in scarlet, with Mrs Jenkins in her Sunday best sitting beside him. They're quite a sight.'

'How lovely,' sighed Jane. 'I do hope we get to see it.'

Cordelia saw the happiness in Jane and knew she'd found her niche, and could only hope that Sarah was as successful in getting the job with the WTC. But there was sadness behind Sarah's smile, and Cordelia suspected that she was homesick and desperately worried about her parents and her fiancé.

The situation in the Far East was worsening by the day and it seemed that only a miracle could save those still trapped on those thousands of tiny islands in the

Pacific. And yet miracles had been known to happen, and she had to remain positive – for without hope they would all be lost.

Ron had listened to all of Peggy's arguments and had decided he would make his own mind up about things. He'd waited until Peggy was out of sight and had then returned to his watching post deep in the shadows of the alleyway opposite the Anchor. The police had been inside for some time, and Ron fervently hoped they were going to arrest Findlay and get rid of him once and for all. He was ruining the reputation of Rosie's pub with his out-of-hours drinking sessions and the number of women he entertained upstairs at night.

His patience was finally rewarded as the front door opened and the two policemen stepped outside. But it seemed Findlay wasn't going to be carted off, for they were shaking his hand and thanking him for his co-operation. 'It looks like he's managed to weasel his way out of trouble again,' Ron muttered furiously to Harvey, who was lying quietly at his feet.

He watched as the police car drove away and Findlay closed the front door. Peggy had been right in one respect, he conceded. Confrontation was not the answer, but there were other ways to skin a cat, and he had a plan. The only problem was that Findlay rarely left the pub, and there always seemed to be some woman in there. It was a waiting game, and Ron had to call upon his many years of covert experience to remain patient and watchful.

Harvey got to his feet, yawned and stretched and then cocked his leg against the wall. He was obviously getting bored by the whole thing, and Ron was about to take him home when he heard a door slam.

Findlay was coming out of the Anchor's side door. Dressed in tailored twill trousers and tweed jacket, he had a bright yellow cravat tucked into his open shirt collar, and a brown fedora angled rakishly over one eye. He stood in a shaft of sunlight taking the air and looking very pleased with himself, and then cupped his hand round a match and lit a cigar. With the cigar wedged into the corner of his mouth, he put his hands into his trouser pockets and strolled off towards the hospital end of Camden Road.

Ron waited until he was out of sight and then hitched up his gas-mask box and patted the pockets of his poaching coat to check he had his torch. A swift glance up and down the road showed no one was about. 'Come on, Harvey,' he whispered. 'Now's our chance.'

With the dog trotting at his heels, he swiftly crossed the road and melted into the shadows by the side door to the pub. He had a key, for Rosie had given it to him over a year ago so he could get in to change the barrels if she happened to be out. The key turned and he pushed the door open, wincing as it creaked on its dry hinges, and slid inside, the dog hard on his heels. The outside noises were muffled once the door was closed behind them, and Ron stood there for a moment, alert to any sound coming from upstairs. Then he moved into the bar.

The tables were cluttered with dirty glasses, the ash in the hearth hadn't been cleared for days, there was a layer of dust on everything and the flagstones were sticky with spilled beer and squashed fag ends. He looked at the long oak bar which had been Rosie's pride and joy, and almost wept at the sight of the deep scars and gouges that now marred it. The brass beer pumps hadn't been polished in an age, the tankards were missing from the hooks, and the mirrors behind the optics and bottles were fly-spotted and smeared. Now both middle-aged barmaids had been replaced by a couple of tarts from London, it seemed the place was going to wrack and ruin.

He couldn't bear to look and turned away. 'Stay here,' he ordered Harvey as he reached the top of the cellar steps. 'Growl if you hear someone coming.'

Harvey sat alert in the doorway as Ron quickly went down the cellar steps. He knew where the false wall was, for he and Jim had been in partnership with the previous landlord, and had stored their contraband here from time to time when it got too dangerous to keep it at home. Rosie had provided the same favour on one rare occasion, but he'd never asked her again, for he couldn't bear the thought of her getting into trouble.

He switched on the single light and made his way around the barrels and crates to the very back of the cellar, where the low-watt bulb barely cast any light. The sturdy wooden shelves fixed to the far wall were lined with cardboard boxes, dusty bottles, abandoned, rusting tools and tins, and piles of old newspapers.

This general clutter of several decades was covered in spiders' webs and mouse droppings and looked undisturbed, but Ron knew that was all part of the camouflage, for everything on this particular part of the shelving had been nailed or stuck into place.

He reached between two empty oil cans and fumbled for the lever. Pulling it down, he heard a click and stepped back as the door opened silently on well-oiled hinges. It was pitch-black in that secret hideaway, and smelled strongly of mice and damp. Ron turned on his powerful torch.

'I thought so,' he breathed in relief and satisfaction as he swung the torch-beam across the stacked cases of rum and whisky and the airtight drums which probably held thousands of packets of stolen cigarettes. Findlay had somehow discovered this hidey-hole and had put it to good use – but it would be his downfall.

He reached for a case of rum which was clearly marked 'Property of Her Majesty's Royal Naval Reserve' and carried it quickly up the steps.

Harvey whined and wagged his tail, and Ron praised him and told him to keep watch as he hurried up the stairs to Rosie's rooms. His rage with Findlay was stoked by the stink of cheap perfume that pervaded every corner, the stains on her carpet and the litter of overflowing ashtrays and empty bottles which was strewn over every flat surface. Rosie had taken such care to make this a homely, pretty place to relax in, and Findlay had turned it into a pigsty. It would break Rosie's heart if she saw it.

However, this neglect and lack of cleaning served his purpose very well. He carried the case of rum over to the couch which stood beneath the diamond-paned window and pulled it forward enough so he could ram the box behind it. His nose wrinkled in disgust at the unwashed smell of the cushions, the grubby upholstery, and the tobacco stink in the curtains. How anyone could live like this, he couldn't fathom.

He ran back down to the cellar and began to heave the cases of alcohol out of their hiding place, setting them behind the stacked crates so they wouldn't immediately be seen by Findlay when he next came down here. Then he took several cartons of American cigarettes out of an airtight tub and hid them behind a stack of old magazines which had been used by the mice as a nest.

Slipping four cartons of cigarettes and three packs of tobacco into his coat pockets, he added a couple of bottles of rum and whisky and then pushed up the lever to close the door on the rest. He didn't want the police finding this hiding place – it might come in useful at some point – but there was enough evidence down here to nail Findlay, and that was what mattered.

Ron had turned off the light and was halfway up the stone steps when he saw Harvey stiffen and heard the soft, warning growl deep in his throat. He tiptoed the rest of the way and laid his hand on the dog's head to silence him. Someone was turning the key in the front door.

As Ron silently reached the side door and turned

the knob, he heard Findlay's voice and the answering shriek of laughter of some woman. He heard the click of high heels on the flagstone floor as she crossed the bar – and he slid through into the alleyway, Harvey streaking like a shadow behind him.

Closing the door silently on yet another drunken cackle from the woman, Ron smiled to himself and hurried down the road. Findlay would be occupied for a while yet – but he was in for a very nasty surprise.

Rita rushed into the kitchen just as they were all about to sit down for tea. 'You'll never guess,' she said breathlessly as she ripped off her helmet and goggles and undid her leather flying jacket. 'The police are swarming all over the Anchor and carting out boxes and boxes of stuff.'

Peggy turned from the stove. 'Any sign of Findlay?' she asked hopefully.

'Someone told me he'd been arrested along with some woman. They're being questioned down at the Police Station.' She washed her hands in the sink and shook them dry. 'It's all very exciting, isn't it? I've never seen a police raid before, and it's drawn quite a crowd.'

'Well, it's about time he had his come-uppance,' Peggy said flatly. 'That one has sailed too close to the wind for too long, if you ask me.' She glanced at Ron, who seemed to be taking this piece of news very calmly. 'You don't seem very surprised, Ron,' she remarked. 'I hope you haven't done anything silly.'

'Me?' His eyes widened innocently as he opened a fresh pack of tobacco and started to fill his pipe. 'I'm just pleased he's been caught at last. Cliffehaven can do without men like him.'

'But if he's been arrested the pub will be shut and Rosie will probably lose her licence,' said Peggy.

'I'll have a word with the police in the morning,' he said as he eased back in his chair to enjoy the ill-gotten tobacco that was burning very satisfactorily in his pipe. 'Brenda and Pearl will be quite happy to take over the bar again until Rosie gets back, and I can carry on doing the barrels and seeing to the deliveries and the books.'

'You've got it all worked out, haven't you?' said Peggy with more than a glimmer of suspicion in her eyes. 'And what if the police revoke the licence anyway and keep the pub shut? What will you do then?'

'Ach, you worry too much, woman,' he said dismissively. 'The police don't want an empty pub on their hands, and Rosie's done no wrong. They'll listen to reason from a respectable citizen like me, you see if they don't.'

Peggy eyed the tattered shirt, the baggy trousers and whiskery chin. 'If you want to look even remotely respectable, I suggest you shave and find some decent clothes to wear. Which reminds me.' She turned and fished a parcel out of her shopping bag. 'I used some of your coupons to buy you two new shirts. You owe me three bob.'

Ron bolted upright. 'Three bob? Good God, woman, what've you bought?'

Peggy turned back towards the stove so he couldn't see her smile. The old so-and-so had been up to something, she just knew it, and if he'd been the reason why Findlay was now in a police cell, then he'd done the whole town a favour. As to the shirts, they would last, as long as she made sure he didn't wear them while he was mucking about in his garden.

She continued to smile as she tested the stew she'd made from boiling a large meat bone with vegetables and pearl barley. Tea was ready.

Ron had shaved and dressed in his best suit and one of his new shirts, and even polished his shoes. Bundling up his old clothes with a bit of string, he'd tied them to the handlebars and cycled to the Police Station, Harvey's howls of anguish at being left behind following him down the street.

It hadn't taken long to get all the information he needed from his old pal, Sergeant Blake. Findlay would be charged not only with running a disorderly house, but with black-marketeering, tax evasion, and theft. Having several previous convictions for similar offences, he was looking at a very long sentence behind bars.

With Sergeant Blake's help, Ron had managed to persuade the Station Inspector to let him run the pub until Rosie got back, and although it would seriously curtail his poaching and the amount of time he could spend with his young ferrets, he didn't mind the sacrifice. Now he was returning from his visit to Brenda and Pearl, with their assurances that they'd come in and help to clean up the place before they opened up that evening.

He had everything organised and was feeling very pleased with himself as he cycled back to the pub and let himself in at the side door. It was quiet and still, and now he knew Findlay was out of the picture, Ron was ready to return Rosie's little parlour to its former glory.

He changed into his old clothes, rolled up the sleeves of his ragged shirt and looked around. He would start by taking the covers off the chairs and the cushions, then he'd get the curtains down and open the windows to get rid of the stink of Findlay and his tarts.

Once this was achieved, he found a cardboard box and began to empty the ashtrays and gather up the old newspapers and magazines that were lying around. The discarded bottles filled three crates, and in the tiny kitchen he found enough empty cans and packets and old fish and chip wrappings to almost fill the dustbin. He found a bra and a pair of lacy knickers stuffed down the back of the couch, and these went straight in with the rest of the rubbish.

He had to steel himself to go into Rosie's bedroom, for he'd never been in there before and felt like an interloper, and dreaded what he might find. But Findlay was obviously particular about where he slept, for the room was surprisingly tidy and his clothes were neatly hung in the wardrobe or folded into a drawer.

451

The sprigged wallpaper was a bit faded, but it was as feminine and pretty as the curtains and eiderdown. There was the wardrobe and a dressing table, and the window looked out over the scrap of back garden beyond the rooftops to where a line of glittering blue formed the horizon between sea and sky.

Ron stripped the bed, flung the windows open to get rid of the man's smell and then added the curtains to the pile of washing. Findlay's clothes didn't take long to pack in the two suitcases he'd found on top of the wardrobe, and Ron tossed in the hairbrushes and the collection of tiepins, collar studs and cufflinks he found in a dish on the dressing table.

He tried not to linger over Rosie's dresses and coats hanging in the wardrobe, or her sweaters and blouses and delicate underwear which were still neatly folded in the chest of drawers. He missed her so much that it was a physical ache. Despite the fact that she'd left without any explanation or goodbye, he had to keep believing that she still loved him back.

Needing to expunge Findlay from Rosie's flat, Ron swept everything off the shelves in the bathroom straight in with the rubbish. He laughed out loud when he discovered a spare set of false teeth hidden in the dressing-gown pocket, and felt an enormous amount of satisfaction when he committed them to the rubbish bin. The little rat would just have to manage with one set from now on, for Her Majesty's prisons would provide a shaving kit and flannels, but he doubted very much that they would stretch to new dentures.

Having finished packing the suitcases, Ron was about to fasten and buckle the straps when he caught sight of a book on the bedside table. He was surprised the man had time to read, and was intrigued to see what sort of thing he liked. He picked it up, saw that it was some cheap western with a lurid cover and tossed it into the case. But as the pages fluttered something fell out and slid to the floor.

Ron stood looking at it for a long while, and then slowly bent to pick it up. The envelope had been opened but it was addressed to him, and the handwriting was unmistakably Rosie's. He closed his eyes against the tears of rage and took a moment to find calm again. If he'd had a moment of doubt over grassing on Findlay then this was his redemption.

Sinking to the floor, he drew out the sheet of paper which had the scent of her still on it. It was dated the day she'd left Cliffehaven.

My dearest, dearest Ron,

I'm so sorry if I've hurt you these past weeks, but when I explain what has been happening, I hope you will understand and forgive me.

My husband's family have become very religious since Jack was committed to the insane asylum, and have never approved of me moving so far from him and trying to make a new life for myself. They have always felt that, as Jack's wife, I should keep close and carry on as if things might get better and that we could live as husband and wife again. This is not even a remote possibility – in fact there has been little evidence up to now to show that he even knows who I am. But I can understand how his parents need to believe that their son isn't doomed to spend the rest of his tragic life in a secure cell.

Their last letter was extremely upsetting, for they accused me of abandoning Jack and taking up with another man. They quoted long passages from the Bible, calling me a Jezebel and the devil's harlot, and warned me that my sins would find me out, and that I'll burn in eternal hell if I don't repent. I don't believe in all that tosh, but it still upset me to realise how little they respected me after all these years. I don't know if someone told them about you, or whether they picked it up from my letters, because I realise now that I must have mentioned you many times over the past months. But it made me stop and think. I need to distance myself from you so that I'm not distracted by my feelings for you. Am I being fair to you, to Jack, or to myself, by loving you when I know there can be no future for us all the while Jack is still alive? I cannot wish my husband dead, Ron, for I loved him once, and owe him my loyalty.

I would have come and told you all this if I'd had the chance, but the sudden turn of events means I have to leave Cliffehaven almost immediately, and I have to trust my brother to give you this letter, which comes from my heart.

I received a telephone call an hour ago, and I am writing this while I wait for Tommy to arrive so I can *leave him in charge of the pub and catch the last train. Jack's hospital took a direct hit and only a few of the patients and staff got out alive. The survivors have been moved to another secure hospital, but Jack was completely traumatised by the air raid, and the doctor who rang told me that he'd begun calling out for me, begging me to come and save him.*

Of course I agreed to go to him immediately, but I'm frightened by what I might find, and have no idea how long I shall be away. I will be staying in a boarding house I've used before, and the address is at the top of this letter.

I do love you, Ron, even though I know I shouldn't, and if you can forgive me for the way I've treated you recently, then please write. I need your friendship, love and support more than ever now, and I'm fearful that I might have lost it.

Rosie x

Ron sniffed back his tears and tenderly tucked the letter back in the envelope and placed it in the breast pocket of his shirt. His first instinct was to catch the next train out of Cliffehaven and rush to be with her. But reason slowly took over and he knew that was not only impossible, but unwise. Rosie needed to come to terms with what was happening to her poor insane husband, and he had to stay here and look after the family.

He fastened the straps and buckles tightly round the cases and vented all his frustration and fury on them by throwing them as hard as he could down the stairs. He stomped after them and kicked them into the cellar, where he hoped they'd rot. Slamming the door on them and feeling much better, he checked the time. A letter could take days to get to her, and he couldn't bear the thought of her all alone and believing he hadn't cared enough to reply.

Locking the side door behind him, he swung onto his bike and set off for the Post Office. He would send her a telegram to say he'd only just got her letter, and that there was nothing to forgive. Then he would rope in Peggy and any of the other girls who might be at Beach View and get stuck into cleaning up the Anchor, ready for this evening's session. There was nothing like a bit of hard work to blow away the cobwebs.

He was grinning like a Cheshire cat as he sped towards the Post Office. Life was suddenly bright again, and once he'd given the two London tarts the sack and everything was clean and shipshape at the Anchor, with Brenda and Pearl installed back behind the bar, he would sit down and write his darling Rosie a long, long letter.

Chapter Twenty-Four

Sarah had begun to fear that she hadn't got the post with the WTC. It was almost the end of March, and Mr Cruikshank had told her that the Corps was due to be up and running by April, so their choice of candidate would have to be made within ten days. Now there were only three days left to this deadline, and hope was fading.

Jane must have seen her worried expression, for she came over to the bed and gave her a quick hug. 'Don't worry, Sarah,' she said. 'They would be very silly not to employ you, and I'm sure you'll hear soon.'

Sarah kept her doubts to herself as she hugged her back. It was four in the morning and Jane had lost none of her enthusiasm for the dairy. In fact she was relishing the responsibility of doing her job well, and was excited about the pay packet she would receive at the end of this first week. Sarah didn't want to put a damper on things by voicing her worries.

After Jane had left for the dairy and her beloved Mabel, Sarah lay in bed for a while longer in the hope she might get back to sleep. But her thoughts were whirling and making her restless, and she eventually gave up on the idea and threw off the blankets.

Shivering with the cold, she quickly dressed and slipped on her new shoes.

She had dithered over buying them, for although they were wonderfully comfortable, they'd been quite expensive. And then she'd rummaged through her handbag and found a pound note she must have tucked away in the inside pocket and forgotten about. Without further hesitation, she'd bought the shoes and worn them home, stopping on the way to donate her Glasgow ones to the WVS. Someone with smaller feet would appreciate them.

The room was icy, for they'd run out of sixpences for the meter, and had decided it was wasteful to use their last bit of money on such things while there was a lovely warm kitchen downstairs. She quickly made the beds and tidied away Jane's clothes which had been strewn about the room, and then hurried into the bathroom. If there was no letter for her today then she would have to go back and see Vera. She simply couldn't afford to be out of work any longer.

Peggy came into the kitchen an hour later with a red-faced and squalling Daisy in her arms. 'Thanks for laying the table and starting on the breakfast, Sarah,' she said above the racket. 'Pour me a cuppa, dear, while I sort this one out.'

Sarah poured the tea and hurried to fill the washing-up bowl with warm water as Daisy continued to yell. A bath usually soothed her, but she was clearly in a grumpy mood this morning, which was unusual.

As Peggy gulped down the tea and then wrestled

to undress the baby, Sarah had a sharp image of her mother. Where was she now? Had she and the baby survived? Were they safe – and how was her mother coping without their beloved Amah to help? There had been no word from any of them, only disturbing rumours of massacres, torture and imprisonment – not just of Government officials and military men, but of women and children too. As time had gone by, it was getting harder to believe that any of them could have survived.

Peggy had swiftly washed the still squalling Daisy and wrapped her in a towel. 'Would you put some porridge in her bowl, Sarah? Perhaps if she's eating she'll stop making such a noise. The whole house must be awake by now.'

Sarah put some porridge in the little bowl which had Peter Rabbit running round the rim, and added a couple of drops of cold milk to cool it down. 'Something's certainly upset her this morning,' she murmured sympathetically.

Peggy fastened the terry-towelling nappy with a large pin and pulled some waterproof pants over it. 'She's teething,' she said grimly as she wrestled to get the baby's clothes on, 'so we can expect this for a while yet.' She took the bowl and spooned some of the porridge into the wailing mouth. Blessed silence fell as the baby clamped her tiny jaws around the spoon and rubbed her gums against it.

Sarah could see the high colour in the baby's cheeks and the almost frantic way she was gnawing at that spoon. 'Poor little mite,' she murmured. 'It must be agony.'

Peggy nodded as she held onto the spoon to stop Daisy from ramming it down her throat. 'I'll have to get a teething ring from the chemist. These old spoons are probably too sharp, and I don't want her to cut herself.' She looked over at Sarah. 'What are your plans for the day?'

'I thought I'd go down to the recruiting office and see Vera. She said there were lots of administration jobs going, and I can't sit about here doing nothing while Jane's at work.'

Peggy smiled. 'There are plenty of jobs here to keep you occupied until you find something that suits you – but I can understand you must be feeling rather at odds with things now Jane is the breadwinner.'

Sarah nodded. 'It's not a situation I ever envisaged,' she admitted with a wry smile. 'Mother and Pops never expected Jane to do more than perhaps help out at the local kindergarten, or get involved in some sort of charity work. I've always been her big sister – her guardian, if you like – and I was expected to work for Pops and be the responsible one should anything happen to my parents. It feels very strange to have the shoe on the other foot.'

Peggy smiled as she spooned more porridge into Daisy. 'I'm sure it does,' she murmured, 'but you must be thrilled at how well she's getting on.'

'It has been a revelation,' Sarah replied. 'I'm beginning to wonder if we'd given her more of a free rein back in Malaya, she might have shown these signs of improvement much earlier.'

'Her injuries must have been severe for your family to cosset her so.'

Sarah nodded and returned to stirring the porridge before carefully easing it off the hot plate and covering it with the saucepan lid. 'At first we didn't think she'd survive. She was in a coma for three weeks, and was very poorly for a long time after that. The doctor told us there were bound to be repercussions, and he warned that she would probably be retarded for the rest of her life and would therefore be very vulnerable.'

'Well, he got that wrong, didn't he?' said Peggy acidly. 'It does make me cross when doctors talk like that – it takes away hope to brand people in such a way. Call someone useless often enough and they'll start to believe it and act accordingly.'

Sarah smiled down at Peggy in gratitude. 'Jane has certainly proved him wrong, but she's still very naïve, and childlike in many ways.'

'She's just taking a bit longer to mature, that's all,' said Peggy comfortably. 'I wouldn't mind betting that now she's got a job and her own money, she'll come along in leaps and bounds.' She caught hold of Sarah's hand. 'Getting away from Malaya was probably the making of her, Sarah, and although I know how homesick and worried you must be for the rest of your family, your sister will be all right.'

Sarah nodded. 'Thanks, Peggy,' she said rather

unsteadily. 'It's good to hear you confirm what I've suspected for a while now.'

Peggy smiled back at her. 'I think I heard the newspapers arriving. Why don't you fetch them while I finish feeding Daisy? You can read out the headlines while I give her a bottle.'

Sarah fetched the papers from the wire cage that hung beneath the letter box and carried them back into the kitchen. The house was beginning to stir, for she could hear footsteps overhead and the rattle and bang of air in the pipes as someone flushed the lavatory. The kitchen would soon be bustling with everyone chattering over their breakfast and preparing to leave for work. The peaceful interlude with Peggy was almost over, but it had renewed her optimism, and she felt ready to face whatever the day had in store for her.

Peggy flicked through the pages of one of the newspapers as Sarah doled out the porridge and the girls chattered around her. Daisy was at last in a better mood and was lying in her playpen gurgling at Harvey, who was watching her, nose on paws, ears and eyebrows twitching at her every sound.

If only the rest of the world was as peaceful, Peggy thought sadly, as she read about the awful German bombardment of poor little Malta, and the terrible struggle the Russian soldiers were having to survive not only enemy attacks, but dwindling supplies and a bitter winter. There were reports of atrocities in Hong Kong, and the fall of Rangoon and Java. The Japanese had landed in New Guinea, but their attacks on Darwin had been brought to an end by the arrival in Australia of three United States fighter squadrons. Sir Stafford Cripps was on his way to India to discuss Government policy and – just to put the tin lid on it – there was to be no more white bread after the sixth of April.

Peggy folded the paper, shoved it across the table to Ron and lit a cigarette. 'I don't know about you,' she said, 'but it would be nice to have some good news for a change.'

He stirred sugar into his tea and looked rather smug. 'I got a letter from Rosie yesterday in answer to my telegram, and that cheered me up no end.'

Peggy had heard all about Findlay's spiteful actions and was pleased that Ron and Rosie were in communication again. 'A letter from Rosie is hardly going to end this blessed war though, is it?'

He chuckled. 'It makes it easier to bear, Peggy.'

She waved goodbye as Rita, Fran and Suzy left for work. Sarah was now upstairs cleaning the bathroom to fill in time before she went down to see Vera, and Cordelia was busy writing letters at the other end of the table. 'Yes, I suppose it does,' she murmured. 'Jim's letters remind me of how far away he is, but at least we're in the same country and I know he's still alive. Poor Sarah doesn't have that luxury, and I think she's finding it very hard to keep up a brave front for her sister.'

Ron looked down at Harvey, who was now stretched out on his back close to the playpen, his tongue lolling.

'Aye,' he murmured. 'We're lucky, Peg – and we must never forget that.'

Sarah heard the clatter of the letter box and rushed downstairs. There were several letters and a couple of postcards, but the only one that mattered was the buff envelope with WLA stamped in the left-hand corner.

She turned it over and over in her hand, almost afraid to read what was inside, then told herself she was being ridiculous and tore it open. There was a single page and it didn't take long to read. 'I've got it,' she called as she ran into the kitchen. 'I've got the job and they want me up at the estate office this afternoon at two.'

'Congratulations, dear,' said Cordelia as she reached out her arms to her. 'We all knew you'd get it.'

'That's more than I did,' she confessed as she stepped over a recumbent Harvey and gave her a warm hug. 'Oh dear,' she stuttered. 'I'm feeling quite emotional about the whole thing. Fancy getting so excited about a silly office job.'

'You have every right to get emotional,' said Cordelia firmly. 'You've been through a lot and this is a new beginning.' She beamed up at her. 'I think we should all celebrate with a cup of tea and a biscuit.'

Sarah sat down and Harvey took advantage of this and immediately put his head in her lap as if he wanted to congratulate her too. She smiled and stroked his silky ears as Peggy gave her a cup of tea and Ron shot her a wink.

'It's cupboard love, Sarah, don't you be fooled. The old rascal's after that biscuit in your saucer,' he drawled.

She laughed and broke off a corner of the biscuit which Harvey greedily snaffled from her palm. 'The rest is mine,' she said to him firmly, 'so you might as well go back to guarding the fire.'

'He'll be coming with me to the Anchor after we've had our walk,' said Ron as he left the table. 'I'll see you all later – and well done, Sarah.' He grabbed his cap from the hook on the back of the door, whistled to the dog and tramped down the cellar steps.

'It's good to see that he's his old self again,' said Peggy to no one in particular. 'I was getting quite worried about him.'

Sarah felt as if some of the weight she'd been carrying since they'd left Singapore had been lifted from her shoulders, and she leaned back into the chair and lit a celebratory cigarette. Tomorrow morning she would be just like her sister and the other girls, and truly fit in, for now she too had somewhere to go and something important to do in the home-front battle against Hitler.

It had been easy to find her way this second time, and she was surprised at how much quicker it had been now that she wasn't hampered by sandals and a blister. She arrived at the main gates out of breath, her calf muscles complaining at the unaccustomed exercise, but with ten minutes to spare.

There was no sign of the gamekeeper or his dog, but she didn't linger on the driveway. Taking the narrow path through the encroaching rhododendrons, she let the peace wash over her as she took in the different colours and listened to the birdsong. She was going to like working here, she decided.

Mrs Cruikshank was behind her desk, thumping away at the keys of the Imperial typewriter. She looked up and grinned as Sarah stepped through the door.

'It's lovely to see you again,' she said as they shook hands. 'I'm glad they saw sense and didn't employ the other girl. She wouldn't have been at all suitable.' Without going on to explain what she meant by that, she beckoned Sarah to follow her as she went into the other room.

It looked very different to when Sarah had come here for her interview, for it had been turned into a sort of canteen and storeroom. 'Who'll be doing the cooking?' she asked as she eyed the collection of cooking pots and pans, the industrial-sized gas rings and the enormous tea urn.

'Mrs Oaks. She's been Lord Cliffe's cook since before the first war. She'll provide the lunches, and in the evenings everyone who's billeted here will take it in turn to do the supper. There will be ten girls arriving tomorrow and they will be billeted in the dower house. The Dowager passed away some time ago, and the house has been standing empty ever since.'

'Does Lord Cliffe have any family?' asked Sarah,

who was still intrigued by the people who owned this wonderful place.

'His Lordship has been a widower for many years and shown no desire to marry again. Both his sons are in the military, and their wives and children have moved to their other estate in Wales for the duration. His daughter is in the Observer Corps.'

She gathered her thoughts and continued her inventory of where everything and everyone was on the estate. 'The lumberjacks are down in the woods in a series of log cabins with their foreman, Alf Billings. He's a retired sergeant major with long experience of working the horses in the forest, and it's his job to keep everyone in order and make sure there are no shenanigans after lights-out. Apart from the farm labourers, who are now mostly made up of Land Army girls, we have two young lads working for us until they're old enough to be called up, two conscientious objectors, and three experienced lumberjacks who are over fifty and therefore too old to be called up.'

'That's quite a workforce,' said Sarah. 'But won't the others find it galling to have to work alongside conscientious objectors?'

'They might not like it, or approve of what they are, but the work is essential to the war effort and they'll just have to get on with it,' said Mrs Cruikshank. 'Alf and my husband will keep an eye on things so they don't get out of hand, never you mind.'

She turned away and headed for a table where great stacks of clothing had been neatly laid out. 'The WTC uniform is exactly the same as the Land Army one, but you get a beret instead of a felt hat, and of course a WTC badge.'

She began to rifle through the sweaters and trousers and held them up against Sarah to gauge their size. 'You're very small and slight,' she said, 'but there's bound to be something here that will do. What size are you, anyway?'

Sarah shrugged. 'I lived in Malaya and everything was made especially for me, so I'm afraid I have no idea.'

Mrs Cruikshank smiled ruefully as she continued to pick out the clothes. 'You'll find these probably won't fit quite as well as what you're used to, but I'm sure you or Mrs Reilly can make any necessary alterations.'

Sarah eyed the sweaters and woolly shirts, and the mannish jodhpurs, and almost laughed out loud. Vera had warned her that the uniform was far from glamorous, and she hadn't been exaggerating. They were so far removed from the delicate silks and cottons she'd been used to that it would be like dressing up for a male part in some strange play. Her mother would have a fit if she ever saw her in this lot.

Mrs Cruikshank handed a clipboard and pencil to Sarah. 'I'll call each item out and you tick it off. Might as well get used to it before the others get here, for this will be part of your duties tomorrow.'

'Two green jerseys; two pairs of riding breeches; two overall coats and two pairs of dungarees.'

Sarah ticked them off in horrified fascination as the

dowdy, workmanlike clothes were carefully stacked in a second pile.

'Six pairs of woollen knee-length socks; three beige woollen shirts; one pair of boots; one pair of brown shoes, and one pair of gumboots,' continued Mrs Cruikshank. 'You probably won't need most of this, but it's the uniform, so you have to have it,' she said with a shrug before she continued with her list. 'One green beret; one Melton overcoat; one mackintosh; a green armband and metal badge, a hat badge and two towels.'

The heavy woollen overcoat reminded her of the pea jackets the sailors had worn when the weather had turned cold on the ship coming over here. 'Won't all this be very warm when summer comes?' asked Sarah, who was still rather taken aback by the drabness of it all.

Mrs Cruikshank grinned. 'Undoubtedly, but when it's raining or snowing and the wind is howling across the hills and you have to walk here every morning, you'll be glad of it, believe me.'

She took the clipboard and placed it on the other end of the table. 'You'll be responsible for this lot once I've gone, so keep the door locked and the key in your pocket. If someone needs to replace anything there are dockets to fill in. There's a locker in the office which has its own key. I'd advise you to keep what you're not wearing in there. You won't want to be carting that lot home tonight – it weighs a ton. Now, follow me and I'll show you around outside.'

Sarah nodded and trotted after her. For a big woman, Mrs Cruikshank could move quite fast, and Sarah had to almost run to keep up with her as she led the way into the forest.

'My husband has moved his office down here for the duration so you won't be too disturbed,' she said as they passed a log cabin set on a bank above a fast-running stream. 'The men's camp is through the trees over there in the glade.'

They kept walking along the winding forest track until they reached a low hill which gave them a panoramic view through the trees to the rest of the estate. 'That's Cliffe Farm down there,' said Mrs Cruikshank as she pointed to a jumble of red-roofed buildings in the distance. 'The horses are stabled there, and the Land Girls are billeted in the actual farmhouse.'

She turned and pointed further into the forest. 'The gamekeeper's cottage is much deeper into the woods where he can keep an eye on the pheasants and deer. He isn't a part of the Forestry Commission or the MOS – he's Lord Cliffe's gamekeeper and his duties are to safeguard the estate from poachers and see to the fishery.'

She turned to Sarah and smiled. 'You won't see much of him. Groves is a solitary man with an unpleasant manner, and we all steer clear of him.'

'He frightened the life out of me when I came for my interview,' said Sarah. 'I certainly wouldn't like to bump into him or his dog after dark.'

Mrs Cruikshank patted her arm. 'I feel the same way, so you're not alone.'

'Does Lord Cliffe still live in the big house at the end of the drive?'

'He's in London mostly these days, but he moved his personal things into the east wing last month. The American Army has requisitioned the rest of the house, and their officers are due to arrive any day now.'

'Isn't that a bit risky with a lot of girls working on the estate?' Sarah asked, grinning.

Mrs Cruikshank laughed. 'It certainly is, but one does hope that as the Americans are officers they will behave like gentlemen – and that our girls will remember they are ladies.'

Sarah giggled. 'I hardly think any man worth his salt would find us at all attractive in that horrid uniform,' she replied.

'Perhaps that's why the powers that be in the Land Army designed it that way,' said Mrs Cruikshank with a twinkle in her eyes. 'After all, everyone is here to work, not flirt. Come on, let's go back to our office so you can try your uniform for size. Then we can have a cup of tea and I'll bring you up to date with all the dockets and bills of lading, and show you how to do the wages.'

Peggy was cooking rabbit stew with pearl barley and dumplings, which smelled a great deal more pleasant than the brew of boiled potato peelings and meal which she'd prepared for the chickens.

Having opened the window to let the stench out, she'd quickly closed it again on the brisk wind that had got up during the afternoon. It might almost be April, with crocuses and daffodils enlivening the hedgerows and bomb sites, but it got very chilly once the sun was low in the sky. Spring was obviously just around the corner, but she did wish it would hurry up. There was nothing like a bit of sunshine to make things seem better, and the winter had dragged on for long enough.

She left the stew to simmer away in the slow oven while she warmed herself by the fire and re-read the letter from Jim that had come in the second post that morning. Once again it was in tatters due to the censor, but he was delighted with the photographs she'd sent him, his back was better, and he was finding the manual labour a bit easier now he'd got used to it – but he still hated obeying orders and being shouted at by the sergeant major.

His endearments touched her heart, but it made her blush to think that someone else had read those very private words. It was unsettling to realise a stranger could legally pry into the intimacies of her marriage – but then she had to accept it was the price everyone had to pay if the spies were to be caught.

She looked up at the mantelpiece where she'd placed the photograph he'd sent. He'd had it taken after his initial training period, and he looked very handsome in his uniform, with the beret pulled over one brow. It was true what they said, she thought with a soft smile

– a man in a uniform was very attractive. It sort of tidied them up, made them straighten their shoulders and hold their heads erect. But if any girl dared flash her eyes at her Jim – or he got carried away with how handsome he looked – there would be fireworks and no mistake.

She sat in the warm kitchen and tried not to think about what he might be getting up to so far from home. He'd always been a flirt, and had sailed close to the wind several times over the years, but ultimately he'd always stayed faithful, and she had to believe this would continue.

Her thoughts were disturbed by the slam of the front door. The girls were coming back from their shifts, so it was time to go and wake Cordelia from her afternoon snooze. She was about to leave the warmth of the fire when Jane came into the kitchen, still dressed in her dairy uniform of trousers, jacket, white overall coat and long striped apron, the cap set rakishly on her head.

'Peggy, do you think I could ask you something?'

Peggy felt a jolt of alarm as she saw the serious expression on her usually sunny face. 'Yes, of course, dear. What's the matter?'

Jane took off the cap and shook out her long hair as she sat at the table. She clasped her hands in her lap and chewed her bottom lip before asking hesitantly, 'Do you know what Anthony does at Castle Hill Fort?'

'Not really,' Peggy admitted. 'His mother goes on about his important, secret work for the MOD, and he does keep things close to his chest, so I suppose it's classified. Why do you ask?'

'He was waiting outside the dairy when I finished work,' Jane said quietly, 'and we went for a walk up into the hills so we could have a long private talk about things. He didn't want anyone to see us, or overhear what he had to say.'

Peggy was rather startled that her nephew should think it appropriate to go into the hills alone with such a young girl.

Her expression must have given her thoughts away, for Jane smiled. 'There was nothing sinister about it,' she said. 'Though I was a bit wary that Suzy might see us and get the wrong end of the stick.'

'So what did he want to talk to you about that he couldn't say here?' asked Peggy.

'He seems to think I would be very useful to the MOD, and asked me if I would be interested in going away to do some specialist training.'

Peggy realised she'd been the one to grasp the wrong end of the stick, and she quickly closed the kitchen door so their conversation couldn't be overheard by anyone coming into the hall. She sat down next to Jane. 'What sort of training?' she asked softly. 'Was he specific?'

'He said it had to do with my ability to solve mathematical problems and codes, and that those skills were very important in helping to win the war. He didn't go into any real detail because he said he wasn't allowed to – but if I was interested in doing something really vital to the war effort, he could arrange for me to see one of his colleagues.'

'And what did you tell him, Jane?'

'I said I would have to think about it,' she replied. She looked at Peggy, her expression earnest and a mite fearful. 'I'm not supposed to tell anyone about this,' she confessed, 'and I feel a bit disloyal about keeping it from Sarah. But she's got enough to worry about, and without Mummy and Daddy here, I felt I could come to you, Peggy. I trust you, you see, and I think you're the best person to give me honest advice.'

Peggy's soft heart went out to her. 'I'm flattered you trust me enough to confide in me, Jane – and I promise this conversation will go no further.' She took Jane's cold hands and rubbed them warm. 'You were quite right to tell Anthony you needed time to think this over,' she said quietly. 'It sounds as if it's a very responsible sort of thing he's asking you to do.'

Jane gave a deep sigh. 'I can only guess that the training must be something to do with breaking codes – and I think I'd really like that, and be rather good at it. But you see I'm only just finding my feet here and getting used to making decisions and holding down a job, and I don't think I'm ready yet to take such a big step.'

'Did you tell him about your accident, and how you feel about his offer?'

Jane nodded. 'He said the accident didn't matter a jot, and of course I must take my time to think everything through. But he urged me to meet this other person so I had a better understanding of what the training would entail and where it would lead.'

'If you don't feel ready to do that, then you've done the right thing by refusing to meet this man.'

Jane lifted her chin, her wide blue eyes bright with unshed tears. 'But I feel I've let Anthony down, Peggy,' she whispered.

Peggy drew her into her arms. 'You haven't let anyone down, Jane,' she murmured, kissing her soft hair. 'You simply need time to settle into the way of life here, and it was a bit unfair of Anthony to put you in such a difficult position.'

'I thought so too,' she said with a sniff, 'but I can understand why he did. You see, I passed all the tests with flying colours and he said I had a very rare and special talent.'

'I have no doubt of it,' said Peggy with a sigh, 'but that doesn't mean you have to feel guilty about turning down his offer.'

Jane lifted her head from Peggy's shoulder. 'But I do, Peggy. I can't help it. And yet I know deep down that I must get used to working and being myself before I start to think about being completely independent. I've had people telling me how I should think and what I should do ever since I had the accident, and this new freedom is quite a heady thing and it may take some time before I can adjust to it.'

'Then that is what you must do,' said Peggy as she gave her a clean handkerchief.

'I do love delivering the milk, and I absolutely adore

Mabel and the other horses, but I can see that it isn't nearly as important as code-breaking,' Jane muttered as she blew her nose. 'Do you think I'm being awfully silly to want to stay at the dairy?'

'All jobs are important in times like these,' said Peggy firmly, 'so I don't want you thinking otherwise. And of course I don't think you're being silly – you're still only seventeen, and far too young for anything more responsible.'

Jane was silent for a moment. 'Anthony gave me a super reference,' she said as she pulled the envelope out of her trouser pocket. 'I thought I'd go and see Vera tomorrow and ask about an afternoon job. I don't earn much at the dairy, and with Sarah not working, we need the extra money.'

Peggy smiled. 'Sarah's got the job with the WTC – she's up at the estate now, in fact, and starts properly tomorrow.'

Jane gave her a beaming smile. 'That's wonderful news,' she breathed. 'I'm so glad she doesn't have to worry about it any more.'

Peggy smiled. 'And are you happier now we've had this little talk, Jane?'

'I am,' she replied, 'and once I've really settled in and am feeling a bit more sure of myself, I might have another talk to Anthony and then meet his colleague.' She gave an impish grin. 'Never say "never", Peggy. Who knows what I might be doing this time next year?'

*

Sarah's walk home from the estate didn't seem to take long at all, despite the unwieldy bundle of clothing she carried under her arm. The day was bright, the work at the estate office was manageable, and she was looking forward to welcoming all the other girls tomorrow.

She strode along the flat ridge which eventually dipped towards the town and Beach View, feeling warm and rather liberated in the WTC jodhpurs, shirt and sweater. Through trial and error, she and Mrs Cruikshank had managed to find jodhpurs that fitted her, and they'd both been pleased and rather surprised at how well they suited her. The new brown shoes that were issued with the rest of the uniform were a bit stiff and needed wearing in, but so far they hadn't rubbed her heel or pinched at all, and she put that down to the thickness of the knee-length socks.

She hitched the bundle under her arm and adjusted her handbag and gas-mask straps on her shoulder. Her arm was aching now, for the bundle was heavy, and contained not only her own clothes and shoes, but the newly issued overcoat and mackintosh. The weather was so changeable, it was best to keep both at hand for the following morning.

Sarah reached the track which led steeply down to the lane that ran behind Beach View Boarding House, and her pace quickened in her eagerness to show off her uniform and tell the others about her first day.

There was no sign of Ron or welcoming bark from Harvey, and she realised they were probably both at the pub, for it was almost opening time. She ran up the cellar steps into the kitchen where everyone else was gathered for the evening meal.

'Well, look at you,' said Peggy. 'Don't you look smart!'

'You look as if you're going riding,' said Jane admiringly. 'Those breeches are jolly flattering, Sarah.' She grinned and rushed to give her a hug. 'I don't need to ask if you enjoyed your first day,' she said. 'Your face says it all.'

'Goodness,' muttered Cordelia as she peered over her half-moon glasses. 'Are you in charge of the stables, dear? I thought you were supposed to be in the estate office?'

Sarah dropped her bundle of clothing on a chair and bent to kiss Cordelia's cheek. 'I am in the office,' she said, 'but I will be expected to muck in when there's a delivery day, or if someone needs help.' She grinned. 'I was worried the uniform would make me feel as if I've dressed like a boy, but actually it's very comfortable and lovely and warm.'

Cordelia looked from Sarah to Rita and then Jane. 'I don't know what the world's coming to,' she muttered, 'with you young things rushing about in trousers and boots – riding motorbikes and cutting down trees and delivering milk. Whatever next?'

'Well, I think we all look jolly good,' declared Jane, 'and as the men aren't about to do these jobs, it's only right we should take over.'

'So, what's it like up at the estate?' asked Suzy as she finished laying the table.

Sarah described the house and the forest and how peaceful it was up there. 'They've got a lot of people working on the estate already,' she said finally. 'There's a farm as well as the forest to manage, and ten more lumberjills are due to arrive tomorrow.'

'Lumberjills? Is that what you're all going to be called?' asked Fran.

Sarah nodded. 'Why not? The men are lumberjacks, after all – and Jack and Jill went up the hill – and cut down all the trees.'

There was a murmur of laughter at this. Sarah picked up her bundle of clothes. 'I'll take these upstairs and out of the way,' she said. Then she turned in the doorway and grinned. 'Oh, I almost forgot,' she said. 'The American Army officers are to be billeted at the manor house. They're due to arrive quite soon.'

'Oh, you beast,' squeaked Fran. 'You left the best bit of news until last. How many will there be, and will you get the chance to meet them?'

Sarah shrugged. 'I have no idea,' she replied, 'but I'm sure they'll be far too busy to take much notice of anyone.'

'But they're bound to have dances and things,' persisted Fran. 'The Canadians and Australians do – it's all part of introducing them to the area and giving them a bit of entertainment before they have to go off to some beastly battle.' She hugged herself and giggled. 'Goodness to mercy, how thrilling. Yankee officers – and right on our doorstep.'

'We'll have none of that,' said Peggy, trying to look

stern. 'They're here to help us win the war, not to provide you with dancing partners – and I don't want any of you girls having your heads turned. You're to keep your hands on your ha'pennies and your knees together, you hear me?'

'It's only Fran getting excited,' said Rita dryly. 'Personally I think they're overrated if the ones at the old airfield are anything to go by.'

Sarah left the kitchen as Fran and Rita argued about the merits and pitfalls of having the Americans stationed in Cliffehaven. She was still smiling as she unpacked her bundle and carefully hung everything in the wardrobe. The arrival of the Yanks had been a talking point for ages now, and the expectation and excitement was almost tangible. Sarah had a feeling that Cliffehaven was about to see great changes.

Having put everything away, she changed back into her own clothes and brushed out her hair. The precious photographs she'd brought with her were displayed on the narrow mantelpiece above the gas fire, and she took them down and sat on the bed as she looked through them.

They were snapshots of sunny, careless days when life had been easy and the dark shadows of what was to come had yet to appear in those cloudless skies. She looked at her parents standing on the veranda, captured in the moment just before their guests were to arrive for dinner, smiling and happy as they raised their glasses to the camera. There was one of Amah with baby Jane in her arms, and another of herself with both of them on some lovely palm-fringed beach. She'd been a skinny little girl with fair plaits, a freckled nose and a wide smile.

She set them aside and picked up the photograph of her and Philip. They were celebrating their engagement, and he looked so handsome in his tuxedo that it brought tears to her eyes. The Americans could come in their droves for all she cared, for Philip was the only man she wanted; the only man who could touch her heart and make her feel treasured.

'We'll be together again one day soon,' she whispered to him as he smiled back at her from the photograph. 'Just keep me in your heart until then.'

Chapter Twenty-Five

'The Yanks are coming,' announced Tuppence Bailey excitedly as she crashed into the office and stood panting in the doorway, 'Molly Douglas saw their jeeps coming down the lane. Hurry up or you'll miss them arriving at the house.'

Sarah grinned. Tuppence Bailey was a sturdy country girl of eighteen whose real name was Maud. She had told everyone that on the day she'd been born her father had decided she looked as bright and shining as two pennies, and the nickname had stuck. She much preferred it to the rather dreary Maud, but her mother had insisted upon it in the hope that her wealthy, ancient spinster aunt Maud might leave her part of her fortune.

Tuppence was an energetic, fresh-faced girl who always seemed to be excited about something, and Sarah had come to like her very much over the past four weeks, for she was great fun to be with. So she left her desk and locked the office door behind her before following Tuppence down the path.

Sarah was curious enough to want to see what these Americans actually looked like, for the rumours about how handsome they were had been circulating ever since the first influx had arrived in Ireland and Liverpool – but it was almost an idle curiosity, for she hadn't looked properly at another man since she'd waved goodbye to Philip in Singapore harbour.

Tuppence joined the other lumberjills who were already hiding in a giggling huddle within the foliage of the enormous rhododendrons, and Sarah eased in beside her. She felt faintly ridiculous squatting there, but the other girls were such fun, and their excitement was infectious, so it didn't seem to matter a jot.

'They're coming,' hissed Molly Douglas, who was so excited she could barely keep still and kept treading on the others' toes in her heavy studded boots.

Sarah heard the rumble of several engines and then the crunch of wheels on the gravel driveway. She leaned forward with the others as three jeeps roared into view with the yellow star of America painted on their bonnets. A gasp went up as they saw the soldiers sitting rigidly in the front, the officers in the back lounging in a much more relaxed manner. Two staff cars arrived with the American flag fluttering from the wing mirrors, and these were followed by four more jeeps.

'Cor, I don't 'alf fancy that one,' growled Eastend Shirley, her eyes like saucers as a tall and very handsome Colonel stepped out of a jeep and returned the soldiers' snappy salutes.

'He wouldn't fancy you or any of us in this awful get-up,' retorted Tilly Rogers. 'But I have to say that if this is an example of what the Americans look like, then we're in for a treat, girls.'

'That one over there looks like Clark Gable,' breathed Tuppence.

'They all look like film stars,' replied Sarah as she took in the immaculate uniforms which fitted the broad shoulders and slender hips to perfection. Even the ordinary soldiers looked dangerously attractive in their camouflage battledress as they stood to attention in front of the mansion.

As the oohs and aahs went through the other lumberjills like a breeze through a field of wheat, Sarah gazed in awe at the tanned faces and lovely white teeth of these Americans. By contrast, the English soldiers who came into town from their barracks nearby were a pasty lot in their ill-fitting and unflattering uniforms, and they all seemed to have bad skin and teeth. And although the Canadians were regarded as quite dashing, and the RAF boys could still command huge attention, they didn't begin to compare to these glamour boys.

'I tell you what, girls,' whispered Tuppence, 'our chaps are going to have to smarten up if they're to get a look-in from now on.'

'I know who I'd rather dance with,' sighed Molly as her adoring gaze followed one of the Lieutenants. 'I bet *his* hands don't get sweaty – and I wouldn't care if he stomped all over my toes.'

There were stifled giggles and they all shifted forward to get a closer look. The soldiers were now standing guard around the perimeter of the turning circle as the officers climbed the steps to the front door where the robust Lord Cliffe was waiting to greet them. He was a man in his vigorous sixties, with a snowy moustache and thick white hair, and the medals on his chest glinted in the sun as he gave the senior officer a smart salute before shaking his hand.

'I didn't realise the old boy was back from London,' whispered Tilly. 'And where did he get all those medals from?'

'He was awarded them in three of the deadliest campaigns during the first war,' said Sarah, who'd been told the history of Lord Cliffe by Mrs Cruikshank. 'One of them is the Victoria Cross.'

There was an appreciative murmur and then all eyes turned back to the driveway where more jeeps and several lorries were drawing up. Soldiers jumped down and ran smartly to the back of the house with cases and bags as others unloaded heavy packing crates, their voices twanging with the accent they all recognised from Hollywood films.

The Americans had arrived and had more than fulfilled every expectation. Cliffe estate was coming alive with their noise and bustle, and as the girls watched enthralled, it was clear the old place would never be quite the same again.

Despite having told Cordelia a month before that she had passed her check-up with flying colours, Peggy knew that sooner or later she would not be able to avoid the truth. She was feeling decidedly under the weather today, but she didn't have time to be ill, there were too many more important things to be getting on with. Things would sort themselves out one way or another – they always did.

She tucked Daisy into her pram and struggled to get it down the cellar steps and into the back garden. Feeling rather light-headed, she sank into a deckchair and waited for the feeling to pass. It was a beautiful late April morning, with the birds singing and the sun shining down warmly onto the vegetable patch. Summer was almost here and the Germans hadn't bombed Cliffehaven for weeks, although there had been some raids close by and several false alarms which had sent them all scurrying into the Anderson shelter.

Peggy closed her eyes and enjoyed the feel of the warm sun on her face. It was peaceful this morning, but she knew that as the day waned and darkness fell the RAF would be leaving their airfields in droves to continue their relentless night bombing of north-western Germany and France. Night after night they'd heard them flying overhead, and each time she'd wondered if Martin was up there and prayed that he and all the other brave boys made it home safely. And yet so many of Bomber Command had never made it back, and the odds on any of them surviving had shortened dramatically.

She heaved a deep sigh and got to her feet, cross with herself for sitting about getting morbid when she had better things to do. Checking that Daisy didn't have the sun on her face, she plodded up the cellar steps and hunted under the sink for the bucket and scrubbing brush. The new kitchen lino was filthy, and she'd been meaning to give it a good scrub since yesterday morning.

Peggy had finished the kitchen and made a start on the hallway tiles when Cordelia came back from Camden Road with a string bag full of shopping. 'You look worn out,' said Peggy as she took the bag and helped her off with her coat.

'I could say the same thing about you,' said Cordelia, regarding her evenly. 'Why don't we both sit down and have a cuppa?'

'That sounds like a good idea, but mind your step – the floor's still wet.' She followed Cordelia into the kitchen and put the kettle on the hob before rummaging in the string bag. 'Goodness,' she gasped. 'Sausages *and* a joint of pork?'

Cordelia beamed. 'It's Monday, Peggy, and Alf slaughtered one of his uncounted pigs yesterday – he thought we might appreciate a treat.'

Peggy was smiling as she quickly stowed the precious meat on the top marble shelf in her larder and shut the door so Harvey couldn't get to it. A great many people now kept livestock, and the inspectors from the Ministry of Food would count them and oversee their official slaughter and then take half the animal away, explaining that it was necessary because of the rationing.

No one ever found out what happened to this meat, and there was a deep suspicion the inspectors ate it –

so on Sundays, which was their day off, there would be an unofficial slaughter of the uncounted beasts by the breeders so they could keep the entire proceeds of their labour.

Peggy's mouth was already watering at the thought of roast pork, and the dripping she could spread on toast with lashings of pepper and salt – although there wasn't any pepper to be had now, and the salt was getting low. She made the tea and had just sat down to enjoy it when someone rapped the knocker on the front door. 'I'll go,' she said quickly. 'You've done enough for one day.'

The plump little woman on the doorstep looked vaguely familiar, but Peggy couldn't place her. 'Can I help you?' she asked.

'Mrs Reilly?' At Peggy's nod, she gave a sigh of relief. 'You obviously don't remember me, but we have met once before. I'm Olive Farmer, Amelia Fuller's neighbour.'

'Of course,' said Peggy and she smiled in recognition of the nosy neighbour. 'Won't you come in? We've just made a pot of tea, and that's quite a walk you've had all the way from Mafeking Terrace.'

'Thank you, dear,' she said as she wiped her sensibly shod feet on the doormat. 'I could do with a cuppa and no mistake.'

Peggy noticed how her eyes were taking in everything as she slipped off her coat, but she said nothing as Peggy led the way into the kitchen. 'Cordelia,' she said clearly. 'This is Amelia's neighbour, Olive Farmer.'

Olive stuck out her hand. 'Pleased to meet you again after so many years, Cordelia. I don't get out much these days, but I remember you used to help do the cricket teas when our husbands were playing for the local team.'

Peggy saw to the tea as the two elderly ladies reminisced. Something important must have brought Olive here, and she was intrigued as to what it could be. She placed the cup and saucer by Olive's elbow and put a few biscuits on a plate – they'd been in the tin for quite a while and were a bit stale, but she was sure they wouldn't mind, as biscuits were such a rarity these days.

'It's nice to see you again, Olive,' said Cordelia as she sipped her tea. 'But I suspect you haven't come all this way to talk over old times. Has something happened to Amelia?'

The woman's bright expression faded and she fiddled with her teaspoon. 'I'm sorry, Cordelia, I'm afraid it has.' She set the cup aside. 'She'd been acting strangely for some time, and we all put it down to her getting old and crotchety like the rest of us. But she began shouting at anyone who walked by, and actually assaulted the poor postman with a frying pan when he knocked on her door to deliver a parcel.'

'Oh dear,' said Cordelia. 'That doesn't sound right at all – even for a bossy woman like Amelia.'

'We realised something was very wrong when she began to wander barefooted down the street in her nightdress, saying she was on her way to open up the school. She got quite violent when I tried to coax her back indoors, and in the end I had to call the doctor.'

'She's lost her mind, hasn't she?' said Cordelia, her voice wavering. 'How sad. How very sad. Poor Amelia.'

Olive nodded and patted her hand. 'She's safe now. The doctor got her into a very good nursing home, and she'll be well cared for there. I have the address if you'd like to visit her, but it is some way further down the coast.'

'There doesn't seem much point,' sighed Cordelia. 'My sister and I have never really got on, and it's been years since we spoke. She probably won't know who I am anyway, if she's that confused.'

Cordelia twisted the handkerchief in her trembling fingers. 'I feel sorry that she should come to this, and more than a little guilty that I didn't at least *try* to make things better between us. But I have to confess I didn't like her one bit, and the way she treated my nieces just confirmed to me what a nasty woman she could be.'

'She was certainly her usual acerbic self when they came knocking on her door. I remember her telling me how she despised people who turned up unannounced wanting help when their precious lives abroad had been disrupted. She couldn't stand foreigners, you know, and regarded anyone who lived abroad as beneath her contempt.'

'That all started when she fell in love,' said Cordelia softly. 'He was a handsome fellow, I remember, and she was certain that he was about to ask her to marry him. But he had no plans to get married and was in fact going out to India to work as a Government administrator. Amelia was not only heartbroken, but furious – convinced she would become a laughing stock amongst her peers.'

Cordelia gave a deep sigh. 'She refused to see him again before he left, but he'd clearly regretted the way they'd parted, for he wrote her many letters, begging her to forgive him, and asking her to go to India where they could be married. He came back three years later having found life in India rather too dangerous with all the fighting going on, and Amelia refused even to speak to him. She had never forgiven him, you see.'

'How sad,' murmured Peggy.

'Yes, it was,' replied Cordelia, 'but Amelia only had herself to blame.' She looked across at Olive. 'Thank you for taking the trouble to come all this way. I do appreciate it.'

'Well, there were one or two things which I thought you should have. With the bungalow empty, it didn't seem wise to leave this lot lying about.' She pulled a great wad of papers from her large handbag and dumped them in Cordelia's lap before digging deeper and drawing out two small jewellery boxes.

Cordelia opened the boxes. 'Mother's pearl earrings, and her wedding and engagement ring,' she sighed as she looked at them tenderly. 'I'm glad she kept them.' She closed the boxes and riffled through the official-looking letters and documents before setting them aside. 'I'll read through those later,' she said.

'There was something else,' said Olive as she reached into her handbag again.

Cordelia and Peggy stared at the two airmail letters which were unmistakeably addressed to Sarah and Jane. 'But these must have arrived weeks ago,' breathed Peggy as she examined the dates franked across the stamps.

Cordelia's expression was grim as she held the flimsy blue letters. 'Amelia knew where I was,' she said flatly. 'She also knew the girls were trying to find me, and could have easily sent these on.'

Peggy's heart went out to her, for it must be awful to realise how cruel her own sister had been.

Cordelia's lower lip trembled as she carefully placed the precious letters on the mantelpiece. 'Those girls were desperate to know what happened to their parents – and all the time my spiteful sister kept these to herself.'

She turned to face Peggy and Olive, the anger sparking in her eyes as colour flooded her cheeks. 'I'm not usually vengeful,' she said unsteadily, 'but at this very moment I feel furious enough to kill her. How *dare* she do that to my poor little girls?'

Peggy couldn't think of anything to say, and Olive was looking exceedingly uncomfortable. She gathered up her bag and gloves. 'I'd better get back home,' she said as she got to her feet. 'The tram will be at the end of Camden Road in fifteen minutes, and I don't want to miss it.'

She hurried into the hall and let Peggy help her with

her coat. Thanking her for the tea, she hurried away and Peggy closed the door and returned to the kitchen.

Cordelia was sitting in her usual chair and staring into the fire. 'Olive Farmer always was nosy,' she muttered. 'I bet she couldn't wait to get into that bungalow so she could rummage about.'

'It's a good thing she did,' said Peggy as she freshened the tea with more boiling water. 'Otherwise we would never have known about those letters.'

Cordelia looked up at Peggy and gave her a sweet smile. 'I can't wait to see their faces when they come home,' she said delightedly. 'Do you think Ron could be persuaded to give us a bottle of something from the pub to celebrate?'

'I think that's a very good idea,' replied Peggy. 'But it might be wise to put any celebrations on hold until we learn exactly what is in those letters.' She put a gentle hand on the older woman's shoulder. 'It might not all be good news, Cordelia.'

Her smile faded and she nodded. 'You're right,' she murmured. 'Oh, what a terrible world we're living in, Peggy,' she said with a wavering sigh. 'When will we ever feel safe again?'

Peggy put her arm around her and held her close. There was no answer she could give, only a warm embrace and the silent assurance that she would never have to bear these awful times alone.

Sarah walked happily up the hill and stood for a moment to appreciate the view. She never tired of it, even though she saw it every day, and the blue of the sky and the sparkle on the water seemed to welcome her.

'Hello, sea,' she murmured. 'You're looking very pretty today.'

Smiling at her silliness, she swung the gas-mask box from her hand and continued across the ridge. It had been a strange sort of day, but great fun, for the Americans had spotted them hiding in the rhododendrons and had insisted they come out and introduce themselves.

She had been quite surprised at how silly the other girls had become with their giggling and flirting, and was getting a bit worried that they'd all get into fearful trouble if the officers caught them. Not wanting to be a part of this fawning, silly gaggle of girls, she'd discreetly left them to it. She had no interest in flirting, and certainly didn't want any of those Americans thinking she was the sort of girl who swooned at the offer of a stick of chewing gum.

She was behind her desk when she heard the forestry foreman thunder past in his truck, and moments later he was bellowing at the girls to get back to work. Peeking out of the window she saw them scurrying back into the forest, still giggling. They didn't seem at all put out, and were no doubt already arranging to meet some of the Yanks after work.

Sarah was still smiling as she continued on her way. The handsome two-star General had come to her office to introduce himself, and she had welcomed him calmly and offered him a cup of tea. The sophistication of years of living in Malaya had served her well, for her mother had insisted she socialise from a very young age, and two-star generals were not a challenge.

He'd turned out to be quite charming, talking of his wife and family back in New Hampshire, and his hopes that their arrival wouldn't disrupt the routine of the estate too much.

She reached the steep slope that led down to the alleyway between the houses, eager to tell the other girls about the invitation to a cocktail party at the mansion the following night. It might be fun for all of them, but most of all it would be interesting to see how Rita reacted to such an invitation. She was a strange, rather prickly little thing, but she had a marvellous sense of humour, and if she could be persuaded to put on a dress for a change, she would be quite pretty, she was sure.

'Hello, Sarah.'

She looked up and waved at her sister, who was approaching Beach View from the other end of the lane. Jane had been taken on part-time by Solomon's factory to deal with the accounts for three hours every afternoon, and Sarah still couldn't quite come to terms with how smart and grown-up she was looking now in her skirt and blouse, a cardigan draped over her shoulders and her hair coiled fetchingly off her face. Her little sister was slowly blossoming into the young woman she was meant to be, and Sarah's heart swelled with pride.

'You were so deep in thought you didn't even see me,' said Jane, and laughed as she tucked her hand in the crook of her arm. 'Had a good day?'

Sarah nodded and told her about the arrival of the Americans and the invitation to the cocktail party the following evening.

'What fun that will be,' said Jane, her face alight with enthusiasm. And then she came to an abrupt halt. 'But what on earth can we wear?' she breathed. 'Neither of us has anything suitable for a party – and besides, won't it be a bit dangerous going over the hill late at night?'

Sarah shrugged. 'I'm sure we can borrow something from one of the others – if not, we'll just have to make do with what we have.' She opened the back door and pressed a finger to her lips. 'As for transport, the General promised to send a jeep to pick us up and ferry us home,' she whispered, 'but don't say anything until everyone's home from work. I want it to be a complete surprise.'

They went up the steps into the kitchen to find it deserted. Daisy was cooing in her pram, which Peggy had parked in the hall, but all was still. Assuming Peggy was upstairs waking Cordelia from her afternoon siesta, they quietly made their way to their bedroom and Sarah pushed open the door to find Peggy sitting waiting for them.

'I hope you don't mind me coming in here when you were away,' she said quickly, 'but I thought it would be best if I gave you these in private.' She handed them the letters with a short explanation and quietly left the room, closing the door behind her.

Sarah dropped her gas-mask box on the floor and they both sank onto the nearest bed. 'I can't believe it,' she murmured as she held the two letters and saw they'd been addressed to Amelia. 'We've waited so long and now I'm almost frightened to read them.'

'If you don't open one, then I will,' said Jane impatiently. 'Mummy must be desperately worried that we haven't replied, and I want to know why she's in Queensland and not here.'

Sarah chose the earlier letter, eased it open, and began to read it out.

My darling girls,

I am writing this in the hope that it will get to you somehow, for we received no reply from Jock's telegram to the great-aunts. My thoughts have been with you from the moment I recovered from the fever, and I pray each day that you got to England safely and are being well looked after.

As you can see by the address, I have managed to get to my parents' home in Cairns, and will stay here until the war is over and we can all be together again. I won't go into too many details, suffice it to say that your baby brother, James, arrived earlier than planned and your father managed to get both of us on one of the last ships leaving Singapore. I so desperately wanted to be in England with you, but I had no choice – and I count myself lucky that the ship was going to Australia and not South Africa. At least I'm familiar with things here, but you must be finding it very strange having to settle in a different country where everything must seem confusing.

I have had no news from your father, or from Philip, my darlings. The last time I saw them was on the docks in Singapore as my ship, the Narcunda, set sail. They looked very forlorn standing there and we were all in tears, for none of us knew when we might see one another again – or indeed if we would ever see each other again. The Japs were fast approaching the causeway by then, and all hell was breaking loose as their bombers tried to sink every ship in the harbour. The ship behind us was torpedoed, so the Narcunda set sail immediately and made a run for it, hiding behind one of the islands overnight to return and pick up the last few women and children that had been left behind. It was a terrible time for everyone – a time of tears – a time of dying and of farewells. I can only pray that Jock and Philip come through, but it is in God's hands now Singapore has fallen.

I love you, my darlings, and know that you will stay strong throughout this time of uncertainty and do the best you can. The mail is erratic, and I don't know how long this will take to reach you, but I long to hear from you.

With all my love,
Mother.

Sarah folded the letter as the tears ran down her cheeks. 'At least she and the baby are safe,' she whispered.

Jane was crying too as she picked up the second letter, which had been posted almost three weeks after the first. She blew her nose and calmed herself before opening it and reading it out loud.

My darlings,

I am still waiting to hear from you, and each day is torture as the mail arrives and there is no letter. I realise the mail is unreliable and that it could takes weeks to arrive – but now I'm fearful that you have not received my letter, or are unable for some reason to reply to it. Please, my darlings, send a telegram and put me out of my fear and misery, for I cannot sleep or eat with worry.

I have had no confirmed news about your father, or Philip, only rumours that have come to me through Jock's contacts in the military – and I don't wish to distress you, but you have a right to know as much as I do, for I am certain you have been worried sick about them.

According to these rumours they are both alive, for which I can only thank God. Jock is in Changi prison along with several other volunteers, and it is thought that Philip was one of several hundred troops who were captured during a skirmish shortly after the fall. These prisoners-of-war were put on ships and sent north to a prison camp somewhere in Siam – but no one has

*yet confirmed that Philip was amongst them – and
of course the only witnesses to what really happened
are still in Singapore, with no possibility of getting
information to the outside world.*

'Oh, Sarah,' sighed Jane through her tears as she
gripped her sister's hand. 'Poor Philip, and poor
Daddy. I can't bear to think of them in prison.'

'As prisoners of war they will come under the rules
of the Geneva Conventions,' said Sarah as she tried
very hard to quell the awful fear that was threatening
to overwhelm her. 'They will come through this,' she
said fiercely. 'I just know they will.'

Jane grasped her hand. 'Of course they will,' she
murmured. 'We must believe that, Sarah, we really
must.'

Sarah clung to that belief, trying so very hard not
to let it slip away from her. 'Finish the letter, Jane,' she
urged.

Jane took a deep breath, but her hands were shaking,
and her voice was unsteady as she returned to their
mother's letter.

*We must all stay strong and optimistic, no
matter what happens, my dearest, sweetest girls. The
Americans and the other Allies will defeat the Japs and
the Germans, and although it may take time, we have
to believe that the end is now in sight and the enemy
will be vanquished.*

I will write again, and keep writing in the hope that
I will hear from you very soon.
　　I love you both with all my heart,
　　Mother.

Sarah took a deep restorative breath, determined to remain positive. 'We'll write a long letter tonight, and then in the morning you must go to the Post Office and send a telegram so that Mother knows we're safe. We can work out what to say when we've finished the letter.'

Jane rested her head on Sarah's shoulder as they sat together on the bed. 'I'll do it the minute I finish my milk round,' she promised, her voice thick with tears. 'Daddy and Philip will be all right, won't they, Sarah?'

Sarah heard the fear in her voice and held her close, finding comfort in their embrace. 'We have to pray that they will,' she replied softly.

They sat in silence, each with their own thoughts as Peggy's old clock ticked away the seconds. Sarah drew back from the embrace eventually, and tenderly kissed her sister's forehead.

'Mummy wants us to stay positive, Jane, and we must try our best for her sake. After all, she and baby James have survived, and so have we. We're safe here at Beach View – safe with Peggy and Cordelia, and it's up to us to make the best of things until our family can be together again.'

As Jane lifted her head and looked into her eyes,

Sarah knew that as long as they had each other they would stay strong. 'Mummy and Daddy's love has given us the strength to get this far, and we must not give in to fear or doubt,' she said firmly. 'We will come through this, Jane. We're Fullers – and the Fullers never give up.'

ALSO AVAILABLE IN ARROW

There'll be Blue Skies

Ellie Dean

**It's 1939 and the first evacuees are arriving at Beach
View Boarding House . . .**

When sixteen-year-old Sally is evacuated to the English south
coast, she is terrified by what lies ahead of her. All she knows is the
sights and sounds of London's East End – but Sally swallows her
tears as they leave the familiar landmarks behind, knowing that she
has to be a Grown-Up Girl and play mother to her six-year-old
brother Ernie. Playing mother is nothing new for Sally – their real
mother Florrie, a good-time girl, hasn't even come to the station to
wave them off and Ernie, crippled at an early age by polio, is used
to depending on his older sister.

When they arrive in Cliffehaven, they're taken to live at the Beach
View Boarding House where they're welcomed by the open-hearted
Reilly family headed up by warm, loving Peggy, and life begins
to improve. Sally gets a job in a uniforms factory to help pay her
way – and to pay for Ernie's expensive medicines – but then Florrie
arrives in Cliffehaven, bringing disaster with her. And Sally is forced
to work out where her true loyalties lie . . .

arrow books

Keep Smiling Through

Ellie Dean

She swore she would never lose heart.

June 1940. Despite losing her mother at a young age and with her father away on important war work, seventeen-year-old Rita Smith has plenty of people to turn to in the close-knit community of Cliffhaven. Until Italy sides with Germany and Rita's closest friends and neighbours are interned as enemies of the state.

As war rages across Europe, Rita is more determined than ever to do her bit for the war effort. Although she is forced to give up her dream of joining the WAAF, she volunteers as a fire warden. When her own home is destroyed Rita vows she will not lose spirit and throws herself into doing her bit for her country, longing for the day when she is reunited with those she loves best ...

arrow books

Where the Heart Lies

Ellie Dean

Can love survive in a time of war?

February 1941. Julie Harris is working in London's East End as a midwife when a bombing raid destroys her family and the house she grew up in. All she has left is her motherless baby nephew William.

Determined to uphold her promise to her sister to keep William safe until his father, Bill, returns from the war, she accepts a post as a midwife in Cliffehaven on the south-coast of England. Here they are taken under the wing of the Reilly family at the Beach View boarding house.

But all too soon Julie learns that Bill is 'missing in action' and William falls dangerously ill. As she begins the long vigil by William's beside, she fears she will lose the little boy she has grown to love as her own . . .

arrow books